Whips

Cleo Watson

Whips

corsair

CORSAIR

First published in the United Kingdom in 2023 by Corsair

1 3 5 7 9 10 8 6 4 2

A CIP catalogue record for this book
is available from the British Library.

HB ISBN: 978-1-4721-5726-3
TPB ISBN: 978-1-4721-5727-0

Typeset in Garamond by M Rules
Printed and bound in Great Britain by
Clays Ltd, Elcograf S.p.A.

Papers used by Corsair are from well-managed forests
and other responsible sources.

Corsair
An imprint of
Little, Brown Book Group
Carmelite House
50 Victoria Embankment
London EC4Y 0DZ

An Hachette UK Company
www.hachette.co.uk

www.littlebrown.co.uk

It has become fashionable to be cynical about politicians and this book will hardly do much to help. Still, I would like to dedicate my first novel to the many brilliant Parliamentarians who are far too decent, hardworking and incorruptible to feature in these pages. I hope anyone thinking about standing as an MP – particularly any women – throws their hat into the ring.

Whip (noun)

1. a strip of leather or length of cord fastened to a handle, used for flogging or beating a person or for urging on an animal.
2. a dessert consisting of cream or eggs beaten into a light fluffy mass with fruit, chocolate, or other ingredients.
3. an official of a political party appointed to maintain parliamentary discipline among its members, especially so as to ensure attendance and voting in debates.

Oxford English Dictionary

Author's Note

There has been a fair amount of speculation in the run-up to the publication of this book about whether any of my characters are based on real people. I would like to state – emphatically – that this is a novel. The fictional men, women, media outlets and businesses I've written about have not been drawn from flesh and blood MPs or journalists etc. In the great universe of political and media misadventure a lot of crazy stuff has happened, far crazier than any fiction I'm capable of dreaming up, but I'd like to reassure the reader that any seeming inspiration from real events or people is inadvertent. Honestly, not everything's about you.

Prologue

Big Ben strikes 11 p.m. A Wednesday night in the House of Commons. Business for the day has finally finished and the draughty corridors carry only the occasional echo of unsteady footsteps. In the now empty Chamber, Members of Parliament spent the day as their predecessors did before them – perhaps one of the few settings left where this remains the case, if you excuse the modernising measures of TV cameras and microphones. They have debated, they have voted, they have legislated. They have slouched and yelled. Dust, disturbed by the day's hot air, is settling once again onto the empty green leather benches. The ghosts of Churchill and Lloyd George and Pitt complain about the standards of modern oratory in the press gallery. A nesting mouse peeks out from behind the throne-like Speaker's Chair.

On the Terrace by the Thames, groups of drinkers and smokers defy the cold in coats and alcohol jackets. Signals are misread or ignored. MPs who struggled to get dates at university now have carbon copies of the girls who rejected them sitting in thigh-grabbing distance, intrigued by their newfound power sitting on the Public Accounts Committee. Patient researchers persuade their drunk, toddler-like employees to stop spatting on Twitter. Cheerful informal audiences watch their friends play at debating. Someone, buoyed by the cheap wine and jovial surroundings, always says a little more than they mean to.

There's only one topic of conversation. On Saturday, the beleaguered Prime Minister is hosting a summit of her MPs at Chequers, ahead of a last ditch vote on her China Trade Deal. Beneath the remarks of even her most loyal supporters lie layer upon layer of sub-plot, meaning and doubt. Her least loyal MPs, who have long awaited their opportunity to represent the government in a morning media round, are rather more gallows than humour. What drives them all, like feverish Italian spaniels sniffing for truffles, is power. They need to figure out where it lies and how they get it. What each of them knows, regardless of loyalty, is that a PM in crisis provides opportunity for all.

Also on the Terrace, feeling like prefects at a school disco, are government Whips, tired after a busy day of coaxing, pleading or threatening groups of MPs – their 'flocks' – to vote on government business. The bread and butter of their work now done, like the only sober people at a party they can make a study of MP behaviour: who has passed out yet again? Who is following that young researcher around like a puppy? Who is struggling to pay their bar bill? Who is unhappy – and loudly so – about the direction the Party is going in? The Whips are the canaries in the coal mine for prime ministers who want to hold on to power. Deafness to the mood music's change of key can be premiership ending.

While the MPs are the actors, the scenes of Parliamentary theatre are set by its own stage crew. Cleaning, bar and catering staff, IT and maintenance teams, security workers and police officers, clerks and researchers. Beneath the crumbling facade of what the public see – and make no mistake, it is

2

crumbling – they strive away in subterranean kitchens and hidden cupboard-like offices, even in the walls themselves, to make sure the show goes on.

Away from the chatter of the Terrace, the hot steam of the kitchens and the cloudy breath of the police officers guarding the gates, sit extensive corridors containing MPs' offices, spread across the Parliamentary Estate. By day these are thrumming with activity as phone calls, meetings, emails and diaries are attended to. When the House sits in the evenings and most of their staff have gone home, MPs often congregate in each other's offices, drinking and discussing ideas between votes, or quietly working through piles of correspondence alone – allegedly. Once voting is complete, the corridors steadily empty out like an estuary and Members head home or to the Terrace or to another bar, leaving an eerie calm.

Tonight, just after 11 p.m. on a Wednesday, one office is still occupied. Dimly lit by a single lozenge-shaped green lamp, a man sits at a large desk with his shoulders hunched forward, palms on the table, deeply absorbed in his exertions. In the few inches between his face and some documents on the leather-bound surface is a woman on her back, her FitFlop sliders braced against the arms of the chair, her skirt pulled up to reveal a convenient hole torn in the gusset of her flesh-coloured M&S tights. As ever, she is WhatsApping: gossip for journalists; instructions for her advisers and officials; congratulations to an MP for a speech in the Chamber she's pretending she heard. The blue light from the phone screen, held aloft, picks out her frowning face and frizzy hair immediately recognisable in Westminster circles. Natasha Weaver MP, Secretary of State for the Industrial Economy and, in one of her colleague's words, 'the perfect example of the modern politician's failure to fall within the Venn diagram of self-belief and self-awareness'.

'Do you really have to text right now?' her companion muffles irritably.

'Yes, I do,' Weaver sighs, continuing to tap. 'Look, I'm pretty short on time so you can just shove it in dry if you want.'

'Charming.'

The man continues, but pretty half-heartedly. Weaver rolls her eyes and starts squirming around a bit to cheer him up. Encouraged, the man responds by rising up to hold Weaver's hands behind her head, so she drops her phone and her back arches. She grunts as the underwiring from her bra digs into her bosoms. The man immediately climbs on top of her. After some frantic effort, the lozenge-shaped lamp smashes onto the floor.

They lie there for a while, panting in the city light streaming in through the window. Once he's recovered, the man gets up to put on his overcoat from the back of the door and turns to help Weaver into hers, but drops it in surprise. She is bending over the desk with her legs apart, her skirt still hiked up over her hips and her palms flat on the surface. Her body is twisted round so that her vaguely manic eyes glitter at him in the gloom.

'Crikey. You're insatiable,' he mutters wearily.

Big Ben dutifully strikes midnight before they finally leave the room, a few minutes apart.

In a darkened window across the road, a silent figure lowers a long-lens camera and carefully stows it in the recesses of a backpack, wondering if Weaver will learn to close her curtains when she's entertaining.

Part One

30th March

Chequers

The Prime Minister stares at the ceiling above the bed, watching the intricate cornicing become gradually clearer as the sun rises and the day begins. Although, yet again, she has barely slept at all, she finds that listening to the steady intonation of two sets of breath – her husband, Michael, next to her, and their aged chocolate Labrador, Dennis, on the floor at the foot of the bed – is comforting. She must stop grinding her teeth, she thinks.

The clock radio jumps into life. The female newsreader's cool voice announces the headlines:

'Good morning – this is the BBC news at 6 a.m., on Saturday 30th March. The Prime Minister, Madeleine Ford, is today hosting a lunch for Conservative MPs at Chequers, her official country residence, ahead of a final vote on her China Trade Deal next week. Party sources say that for Mrs Ford, who has already suffered two losses at the hands of her colleagues over this divisive

7

legislation, this event is a last ditch effort to get their support. In response to a sustained slump in the polls for the Prime Minister, there are rumours of several letters being sent by Tory MPs to the Chairman of the 1922 Committee, Sir Godfrey Singham, expressing their loss of confidence in her leadership. The letters are sent in secret, but should Sir Godfrey receive fifty or more – the threshold of fifteen per cent of the Parliamentary Party – Mrs Ford faces a vote of confidence and a threat to her leadership . . .'

The sheets stir and a sleepy voice mumbles, 'Oh, turn that off, will you? I was having a lovely dream about a dictatorship.'

Dennis thumps his tail on the floor approvingly.

'*. . . Meanwhile, the* Sentinel *newspaper reports that the Transport Secretary, Graham Thomas, is coming under pressure to explain how his Easter trip to the Caribbean was paid for and how he spent his time in the region. The leader of the Labour Party has written to the Cabinet Secretary, calling for a full and transparent account from Mr Thomas, who insists the trip was for official government business followed by a private family holiday. However, photos have emerged overnight of Mr Thomas in a corporate box at the England cricket friendly, with Caspar Dubois, the French rail manufacturing tycoon, whose company was announced as the winner of the East London rail link contract three days ago . . .*'

'Urgh, photos . . .' the PM groans, hitting the button on top of the radio. She takes a deep breath and cranks herself out of bed. 'Shall I ask for a cup of tea to be sent up? I think I'll go for a quick swim. Just to clear my head for later.'

'Ooh, yes please.' Michael pulls himself up against the pillows and fires up Wordle. 'Will you let Den out with you?'

The PM picks up her swimming things, being careful not to disturb the outfit laid out for later, and moves to the door where Dennis waits patiently. They head downstairs, the early morning light hitting the antique carpets and priceless oil paintings that generations of British Prime Ministers have enjoyed at

Chequers, the ancient grace and favour home reserved for their use for as long as they serve in Downing Street.

Chequers is a sanctuary, the most exclusive country house hotel imaginable maintained by Royal Navy and RAF staff. The housekeeper, Sally, is insistent that the team give the PM and her husband privacy. They could cartwheel down the corridors if they wanted to and nobody would know – or say anything, anyway. The cook makes hearty, homely meals that can be enjoyed at leisure. The study, where the PM works with Dennis dozing at her feet, is quiet and cosy. Even the Duty Clerks, who accompany her everywhere, closet themselves away in a small section of the house. Mobile phone signal at Chequers is poor and gives a perfect excuse to put off answering the constant texts until Sunday night. Here, not least in the stunning gardens, there is some space.

Only *some* space, of course. If the Fords venture out into the grounds they are carefully guarded by armed police officers, unseen and unheard but nonetheless quietly communicating over radios and roaming the telescopic sights of their rifles over the countryside. The Duty Clerks, smiling and polite as they hand over and collect papers from the iconic red box, are primed at any moment for the worst to happen: ready to patch the PM in on a secure line in the event of a major incident; ready to hand over her pristine black suit – which travels everywhere with her – to make an immediate statement in the event of the death of a member of the Royal Family; ready to alert the PM's Principal Private Secretary, the Cabinet Secretary and the Deputy Prime Minister in the event of her own incapacity or death.

The PM steps onto the terrace and listens for a moment to the birds singing. From the field of the neighbouring farm, lambs bleat tunelessly. She breathes in the fresh air, watching Dennis lollop off towards the flower beds, his crumbling hips struggling down the steps, and checks the bottom gate is shut – his eyesight is deteriorating and she worries he could wander off – before heading to the swimming pool.

The indoor pool at Chequers, a gift from the Nixon administration in the early seventies, sits alongside the terrace in a glass orangery. Although it raised eyebrows at the time – the Trust agonised over how to protect the integrity of a listed building and avoid snubbing such a generous gift from an American President – the pool, carefully incorporated into the old red-brick walled garden, with its sage-green painted timbers and shimmering glass ceiling, has become a favourite spot for Prime Ministers and their families.

After changing into her costume, the PM slips into the lapping water and begins to rhythmically breaststroke in strong, precise movements. As always happens when swimming – maybe it is just the sensation of being suspended in water – she feels the tension in her shoulders ebb away. Completing her regulation thirty lengths, she reaches the end of the pool and floats with her back to the wall, grasping the edges, feeling like a carved figure at the prow of an old ship.

She wants people to listen to her today, not whisper about the tell-tale signs of her cracking under the strain they are putting on her. It is something she feels particularly subject to as a female Prime Minister – what she is wearing and how she's styled her hair. It constantly amazes her that being described as looking tired or careworn means something quite different when it refers to her rather than her male predecessors. It means weakness and a kind of undesirableness. As a result, she has swum carefully to keep her hair dry, her neck stiff.

On the other hand, if the PM wears anything at all characterful then she's 'OTT'. The idea of wasting time thinking of how to dress to please these people irritates her. *Bollocks.* She suddenly squats down in the water, pushes her feet against the wall and jettisons herself forward, torpedo-like, feeling the cool bubbling jet-stream rinse over her face. The next best thing to skinny dipping. As she bobs back up, her hair slick over her head, she feels a degree of calm and control come over her once again. Aside from these small bursts of rage, she's lived with the white-noise feeling of dread for so long that she almost doesn't notice it any more.

Tipperton

In the foyer of Tipperton Community Hall, Bobby Cliveden sits patiently on a plastic seat, her hands folded over the neat file of notes on her lap. With her slight frame and freckled, round face she is often mistaken for much younger than her twenty-four years and generally treated as such. It used to annoy her, but as she's become more worldly she has often found it useful for people to assume she is naive. Bobby pulls her phone out and checks the time: 9.15. Weeks of chasing down Simon Daly MP – she'd eventually gatecrashed an interview he was doing with the local paper and shamed him into agreeing to a meeting – and he doesn't even have the courtesy to be on time. Hovering somewhere between irritation with him and embarrassment for herself, she fires off a message to a WhatsApp group with her two closest friends from university, Jess and Eva:

He's 15 minutes late! Do you think this is a massive waste of time?

Jess replies immediately:

Are you joking? You know the plan – start reasonably, then if necessary chuck in that you're talking to a journalist about a campaign (he doesn't need to know it's just little old me from a regional paper – and the wrong region!).

Eva chimes in:

And don't be afraid to turn on the water works. Men like him fall apart in front of a crying woman. Trust me, I know! Let him underestimate you . . .

11

Bobby doesn't think that would be hard. She puts her phone away and peers at the tatty posters advertising local book clubs, mother and baby groups and the Brownies on the foyer walls. Frowning slightly, she stands up and smooths over one of the posters of a plain building set in a few acres of leafy, tree-filled grounds, repinning it neatly so that *Stop the closure of Tipperton NHS Mental Health Unit* is clearly visible to passers-by.

Bobby stares at the poster and wonders how many she has personally handed out. The mental health unit in Tipperton has been a linchpin of her family's life for the last decade. She was about eleven years old when it became clear that her father was struggling with his mental health and became an in-patient. Stephen had joined the police force as soon as he'd left school and, once he'd married Bobby's mother, had settled into a job in the county road traffic unit. He'd often joked about how being a traffic cop felt a bit like being a goalie in football: you're either bored, sitting about with your speed gun, or stressed out of your senses dealing with an accident.

This theory was pushed to the brink when he attended the scene of a particularly bad accident, the car in question having veered off the road at high speed, crashed and gone up in a ball of flames. He was surveying the scene when he saw the paramedics pull the bloodied and blackened body of the driver out of the vehicle. He immediately recognised his own brother. Initially Stephen had been almost silent on the subject, angrily shouting, 'Stop pestering me, Liz. What's there to say about scraping your brother's brains off his steering wheel?' when Bobby's mother pressed him. Then the regular nightmares began, with Stephen desperately trying to claw his way out of a burning car wreck, and were followed by whole days when he couldn't get out of bed, exhausted after being too afraid to fall asleep the previous night. His colleagues became worried, as did his friends and family. He would disappear for hours at a time, with Elizabeth fearing the worst. He was put on sick leave from work, then eventually took early retirement.

Finally, when Bobby was doing her GCSEs, Stephen was persuaded to spend some time in the Tipperton Mental Health Unit after going missing for three days – Bobby's mother had to threaten to have him sectioned under the Mental Health Act. She and Bobby found that terms like CBT, psychosis, PTSD and depression slipped quickly and easily into their casual dinner conversation. After a few late-night panicked phone calls from her mother in Freshers' Week, Bobby had taken up a routine of coming home each weekend for the three years of university. After graduating, despite the promise of a job offer in London, Bobby had chosen to stay in Tipperton until the situation stabilised. Happily, Stephen is now in a routine of therapy and medication.

Bobby's lifeline has been her friendship with Jess and Eva, who she met at Cambridge, and who, though far away, give her constant support and light relief. With Bobby's weekend absences, Jess's dedication to the student newspaper and Eva's infatuation with the Union, they agree they're unlikely friends. But with the same college, same course and same tutorial group they were pretty much thrown together. They're very different people – Jess tenacious and tough; Eva charming and witty; Bobby sensitive and empathetic – but for whatever reason, their friendship works, their shared sense of humour, fierce loyalty to each other and a burning ambition doing the rest.

Jess and Eva's progress – Jess as a journalist in Scotland, Eva as a junior government adviser in London – is a constant source of discussion between Bobby and her mother, and the time had felt right for Bobby to fly the nest too. But the mental health unit, which has become a critical part of the Clivedens' lives, and the lives of dozens of local families who depend on it, is due to be closed. If this happens, Elizabeth will have to give up her job

13

to drive Stephen to the next closest facility – over eighty miles away – or reckon with the prospect of simply leaving him there for weeks at a time. Practicalities aside, Stephen generally only takes steps forward these days, but this change in routine and existence could upset the delicate Cliveden family ecosystem.

Bobby is staying put and has taken on the task of starting the campaign to save the unit. For weeks, she has run petitions in the local community, spoken to clinicians and the families of patients and even headed small fundraising efforts. It's only recently that she read that campaigning the government through MPs and departments – and the media, of course – is a far more direct route. With time running out, Bobby is in a hurry to pin down her local MP and get him on the case to advocate for the community.

The MP in question, Simon Daly, is driving down the high street to their meeting. Tipperton's an all right sort of place, he reasons, but nothing like Surrey, where he was brought up. Okay, there's lovely walking in the National Park and the pies are delicious and a pint is very fairly priced. It's quite pretty when it isn't raining. But there's also the many pound shops and morris dancers and the estates of identical new builds on the edge of town. Regardless of all that, the good and wise people of Tipperton elected him as their MP – a pleasantly safe seat in this part of the world – and so anything they think is good, Daly thinks is good. Even football.

He pulls into the car park of Tipperton Community Hall, turns off the engine, and sits for a second, examining his handsome face in the rear-view mirror. The marathon training in aid of the local hospice is really paying off. He had been getting quite bloated from late-night glasses of House of Commons plonk on the Terrace, and clocking up his miles of jogging has the added benefit of looking like a good egg locally.

As ever, at the top of his mind is cash. Like so many in his position, he finds the life of an MP to be a pricey one. There are the obvious things like rent and travel, which he and his colleagues are careful to expense, but there are all kinds of hidden costs like raffle tickets and coffee mornings and donating to sponsored walks and knit-a-thons. He seems to be constantly getting money out of ATMs to give to somebody to bathe in baked beans. And he can't even complain about it! To the average person, an £80,000 salary, plus expenses, is extortionate. MPs crying about struggling to balance their Berry Bros account would hardly expect an outpouring of sympathy from the public. Still, there is no denying that compared to his time as a solicitor at a top London law firm, the pay is measly. He'd given it all up to give something back by becoming an MP – he didn't realise it meant giving the shirt from his back.

Daly exhales heavily and drums his fingers on the leather steering wheel of the Audi, thinking of the cheery air he now needs to put on all morning. He hates this kind of stuff, even if he knows he is good at it. So much of his life in his constituency is spent fobbing off people or stamping on inconvenient problems – local maternity wing closure, ugly solar panel planning applications, petty disputes of one kind or another. The list is endless and he is constantly hit with the uncomfortable reality that his need to be liked by everybody can't be matched by the amount of money or time to go round.

This bothersome issue with Ms Cliveden is nothing new. He cringes in his seat, thinking once again about how it makes him look to have a mental health unit close in his patch, but the harsh reality is that he doesn't really want to kick up a stink. He really wants a new A-road – it was the cornerstone of his selection to become the Parliamentary candidate – and it's really much cleaner to focus his energy on one department – and the Treasury, of course. It is also the case, though he will never say this is a factor, that his strongest supporters and biggest donors in the constituency are pretty much all pro-closure in private – some of them vehemently so. His most generous donor, Jeffrey Cuthbert of Cuthberts, a local developer, is the most strident on the subject and has often made the observation that people like to say the NHS is bloated and that small cottage hospitals need closing to merge into proper, state-of-the-art facilities with every feasible therapy and treatment – unless it's their own. Regardless, the local paper is now sending his office questions about this on a daily basis, and there is a growing local social media campaign. Time to take care of it.

Leaving the leather-clad sanctuary of the car, Daly steps into the hall through a side entrance and finds Moira, his trusty constituency office manager, making tea in a small kitchen. Six years ago he'd inherited Moira from his predecessor. Now in her early sixties, she has worked for the Tipperton Conservative Association for nearly twenty-five years and makes Daly's government role of Parliamentary Under Secretary (a junior minister, known as a PUS) in the Foreign Office possible by running the part of his job that he's actually been elected to do, while he travels the world. *Mrs Muscle*, he calls her privately. *Does the jobs you hate.*

'Moizy, darling, you look sensaish. The new diet is really working.' Moira rolls her lilac-shadowed eyes and gives an irritable shake of her head, which makes the mass of yellow hair on top of it wobble. 'Has that Roberta Cliveden woman arrived yet?' he asks, leaning against the counter and selecting a biscuit from a tin.

'She's been waiting in the foyer for nearly twenty minutes,' Moira says tersely, filling a milk jug. 'I need you to get it over with quickly because we have to talk about staffing before all your other meetings. We're absolutely racing through people down in Parliament. They're either incompetent airheads or they just ... *leave.*'

Daly hates the judgemental tone she uses, the old trout. She can't have it both ways – she voted for the smooth, young Simon Daly as the Conservative candidate along with the rest of the Association. He'd promised they'd get an eventual Cabinet minister. He didn't promise to be Tipperton's answer to Mother Teresa.

Like many of his fellow MPs, Daly lives a strange, double life. Within the boundaries of the constituency of Tipperton, he is the dutiful husband, son-in-law and local representative. When Parliament is sitting during the week, Daly stays in London and travels abroad frequently as part of his Foreign Office job. As a result, bar a few weekends and patches of the long Parliamentary recesses, Daly lives as a freewheeling bachelor, with every conceivable perk. There have been girls. There's no point in denying it. But he's not an idiot – all consensual and cheerful and completely hidden from his wife, Susie. Besides, he's such a small potato as a PUS that there's no real scrutiny of his behaviour. Yet.

Daly gives Moira's thick body a glance. Nag, nag, nag. He is sick of her being on his case. *He* is the MP: he has the star quality, the knack of charming everybody, the ability to get away with things that a wrinkled old spud like Moira can't. On life's silver screen, he is the lead actor – Moira is just in a supporting role. Maybe even an extra.

'So anyway,' Moira continues, 'I've lined up some candidates and I want you to read their applications and decide who you want to speak to before this lunch—'

'Aha, yes!' interrupts Daly, delighted to have a new topic of discussion. 'With the Prime Minister. Ever been to Chequers?' When she doesn't answer, Daly shrugs and pulls out his phone. 'Whatever, yes . . .' he sighs, 'great.'

He moodily crams a second biscuit into his mouth as he scrolls through his messages and smirks at a new video on his

'Legislative Lads' WhatsApp group of a porn star popping a champagne cork out of her vagina:

See you at Chequers. Here's to a corking party.

'I'm serious.' Moira turns to face him, hands on hips. 'Since Annie resigned,' she raises an eyebrow, 'the Parliamentary team is completely snowed under. Do you know there is a backlog of fourteen hundred emails? I had Lucy on the phone yesterday at her wits' end. She is seriously worried someone is going to speak to the Ombudsman or something.' Moira looks directly into Daly's bored face. 'Simon, this Graham Thomas stuff has really spooked everybody. There is an important lesson here in having a well-run office. The silly old bugger has had so many warnings from the Parliamentary Standards people – things like these returns do actually matter. All he had to do was tell his team what he'd been up to so they could write it up. It hardly gets noticed if done properly.'

'Yes, yes ... Damn shame Annie left us so abruptly ...' muses Daly, thinking of Annie's lithe figure. Moira stares at him, baffled that that is his key takeaway from what she's just said. 'Still,' he says airily, brushing the crumbs off his fingers and putting his phone away, 'we must struggle on without her. I will return shortly to fulfil all your wishes, Moiz.' He winks from the door. Moira, not for the first time, gives his retreating back the middle finger.

Bobby is skimming her notes when she hears a door open.

'Ah, you must be Miss Cliveden,' says Daly, striding over and flashing a winning smile. Bobby stands and offers her hand, taking in his sleek hair and tanned face.

'Nice to meet you, Mr Daly. I'm Roberta. But I prefer Bobby. Anyway, thank you for your time.'

'Please,' Daly gestures to a desk and chairs at the far end of the hall. As they walk he looks at her sideways. She looks barely out of school, he thinks with a smirk. I can't believe I was worried about this campaign.

'So before we get started, tell me a little about yourself,' he twinkles, pulling a chair out for her to sit down.

'Well, I grew up here,' Bobby picks up the cup of steaming tea that Moira has placed in front of her, 'and then since graduating from university—'

'University! Good for you,' Daly chips in, 'somewhere local?' Daly himself went to Oxford, where he studied PPE. An essential stage of the assembly line for future Prime Ministers. He casts an eye over Bobby. Hull, most likely.

Eva's text flashes before Bobby's eyes: *Let him underestimate you.*

Bobby pauses for a moment then continues. 'Since graduating from university I've been temping at some local businesses, tutoring and helping my mother care for my father, who is a sometime resident of the Tipperton Mental Health Unit, and – as you know – I'm campaigning to keep the unit open.'

Daly nods seriously but says nothing.

'Anyway,' says Bobby, 'we need your help and seeing as my letters and calls have gone unanswered I've come to see you in person.'

'And, uh ... tell me more about your campaign.' Daly leans back in his chair and puts his hands behind his head. She really is cute. All thoughts of Annie have now gone.

'Well, Mr Daly—'

He waves the formality away. 'Please, call me Simon.'

'Well, Simon,' Bobby says evenly, taking a deep breath, 'as you're aware, the unit caters for people with all kinds of mental health needs. My father, for example, has been in and out of there for nearly a decade. He was a police officer and has PTSD and depression. Some of his fellow patients have addiction issues, childhood trauma, schizophrenia ... It's a complicated picture. Some patients need to stay in a ward for a while, many are day patients and live locally like my dad and some just come in as and when. It isn't exactly a secret that there simply aren't enough beds to go round nationally, so the resource here is precious.' Bobby opens her folder. 'I'm sure you're aware that the unit was built through a PFI contract twenty-five years ago, and it's coming to an end next year. The NHS Trust has concluded that it can't continue to keep it running. The nearest facility after ours is an eighty-mile drive away, which is hardly feasible for local families.' Bobby sits back in her chair and shrugs her shoulders. 'I keep trying and failing to find ways to keep it open and time is running out. The contract collapses imminently. So I've come to you.'

Christ, this is tricky, thinks Daly. He is tempted to ask why the NHS Trust doesn't think carrying on the unit is viable, but already knows it is from repaying the massive debt owed to the PFI contract consortium who built (or in this case converted a listed building) and maintained it. He knows those things are a bad business and honestly doesn't have a clue what to suggest.

'And how can I help you?' asks Daly, his eyes idly roving over the neatly typed papers on the table. 'Did you know my wife was studying to become a therapist when I met her? It is an issue very close to both of our hearts.' Doesn't hurt to look a bit clued in.

'I didn't know that, but I'm so glad you're keen to take an interest.' Bobby smiles at him. 'Truthfully, I'm not sure where to begin. I'm new to campaigning. And policy. But I suppose it would help if you lobbied the Secretary of State for Health – plus perhaps the Chancellor and Prime Minister – to help. Maybe ask them to ring-fence money for these units across the country. I doubt we are the only place facing this problem.' Bobby speaks faster, her enthusiasm blowing away her nerves. 'Perhaps they could make these buildings protected spaces. Or we could persuade someone to buy the building off the NHS and the government could create a tax break for property owners who lease assets to these kinds of facilities at a reduced rate? I'm sure as a government minister with such an interest in this your help would—'

'Now, Bobby,' Daly interjects. 'This campaign of yours is extremely impressive and I've followed it with interest.' He pauses, scratching his chin as he thinks about what to say next. 'You should be very proud of yourself. I've already spoken to the Secretary of State for Health who insists it is a local decision—'

'But you're the *local* MP.' Bobby tries to keep a tinge of irritation out of her voice. 'Surely this matters to you?'

'Of course it matters!' choruses Daly, looking hurt that she could so badly misunderstand him. 'It matters to me greatly. But if the NHS won't change its mind and there's no more money to fund the unit, then we're talking about a likely change in the law here. The government has a limited budget and an extremely full legislative agenda . . .' he trails off. 'I can of course write to everyone I can but,' he smiles sadly, 'I can't really do anything more than that.'

'Well . . .' Bobby can feel her frustration threatening to bubble over. She has been trying to track this guy down for months. He could have told her this ages ago and now the clock is running down. 'Well, I don't quite know what to do now.'

'Like I say, you've run a fantastic campaign,' Daly claps his hands together and rises from the desk, 'something to be really proud—'

'Could I ask you for some advice, Simon?' Bobby asks abruptly, the plan she'd made earlier with Jess and Eva leaping into her mind. Daly raises his eyebrows. 'I was contacted by a journalist yesterday, who is extremely interested in what we're doing.' Bobby sees Daly's eyes widen. *Bingo.* 'They seemed to think it is a bit of a human interest story for them. All very emotive. They think it might be worth doing something nationally.' She gestures at the documents on the desk.

I bet they do, thinks Daly.

'Anyway, I'd sort of agreed that they can come up here and talk to us about it.' Daly's sense of unease grows. 'And ...' Bobby glances at him sideways, forcing a small wobble into her voice. 'And now I feel like I've led them down the garden path ...' She sniffs loudly. 'All I'll be able to tell them is the unit is going to close and I've let my dad down.' She slams her small fist on the table and is surprised to notice real tears come to her eyes. She lets them pour out. 'I've wasted all this time since Cambridge for no reason!'

Daly thinks for a moment. He is so absorbed that he almost fails to register the word 'Cambridge'. Hull, indeed. Maybe he should attend the Parliamentary unconscious bias training after all. Anyway, one story is hardly going to scupper him. Everyone has to sit through a sticky news cycle from time to time. He can ride this out.

'Don't worry, it's just one journalist,' he says, mainly to himself.

'Well, that's the thing,' Bobby sniffs, seeing exactly where Daly is going, 'they're talking about a whole campaign around it. They've got behind hospital closures before and,' she searches her mind for something plausible, and lets out another sob, 'they're doing a big push on mental health this year.'

Daly immediately jumps up and steps around the desk, pulling a handkerchief out of his pocket. He kneels down and hands it to her, thinking fast. Problems, problems.

'Don't worry, Bobby,' he says kindly, patting her on the shoulder. 'I'll help you.'

'But,' she sobs, 'if the campaign isn't going anywhere, this journalist will think they've been called up here for no reason ...'

Oh, they'll have a reason, Daly says to himself. A government minister, who has made mental health treatment for victims of conflict abroad a core part of his brief – and which he speaks so feelingly about at the despatch box – simply

22

nodding through the closure of a centre that caters for the most vulnerable right here in his constituency without a fight ... the story writes itself.

'Now, Bobby.' Daly wills himself into action, his eyes roaming around the room, grasping for an idea. 'Now ...' He hears a cupboard door close in the kitchen and thinks of Moira working away in there and a thought strikes him.

'Bobby,' he clears his throat and holds her by both shoulders, 'I've got a plan.'

Bobby looks at him in full Bambi mode, her watery eyes hopeful.

'What we're going to do is this. You're going to come and work for me in Westminster. Move down to London and, uh, really take this campaign to where it matters.' He clears his throat loudly while his mind continues to race ahead, trouble-shooting as he speaks. 'We can tell this journalist that we're going to fix this local issue and take it national' – so in the meantime they can politely shut their pie hole while we work it all out, Daly thinks – 'and change the law!'

There is a stunned silence. This is the last thing Bobby had expected to happen. She just thought she could push Daly into writing some letters and do some mild cage-rattling. She's always had a pretty dim view of politicians and it has certainly never occurred to her to work for an MP. Not least a Conservative MP. And definitely not *this* Conservative MP. But this seems like the only way to save the unit. She can keep her eye on this slippery character and come home as much as she did at university ... and her mother does keep saying that she wants her to use her degree properly ... But does she really want to work for an MP? Well, a small ambitious voice niggles at her, Daly is definitely one to watch. Who knows where this could lead?

'Th-thank you,' she stutters, 'thank you so much. I ... I ... I'd love to.' Bobby begins laughing, wiping her eyes.

Daly's face floods with relief and his bounce instantly returns. You son of a gun, you've done it again.

'Of course.' He pats her shoulder and moves back around the table. 'Moira!'

Moira pokes her head round the door.

'Moira, the brilliant Bobby has agreed to come and join my Parliamentary office – could you call Lucy and let her know?' Daly grins broadly. 'Moira is a total hero and makes everything at this end tick. Lucy is the Parliamentary office manager, in London. There are some forms and things I'll expect you have to do but Moira and Lucy will help you with all that.'

Moira smiles tightly, casting her eye over Bobby's athletic frame, taking in her glossy brown hair and slim legs.

'Well, that is good news, Simon. You are a dark horse, I must say: I wasn't even aware this was a job interview . . . What would you like me to say to the other seven people we'd short-listed? And I'd *love* to see Bobby's CV and references. She must be an impressive candidate to have been taken on so fast!'

Daly's grin stiffens. 'Well, Moira, I know talent when I see it: you're my Tipperton office manager after all, so clearly I only work with the crème de la crème of administrative staff.' Moira doesn't smile. 'Bobby recently graduated from Cambridge – more sciences than classics – but hardly the airhead, don't you think?' Daly gabbles. 'And, as you say, we really need a sharp mind and attention to detail . . . Cancel the others, there's a love.'

Daly turns his back on Moira's hard look.

'Oh, Bobby, you must also speak to Moira about standing as a Parliamentary candidate. Moira's done it *loads* of times, haven't you, Moizy? Stood in some absolutely dreadful places. Keeps trying, though.' Moira stares at her feet. 'Still, we've all got to have something that gets us out of bed in the morning.' Daly winks at Bobby, who ignores him. 'So . . . how soon can you start?'

Twenty minutes later, the conversation finally sinking in, Bobby marches purposefully down the high street, returning waves. She knows each shop and café. The leisure centre, the library, the bowling alley. The schools and churches. Everything is gleaming in the morning sunshine. Bobby can't believe that the plan has worked! She can't wait to get home and tell her mother what has happened – and that she's moving to London. Her heart is full. Well, nearly full. It was going to be a wrench to leave her parents, but this is her best shot at securing the unit permanently.

She thinks about Moira, who does not seem pleased with Bobby's appointment. Bobby wonders if Moira had seen through her tearful act. They had a brief introductory chat while Bobby filled in a form and it was clear that Moira has a low tolerance for fools. She will be checking Bobby's work and expecting the highest standards – and Bobby is not to take any decisions relating to the constituency without checking with Moira first. It was like meeting the Mother Superior. The only time she had softened was when Bobby explained her connection to the unit. But it had only been momentary – Moira had sighed heavily and carried on passing Bobby forms.

Back in the community hall bathroom, Daly sits in a cubicle and wonders to himself why exactly he just created this new rod for his back. Does he really need another Annie-type situation? And how on earth is he going to save this unit? He hasn't a clue where to start. Still, he's got form in navigating his way through messes. Something will turn up.

Glasgow

At 10 a.m., some three hundred miles away, Jess Adler sends Bobby a congratulatory WhatsApp and marches up to a doorstep in a Glasgow suburb. She pauses to straighten her coat and smooth her hair before knocking, holding her press accreditation in one hand and her phone, set to a voice recorder app, in the other. This is easily one of the most testing parts of her job as a crime and justice correspondent at the *Glasgow Tribune*. Sifting through death notices to find one of interest (which in this case means 'young' – the woman who has died was still at college), then interrupting a family's grief to try and learn more about the loved one they've lost. At least with cold-calling from a phone bank, you don't risk getting punched.

Jess has been at the *Tribune* for the three years since she left university and is keenly aware that some of her Cambridge peers wonder – with a smirk, she suspects – why she hadn't landed a job on a serious London-based broadsheet straight after graduating. She had been one to watch in her year, after all: editor of the university newspaper, a gymnastics blue, a first in History. And yet here she is at the *Glasgow Tribune* rather than *The Times*. It is a choice she's made, but her competitive side prickles at the thought that the public schoolboys she'd bossed about at *Varsity* have landed coveted roles at top London papers, via a conveyor belt of unpaid summer internships that Jess couldn't possibly have afforded to do – or had the address book for. She notices that this gang have quickly embraced the so-called Westminster Bubble, feverishly watching their Twitter follower numbers go up as they share their self-important analysis of 'what the public are thinking' from the latest snap poll.

Jess tries not to lose herself in these sorts of sour reflections. She has chosen journalism, and she has chosen to do it from the bottom up. Patient, tough and a firm believer in graft – one of the few things she has in common with her parents – she likes what she does. Far from reporting the gossipy stories swirling around SW1, she is seeing for herself the drivers of devastating poverty, drug use and violent crime. Her doughty editor has let her run a series recently on women who have been in abusive relationships and their journeys through 'the system'. Seeing them go into court, watching them lose their nerve and refuse to give evidence against the smirking, pseudo-contrite Mickey sitting in the dock. Listening to meetings between them and their social workers as they discuss the removal of their children. She is learning how 'the system' – the police, the social services, the courts – can let people down again and again because of anything from chronic underfunding to institutional rot.

Jess documents all of it in the hope of a longer-term project. It feels like a vital story, and she is an important witness to it. She wouldn't want to be doing anything else. She remembers the excitement she'd felt at getting to interview a Cabinet minister at university. A load of waffle. Nothing could feel less important now.

The youngest of seven children, she has always been determined to make her mark on parents who are understandably distracted by her six other siblings and the grinding work of a sheep farm in the Borders. Jess was the only Adler child to get into Cambridge, the only one to go into journalism and, now, the only single one. She loves her parents and her siblings but has developed a revulsion for conformity. Her oldest brother once mockingly referred to Jess as a libertine, after she returned home from a teen holiday with experimental hair dye, a belly button piercing and a couple of small tattoos. Jess has found herself embracing that persona, instinctively pushing against her family's roster of early, long-term relationships based on *Strictly Come Dancing* Saturday evenings and cosy Sunday roast lunches. Jess wonders whether this is what drew her to Eva (something of the exotic, rock 'n' roll about her adolescence compared to Jess's summers of pony club and young farmers) and Bobby (the perfect, ready-made younger sibling Jess never had, ready to absorb worldly advice like a sponge).

27

Jess's thoughts are interrupted by the sound of steps moving towards the front door. She prepares her best, most sympathetic smile. *I'm so sorry to disturb you at this time, and on a Saturday . . .*

A man in a loud check suit answers. It is Geordie Adams, a rival from the *Herald*. Jess's smile falters.

'Piss off, mate. I've beaten you to it.' Geordie sticks out his tongue. 'Drinks on you later.' The door is slammed in Jess's face. 'Just some bloody gawpers. Have sent them packing. Now . . . do go on . . .' Geordie's voice trails off down the hallway.

Bollocks.

This happens sometimes, but her editor, Magnus Campbell, will still be furious. Jess walks slowly back down the path, racking her brains for a different angle that Geordie might miss to pacify Magnus. She's certainly lost the family story now. She pauses on the street for a moment, jingling her car keys and thinking of Geordie's leering face at the door.

Suddenly an idea comes to her and she strides over to her car, typing into Google on her phone as she walks.

Ninety minutes later, Jess leaves the salon where the young woman had been a trainee and dashes to a café to type up her words. As she had suspected, no other journalist had thought to go and interview the young woman's friends. Through her careful and sensitive questioning, Jess gains the group's trust and has emerged with a vivid picture of their dark party culture – plus a sense that the young woman's family might not know the full story.

Jess is just hitting send when her phone rings. It's Magnus.

'Hello, boss. Tell everyone to keep their pants on, I've just sent it through,' Jess says cheerfully. 'I suppose you've heard Geordie got to the family. I've just been to the salon—'

'I don't care. I need you to come back to the office,' Magnus cuts in brusquely.

28

'Um, right. Okay.' Jess fumbles getting her key into the ignition. 'I'll head back now. Fifteen minutes.'

The line goes dead. Jess tells herself there is nothing to be worried about. True, she is coming to the end of a two year contract and is waiting to hear if it will be renewed. True, Magnus had hardly sounded friendly on the phone, but when did he? He has a disconcerting habit of just hanging up when he's finished speaking. He has a knack for making you feel uneasy: it is hard to know where you stand, when he is so unpleasant half the time and jovial and kind the other half. He certainly hadn't sounded jovial just now. Jess feels a knot of anxiety travel up from her stomach into her chest as she follows the road along the Clyde to the *Tribune* offices.

After parking, she dashes to the bathroom in the foyer to touch up her makeup with slightly shaky fingers. She looks into the mirror at her angular face, her pale skin set off by her dyed black hair, and meets her own gaze as she used to do countless times before gymnastics competitions. It always steadies her, and as she exhales a deep breath she lifts her chin in a defiant attitude. She's got the *Tribune* some brilliant stories, her copy hardly needs a scrap of editing and, she knows, her ability to judge the right moment to tease Magnus has made her one of his favourite reporters. Everything's fine. She straightens her collar and sweeps towards the lifts.

She reaches Magnus's office and knocks on the door.

'Come in,' he barks.

Jess walks into the room with her arms folded. When Magnus doesn't look up from what he's reading she reaches behind her and pushes the door closed with a loud snap. 'You wanted to see me.'

'Yes,' he grunts, digging around in his breast pocket and pulling out an e-cigarette. He leans his considerable weight back in his chair and surveys Jess sullenly through his dense

29

eyebrows. Magnus has a thick, wild head of grey hair and a matching wolfish beard, streaked with yellow. He puffs out a wisp of rhubarb and custard vapour, his chosen way to keep up his nicotine levels between his lunchtime and evening cigars.

'Your contract has come to an end.'

Jess shifts her hands to her hips, determined to fight. 'Yes, I know.'

'We aren't renewing it.'

She bites the inside of her cheek.

'Right, well ... Thank you for the opportunity.' Jess turns to the door.

'I haven't finished.'

Jess stops and closes her eyes for a moment, then faces him again.

'We haven't renewed your contract because I've recommended you for another role.'

She frowns, confused. 'Doing what?'

Magnus takes another deep, rattling inhalation on his e-cig that reminds Jess of the caterpillar from *Alice in Wonderland*, and says to the ceiling, 'Junior lobby bod for the *Sentinel*.'

He dips his chin to look at her stunned face.

'Well, this is a first,' he smirks. 'I've finally shut you up.'

'I, uh ... I don't know what to say.'

'Well, don't say thanks, not yet anyway.'

Jess raises her eyebrows.

'The situation is this ...' Magnus sits upright, grunting with effort. 'Ed Cooper is the political editor there, and his position is about as solid as they come.' Jess steps closer to the desk to listen. 'StoryCorps execs, who oversee the paper, are determined to have a woman in the junior correspondent role – the way things are now I suppose – but the latest has just left after eleven months, which I'm told is the record time someone has put up with Ed. I got word they're after someone tough,' he gestures towards her, taking another puff, 'to pick up the mantle until the end of the year – maybe beyond. It's a weird arrangement, but Ed is a weird guy and they want to hold on to him and be,' he shakes his head irritably, '*diverse* . . . So I thought: two for the price of one. Do someone down there a favour, and give Ed a headache.' He leans back and smiles at the ceiling again.

Jess opens her mouth to speak, but he cuts in.

'I should be clear, though.' Magnus takes yet another drag and lets his breath whistle through his teeth. 'I know Ed Cooper,' he growls at the ceiling. 'He is a total bastard.'

Jess waits to see if he will say anything else, but he just continues to gaze upwards. Magnus has always snidely referred to the Westminster press lobby as 'Twatter' – chatter and Twitter – and Jess has firmly taken the same view. So why recommend her to go down there, if he thinks the work his newspaper does is far superior?

'Well, Magnus,' she says, 'thank you for putting me forward for this . . . I like doing what I do here, though . . . the stories I've been doing on domestic abuse – I, I think they're getting a bit of cut-through now. It's a flattering offer . . . ' Jess trails off.

Magnus holds up the sheet of paper he'd been reading. It's the piece she sent through earlier.

'You're a good writer and you get me great stuff. The stories you're doing are powerful. Sad thing is no one reads them. It isn't like when I started out. We could afford long-term projects like what you've been working on . . . Look, just take this in the spirit it's meant – this is a run at the big time.'

There is an awkward pause, as Magnus pulls himself up from his chair and walks around the desk until he stands in front of her, his blue eyes suddenly fiery.

'I'm serious about what I said about Ed, though. I know I'm hard on you but I am Miss Honey compared to him. There can be no teasing, no piss-taking, no room for manoeuvre.' He looks at Jess, hard. 'He will belittle you in front of other people. He will treat you as his skivvy. He will nick your stories. And there's nothing you can do about it because there is no such thing as fair play or complaining where you're going.' He smacks his fist into his palm with each word. 'You have to box smart.'

After one final hard look he turns back to his desk. 'Now, you'd better get packing. You start next Monday.'

Shocked again by his abruptness, Jess stumbles towards the door then stops.

'Magnus?'

'Yeah?' He's back to studying the ceiling.

'This Ed Cooper character. Just on . . . handling. What if I got past him to the editor?'

'Philip? He's a good guy but I wouldn't count on him being able to vouch for you. Ed has some clout with the high-ups down there. He'll make your life a living hell if he thinks you're undermining him.'

'Hm,' Jess thinks for a moment. 'Is he, uh, married?'

Magnus chuckles throatily. 'I like where your head's at.'

'Well, is he?'

'He is. But he's not met you yet, kid.'

'Understood.'

As the door is about to close he shouts out one last time: 'Remember, box smart!'

Claybourne Terrace

In Pimlico, Eva Cross stands in front of her bedroom mirror, studying herself carefully. She is wearing a matching set of red lace bra and knickers and holds a long-sleeved navy woollen polo-neck dress against herself. The dress is a gift from her mother from when she started her job, and is easily the most expensive thing she owns. She has promised that she'll wear it only for special occasions and, seeing as today is her first event at Chequers, it feels this should be its maiden outing.

Eva turns to the side view and rubs her tummy, frowning. She ruefully thinks about the salty reception canapés and warm white wine that have lately become her evening meals in her role as a junior adviser in the Prime Minister's political office. Because Eva's room is the only area in Number Ten without any civil servants (her team does strictly party political business for the PM in her role as Leader of the Conservative Party), fellow political appointees known as Special Advisers – SpAds for short – often congregate in there to gossip and gobble up the leftovers from the reception celebrating Chinese New Year or marking International Women's Day or welcoming the report into the life cycle of the toad in the State Rooms upstairs. No booze today, Eva thinks, need to be on high alert. It's just so easily done when you're cornered by someone boring.

A sleepy voice from the bed interrupts her thoughts. 'Hang on, I've not seen those before. When were you going to show them to me?'

Eva draws herself up and looks over her shoulder coquettishly. 'You're seeing them now, aren't you?'

'Yes, but I wish to *really* see them . . . explore them,' the man says, nestling in among the pillows.

'Well, Jamie, you can look now and touch another time.' Eva turns sideways so Jamie can see the curve of her breasts and bottom. 'Anyway, I had to get new stuff. I've done a bit of filling out recently so I thought I may as well do some tarting up at the same time.' She snaps a red bra strap.

There's a click and an intake of breath and Eva sees reflected in the mirror Jamie's handsome face watching her through a wisp of cigarette smoke, his arms folded sulkily across his bare, tanned chest.

Eva met Jamie Whitmore at the Henley Regatta a year ago, when he accidentally poured a glass of Pimm's down her backless dress. She hadn't been able to resist his arrogant apology ('Oh dear, I seem to have made you wet. Care to get wetter?'). He is funny and attentive and has the gift of being able to make easy conversation with anybody. Eva is clever and connected and pretty. They both know that they're two bright young things, and with Jamie's job in the City sitting squarely away from politics, Eva feels she's safe to live out her private life in peace. In SW1, nothing shuts down tedious enquiries into what your boyfriend is like more than, 'Well, he works in finance.'

Eva knows she is an object of fascination in Westminster. Two weeks after she turned thirteen her father, Percy Cross, had become Prime Minister of the United Kingdom of Great Britain and Northern Ireland. For exactly two years and 299 days – the same incumbency as the Duke of Wellington, Percy's idol – Eva had lived in Downing Street, growing up in the public eye and dogged by strange rumours of her father's affairs. Just shy of her sixteenth birthday, Percy had been forced to resign in disgrace after photos emerged of him having a particularly graphic stretching session with his personal trainer in some bushes in St James's Park. The fallout had been terrible. The national media had camped outside the school gates and the rental home her mother, Jenny, had moved her to. Eva had endured excruciating bullying and her parents' marriage had fallen apart.

Now, the Cross surname is synonymous with sex. Percy, rollicking around the after-dinner speaking circuit leaving women, towering debts and empty bottles behind him, is only too happy to mix the private with the public. He makes his living off poorly researched hagiographies of his favourite historical figures and *GQ*, *Playboy* and *Telegraph* columns that depend on his back catalogue of risqué anecdotes to capture

34

the growing mass of readers who so enjoy his witty takes on navigating Pornhub categories as a silver surfer.

Eva has learned from painful experience that people she thought she could trust will talk and the media can turn on a sixpence (glossy features in *Tatler* one day, embarrassing university stories from so-called friends in *The Sun* the next). She didn't even find safety with her mother, who used the chubby, teenage Eva as Exhibit A in her First Lady Vlog, which chronicled a whole series about her developing daughter – a low point being 'Eva's first period'. Jenny has since launched a TV career off the back of her split from Percy, pitching fad diets and cleanses and revenge bodies to fellow middle-aged divorcees, and has announced her decision to publish her memoirs, which promise to be toe-curling. So yes, Eva has good reason to keep her private life hidden away.

'What are you doing today?' she asks, balancing on an armchair and pulling on a pair of black tights.

Jamie blows a smoke ring. 'Playing tennis and counting down the minutes until I see you next, I s'pose.'

'I'll leave you some keys,' Eva zips up a high-heeled suede boot, 'I've got Dad's set. Which reminds me, do you think he'll care if I invite Bobby and Jess to stay here? Just until they find their feet. It's his house, but he's away for a while, so the company would be wonderful.'

'What about me?'

'Well, you aren't a paying guest. And no, sexual favours don't count,' Eva smirks.

'Where is he, anyway?'

'Gone off to do this professorship or something at a college in California until the end of the summer. The college admissions scandal is nothing compared with the reality that they're paying Dad actual money to teach.' She looks thoughtfully at her booted feet. 'I hope they like Latin.'

'God help those West Coast freshmen,' intones Jamie, 'you'll have a stepmother who's younger than you at the rate he's going.' He puts on a gruff, irritatingly good impression of Percy's voice and cups his hands on imaginary breasts, '*Salve puellae.*' Jamie, who rather likes Percy, is always careful to stay on the upbeat, jolly side when the subject of Eva's father comes up. His own relationship with his parents being normal, Jamie doesn't know how else to deal with the occasional outburst Eva has about hers.

Eva stands up.

'It's pretty cosmic though, right? Bobby and Jess coming to London at the same time – and for political jobs too!'

Eva hopes Jess and Bobby will come and live with her. She wouldn't admit it, but she's lonely and she doesn't have another way to find housemates. Upon starting at Number Ten, she had been presented with a summary of her online activity, prepared by a mole-like researcher from Conservative Campaign Headquarters (CCHQ), detailing every excruciating teenage musing, fancy dress or bikini picture ready to be found by a nosy journalist or troublesome Labour HQ researcher. Panicked, she had immediately deleted every account she held, which means she has shrunk her world right down. There's no way she could issue a social media callout for flatmates. Admittedly, she is in touch with everyone she really needs to be, but that is quite a modest circle of family and friends, plus the politicos she mixes with after work at house parties and pubs.

Jamie's eyes follow Eva as she walks in front of the mirror once again. The navy dress hugs her body but, with the long sleeves, high neck and black tights, only the skin on her hands and face are exposed. She pulls her sandy blonde hair back into a modest bun at the nape of her neck, and adds a pair of small pearl earrings. She looks simultaneously sexy and demure. Enough to spark a man's interest, but not enough for a woman to be threatened. She wonders how many of the other women going today are performing this exact same dance right now: clothes piling on the bed; lipstick being applied and wiped off; the narrow path between trendy and try-hard lost in a mapless wardrobe of trusty navy and cream.

'E-va, isn't there time for just a quick one?' Jamie butts into her thoughts, a begging tone in his deep voice.

'Oh, don't whine,' she snaps, but softens when she sees his face in the mirror. 'Sorry, I didn't mean to sound cross,' she narrows her eyes and grins, 'but you didn't even say please.'

Without losing eye contact Eva walks slowly around the side of the bed until she stands before Jamie, then she leans in and removes the cigarette dangling from his mouth, stubbing it out. She creeps her right hand forward until she clasps his fingertips and uses them to slide her skirt up her thigh, towards her hips. Jamie feels his mouth go dry and swallows hard, as she silently skims a leg over him, continuing to look into his eyes.

Jamie wraps his hands around Eva's waist and feels himself stiffen as she pushes her weight into his lap. He moves his hands further down until he is gripping her, a cheek in each hand. He moans softly as Eva gently kisses up his neck from his collarbone to his ear. His fingers are massaging beneath her, Eva's breath responding to his touch through the tights. Jamie finds it tricky, but manages to manoeuvre his hand under the waistband. He can tell he's doing a pretty good job, based on Eva's increasingly loud gasps. Then Eva's phone buzzes. Jamie groans.

She sits up abruptly, completely recovered, and reads a message. It's her boss, Peter Foulkes, the Prime Minister's Political Secretary:

Come on, missus. I'm outside.

'I've got to go,' Eva says, tapping out a quick reply.

'Oh please no,' Jamie says desperately. 'I was just waking up. It isn't fair.'

Eva smiles down at him and he feels a brief flicker of hope as she leans down, her warm breath tickling his neck. He can feel the kiss coming. Instead she bites his ear, hard.

'Ouch!' Jamie cries angrily, as Eva jumps off the bed, laughing.

'Now, be good,' she says silkily, lighting a cigarette and popping it into his mouth.

Eva gathers up her handbag, jacket and a large folder containing the biographies of all the MPs and their partners coming to Chequers, and heads down to the waiting car. Jamie sits helplessly in bed, moodily staring into space through a haze of smoke. He gets tired of Eva rushing off the whole time. He can't remember the last time they'd gone out for dinner or watched a film when she hadn't been texting or talking on her phone. Still, she's extremely good at leaving things on a cliffhanger so that he can't wait to see her again. He finishes his cigarette and reads the news.

As she walks down the stairs Eva checks her phone and fumbles for her keys. Just the usual messages from SpAds and MPs on the endless, *endless* WhatsApp groups.

She opens the group with Jess and Bobby on it and smashes out a message:

Girls, it's quite spooky this is all happening at once! So exciting. I guess you might need somewhere to camp out. My dad is away all summer ... want to come and stay with me? x

A car honks outside. Eva shoves the phone in her bag and swings the door open, heading out into the day.

Notting Hill

A couple of miles away, Eric Courtenay MP, Minister of State in the Foreign Office, pushes open his front door and chucks a selection of newspapers from the corner shop onto the kitchen table. Now in his mid-forties, Courtenay is tall and athletic with thick, steel grey hair and icy blue eyes. Clad in sleek, grey designer gym kit, he sweats slightly after his run, which has conveniently been pictured by a friendly photographer (Courtenay's team takes every opportunity they can to frame him as fit and vigorous, his Scandinavian features in sharp contrast to some of his paunchier colleagues).

Courtenay steps over to the sink and runs the tap, stretching his hamstrings against the sideboard while he waits for the water to run cold. His wife, Clarissa, wrapped in a cream silk dressing gown, her raven hair in rollers, glances up from the front pages, china teacup in hand, to see what kind of mood her husband is in. Sometimes he returns from a run very horny. But today, no dice. He must be thinking about the torturously sociable couple of hours ahead of him.

Clarissa daintily refills her teacup. A stranger wouldn't guess that her refined attitude is anything but second nature to her. Raised in a Cheshire village where her parents ran a garden centre, Clarissa knew from an early age that she wanted to be important and powerful, and had decided in her teens that she would escape to work in television. As a teenager, Clarissa had come alive to her mysterious ability to enthral pretty much anyone she encountered, especially men. She had made good use of her black magic to scrape a job on her local newspaper straight out of school, before navigating the climbing wall of regional and national media to eventually land a senior executive role at StoryCorps, Lord Finlayson's London-based media empire. In response to the many questions about how she had achieved such a meteoric rise to prominence from obscurity, Clarissa chooses to say, 'I cut my teeth – literally – doing grunt work,' and leaves out the bits about blackmail and shrivelled blowjobs.

She had met Courtenay, her second husband, in a TV studio

when he had come on as a guest for a programme she had dropped in to revive (their viewing figures were down). He was leaving the Army and had talked about the lack of opportunity for ex-servicemen and, stunned by his remarkable good looks and the gentle way he spoke, Clarissa had immediately spotted his potential. She had been languishing slightly at StoryCorps, tiring of the daily fights and back-stabbing and being at Lord Finlayson's beck and call each time he'd popped a Viagra. Meeting Courtenay had given her a new idea on how she was going to become truly important and powerful. Within the year she had persuaded Courtenay to leave his wife (perhaps the easiest challenge she'd ever faced, Clarissa had boasted at the time) and had become Mrs Courtenay.

When Courtenay won the safe seat of Chatterham in Oxfordshire, Clarissa resigned her role at StoryCorps, while remaining on excellent terms with his Lordship, and kept on a handful of strategically useful advisory roles – plus a healthy balance of favours, friends and enemies. She finds she needs every ounce of the cunning, charm and ruthlessness that she had needed in her old life – plus the sharp teeth – to support Courtenay in his rise through the Conservative Party and her own rise in society. She wants to mix with people of unimpeachable importance: Royals, world leaders, ideally Amal Clooney, and she feels sure that securing her husband – and it has to be her husband; God knows she has too many skeletons buried among her fur coats – the keys to Downing Street is the way to go. The First Lady, if the UK officially had such a person. As she admits only to herself, though, Courtenay isn't exactly the Brain of Britain and certainly no strategist. But he has a certain charisma and an officer's ability to take orders and has been happy enough so far to muddle along with her plans. Courtenay is Clarissa's vehicle to greater things – but she is the driver.

Clarissa holds up the front page of the *Telegraph*, which

reads *PM's appeal to Party* and includes a photo of the Prime Minister awkwardly folding herself into her armoured car.

'Good Lord, look at the old dear. I really can't think of anything worse than having to watch her wheeze through today. Still,' she winks at her husband, 'we can measure up the curtains.'

Courtenay changes legs on his stretches and frowns. 'Darling, I wish you wouldn't say things like that. Don't you think it's tempting fate?'

'Oh, Eric, for goodness' sake. Do you think we're the only people talking about this? It's clearly going to be a screaming mess for her, and mark my words: this evening, West London will be deafened with the sound of Tory MPs firing up their laptops all at once, tapping away at "My vision for Britain" Google docs.' Clarissa clacks her coral fingernails on an imaginary keyboard. 'There'll be a strain on the Grid!'

Courtenay pulls up a chair next to her. 'I know, I know. It just all feels so far off and huge and … and I don't know. I obviously think she is getting it totally wrong on China, but I suppose I do feel sort of sorry for her. What a position to be in.'

Clarissa looks him squarely in the eye and prepares to trot out her usual mantra. 'Well, don't. This is politics, Eric. You have to be tough about this sort of thing. Have you taken a look at the polls lately? The Party – and likely the country, if that red maniac gets in – is screwed if she remains in charge. China is a perfect example of her getting the big calls wrong. Don't think of this as being ruthless.' She draws a cross through the PM's careworn face. 'It's being merciful.'

Courtenay nods reluctantly and stands up to put his glass in the dishwasher. Clarissa wonders, not for the first time, if he has actually understood what she's just said. He really doesn't have a political bone in his body. It astounds her that so many really quite successful MPs are like this – completely lacking the lizard-brained political nous necessary to truly win in politics. Relying on competence. It's like they're old radios that are struggling to tune into the frequency of the rest of SW1. Enough are switched to the Courtenay station, though. By Clarissa's reckoning her husband would have the support of at least thirty MPs without breaking a sweat if he ends up running for leader.

She picks up the *Sentinel*, which features a grainy photo of Graham Thomas MP, Secretary of State for Transport, in a panama hat on the front page. One of the older MPs – he must be approaching 70 – his shiny face, even in black and white, looks blotchy and slack with drink. The man with a friendly, conspiratorial arm around him, Caspar Dubois, looks smooth and in control. In the corner of the picture is a young boy aged around eleven years old, looking bored. She opens the paper and scrutinises the other pictures: Thomas and Dubois shaking hands, Thomas and Dubois toasting with full champagne flutes, Thomas downing his glass while Dubois looks on triumphantly. The boy stares intently at an iPhone. The journalist in her can't help but smile. Hacks don't often get 'gotcha' stuff like this these days. She casts her mind back to the last good, solid scoop with actual photographs . . . the Fake Sheikh? Percy Cross in the park?

Clarissa taps a nail against her tooth thoughtfully, watching her husband as he heads upstairs. Once she hears him on the landing she slides her phone out from under the pile of newspapers and calls Nigel Jackson MP.

'What's new, pussycat?' Clarissa says. Or rodent, if she were being truthful. 'Tell me, have you seen the *Sentinel* today?'

'Hello, Clazz.' She hates that Jackson calls her that. But she always lets it go – he has that political lizard-brain stuff in spades. 'I have indeed. Quite the pickle Graham's got himself into.'

'Absolutely. What do you think?'

Clarissa hears Jackson suck his teeth, a habit he has never kicked from his days as a bloodstock auctioneer. 'So he could be in hot water—'

'Come on, Nige,' Clarissa lowers her voice as she hears a creak from upstairs, 'I mean where does *she* go with this?'

'Well, we've got a few considerations to take into account,' Jackson says, enunciating each syllable pleasurably. 'First off, let's establish the facts: the Secretary of State has gone on an official trip, followed by a private holiday. While there he appears to have had a meeting with an individual who is later awarded a chunky contract directly from the Secretary of State's department. Which part of the trip is which? If this was an official meeting, he failed to report what was discussed at that meeting and he didn't take a civil servant with him to take notes and keep it all proper. Even if this was just a friendly chat, did the Secretary of State just happen to bump into his mate at the cricket on the other side of the Atlantic Ocean?'

'Doubtful,' snorts Clarissa.

'Right. So I think we can assume they decided to meet there. In which case, did Graham buy his own tickets for the box sponsored by Dubois's company? He's not saying so. If he has accepted a favour from Dubois, he has to declare it. So far he's made no declaration either through his department or the Cabinet Office, which would indicate that in his view he was *not* there on official business. But he also hasn't noted the interest through the Parliamentary Standards route, saying he accepted the favour as an MP. Can he safely argue that cricket tickets are in no way connected to the whopping Dubois contract?'

Clarissa listens intently, fixing her eyes on the picture of the PM with the line drawn through her face.

'We both know these things can kill you but they most often don't. Even if it turns out that Dubois paid for the tickets, a five-star hotel and a private jet, Graham can probably get away with a late declaration, a smack on the wrist from the Parliamentary Standards people, an internal Cabinet Office investigation that returns nothing, blah blah.'

When Clarissa doesn't speak, Jackson continues.

'Second on the list. What do the public think?' Jackson chuckles. 'Tory wanker, clearly guilty, can't have this person in the Cabinet. Ford should show some bottle for once and bin him. Which of course she should. But she can't. Not if she wants to hold her MPs together. You see, Clazz,' Clarissa grits her teeth, 'with the polls where they are, and as much as she will hate it, she can't afford to do anything but show her MPs loyalty to one of their own. They're looking for an opportunity to ditch her as it is – think Maggie in the nineties – and Graham's a popular guy who, until tomorrow's papers arrive at any rate, hasn't actually *unequivocally* been proven guilty of anything. Terry Groves will caution against anything dramatic while he wheezes on as Chief Whip. So then, of course, she only slumps more in focus groups and opinion polling and whatnot because she went against the public mood and looked weak. Vicious cycle, innit.'

Clarissa nods to herself.

'Are you still there, Clazz?'

'Yes, I'm here. I'm nodding.' She pauses, struck by a thought. 'You say Graham is popular?'

'Yeah, with MPs anyway. The country obviously thinks he's a tool, but he could get far in the first stage of a race – the bit when it is just MPs voting – if there were a leadership contest. We have a few goes of that to whittle down to two contenders for the Party members to vote on. He's got a bit of a base there, too. All the older members like that travel pass he cooked up last year.'

'Will he run?'

'Hm, if he survives this then I should think so. I'd advise him to. Throw your hat into the ring and then withdraw to back who you think will win. Bring some people with you and you've probably got yourself a nice Cabinet role there. Kingmaker.'

Clarissa draws a target around Graham Thomas's ball-like head, holding the pen tightly.

'Sounds like there's some work to be done,' she says quietly. 'We can cause havoc for the PM this weekend. Tell the Courtiers it's time to get the alternative whipping operation up and running in earnest. In the meantime I'll tee up the Sundays accordingly to make sure back bench grievances are front and centre.' She lowers her voice to a near whisper. 'It's already obvious she's toast – but we can't have Graham stumbling out of this in good enough shape for a genuine leadership bid.' She blacks out Graham's eyes to empty, yawning holes. 'See you later – time to get on your party clothes.'

Chesham

At the Three Horseshoes pub the Chief Whip, Terry Groves MP, and his wife Sheila, a cheerful, stocky couple in their late sixties, are sitting down to a late breakfast. As they make their way through a stack of toast and marmalade, MPs and their spouses who have also stayed overnight quietly come over to respectfully wish the Chief and Mrs Groves a good morning. The Chief's role gives him the gifts of promotion, patronage and punishment. He acts as adviser to the Prime Minister and therapist to his back benchers and is in charge of nursing the government's legislation through Parliament and into law. He is one of the few Conservative MPs from the North East, and the only one to have worked in the dying steel industry.

Though he is widely respected in the Party as a reasonable, no-nonsense man, his job has become increasingly difficult in recent months as he fights to persuade his Party's MPs to back the

Prime Minister in crucial China Trade Deal votes. Tory MPs are divided pretty well in two over it: half are committed Sinophiles or simply pro-trade with the superpower, clocking jobs and growth in their constituencies and the reality that British businesses need access to technological and manufacturing expertise on the other side of the globe; the other half raise human rights concerns, cybersecurity, military aggression against Taiwan and a nervous sense that Chinese companies are creeping into British structural security systems like telecoms and energy.

The Chief often wonders which way he would vote if he was free to follow his conscience. He's certainly suspicious of the Chinese state's knack for funnelling money into anything from APPGs (All-Party Parliamentary Groups – unregulated groups of Parliamentarians that stand under the banner of anything that interests them, from Portuguese to pottery to polycystic ovaries, which are potential loopholes around lobbying rules) to former Commonwealth states, who gladly take funding for roads and hospitals in exchange for access to precious metals. Closer to home, cheap steel imports from China have, in his view, contributed to the near collapse of his first industry. However, Chinese investment in his patch might also reignite British steel production through new plants run on nuclear power. And the old steel jobs might move to car manufacturing. Besides, is he just unleashing his inner conspiracy theorist with all this 'creeping tentacles of Beijing' stuff? The Prime Minister, managing an economy that's still feeling the pinch from a deep recession a decade ago and sensitive to the moral pride of the UK, has tried to stitch the two sides together. Her draft deal is fundamentally a Free Trade Agreement but there are specific clauses about human rights, slave labour and curbs on Chinese investment in key UK state infrastructure – all of which is making negotiations on the Chinese side very sticky.

That's not the Chief's problem, though. His focus is just on getting the China Trade Bill through the Commons. He has reasoned arguments, threatened the end of pork barrel offerings (the promise of bridges, road junctions and station upgrades in constituencies), dangled jobs and future careers and, frankly, pleaded with back benchers. Meanwhile, the opposition parties talk about the cost of living, NHS waiting times and school funding, making the Conservative Party look preposterously obsessed with a niche issue in the eyes of the public. He feels sure that bringing the whole lot of Conservative MPs together today is his last shot at winning them over. Show them what they have in common – although he fears that might be the shared wish for a new party leader.

'What's wrong, love?' asks Sheila, noticing that he has a piece of toast frozen in mid-air, marmalade plopping off it.

'Oh, nothing. I just hope it goes all right today. I reckon I'm out of tricks now. Plus this stuff with Graham is really the last thing I need. How stupid can he be?'

'There's nothing you can do about that. And as regards everything else ... Well, you've done your best, Terry. You can't say fairer than that.'

The Chief pats his wife's hand. 'I know, love. It's just hard to argue for something that I'm not really sure of myself. But she's the boss and I can't see another way through.' He takes a long gulp of tea and smacks his lips. 'I hate the idea of these toe rags closing in around her. I just can't stand the stupidity and ...' he wipes his mouth and shrugs moodily, 'disloyalty. They're using this bill to rumble her whole premiership.'

A man clatters into the pub, a woman trailing reluctantly behind him. Sheila is immediately struck by the man's ability to catch the attention of the room, despite only going through the innocuous task of requesting a table. She watches him glance around the diners, nodding to various people, before catching sight of her husband.

47

'Ah, Chief!'

Sheila notices her husband recoil like a tortoise retracting into its shell as the man, wearing a navy blazer, pink striped shirt and beige chinos, lunges forward. Richard Hendrick MP, the Secretary of State for the Department for Education, has a thinning head of carefully styled, expensively cut curls and a wide smile that shows every one of his rather small teeth.

'Good morning, good morning. Chief. Mrs Chief. How are we?' Hendrick says ostentatiously.

The Chief responds with a brief smile.

'Excellent. We've just come from London and this is the only chance we've got for a quick coffee.' Hendrick raises his voice even louder. 'I was doing the media round today. Next week's vote, Graham's little trouble, a bit on my own brief . . . A tough gig but I think I got through okay,' he guffaws before leaning in conspiratorially. 'Got a good feeling about today. Do let the PM know, I'm one hundred per cent behind her. If there's anything I can do, just tee me up.' He does a pretend golf swing, nearly smacking a passing waitress.

'Thanks, Rich. I'll let her know.' The Chief nods again. He notices the man is looking expectantly at him so raises his cup in a little salute. 'See you there.'

Hendrick loiters a few more seconds, smiling obsequiously at the Chief before retreating slowly back to his table.

'Well, you aren't his biggest fan,' Sheila chuckles.

'You know what Rich is like,' the Chief sighs. 'He might be in the Cabinet and saying supportive things in public but mark my words: he'll disappear like a submarine if we lose this vote on Tuesday and we won't hear a thing from him until he announces his leadership candidacy. He's already having secret fundraising dinners. I told you – I hate disloyalty. And ill-discipline. If I really had it my way I would tell the PM to sack Graham. If she were in a stronger position they'd respect her for it. But we are where we are and she has to play nice – including to that wazzock.' He inclines his head towards Hendrick's table.

Sheila looks over, just in time to hear him order 'a *skinny* cappuccino, please. That means skimmed milk. The red top. I'm on a *very* specific diet that rules out excess dairy'.

'I don't fancy his chances of the big job, though,' the Chief says quietly into her ear. 'His nickname with his colleagues is "the hermaphrodite".'

She looks back at him, nonplussed.

'Because he's both a dick . . .' he lowers his voice further, 'and a cunt.'

Sheila has to cover her mouth with a napkin to stifle her shrieks.

Wendover

Daly eases his Audi into sixth gear and glides along the road. His wife Susie grips her door handle just a little tighter as they speed up to ninety miles per hour.

'Well, Suse,' Daly glances at his reflection in the rear-view mirror, 'it is good of you to come today. I'm afraid it's going to be terribly boring.'

'Oh, I don't mind,' Susie says brightly. 'I'm looking forward to seeing Chequers. I've heard the gardens are wonderful. And it's so nice to be away from the constituency to meet some more of the folks you spend your time with. Apart from the occasional fundraising thing I help the Conservative Women's Organisation with, I hardly know anyone from Parliament.'

Daly keeps his eyes on the road ahead, wondering to himself once again whether Susie is letting on that she knows more than he thinks. Since Daly won his seat six years ago, Susie has given up her work on a PhD in psychiatry and has lived full time in his constituency and, under Moira's watchful eye, has fully immersed herself into the community and the Conservative Association. She has joined the WI, bought raffle tickets, joined book clubs, helped at bake sales, and attended agricultural shows and school plays. She has manners and money (via her very generous – and now ennobled – father, who took a shine to Daly and shored up his political career) and has been willing to shelve her studies to support him. The perfect MP's wife in every regard, which unfortunately for Daly includes a sensible and unsexy floral dress and cardigan.

Daly occasionally feels guilty about taking her for granted, but not often. She never makes a fuss about anything, and he is mostly inclined to forget about her as soon as she is out of sight. He absently rubs her thigh with his left hand. He's probably just being sensitive.

'Both hands on the wheel at this speed, darling,' Susie says primly.

Daly wonders how long he can keep up his second identity. He feels like a bit of cartilage between the bones of clingy women with whom he's had ill-advised affairs and Susie, who is taking an increased interest in his life in Westminster. Just this morning, she expressed a hope of replacing Annie in his Parliamentary office to spend some time with him in London. He truthfully said that Annie could do things that Susie can't (notably, getting both of her feet behind her head). Thankfully Bobby has come along just in time, with the same youthful grasp of social media and mail merge and who knows what else . . . Talk about hitting two birds with one stone. He smiles, keen to hit two birds whenever he can.

Daly mentally gives himself a slap. Bobby is not to be touched. If all goes well, he will be promoted to Cabinet level soon under Eric Courtenay and he needs to keep his paws clean. To focus, he turns his mind to his task for the day: drip poison on the PM's China Trade Deal ahead of next week's vote and gauge the true level of support for Thomas. Jackson had called round the Courtiers – the name for the Courtenay hardcore supporters – earlier and was very clear about what is needed:

'Piss over everything. The P is for persuasion. We need the waverers to get off the fence. They need to know the time has come to give her a push. Make it clear we're all screwed otherwise. Regardless of the China stuff. I is for information. What needs to happen for each MP to move and to back Eric? What is each person's deepest personal desire? What is their big dirty secret? We need to know. S is for solid numbers. I need to know who's a human and who's a committed Courtier, who's against us – and who's just a useless bedwetter in the middle. That's where the big dirty secrets come in . . . '

'And what about the final S?'

'Jesus, Simon, who gives a shit about spelling? But yeah, all right. The final S can be for . . . uh . . . sow some chaos. Yeah. The more confusion the better – and anything that scares people . . . keep pushing human rights stuff, selling off Britain. And the dodgy polling, the public mood . . . '

It's heady stuff. He's tired of languishing at PUS level under this PM. Should Courtenay, one of his oldest friends, become PM then Daly is guaranteed a good job. Chancellor has been floated. He just needs to be as loyal and helpful as possible. He keeps saying to Clarissa and Jackson he'll help Courtenay win 'by any means necessary' but is anxious they aren't using him properly.

Daly's ringing phone cuts into his thoughts. Via the car speaker a faraway, crackling voice comes through. 'Si . . . Si? Can you hear me?'

'Yes, hello. Hello? This is Simon Daly.'

'Oh, thank God,' breathes the voice. 'Si, it's me – George. I'm calling from a payphone as there isn't any bloody signal around here. We got to Wendover station and I completely forgot to book a cab. Can you pick us up on the way through?'

Daly chuckles. 'Yes of course, mate. See you in fifteen minutes.' He hangs up. 'Classic Sack.'

George Sackler, MP for East Devon and Daly's office neighbour in Parliament, is perhaps the most disorganised person in Westminster and famously late for everything – assuming he even turns up to the right place.

'Oh, it'll be great to see Millie again,' says Susie, smiling. 'She's lovely.'

Daly momentarily allows his thoughts to wander to a few nights ago, when he and Millie had a bottle of Bollinger to themselves in a private room at the Cinnamon Club. Very lovely, thinks Simon, suppressing a grin.

Chequers

As the car stops at the barrier, Eva spots a pair of police officers stepping out of the bushes, armed with huge guns and walkie-talkies. She and Peter hand their IDs over to have their names checked off a list by one officer, who radios their arrival up to the main house, while another checks under the car for explosive devices. As the barrier lifts, Eva exhales a breath she didn't realise she's been holding, prompting a knowing smile from Peter.

Peter Foulkes OBE, a native of the North West, is known as a hot property in politics. He has a careful understanding of how MPs, Peers and the public think, a *Mastermind* memory of the history of the Conservative Party, its politicians and campaigns and a cutting, camp sense of humour that even the stuffiest person can't help but love. He was the first person the now PM hired upon joining the Cabinet nearly a decade ago. She says he can see around corners.

Peter took Eva under his wing after meeting her during her stint as President of the Cambridge Union, a post he also held eight years previously. He came to a debate in traditional black tie, his svelte frame and peppery hair prompting an immediate crush – right up until the moment he introduced his boyfriend to her. After Eva graduated he hired her straight into the Prime Minister's political office, where she has learned everything from how to correctly address a bishop to the rules around a Parliamentary by-election. Eva adores Peter and knows she is good at her job, but she can never shake off a mean voice at the back of her mind that insists she has only won her role because of who her father is. But as she repeatedly reminds herself: in reality, being Percy Cross's daughter can only damage her career prospects.

The car moves slowly up the driveway, crackling over the gravel, towards the beautiful red-brick building. On the far lawn there are billowing white tablecloths and buckets full of ice and wine bottles. Catering staff buzz about, laying cutlery and flower arrangements. It dawns on Eva that the event is being held out of doors as there would be no space for all the Tory MPs and their partners indoors, yet it has to be held at Chequers for some privacy from the media. She hopes the weather holds at least. She and Peter climb out of the car and, as they step through the imposing front door, are greeted by a grinning Dennis, whose whole body ropes back and forth as he wags his tail.

'Hiya, old chap, where's the big boss?' Peter crouches down to stroke the dog's head.

They hear footsteps coming down the stairs.

'He can't understand your accent, Pete. He was born in

Surrey,' laughs the PM's husband, dressed in a navy cashmere sweater, dark grey corduroys and brown suede loafers. He always dresses stylishly, Eva thinks. 'She'll be down in a minute. Just getting her war paint on. Can I take a look at that folder? I don't want to get anyone's name wrong. Feels like the bloody G20 spouse programme all over again . . .'

Eva hands it over and Mr Ford settles onto a sofa. Dennis pants at his feet, eyes fixed intently on the stairs.

Wendover

Daly pulls up to the station and beeps his horn. Sackler jumps up from a bench and bounces over. As usual, he lives up to his Parliamentary nickname: Sack. His suit looks like he's pulled it out of a bush. His hair desperately needs a cut. His razor has somehow missed great patches of stubble on his jaw. What Sackler's dentist refers to as his 'good time teeth' sum him up: he is irrepressibly cheerful and permanently shabby.

'Good Lord, Si. It's the Batmobile!' Sackler walks slowly around the car, taking in its smooth sides and gleaming alloys.

Daly gets out of the car and saunters over to his friend. 'So, Sacky,' he says quietly, 'have you given what I said much thought?'

'Si, I told you last week,' Sackler tuts, changing direction to walk away from Daly, 'I want to hear what she has to say later before I do anything.'

'I know, I know, mate,' Daly circles around to meet him, 'but you know what I said. There's limited time to get you a decent job. If you don't row in behind Eric soon, you'll get trampled by the rush of the other Johnny-come-latelies and the opportunity will have passed.'

Sackler bends down to tie his frayed shoelace. 'Simon, has it occurred to you that I don't care about being a minister?' He squints up and smiles sadly into the face of his friend, towering over him. 'You know I'm not one for greasy poles. I'll leave the arse-kissing and arm-twisting to you and your,' he twiddles his fingers in air quotes, 'Courtiers.'

Daly's mouth sets into a thin line. He decides to change tack. 'Look, Sack, we all like the PM. God, we both voted for her to be leader in the first place! But we are haemorrhaging support now. She's too slow to make a decision, dithering and hand-wringing, and then once she's made up her mind she's too stubborn to change it, even if it's for the better. This China stuff is a typical fudge.'

Sackler straightens up and moves thoughtfully round to a rear passenger door, his hands in his pockets. Reluctantly he looks at his friend and shrugs.

Daly opens the driver's door. 'All right, well, as you say – let's see how she does later. But Sacky,' he steps one shiny shoe into the footwell, 'please tell me you won't back Graham if he runs.'

Sackler lets out a honking laugh. 'Christ, no! Look – if today is going to go as badly as you say, you'll have my support by the time we're fastening our seatbelts to leave.' He grins at Daly, who smacks the roof of the car smartly and lowers himself into the driving seat.

Sackler clambers in behind Susie and squeezes her shoulder. 'Hello, my dear, great to see you. Mills is just coming – popped to the lavs.' He fiddles with his seatbelt and then motions to a woman coming out of the small pebble-dashed building. 'Ah, there she is. Come on!'

Daly looks up from the latest offering on the Legislative Lads WhatsApp group just in time to get a full view of Millie Sackler gliding across the tarmac, her auburn curls bouncing over her shoulders, her wide, lipsticked mouth in a beaming smile. She wears a silk, rose-printed wrap dress that is demure despite firmly planting the word 'unwrap' in the mind. The mother of four will celebrate her fortieth birthday in a few weeks and she's feeling self-conscious about it. Still, being with Sackler means she'll always look comparatively young and glossy. And her latest flirtation is doing her the world of good.

Millie slips in behind Daly and he feels the hairs rise on the back of his neck as she leans forward and plants a kiss on his left cheek, brushing against his ear.

Daly starts the ignition and, as Susie and Sackler merrily begin talking about the day ahead, he sneaks glances at Millie via the rear-view mirror. Each time he looks, she unabashedly meets his gaze.

After a couple of minutes Millie speaks. 'Do you mind if I have some chewing gum?' and leans forward towards the handbrake to the packet, exposing her tanned cleavage down the long V of her dress.

Christ, Daly thinks, keep your eyes on the road. But he can't resist risking another glance at her face as she lolls back in her seat. He notices his heart rate increase slightly as he sees she is smirking at him.

Suddenly Susie bursts in on his thoughts. 'Si, I know we're nearly there, but I could really do with a quick sip of water. Can you pass me that bottle in your door?'

'I'll get it,' says Millie. 'With these winding roads, let's keep the driver with two hands on the wheel.' As she leans forward for the bottle, her hand out of Susie's view, she lets a finger slide along Daly's thigh and breathes in his right ear. 'And two eyes on the road.'

Daly can feel himself getting hard, incredulous that Millie could be so daring, inches from his wife and her husband.

'Oh thanks, Millie, you're so kind,' says Susie. 'Mustn't spill it on myself. How silly it would be to turn up to Chequers with an embarrassing stain!'

'Tell me about it,' Millie replies languidly to the rear-view mirror.

Chequers

Eva stands by the grand piano, her attention on one of Chequers' most prized possessions – a pearl and ruby ring that belonged to Queen Elizabeth I with two portraits concealed inside it, one of Elizabeth herself and the other of her mother, Anne Boleyn – when the Prime Minister enters the room. She's wearing navy trousers, red suede pumps and a Breton striped top. The two women don't know each other well – Peter goes to all the regular PM meetings – but the PM has a soft spot for Eva. Scandal aside, living in Downing Street isn't easy and as a teenager it must have been suffocating. It is also Eva's father who promoted the PM to her first Cabinet role: Party Chairman. When the time came to think seriously about the proof of affairs and debt and mismanagement – and what that meant for the Party's electoral chances – the career-minded and clean-nosed Ford cast a vote of no confidence in Percy. She even used his reputation to her advantage, becoming his successor after she ran a campaign that focused on her previous career as an accountant, her many years as a local councillor and her fanatical insistence on never accepting a free lunch – not so much as a free coffee.

Eva, as is often the case in these relationships, knows she and her boss have more in common than the PM realises. Both tall and pale, Eva acts as a body double for the PM when the broadcast team are preparing the lectern height and camera shot for a speech or press conference. They also have the same coat and shoe size – something Eva learned one Friday last winter when, ahead of a weekend in the country, the Downing

Street operations director had burst into their office. The PM was going on an emergency visit to a flood site and her wellington boots and raincoat were nowhere to be found. Could Eva do without hers this weekend? Eva's not sure the PM ever knew the truth.

'Hello, Prime Minister,' Peter says, rising smartly from a chair. 'I think the guests have started to arrive so we probably ought to head out shortly. The Chief Whip is going to join us first to discuss a couple of things. You know Eva of course.'

Eva steps forward from the piano and the two women smile at each other.

'Here he is!' Peter calls, as the Chief waddles awkwardly into the room, smiling at the PM and her husband. 'Thanks for joining us.'

'So, PM.' Peter unfolds a sheet of paper and clears his throat. 'I'm afraid David Marlow's wife is still in hospital, so he can't come. We also aren't sure if Natasha Weaver's husband is coming – her office hasn't confirmed. David Carmichael's due in theatre today for his knee op, so he's out. A couple of people are bringing their babies. And,' Peter steps awkwardly from foot to foot, 'David Jarvis will be bringing his new partner. The young chap.'

'He's left Harriet?' Michael stammers. 'For a *man*? We used to go on holiday with them!'

'Yes, I'm afraid so. But it all seems much the best thing for both of them. They're remaining friends. Their children are grown up . . .'

'Difficult for all of them to have it so public, though,' says the PM.

'But better than living a lie,' says Peter firmly. 'Look, it obviously isn't ideal but I spoke to Harriet yesterday and she sounded relieved, frankly. Just dreading the gossip in the Sunday papers.'

'Well, aren't we all,' the PM mutters darkly.

'Which brings us to the other matter,' the Chief says in a low voice, despite nobody else being around. A force of habit in his job.

The PM's husband instinctively takes a couple of paces back from the group.

'Pete can correct me, but my understanding is there isn't definitive proof that Graham has done anything wrong, although he has been very stupid. And . . .' the Chief hesitates until he catches the PM's firm, intelligent gaze, 'I don't feel he has been entirely honest with me so far. The timing of this deal . . . the holiday . . . the tickets . . . how this Dubois chap got his personal mobile number. It makes me very nervous that there is more to come beyond these photos.'

The PM turns to Peter. 'How did your chat go with him?'

'He maintains that CCHQ has dropped him in all this mess. He says he only met Caspar Dubois because of the Winter Party auction. He was raffled off as a prize for an afternoon of cricket at an England match. It just so happened that he and Dubois were in the Caribbean at the same time and it was the Windies match they ended up seeing, but it was Graham's decision to exchange numbers and so on. The timing is . . . smelly.' Peter pauses. 'And he does technically have time on his side. There is a way he could say his declaration to the Parli authorities is late, or that there was a mistake within his department, or maybe CCHQ can reimburse Dubois for the tickets and close the loop . . .' Peter trails off lamely.

The Chief steps forward. 'In my opinion, Prime Minister, you have no alternative but to wait and see if there is more stuff here. The back benchers are,' he chooses his words carefully, 'in a delicate place just now. Backing Graham to the hilt is the only way to go—'

'But the public—' begins the PM.

59

'I know, PM,' continues the Chief gently. 'But the public doesn't matter when it comes to a confidence vote. It's only about MPs, which is who we have to think about just now. Look, if today goes well you have some wiggle room. I'd suggest that we wait and see what the Sundays print. If there is a smoking gun for Graham, you might have to sack him. If there isn't, you're better off showing the troops that they can expect loyalty in return when they show it to you. Graham's an all right man. He's not the person to make an example of. I . . .' he searches for the right words, 'I don't think you should rock the boat before Tuesday.'

The PM looks hard from her Chief Whip to her Political Secretary. They bow their heads, avoiding her bright blue eyes. Eva knows what they're all thinking. She had asked in the car earlier if the PM couldn't just ask Thomas to resign, but Peter had pointed out that his resignation – particularly if he made it sound like he'd chosen to throw in the towel – could damage her further and maybe even cause an exodus. For now, they're trapped.

Finally, the PM nods. 'Okay,' she sighs, deflating a little. 'Come on then, let's get this over with.'

As they shuffle to the front door, her husband's hand secretly finds hers and gives it a squeeze.

The little group make their way past the PM's armoured Jaguar and accompanying black Range Rovers and wait on the driveway. On the substantial lawn behind the house the waiters stand ready to serve drinks. Small clusters of people are trailing up from their parked cars on the bottom field, the usual spot for foreign leaders to arrive by helicopter. Many of them bend down to pat Dennis, who has gambolled gamely down a little way to welcome them like a doddering butler.

For about an hour the PM and her husband greet their

guests, a flurry of shaking hands and making small talk about children and journeys. Standing at a discreet distance, a couple of plain clothes protection officers keep watch over proceedings, the strange choice to accessorise their chinos and Barbour wax jackets with lapel badges, ear pieces and Oakley sunglasses giving them away.

The PM is acutely aware that not everyone she greets can quite meet her eye. Sir Godfrey Singham MP, Chairman of the 1922 Committee, looks extremely awkward. The PM is particularly worried by this as Singham, to whom letters of no confidence in her are addressed, is the only person who truly knows quite how tenuous her position with the Parliamentary Party is at any given time. Natasha Weaver – without her husband – doesn't stop walking, just robotically babbles her thanks to the PM for hosting. Graham Thomas, still tanned from his holiday, cheerfully thanks the PM for her support before she gets a chance to give it and dashes off towards a tray of drinks. Despite his formal, Army officer exterior, Eric Courtenay's handshake is clammy. His wife's eye contact is so steady, however, that the PM isn't sure she blinks once during their entire conversation.

Finally, the welcome party heads towards the lawn to mingle with guests. As ever, the PM is profoundly grateful for the presence of her husband whose clear, intelligent eyes behind his horn-rimmed spectacles always look interested in even the most mundane conversation. Dennis's grinning face and willingness to shake paws is a handy last ditch distraction if the PM is struggling to make headway with someone's spouse.

Leaving Peter to man mark the boss, who is stuck with an extremely effusive Daly ('You have my fullest support, PM.' The PM can't help but raise an eyebrow), Eva circulates. She realises her poor choice of footwear as she steps onto the lawn and immediately feels her heel sink into the mossy grass.

Cursing under her breath and retracting her earlier comments to Peter about the truly awful array of wedges favoured by the other female guests, she tips forward onto the balls of her feet and, picking up a glass of fizzing elderflower cordial, blushes slightly as she hears someone loudly whisper, 'Yes, Percy Cross's daughter. Can't *imagine* how she got her job . . .'

Eva is trapped for quite some time with David Jacobson MP, who earnestly pontificates on climate, human rights and how he'd be the perfect fit to lead the Aid and Development Office should the PM wish him to serve. Fat chance, Eva thinks, as she assures Jacobson she'll put in a good word. Hoping for a get out, all the while gently padding from foot to foot to avoid sinking any further, she looks around, excuses herself and steps gingerly towards a plump woman in a floral dress and cardigan, who is admiring a flower bed by herself.

'Hello, Mrs Daly?' The woman turns. 'Hi, I'm Eva Cross. We haven't met before, but I work in the PM's political office and wanted to introduce myself.'

'Oh, hello,' Susie smiles warmly. 'Nice to meet you. Isn't this a lovely place? Is it your first time here?'

'Well . . .' Eva hesitates, thinking of an answer. She spent many weekends here when her father was PM, normally watching telly by herself while her parents entertained their friends or the Archbishop of Canterbury, but she'd really rather not discuss that. 'It's my first event, yes. I think, understandably, that the PM prefers not to be reminded of Number Ten when she's here, so we rarely come.'

Eva surveys the crowd, groups of couples chatting animatedly. Not much of a retreat today.

Susie seems to have read Eva's mind. 'Yes, of course. It must be such a pain to have all of us here. Particularly with everything else going on. Now, Cross . . . you aren't related to *Percy* Cross, are you?'

'That's right, I'm his daughter.' Eva, suddenly wishing she had allowed herself at least one glass of wine today, hopes Susie isn't going to reveal she has Percy on her fantasy list for a secret knee trembler, which has happened more than people would guess. 'Dad's currently single, if you know someone looking for a challenge!' She laughs hollowly.

'Do you know, my father still buys all his books,' Susie says kindly, noticing Eva's discomfort. 'He loves them. It must have been awful for you to go through all that rubbish in the papers.'

Eva takes a gulp of elderflower, shoving down a bilious little jolt of rage at her father. 'It was.'

They stand awkwardly together, examining the shrubbery. As though sensing his presence is needed, the PM's dog waddles over to sniff Eva's hand, his tail wagging vigorously in recognition of someone he knows in the large crowd.

'Oh, hello, boy.' Susie rubs behind Dennis's ears, laughing at the whipped cream around his snout. 'How handsome you are. Although it looks like you've been having a go at the pudding table. Is this the PM's dog? He knows you.'

Eva squats down beside Susie, running her fingers through the dog's thick fur. 'Yes, this is Dennis. He has a basket in our office, so we know each other pretty well. It is generally a pleasure, but he's very old so farts a lot and he wags his tail really hard so he quite often knocks table legs and things.'

'Poor chap.' Susie strokes the greying muzzle. 'Well, I think you're just charming. Ah—' She spots a figure walking past with two glasses of white wine and quickly straightens up. 'Simon!'

Daly turns and abruptly switches course towards them, prowling guiltily, like a fox.

Eva gets in a quick 'Hello, Minister', knowing how much men with his ego enjoy hearing those words, before Daly heartily and, Eva thinks, rather guiltily says, 'Ah, you've met Eva, have you?'

'Yes, and admiring Dennis. Isn't he a sweet dog?'

Daly nods and then seems to suddenly become aware he is holding two glasses of wine. He holds one out to Susie.

'No thanks, darling. I'm driving, remember?'

'Oh crumbs, of course,' Daly says, in the same slightly over-cheerful way. 'I'll uh . . . find someone to palm it off onto and find you a soft drink, eh?'

'No, don't worry, I'll go and find something. You stay here.'

Eva and Daly watch his wife disappear, Eva searching her mind urgently for something to say. She doesn't dislike Daly exactly but she knows he is one of Courtenay's Courtiers, and therefore one of the many people on manoeuvres against the Prime Minister. Coupled with his reputation for sleeping around Westminster, Eva feels very self-conscious all of a sudden about the two of them standing alone together.

Daly for his part is staring at the back of Courtenay's head, roughly ten yards away. Over thirty years have passed since they first met as little boys at prep school. Theirs has been a close, or at least old and familiar, friendship egged on by a strange kind of rivalry, the rat race of their lives: Courtenay captained both the football and cricket First XIs at Eton, but Daly was head of school; Daly got his First from Balliol and became President of the Union, but Courtenay had a glittering military career, including as the Prince of Wales's equerry; Daly got selected for his safe seat first, but Courtenay's wife is a far more formidable political spouse than Susie. Daly has always known that he is cleverer than his friend – both intellectually and emotionally – and finding himself running around on Courtenay's behalf feels instinctively weird. Still, with his skeletons it's best to settle for a Great Office of State and be the power behind the throne.

Daly and Eva are both saved from struggling to make conversation by Millie Sackler striding over, pretending not to notice people staring at her well-presented bosoms.

'Hello, Millie, how are you?' Eva tilts her head to kiss Millie's cheek.

'Hi, darling, great to see you,' Millie chirrups, accepting the second glass of wine from Daly. 'Thanks, Si. I wondered where you'd got to.'

Before he can answer they are interrupted by Hendrick, the Education Secretary, practically popping with enthusiasm, trailed by his long-suffering wife.

'Hello, hello!' he crows. 'How are we all?'

'Hello, Rich, good to see you.' Daly shakes his hand. 'Stellar round this morning.'

'Secretary of State. Mrs Hendrick,' smiles Eva, watching out of the corner of her eye as a harried-looking man, his bald pate glinting in the sun, stomps over to them.

'Oh, did you hear it?' Hendrick said brightly. 'Felt like I drew the short straw today! Ah, hello, Tim,' he says to the man, who has now joined the group and is glowering at him. 'Have you met my wife? Tanya, darling, this is Tim Bowers, the PM's press chappie.'

Tim nods his head stiffly at Tanya and turns to Hendrick.

'Interesting round this morning, Secretary of State,' Tim bristles.

'It was rather, wasn't it?' Hendrick grins.

'I tuned in just in time to hear you get into your flow about whether the letter "y" should officially be recognised as a vowel,' Tim continues through gritted teeth, 'which I don't remember signing off on the government comms grid when we agreed your announcement on top-up tutoring. Unless, of course, you have your own secret grid full of unnecessary ways to make us look like total tits while the Leader of the Opposition lampoons us every day on food and energy prices.'

'Tim. Matey,' Hendrick spreads his fingers apologetically, 'I was trying to get off the PM and Graham Thomas stories . . .'

'You used a story about turning the alphabet Welsh as a dead cat?' Tim growls. 'This was only one rung down from when someone forgot to type up the Home Secretary's speech phonetically.'

'Ah yes,' laughs Hendrick, dancing from foot to foot. 'When she said *Führer* instead of *furore*—'

'Shut up,' Tim hisses. 'Has it occurred to you that a small fraction of the British public actually tuned in to hear you babbling like a fuckwit this morning hoping to learn what the government is doing to educate their children better? What's more, some of them, statistically speaking, are actually behind the PM and just want us to get on with the job of improving the country.' Tim looks around at the silent group. 'Well, those same people are now presumably scratching their heads, the only "y" on their minds being why on earth the PM thinks she can appoint such an unutterable *chump* and remain credible as a genuine public servant.' Tim drains his glass of wine and stomps off.

Daly, who has watched the scene with undisguised glee, raises his eyebrows.

Eva looks desperately at her feet, trying to avoid catching Mrs Hendrick's eye, who finally seems to be enjoying herself. Hendrick himself stares mistily after Tim's retreating back, silently mouthing the word 'chump'. Within moments, though, he has recovered and spots an elegant couple stepping graciously through the party.

'Ahhh, Eric! Clarissa!' Hendrick chirps, turning to his wife and pulling her by the elbow behind him. 'Have you met Tanya?'

Millie melts into a fit of giggles. 'That was wonderful! That chap Tim is such a character,' she puts a hand to her brow and surveys the crowd, 'and quite attractive, in his own way.' She sneaks a look at Daly, knowing this is exactly the sort of thing that nettles the competitive young(ish) thrusters who are in a hurry. 'Such aggression.'

'I meant to ask,' Daly says firmly, before Millie can say anything else, 'have you been to Chequers before?'

'I haven't as a matter of fact. This is my first time,' Millie lowers her head to take a sip of wine and looks at him through her lashes, 'a virgin, so to speak.'

Eva valiantly pretends she hasn't heard the exchange.

'How about I show you around the house a bit?' Daly takes Millie's arm. 'See you later, Eva.'

Eva watches them leave, wondering at their audacity. Unimpressed, she turns away and surveys the crowd. She spots Jackson – Uriah Heap incarnate – darting from group to group like a crazed honeybee, fertilising every available flower. The Courtiers are out in force: she ought to get out there to speak to as many MPs as possible and shove the merits of the PM's trade deal down their throats.

Eva steps into the crowd, balancing carefully to stop her heels sinking into the grass. As she walks she nods to various people but keeps moving to find the right target, catching snippets of conversation as she goes. 'Clever to drag us all the way out here. Nobody to hear our screams. I've heard there are already enough letters but Godfrey's not told her yet . . . Did you hear Natasha on that podcast last week? They asked her what she'd do if she was cat-called in the street. The honest answer is "bend over" . . . I don't blame him. I'd sell my children to watch England in the Caribbean . . . I just don't think I can vote for it, Chief. A trade deal should mean we actually get something out of it. It's a sell-out . . . Yes, Percy Cross's daughter. One of many, if the rumours are true . . . Darling, that's Eric Courtenay. I hear he's a shoo-in. Let's go and say hello . . . Anyway, the silly bugger has been sending dick pics to all the candidates he didn't hire. Absolutely amazing nobody has reported him. I only know because . . . Still, I reckon it depends on if there's more to come. If she gets rid of him I wonder who they will bump up? I might go and put a good word in with the Chief . . . Please put a jacket on, Beth, everyone can see your tits . . . He's obviously been silly but anyone can make a mistake. You have to be so careful these days. Bloody expenses scandal . . . Look, nobody in my seat gives a shit about this vote. I just want it over with so I can get back to being shouted at about HS2 . . . This wine is absolutely revolting. They might have stretched to something half decent for once . . . Look at that wretched old thing. Someone should put it out of its misery. And the dog . . . '

Meanwhile, up two flights of stairs, Daly and Millie reach the Long Gallery. They look down, unobserved behind the stained-glass windows, at the party outside. It is cool and quiet indoors and all they can hear is the ticking of a couple of clocks and the murmur of the crowd down below.

'That's a very odd picture.' Millie points at a pane of glass. 'Those look an awful lot like cricket stumps.'

'That's right,' says Daly softly, running his fingers lightly down her spine and over her bottom. 'And those red things are cricket balls. Along here the different former PMs' coats of arms are set into the window. This one is John Major's.' As Millie turns to look, Daly leans in and kisses gently along her collarbone.

She smiles impishly. 'You naughty boy, everyone's just outside.'

'Exactly,' he breathes into her neck, his left hand sliding around her waist, his right inching through the fold of her wrap dress.

Millie leans back into the frame of the window, bending her knee until her foot rests on the window seat and her skirt falls open a little. Daly's fingers explore a little further and Millie hears a sharp intake of breath.

'No knickers ... did you miss the dress code?' he whispers, kneeling down slowly before her.

In the grounds down below, the party in full swing, one of the PM's protection officers nudges his colleague in the ribs and inclines his head at an upstairs stained glass window, where the imprint of a pair of pale bum cheeks is undulating against the glass for anyone to see – if the guests cared to look up from their involved conversations.

'PM, I think it's time.' Peter looks up at the sky, which has darkened ominously. The Prime Minister nods her agreement and someone bangs a gavel. The crowd immediately quietens down as the PM receives a final encouraging smile from her husband. She makes her way onto the makeshift stage, clears her throat and begins.

'It is a great pleasure to welcome you all to Chequers today,' she smiles. 'Thank you for making time to come here on a Saturday, particularly those who have had to travel far. Some even from the Caribbean ...' Thomas waves clownishly back, clearly a few drinks down. The group laughs and the PM immediately relaxes. 'I wanted to ask you here to speak to you face to face away from the cameras and the green benches and the journalists. To speak to you as colleagues. As equals. As friends. To ask you – implore you – to vote for the deal next week ...'

Roughly twelve feet above the platform, Millie is still writhing against the window frame, her fingers knotted in Daly's hair, trying desperately not to cry out. She hears a murmur of approval from the crowd outside, and a moment later a patter of applause but she has no idea what is being said.

Millie takes the opportunity of the sound below to pull Daly up by his tie and push him back into a chair at a nearby desk. She slips into his lap and leans slightly back as Daly buries his face into her chest. She fumbles with his trouser button and zip and has an idea.

'Calm down,' she whispers. Daly takes a deep breath, not least to try and suck his stomach in a bit, feeling more Lurpak than six-pack these days. Millie tilts her head down and kisses him while she twists his tie round behind his head and knots it firmly to the back of the chair.

There is another small, echoing cheer from outside, which only spurs Daly on harder. Who else can say they have screwed their way through a prime ministerial address at Chequers? Then he thinks of Susie in the crowd.

'We haven't got time for this,' he murmurs, starting to lean forward but finding himself leashed to the chair by the neck. 'What...?' He tries to turn to see what's holding him back but can't. He feels around behind his head with his hands. 'Fucking hell, that's a bit much, isn't it?' a note of panic in his voice.

Millie laughs at his wide eyes and moves her hips forward, lowering herself until he is inside her. Daly sighs contentedly into her hair.

'I'd just shut up if I were you,' Millie whispers.

'...and I know this isn't a deal that is perfect for everyone here,' says the Prime Minister. 'That's the nature of compromise. But it is the right one, and voting for it on Tuesday is the right thing for the country. To leave this question unanswered leaves us in a state of eternal paralysis and our communities, our families and our businesses at a constant disadvantage. To say nothing of the risk of an extreme far-left Labour government.' There is a pantomime-like hiss from her MPs.

The PM looks up and is suddenly aware of how dark and heavy the sky has become. The canvas catering tents are starting to flap. The wind is picking up. She needs to hurry but she feels tired. 'The right thing for our country and our Party is to stop this in-fighting and get on with what the British people really want – a safer, healthier, brighter future. Simply put, this deal means jobs and it means peace.' She feels a drop of water on the back of her hand and stops to watch it slide down inside her cuff. *You don't have to do this.* The thought suddenly occurs to her. *You could just . . . leave. Before the letters come and you're hounded out.* Her ears fill with a strange buzzing. She ignores the remaining few speaking notes and instead studies the bruised clouds scudding across the sky. The buzzing changes key, whispers from the audience adding a bass note to the sea-like sound. *You're so tired. This has gone on for months. If you resign now it will all be over soon.* The PM feels completely removed from her body. Then the familiar thump of a friendly tail on the side of the stage snaps her back. *No. I can still win.*

The PM pushes her shoulders back and steps out from behind the podium. 'We are in danger of getting stuck in the present. The *future* is of course what we hold most precious in this Party. We are Conservatives – we are here to conserve this great nation for future generations. Right now we're in danger of conserving nothing and destroying ourselves. Upon becoming Prime Minister, I promised that I would leave this country in a better state than how I found it.'

Out of the corner of her eye, Eva can see Peter flipping frantically through his copy of the PM's remarks, unable to find where she is speaking from. There is a distant rumble of thunder.

'I know some of you think that the time has come,' the PM says clearly, feeling another drop of rain. 'That *my* time has come. Well . . .' Drip, drip. A louder rumble. The storm is moving towards them. She takes a deep breath and looks around the group, as still and silent as statues. 'I think you're wrong.'

The PM gazes down at the upturned faces, hanging off her words. 'Let me be your leader, the greatest honour of my life. Let me lead you through this, the choppiest of times, where the water is deepest and an experienced captain at the helm is critical.' Another roll of thunder echoes around the valley. 'We can do better than simply conserving: we can build and grow. But we have to break this impasse. So on Tuesday, it is time to vote with me or against me once and for all.' She pauses one last time for effect. 'I'm officially calling it: for the government benches, the China Trade Deal vote is a vote of confidence in my leadership.'

There is a sharp collective intake of breath as every MP inwardly updates their threat/opportunity matrix.

'It's time to decide what you want to do.' But before she can say anything else a streak of lightning cracks across the sky. A woman in the crowd shrieks. The drops have become a convincing shower.

'I think we are in danger of drowning if we stand out here shaking on it, though.' There is a ripple of relieved laughter, just audible over the rising wind. There's nothing more to say. 'I . . . I'll see you all next week. Have a safe journey home.'

The PM turns and walks off the platform. The audience of shell-shocked MPs clap respectfully until she has left the platform, then there is a flurry of activity as people rush to seek shelter from what is now a downpour. High heels are yanked off, jackets pulled over heads. Waiters dash about, taking glasses from frantic guests and bundling tablecloths and napkins into black bags. The PM, holding her husband's elbow to avoid slipping, escapes indoors.

Sackler, in many ways improved by the shower, reaches Daly's car to find Susie already waiting, completely soaked through.

'Oh dear!' Sackler shouts cheerily above the rain and the

sound of dozens of engines starting, 'Where is Simon? I hope he hasn't lost his keys. This rain is biblical – we'll drown!'

Susie gives a strained laugh, conscious of her sodden dress sticking to her body, highlighting her paunchy tummy and cobby thighs. An anatomy lesson, her mother would have called it. She clutches her hands across her front, straining to see through the pummelling raindrops. She's feeling cross with her husband, who abandoned her for the entire party and left her to fend for herself. She thought the lowest point had been getting stuck with an old duffer with dreadful breath, who kept asking her if she was 'in foal yet'. Daly might at least have stood with her for the PM's big address.

Two figures come dashing around the side of the house. As they get closer Susie recognises her husband, who in the confusion has managed to untuck his shirt and twist his tie off kilter. As he runs he pulls the car key from his pocket and frantically presses the unlock button. Susie sees the indicator lights come on, pulls open the driver's door and stows herself inside.

'Well, mate,' Sackler yells over the rain hammering on the car roof, tearing a back door open, 'I need more time to think than I thought. She's really upped the stakes now!'

'What?' Daly pauses for a beat, half in, half out of the car. 'What do you mean?'

'Well, we all heard it – she's called our bluffs! Tuesday is D-Day,' Sackler says happily, slamming the door behind him. Millie gets in on the other side.

Daly lowers himself slowly into the passenger seat, cursing quietly. 'Um . . . would you say it was that black and white?'

Susie looks at him wonderingly. 'Come on, Si. China or bust – we all heard her. The trade deal is to be a vote of confidence in her.'

'Well, yes, of course I heard what she said,' Daly says

defensively, thinking fast. 'But I mean – the deal is one thing, but what about the general direction we're going in? She's just bought herself a bit of time. It still doesn't mean this isn't a . . . Well, look,' he motions at himself and his dripping companions, 'a washout!'

'Whatever you say, Simon,' Sackler sighs, 'it's good enough for me. You know, seeing her up there reminded me of when she stood up to the Russians at the G20. She had that fierce, stubborn look on her face. Really statesmanlike. Maybe this means she's back on form . . .' He begins to wring water out of his tie. 'What a bloody relief!'

For a moment they listen to the rain pounding on the roof. Then Millie begins to giggle, Sackler immediately joining in. She is mad, thinks Daly irritably, rubbing his neck and thinking how stupidly risky he has just been. He reluctantly chortles. Susie smiles and looks into the rear-view mirror. She is taken aback by how incredibly pretty Millie looks – the mad run through the rain has knocked ten years off her, giving her a rosy, fresh complexion. Her wet hair hangs down in delicate tendrils. Susie glances at her own face and is horrified to see her carefully applied mascara is leaking down her cheeks, the blusher streaked with raindrops. She pulls a tissue out of the car door pocket, puts the key in the ignition and wipes her face.

Even though it's only about five o'clock, the heavy rain and dark clouds make it seem much later. As Susie backs the car out she thinks she sees a dark shape appear in the glow of her rear lights. She quickly slams on the brakes, but when she checks again nothing is there. She shifts into first gear and joins the long queue of cars at the main gate.

The PM slumps onto a sofa and thoughtfully rests her chin in her cupped hands, listening to the rain lashing against the windows and thinking about the dozens of feverish, chattering conversations taking place in the departing vehicles. She notices she is shaking slightly, certainly from the cold and wet but from something else too. It must be shock at her own instinctive decision, so wildly out of character. Or is it just that, for the first time in months, she stood up to her colleagues? Has she just snapped?

The collection of Number Ten staffers, including Peter, Eva and Tim, stand dripping quietly to the side. Nobody knows quite whether they should smile or not. The PM has momentarily silenced her enemies, but she has also pointed to the secret door marked 'exit', something they all recognise as terminal one way or another.

The PM's husband leans down and puts a bracing hand on his wife's shoulder. 'Sally, do you mind bringing some tea?' The housekeeper immediately bustles off.

He looks around at the assembled group of sopping advisers and wonders whether he should say something, but is saved by the Chief, who strides in, punching the air triumphantly.

'Sorry I took so long – could hardly move for supporters clustering-round.' He turns to the PM. 'Well *done*, Prime Minister. You've pushed them onto your terms. It is risky. Very risky. But I like us being back on the front foot.' He turns to the rest of the group, who are looking marginally more cheerful. 'You all deserve a big drink tonight!'

The PM rises. 'Yes, thanks, everyone. Look ... I don't quite know what came over me. I promise that wasn't planned!' She is suddenly aware of how paranoid members of her team feel when some of them learn a secret after the others. Peter heckles a cheeky 'tell me about it' and the group laughs. 'I truly think it's the right thing. One way or another we have a real opportunity here. If we win on Tuesday, there'll be no more waiting for events to happen to us. We have a lot of work to do ahead of that,' she glances round at the determined faces, 'but for now I want you to get back home safely and relax this evening. After the Whips have done their work, you'll be hitting the phones too. Anyway, at least Graham Thomas needn't worry about the papers tomorrow any more.'

The PM's team laugh again and gather their belongings, shedding raindrops everywhere. After weeks of tension, the relief at a break in the atmosphere swells through the room like baking bread. The PM and her husband stand at the front door, nodding and smiling at each 'well done, PM' and 'see you on Monday' and 'hope we aren't flooded in' as the advisers troop out to waiting cars.

'Honestly, darling, it was like going for a smear test,' Clarissa sighs into her mobile phone, examining her damp hair in her compact mirror. 'You must go, it's extremely uncomfortable and you're never quite as lubricated as you'd really like to be.' She listens to the person at the other end of the phone. 'Yes, exactly. A complete washout. I mean, she's hardly the type to host a wet T-shirt competition ... You should dig out that photo from the log flume at Barry Island last summer. She was dripping!' Another pause. 'Yes, all right. But she's left us all with more questions than answers here. If she scrapes through Tuesday, are we meant to do this again in a year's time? God knows where the polls will be by then – and a year closer to an election. Surely she isn't leading us into that ... Yes, Graham looks pretty safe to me. Or safe for now, in any case.' She lowers her voice a little. 'If it goes wrong then some big questions about her integrity on not sacking him ... yes, yes, I love it! Okay, see you, darling. Bye!'

She hangs up and snaps shut her compact.

'That was Bruce at the *Mail on Sunday*. They're splashing with "Pathetic Fallacy".' Clarissa underlines invisible words with her hands. 'It's absolutely perfect.' She starts the car engine and fastens her seatbelt.

Her husband says nothing, just stares sullenly out of the window, trying to pinpoint the exact moment when a large number of his colleagues turned off the PM. Plenty, including him, feel overlooked. Plenty, including him, are unhappy with her policy decisions. He thinks back to talking to her earlier. He had to really work for her interest, struggling to get any purchase on her. Not in a slippery way, but in a kind of aloof, unclubbable way. Is that the reason so many MPs dislike her? Hate her, even?

Clarissa slams her palms hard on the steering wheel. 'What are you sulking about, Eric?' she demands. 'Do you even realise how far this sets us back? You really needn't be so judgemental about me briefing stories to help *your* career!' Her voice becomes shrill as Courtenay tries to interject. He still hasn't worked out what his wife's snooze button is when she flies into these rages.

'I'm not sulking, my darling. I promise. I'm just thinking. It's just a big decision, isn't it? I knew exactly where I was with the China Trade Deal, obviously. It isn't tight enough on what constitutes military aggression and doesn't even address cyberspying! But it isn't terrible – and to topple a Prime Minister over it . . . '

'Do you know how it feels to do *all* the thinking *all* of the time? That woman has overlooked you in the last two reshuffles for decent jobs. She's just stringing you along and you're somehow grateful. Fuck!' Clarissa hisses, preparing a fresh onslaught. She is caught off guard by a dim form that sidles into her field of vision in the rear-view mirror through the gloom of the storm.

She decides to change tack, taking a deep breath and slipping the car into reverse.

'Look, I know this is hard, honey. And it should be – this is serious stuff. But you have to stand by your principles, don't you, and not be manipulated like this. You were going to vote against the deal anyway … This is surely just a symptom of her wider leadership? She's asked you to vote based on the deal, nothing else. Pretty straightforward, don't you think? Pity the fools who are undecided even on that!'

Courtenay sits in silent thought for a moment, biting his lip, then his face clears.

'You're right, of course. Christ, you're always right. It's a good thing you're around to remind me of what I actually think!' He laughs, relief flooding through him.

Whatever it is behind the car seems to be confused and takes a hesitant step towards the car. As it moves into the pool of light thrown up by the brake lights, Clarissa's eyes narrow in recognition. She is annoyed that her husband has yet again missed so much subtext from the last couple of hours: the PM's pointed remark about experience, which Courtenay definitely doesn't have and which the Party grey beards can fixate on in their future Conservative Home columns about the leadership frontrunner; pushing MPs, who can be quite cowardly and prefer writing secret letters to the 1922 Committee Chairman, out into the open; how the window of opportunity to change leader before a General Election is shrinking.

Clarissa suddenly revs hard and the car shoots backwards. There is a loud clunk. Her husband looks at her, aghast. 'Christ, what was that?'

Clarissa locks her black eyes on him. 'Nothing. Just a bump in the road.' She slams the car into first gear.

'Just think,' she says as she sweeps the car down the drive, 'if you were in the Cabinet, we'd be in a ministerial car with a driver. I'm afraid that, for now, you just have your darling wife at the wheel.'

78

Courtenay summons a lingering thought from the back of his mind. How has he ended up here, being pushed into a world he neither really understands nor takes much interest in? Then he remembers where he'd be otherwise: in a passionless marriage, without the job where he'd had a real, life-or-death purpose, and heading into a mid-life cul de sac. Clarissa had scooped him up and given him drive and excitement again. Generally he is up for the ride but, Courtenay thinks as he fixes his eyes on the road ahead, he does wonder sometimes exactly what his wife is capable of.

A few cars ahead in the queue to leave, a Government Car Service driver glances at his passengers. His Secretary of State, Natasha Weaver, had sprinted through the rain with a man the driver recognised as an MP (was he the guy who won that by-election last year?) and announced that she wanted to give him a lift from Chequers to London. Giving a lift seems reasonable. Besides, the driver is pretty used to accommodating the various waifs and strays that the Secretary of State picks up.

The ministerial red box has been placed directly behind the driver so that his charges are sitting next to each other. Because of the general gloom outside and the tinted windows, it is dark in the back, but he can see their faces lit up by their mobile phones.

Presently, the passengers put their phones away and make conversation about the party – the storm, the gardens at Chequers, the food and wine. Not exactly LBC. The driver listens at first but the wind and rain are so aggressive that he has to focus on his driving, dipping in and out of the aimless chatter.

Unbeknown to the man at the wheel, as soon as the conversation begins ('I suppose it was rather brave to host it outdoors at this time of year . . .'), Weaver playfully takes the man's hand inside her wrap skirt and slides it, inch by inch, up her bare inner thigh (she can't afford to keep buying tights). The man feels his mouth go dry.

'Yes, very risky,' he stammers, 'did you get wet?'

Weaver guides his hand until he slips a finger inside her underwear.

'Soaked.'

After about a minute of quiet she speaks again. 'The poor PM seems to be under a lot of pressure. Arguably *too much* pressure.' He eases his efforts off slightly.

'Well, she's handling it brilliantly,' the man grins. 'What ... direction do you think we are going in?'

'I know there are complaints about going round and round in circles,' Weaver stares at the back of the driver's head, 'but I like that.'

Judging by the polite, strained chit-chat, the driver decides this new MP won't go far. Hardly Mr Charisma. The journey passes without incident although, as they speed along the M4, he is taken aback when there is some loud disagreement about whether guests had arrived at Chequers 'through the back entrance' or not.

The front door thuds shut behind the last person and the PM and her husband slump down on a sofa.

'Well done, love. You really showed them. The Chief thinks you might do it. Either way, you can go on your own terms. Just think, soon it'll be you, me and Den—'

The PM cuts him off, shooting to her feet.

'Oh my God,' she cries, 'Dennis! I haven't seen him since the rain started.'

'Well, I ... neither have I. Dennis ...? Sally, have you seen Dennis?'

'No, sir, not since the lunch,' Sally says, putting a tea tray on a table.

There is a crash of thunder. Without even stopping to put on coats, the PM and her husband run to the garden door and out into the storm, shouting the dog's name. For forty-five agonising minutes they search – the protection team helping – roaming the grounds of Chequers, screaming Dennis's name into the wind and driving rain.

The PM's sodden clothes weigh her down and her suede pumps are ruined. Her jaw aches from clenching it against the wind. She wipes her dripping fringe out of her eyes. Was that a bark? She squints through the gloom.

A streak of lightning splits the sky. Dazed, she heads to the porch of a nearby door to get her bearings. A couple of paces past a sundial, she notices something huddled at its base. She crouches and touches soaking, trembling fur. Dennis has rolled himself, hedgehog-like, into as tight a ball as possible and refuses to uncurl. He is shaking badly and as the PM leans closer she can hear a soft, pitiful whining. She shouts for her husband.

Soon the sounds of heavy booted footsteps and men's urgent voices approach. Someone bends down and hoists the dog into the air, while somebody else pulls the PM up from the ground.

'It's okay, we've got him,' she hears her husband's voice in her ear. 'Don't worry. He'll be all right.'

Claybourne Terrace

Eva slams the door behind her and drops her keys into a bowl on a side table. Holding a carrier bag of food in one hand, she leans her umbrella against the wall and uses her free hand to unzip one muddy boot after the other. Catching sight of herself in the mirror, she looks like a drenched vulture.

Eva pads into the kitchen and opens a bottle of wine, then unpacks her shopping and turns on the oven. She pours herself a healthy glass, takes a gulp and nearly chokes at the memory of Peter, giddy with relief at how the day had gone in the car back to London, gleefully describing the sight of Simon Daly struggling to help Millie Sackler fasten her bra as they scrambled out of the huge Chequers front door into the rain.

After some internal debate about quantities, Eva pricks the whole packet of sausages, picturing her most detested MPs' faces, and lays them out on a baking tray. She starts to pace but is sliding around, so tears off her clinging, laddered tights and throws them straight into the kitchen bin. Why is she unhappy? Peter said it was like seeing the PM he'd first worked for today, that she has defied expectations and 'really given those pricks something to think about'. Team Ford has reason to celebrate, but after one drink in the pub with everybody Eva has slunk home. She doesn't feel much like revelling.

Not to be totally self-centred, but what does this mean for her? SpAds never feel they have job security. Your Secretary of State can be sacked or reshuffled and that's you, gone. There is a strong chance that Eva could be sending out her CV in a matter of days. She doesn't want to leave Number Ten. She is making progress: the senior team values her judgement; she's learning about communications and legislation and policy; she's starting to develop the emotional and, frankly, animal intelligence needed to understand and manage MPs.

Well, Eva thinks, if she wants to give herself the best chance of staying then she needs to work like a dog in the next couple of days to keep the PM in place. Peter says that Number Ten will get an updated list of which way Conservative MPs have said they intend to vote from the Whips Office once they have finished the weekend ring-round of their flocks. He estimates that it will take until Sunday evening. So on Monday morning the Downing Street SpAds will be presented with their own lists of MPs to ring. Just the thought of those phone calls makes Eva feel tired. And scared.

It's times like this that Eva feels most lonely. Although it's like living with a fifty-five-year-old teenage boy, she misses having her father around. It's only been a couple of weeks but she's never lived alone. Before this was university housing and before that had been the school boarding house. She's thoroughly institutionalised. Claybourne Terrace is a big house to be alone in and with the doubts over her future she'll need good company before long.

As if sensing her mood, Eva's phone vibrates and she realises she hasn't checked it since before her arrival at Chequers – then remembers Jess and Bobby. She unlocks the screen. As expected, a lot of WhatsApps from fellow SpAds, curious about what happened at Chequers, plus a few MPs sending messages of support for the PM. And a flurry from the group with the girls, the most pertinent of which are:

Jess: *Yippee! Yes please. xxx*

Bobby: *Thank you so much! This is going to be so fun!!!*

The rest of the messages are the girls making travel arrangements and deciding what to pack. Eva's chest expands with pleasure, her tiredness seems to have evaporated. She shoves the sausages into the oven and makes a decision: with a hectic few days coming up, there's no time like the present to get Claybourne Terrace shipshape.

Eva trots up the stairs, texting Jamie, who has suggested he comes round later to pick up where they had left off that morning:

J, sorry about this but got a hectic few days coming up and need to spring clean pigsty before the girls arrive. Plus I got so drenched that the fancy new underwear set needs wringing out. Will make it up to you xx.

When she gets to her room Eva immediately opens a

window – Jamie has made the bed but there's a stubborn smell of stale cigarette smoke – and rummages around in a box for a scented candle. She peels off her wet dress, sadly thinking of the dry cleaning bill, and her underwear and drops it all into her laundry basket, before pulling on some tracksuit bottoms and one of Jamie's sweaters.

Eva heads back downstairs and gives herself a mental to-do list:

Have supper.

Clean house.

Bath. (Possibly Facetime Jamie, depending how horny she is feeling.)

Bed.

After eating, Eva puts on her headphones and fires up Lady Gaga, then pours the remaining wine into her glass and snaps on some Marigolds. Kitchen and bathrooms first.

As she scrubs and sings, Eva can't shift a strange niggle. She's excited the girls are coming to join her, but what brings them to London? Or rather, who: Ed Cooper and Simon Daly. Eva knows both of their reputations – a notorious bully and a notorious shagger. It's just as well the girls are moving in. They'll need her as much as she needs them.

Chequers

In the cosy living room the PM, now changed into jeans and a thick woollen jumper, sits in front of a roaring fire, a steaming bowl of clear soup in front of her. Her husband is worried she has caught a cold.

It wasn't until they were inside the brightly lit hallway that the PM had realised her hands were covered in blood. The protection team initially panicked until they realised the blood was coming from a deep wound on Dennis's head. He'd been rushed to the nearest emergency vet. An X-ray showed a cracked skull and a broken jaw. The hardest blow was learning that the dog is now completely blind.

The PM stares into the flames and wonders if her dog will cope living between Chequers, the Number Ten flat and their home in the constituency. A lot of stairs. A lot of changing people and smells and noises. She feels her throat tighten at the thought that he hates the dark so much, and now he'll be in darkness forever.

She is about to reach for the red box of papers at her feet when her husband chimes in.

'I don't think so. You need to finish this soup then head up to bed with the crossword. I'll cut it out . . .' Since the newspapers have become increasingly hostile towards her, the PM's team has taken to cutting the crossword out, and digesting the news into a short written summary. 'Come on – you did brilliantly today and I can see how worried you are about Den. You deserve a night off.'

The PM bristles, but nods.

Her husband watches her carefully. She needs as much rest as possible ahead of next week. Perhaps he can get her out for a long walk tomorrow. She has triumphed today: brave, eloquent, reasonable. This accident with their dog rattles him, though. He has a creeping fear that it hadn't been an accident at all and that someone is willing to go to any lengths necessary to get to the top – or sink his wife to the bottom.

31st March

PETROL PRICES SPIKE/

SITUATION WORSENS IN MIDDLE EAST

Glasgow

In the darkness of the car Jess runs her fingers through her hair once again. She feels a swoop of excitement as she turns onto the street and slows to find the right house number. This feels bold. Very bold. But she's leaving town soon, so why not have a final bit of fun?

Jess locks the car and walks to the front door, smoothing down her long trench coat. She presses the buzzer, her heart racing and her breathing shallow and quick. Finally a man's silhouette appears in the doorway.

'Hello, come to say goodbye, have you?' Tommy asks.

Jess wordlessly unties the belt of her coat, revealing her completely naked body, save for a pair of black thigh-high PVC boots.

'Jesus. Come here,' he growls, picking her up.

The dual sounds of her gasping softly into his neck and her boots squeaking together as she wraps her legs around his waist raises the hairs on the back of Tommy's neck. It's like listening simultaneously to Mozart and the scraping of nails down a blackboard.

'I want to ask you something,' she breathes.

'Shoot,' his face buried in her neck.

'Have you used your handcuffs before? You know . . . outside the line of duty?'

Tommy keeps kissing his way down her collarbone. 'Nope. But you're a big shot journalist now. Don't want to damage your reputation by putting you in cuffs.' He moves to her chest. 'That's for the Leveson 2.0.'

'Don't you worry about me.' Jess pulls his hair back until he is looking into her face, wincing. 'You might be the police officer, but I'll be the one taking you into custody.'

He laughs softly, his eyes glimmering, and nods at a bag on the floor.

'Be my guest.' He can tell Jess wants to be in charge tonight. Although she occasionally engages in what she calls Tommy's 'traditional man-splaying', Tommy himself much prefers their sessions when she is in control, not least because of the texts she sends him afterwards, reliving every moment.

He lets Jess slide out of his arms and watches as she pulls the cuffs out of the bag and walks slowly up the stairs ahead of him, letting her coat slip off behind her. She swings the cuffs round one finger. Tommy watches her ascend, lingering on her toned back and perfectly shaped arse above the shiny boots. He shakes his head, grinning to himself, then chases after her.

1st April

UK unemployment hits 6%/
North Korea launches test missiles

Downing Street

Shortly after 8 a.m. on Monday, Eva makes her way across St James's Park to the back entrance of Downing Street. Uncertain about what the day holds, she has fully braced herself. She'd woken up early and gone for a run and taken extra care when drying her hair. She has hot coffee in her thermal cup and Blondie in her headphones.

As soon as she sets foot inside the building, Eva registers the sudden change in atmosphere. She was told before she started that working in Downing Street often feels like a bunker, because once you are inside you are closed off from the rest of the world. She thinks it is more like a plunge pool – sometimes balmy and inviting, sometimes freezing, but always a marked contrast with the outside air temperature. For the past few weeks the mood has felt heavy and lethargic, as though the bricks themselves are succumbing to an illness that is taking down the whole administration. Today it is electric.

Eva often wonders how the PM finds being in the building. From the moment she leaves the flat she is instantly on display, caught on CCTV at regular intervals by the Custodians – the official gatekeepers of Number Ten – like a rare expectant panda at the zoo. Her entire day in Downing Street is carefully planned with meetings, calls and decisions. The quick breaks for the bathroom and lunch are a different kind of work in themselves as she often bumps into a group of schoolchildren on a tour, normally patting an ecstatic Dennis, or a Cabinet minister wanting a quick word. Eva has witnessed the change in atmosphere when the PM steps into a reception in the State Rooms, a ripple of expectation as she circulates among the guests. She is always 'on'.

Eva is hanging up her coat when Peter pokes his head around the door of the office they share next to the Cabinet Room. 'Come on – meeting in the State Dining Room. It's like a palatial war room. Only need sticks and little tank figurines to push around a giant map.'

Eva picks up her notebook and follows him up the famous yellow staircase and through the ugly, industrial kitchens. Peter pushes open a large green baize door and they enter an ornately carved, high-ceilinged room. A huge mahogany table in the middle is surrounded by about thirty people, all chatting quietly. It looks like every SpAd in the building is here. Peter joins the Prime Minister's chief of staff, Leonard Smith, at a large whiteboard by the window, which looks oddly out of place next to the priceless collection of silver and heavy draped curtains. Eva takes an empty seat at the table and exchanges excited waves and nervous smiles with her friends.

'Okay, everyone, listen up.' All eyes are on Leonard, the battle-hardened chief of staff. 'I've called you all together because we have a vote to win and we have tasks for all of you. The Whips have completed their ring-round and the Chief has

89

his numbers. Let's begin with what everyone knows: with 650 MPs in the House, removing Sinn Fein and a handful of other independents expected to abstain, plus the Speaker, we are at about 638. To be safe, we need at least 320 ayes. From what we've seen publicly and from our private intel from the different opposition parties, we're expecting a decent number of Labour rebels to join us. Now we have the offer of a few goodies like Free Ports and specific language on military aggression, the Chief reckons we can bank as many as forty, mainly from coastal areas. Plus, I'm pleased to say, it looks like we have the DUP on board.'

The assembled SpAds listen attentively.

'So that's the easy bit. Short of something crazy, we'll win overall. But the PM needs to show she has the confidence of her own side. After all, Sir Godfrey Singham only needs to receive fifty letters to trigger the 1922 Committee confidence vote procedure. If more than forty-nine of our 331 MPs vote against her tomorrow then we'll be updating our LinkedIn profiles by the end of the day.'

Leonard glares around at his team.

'Peter's going to explain what we need you to do, but in effect, we want to tap up every MP we have and leave nothing to chance. Even David Carmichael is getting wheeled through after his surgery. We're fighting for the PM's political life here, folks, and you're the foot soldiers.' He smiles and nods to Peter, who steps forward.

'Thanks. As Leonard says, each of you will be given a short-list of targets in priority order. They'll also all get a call from their Whip and a member of the Cabinet. It will be people you know well, or who we know have an interest in your policy area. Make sure you see them in person. They've all come up early for business this afternoon, so they won't have much on as it's Monday morning. You'll be given tailored scripts outlining the merits of the deal and why they need to back the PM tomorrow. Do *not* promise anything in return for their vote. Just feed any information back to us immediately. Jobs, gongs, constituency funding, legislative time – they don't get anything unless it is promised directly from the PM or the Chief.'

Peter distributes sheets of paper. Eva runs down her list – there are even members of the payroll, so named because they are government ministers, so generally take a salary, who are expected to be uber-loyalists – and sees her father's name at the bottom of the page. She feels a twinge of paranoia and disappointment.

'Some of you,' Peter ignores her stare, 'will have a handful of names from outside Parliament. It's pretty obvious – we need thought leaders, Peers, columnists and so on to come out in support. The press team is running a separate operation for editors and political editors.'

Leonard turns to the group. 'That reminds me – one thing to add is that vocal, public support is really important. You will have seen that journalists are keeping a close eye on which ministers and MPs have done supportive tweets and so on. If you get a commitment to back us, ask them to say something publicly. Builds a sense of momentum. Plus it weeds out who is just fobbing you off, for starters. Any questions? Good. Okay . . . ' He looks at his watch. 'Let's regroup here at midday.'

Chairs scrape back and people gather their things, but Eva doesn't move. When the last person has left she speaks up.

'Excuse me, Leonard. Peter. I just wanted to ask why my father's name is on my list.'

The two men pause their conversation to look at her.

'What?' asks Leonard.

'My father's name. I was wondering why it's on my list.'

'Eva, you have to get past this nepotism thing. Nobody cares—' begins Peter.

'I care, though. I care what people think.' Eva's hands move to her hips. 'Look, this isn't even about that. I just don't think it's a good idea.'

'Well, why not?' Leonard interjects. 'He's a former Prime Minister. The membership loves him. It would be great to have him write an op-ed or a supportive tweet or something.'

'Yes, I see that. But don't you think the PM herself should call previous PMs, rather than SpAds?'

The two men look at each other.

'Well,' sighs Peter. 'She *is* calling the others . . .'

'Right, I see. Sounds like I either really need to just get past this nepotism thing . . . or you don't even deem him worth five minutes of the PM's time. Why even bother then?'

The two men shift their feet. Finally Leonard speaks up.

'Look, I'll be honest with you. Your father is . . . unpredictable. We thought that if you speak to him in the first instance and gauge where he is it might, uh, avoid a comms risk.'

Eva bites her lip. It's a fair point. Now he has control of his Twitter account, Percy could easily live-tweet his conversation with the PM or blast out something unhelpful in the hope of getting a lucrative op-ed from a newspaper.

'How about we take a view later today, when we know where we are?' Peter says quietly.

The three of them exchange looks.

'Deal.'

Portcullis House

Stopping only to pick up her coat and dab on some lip balm, Eva heads over to Parliament with a small group of advisers. As they cross Whitehall, they joke nervously about who is on their lists. 'At least ours aren't as bad as Leonard's or Peter's – or the PM's! Apparently they're trying to reason with Nigel Jackson a little later on,' someone whispers.

It takes the SpAds a while to get into Parliament as there are so many people protesting against the China Trade Deal. Many carry large placards and a handful have tannoys. Bewildered tourists fight their way through to Westminster Abbey.

'I dunno,' replies somebody else, as they make their way into the glass-covered Portcullis House, 'I have to speak to David Montagu about his Herbal Remedies Bill. Reckons we should all be knocking back milk thistle instead of doing dialysis on the NHS. Quite hard to smile and nod my way through that one . . .'

The list comparison continues and Eva reflects on what a golden opportunity this is for those MPs with poor political instincts but with good, earnest plans to improve their communities. She thinks of the names on her list, many of whom have carved themselves reputations on particular issues, on anything from postnatal depression support to regulation of products advertised by celebrities to city status for their towns: they ask questions of ministers in Parliament at every opportunity; they tirelessly write letters and articles, laying out their arguments; they have put their own careers on the line, choosing to push forward on something they care about at the risk of annoying the powers that be. Today, the smart ones will leverage their votes to get something out of the government to progress their campaigns.

Eva waves to the group and peels off towards the lifts. When she reaches the door marked 'George Sackler MP/Simon Daly MP' she takes a deep breath and knocks.

'Come in!'

Daly is leaning back in his chair, absorbed in his phone

screen. Eva can't see he is watching a gif on the Legislative Lads WhatsApp group of a large pair of breasts bouncing up and down. He glances up, his eyes drawn straight to Eva's chest.

'Ah, Evie! What a treat.' Daly jumps up from behind his desk. 'How can I help?'

'Hello, Minister, how nice to see you again. I'm actually here to see George.'

Thank goodness for that, Daly thinks, having panicked for a moment that Number Ten is on to him. He's just been having breakfast with Clarissa, who has finally given him an opportunity to show his quality: he shall fall on his sword and resign as a minister at the opportune moment – perhaps in the next couple of hours, perhaps in the next couple of days. Regardless, he'll bravely lead a campaign of mass resignations and be regarded as a Party hero for breaking the painful, zombie-like death march off an electoral cliff.

'Been sent on a mission, have you?' Daly grins, knowing all about these sorts of whipping operations, but Eva doesn't react. 'All right, all right. Sack!'

Sackler stumbles in from the adjoining room, applying after-shave and swilling mouthwash. When he sees Eva he intones a doorbell-like 'muh-uhh' of greeting, before grabbing a dirty mug off his desk, gargling and spitting into it.

'Hello! To what do I owe this great pleasure?'

Eva smiles back at him. 'Hi, George, I wondered if you have a few minutes to spare?'

'Why of course!' He gestures through the doorway to the side room. 'Make yourself comfortable.'

Eva looks around what she supposes is their storage room. There's a large printer/photocopier and boxes of headed paper. She sits down on a broken desk chair and hears Daly's stage whisper next door. 'Pretty shit sign that they're sending one of the most junior people in the building over to twist your arm, Sack ...'

Oh fuck off, Eva thinks.

'So, my dear, what can I do for you?' Sackler closes the door and sits down on a stack of newspapers.

'I'm sure you can guess, George. I've come to confirm your support for the PM tomorrow. Will you vote for the deal?'

'Well, Eva. I'm all in favour of free trade of course! And naturally I think the PM is marvellous . . .'

'Brilliant, so we can count on you?'

'Gosh, I . . . well, I haven't *completely* made up my mind—'

'What are your doubts? I'm sure the Chief – or the PM herself – would be happy to meet with you to talk them over.'

'I, uh . . . ah, just a moment.' Sackler leaps up and steps into the next room, closing the door behind him. 'Si, can you just check what time we're due for that meeting . . . ?'

Eva paces slowly around the room, wondering what Daly is saying in such a hushed voice. Sackler is meant to be one of the easy ones. Start the day with a win. She kicks the printer angrily.

A piece of paper sitting on top of it catches her eye, clearly fresh out of the machine.

Following the defeat of the China Trade Bill and the resignation of the Prime Minister, I have consulted with colleagues and am honoured to announce my intention to stand as Leader of the Conservative Party . . .

Eva is stunned. Who on earth can this be from? She picks up the sheet and stifles a laugh at the name printed at the bottom. *George Sackler MP.*

'Righto . . . yes.'

Eva drops the sheet back onto the printer and slips back into the chair.

'Sorry about that, Eva. Just checking when my next meeting is.'

'No problem.'

'So as I say: huge fan of the PM. Huge fan of free trade,' Sackler guffaws. 'If it were down to me personally, I would shout it from the rooftops. But my Association is very worked up about the general direction of things. You know how it is. I'm getting inundated with calls from my members to write a letter to Sir Godfrey. A public statement of support would really put the cat among the pigeons. I think the best thing is for me to keep a low profile and spend some time on the phone, talking folks round.'

Sackler fiddles with a loose thread on his cuff.

'Well, if the Association is the problem, I'm sure the Party Chairman would be happy to get on the phone. We certainly weren't aware there is an issue there.'

'Ah yes, well, they are very discreet in my patch. Besides, I don't want to bother the Chairman with this. So, uh . . . leave it with me.'

'Well, George, thank you for your time.' Eva rises from her chair and puts on her coat. Sackler looks extremely relieved that the meeting is over.

'I'm so sorry about your Association being difficult. I hope you can get them behind you. After all, it would be tricky to progress further up the ranks to the Cabinet if they aren't supportive of you showing a bit of loyalty to the Party Leader.' Eva stops at the door and turns to him. 'I mean really, if you can't persuade them on something like this, there's no chance you could . . . I don't know . . . one day throw your own hat into the ring.' She gives him a hard look.

Sackler's smile sags. 'Ha . . . yes. Quite.'

'Thanks again. Hope the calls go well. Bye, Minister!' Eva waves to Daly as she marches out of the office. The door is quickly pulled closed behind her and the sound of Sackler's babbling voice follows her down the corridor.

Downing Street

The SpAds regroup in the State Dining Room to throw out snippets of information, which Peter details in a spreadsheet of MPs' names, coding them in traffic light colours: green supporters, amber maybes and red rebels.

'Oh, I'm not surprised at all,' Peter says, after Eva relays her conversation with Sackler. 'All MPs think they could be Prime Minister.'

'But surely George knows he has no chance. I mean . . . I just couldn't believe it when I saw that letter. I honestly thought it must be an April Fool!'

'Come on, Eva. Putting this vote to one side, there are two routes for an ambitious MP here if a leadership contest should go ahead: either you run yourself, counting on being bought off with a Cabinet job by one of the frontrunners in exchange for bringing your supporters with you; or coming out in support of a frontrunner early. Maybe even running their campaign. Sack is just playing the game. A rubbish version of it, but still . . . I'll get the Chairman to call his bluff on the Association.'

'Okay.' Leonard, fresh from a meeting with the PM, is keen to get back to business. 'What else have we got?'

'Mary Jones is digging in on her menopause stuff,' the health SpAd says. 'She's been so dogged on it. Can't we just go for it?' There is a murmur of agreement.

The meeting continues. Although a few MPs have crystallised their support in favour of the PM, it is clear that there are still plenty who need persuading.

'It looks like a lot of this can be solved by the Chancellor,' chimes in Tim Bowers, the director of communications, who is leaning against a wall, a phone in each hand. 'New roads, station upgrades, etc. In fact, we need to get all the Cabinet working the phones this afternoon. I—' He is interrupted by his phone pinging. 'Oh, you are joking! Simon Daly has resigned.'

The room erupts in gasps and swear words and the scuffling of everyone digging out their phones. They're all thinking the same thing: is Daly the first in a carefully coordinated deluge of resignations and letters of no confidence?

'His letter has just come through on email ... and it's on Twitter too. Pompous arse ...'

Eva studies the letter, written on House of Commons headed paper:

We need to ignore the red herring of this important piece of legislation, which can be revisited by a future administration. It is time for new leadership ... we are, in my view mistakenly, looking to experience rather than to creative thinking.

Everyone can see it is a thinly veiled call for Eric Courtenay to take over. Within minutes *Crash*, the most visited political gossip website in Westminster, has a *Blue Peter*-style thermometer to measure confirmed numbers of rebels. Online coverage, which has been hedging for any outcome, tweaks to give the sense that the ground is shifting away from the PM. Phones explode with messages from both jittery and bullish MPs.

'Right, we'll see about this,' shouts Tim, jabbing at his mobile. 'Yes, hello, Daly, you little fucker!' he screams into the phone, kicking open the baize door and racing down the corridor. 'This is just a courtesy call to let you know I'm going to bury you ...' His shouts echo down the staircase, the other media SpAds in hot pursuit. They now need to flood the airwaves with supportive voices to head off a sense of momentum against the Prime Minister.

'Well,' Leonard rubs his eyes and picks up his things, 'I'd better go and tell the PM the latest.'

Notting Hill

Courtenay paces around his living room. Occasionally he steals a glance at his wife, who reclines on a sofa, scrolling through her phone. It has been a tense day. Jackson advised Courtenay to stay away from SW1 to avoid journalists, so he had anxiously watched the lunchtime news as it was reported that Daly had resigned. Over the next few hours, a steady stream of Courtier MPs announced that they were considering submitting a letter of no confidence in the Prime Minister, but there have been no further ministerial resignations. Courtenay's phone has dozens of unreturned missed calls from members of the Cabinet, from other MPs, from Leonard Smith at Number Ten, from journalists. Everyone wants to know what he is going to do. He looks out of the window at a lone jogger puffing down the street in the dwindling evening light. Terrible form.

His phone rings: Jackson.

'Hi, Nigel, how are you doing?' Clarissa's head snaps up at his words. Courtenay turns away from her.

'Fine, fine. I just, uh . . . wondered where your head is?'

'Well, I . . .'

'What's he asking?' hisses Clarissa.

'Sorry,' Courtenay clamps his phone harder to his ear, 'I couldn't hear you for a second. What was that?'

'I was asking what you're thinking.' There's a long pause.

'I . . . I'm not sure, to be honest. I saw the Chancellor's clip earlier, about the China Trade Bill being the PM's first priority and Party in-fighting being a distraction from the dire straits the economy is in, and it did get me thinking.' Clarissa looks furious, mouthing to let her have the phone. 'I mean . . . it does look sort of weird, doesn't it? Resign as a minister over a free trade deal . . . there are steeper hills to die on.'

There is another long pause. Clarissa snatches the phone and hits the screen.

'Nige, it's Clarissa. You're on loudspeaker.'

'Hiya, Clazz.'

'What's going on? Obviously Eric's talking out of his arse.' Courtenay pouts.

'Look. Things have slowed down here. I think Simon is the only resignation we'll get. We've got a decent number of letters but we won't get enough. Number Ten has run a pretty good operation today. You know how Simon assured us he had Sack sewn up? They got the PM on the phone to him with his Association Chairman and he's turned turtle.' Clarissa punches a cushion. 'I actually think Eric's instincts are right. He's in danger of looking like a back-stabber, something the membership hate. Number Ten has muddied the waters in making this a confidence vote and the deal itself is essentially harmless now.'

'Harmless? You lot keep telling me it isn't worth the paper it's written on!' Clarissa cries.

Jackson embarks on a lengthy explanation of why things have changed. The government has managed to include clauses on things like sanctions on products from factories known to use slave labour and language on Taiwan and military aggression. Coupled with all the new economic perks (the Treasury has created an online tool where you can type in your postcode and see what the deal means for your area – 'Cornwall can double its GDP!'), it looks increasingly difficult for an MP to explain to their constituents why they aren't supporting the deal during one of the country's worst cost of living crises in recent times. The Courtiers are snookered.

'Nigel, even if we down tools now, Eric looks a bit out on a bloody limb, doesn't he? We've got cameras camped outside the house.' Clarissa's nostrils flare.

'You're the media whizz,' Jackson counters. 'But I've already

100

been telling people he hasn't been well. Mystery bug. Totally wiped out.'

Clarissa rubs her temples, preparing herself to salvage what she can from the situation. She decides her best bet is to brief to as many hacks as possible that the deal changes on military aggression definitions and the specifics around boycotting products made by sweatshop workers are all because Courtenay valiantly dug in against the entire government machine. He'll be voting for the deal, but it is reluctant head over heart stuff.

'That sounds pretty good to me. But what about Simon?' Courtenay asks. 'He's one of my oldest friends.'

'Well, he won't be happy,' they can hear Jackson sniggering, 'but I'll make it clear that when we enter Carthage he shall be honoured above all others. He'll get it. Eric can't have every leadership debate he does torpedoed with "are you against free trade?" Right, so—'

Clarissa hangs up, tired of the old fox's obsequious, sing-song tones. She knows this mustn't happen again. You can't march MPs up a hill just to camp out in gale force winds more than once. She'll call Jackson and make sure adequate amounts of Sudocrem are administered on the slapped bottoms of those who have come out in public against the PM. They mustn't retract letters or issue apologies. They will be proved right to have voiced their doubts. Clarissa knows to make sure the next fight is solely about the PM's leadership and judgement. And soon.

Courtenay looks nervously at his wife's face, mask-like in its expressionless fury.

2nd April

UK HOUSE PRICES HIT RECORD HIGH/
US PRESIDENT KICKS OFF RE-ELECTION CAMPAIGN

United Kingdom

You could draw a heat map of the UK at this moment to register interest in the China Trade Deal vote. In searing red would be Westminster (filled with MPs, researchers, journalists, lobbyists and PR consultants), the City of London (packed with bankers and analysts concerned about the markets) and the webs of most main roads (where cab and van drivers might be tuning in on the radio). A few other red, amber and yellow blotches appear across the country, with a couple of million UK residents paying attention to the significance of the vote, while most try to get through another Tuesday and have little time for the latest Parliamentary psychodrama.

One small red dot hovers over the Cliveden home in Tipperton, where the family have congregated in the living room.

'Bobby, can't we watch this on the news later?' Elizabeth asks.

'It'll only take a moment, Mum.'

'Bobby, for the last time: we're thrilled you're getting on with your life, but this makes no sense to me at all. Why on earth would you want to go and spend time in that ... *zoo*?' Elizabeth waves her iron at the TV, which is tuned to the BBC Parliament channel and shows MPs shouting and gesticulating at each other. 'Hard to think we're in the twenty-first century looking at that place. It's like a cult or something.' She folds a pillowcase. 'Those costumes and the sort of chanting. And all this bloody "as the honourable gentleman knows" and "my honourable friend". I've had to put the subtitles on and I'm none the wiser.'

'Honourable indeed,' mutters her husband, who is cleaning and rewinding a small silver clock on the mantelpiece.

Bobby doesn't answer, completely absorbed in the proceedings on the TV. It's true that her family has never tuned into the Parliament channel before – who does? – but now knowing Daly, a key player in the psychodrama, has made her feel a little invested in the outcome of the vote.

'What's this Daly man even like? He's been our MP for years but I've certainly never met him,' Elizabeth continues.

'He actually seems all right, Mum. I've done a bit more reading about him since that meeting and he's kind of impressive. Last year he was really punchy against the government about benefits. DWP issued this policy that they'd only pay child support for the first two children in a family, even if any additional kids are the result of a rape. He went crackers.' Bobby thinks about the YouTube clip she watched repeatedly last night. It wasn't just that Daly was a good speaker. She'd found herself nodding along at everything he'd said. Perhaps he'll be making a similar speech about the unit before long.

'Oh look, something's happening,' exclaims Elizabeth.

The Prime Minister, who had been speaking from the despatch box, has sat down and the Speaker in his black robe is standing. Bobby can't quite hear what he is saying but there is some shouting from MPs and a couple of minutes of back and forth. She hears the words 'Ayes' and 'Noes' and 'Clear the lobby!' Finally, in a great stampede, all the MPs leave the Chamber. Bobby's father Stephen takes the opportunity to head to the kitchen.

'I wonder what's going to happen,' he says, returning with a tea tray. 'The radio this morning said this might mean the Prime Minister is sacked.'

'It's a shame, really. I like a woman in charge. Although I don't like that necklace,' sighs Elizabeth.

A line of four people has formed and is slowly marching down the centre of the Chamber. One of them steps forward, prompting loud cheers.

The Ayes to the right: 343. The Noes to the left: 295.

The Chamber erupts in roars.

'What on earth does that mean? Ayes and noes. Did she win?' asks Stephen.

The Prime Minister, pats raining down on her back from her ecstatic colleagues, allows herself a few seconds to enjoy the moment. She has won, prompting sighs of relief from her political allies, plus pro-China lobbyists and City bankers, who can now head off for a decent lunch. Her enemies, plus a few hedge funders who had bet she'd lose and some journalists who had drafted very good 'what's next' pieces, slink off to lick their wounds.

The PM is whisked back to Downing Street where SpAds and civil servants gather outside the Cabinet Room and cheer uproariously as she walks down the corridor from the famous black front door. Leonard Smith has ordered in champagne and one of the private secretaries raids the vending machine in the basement for crisps.

Eva has never known the mood in the building to be so

utterly joyous. The PM gives a wonderful speech about bravery and how the vote had been a reminder that they could be gone at any time: she vows to use this as an opportunity to make courageous, bold decisions that help people. No more floundering in crisis and group depression.

The only person Eva can't see celebrating is Peter. Eventually she finds him, sitting at his desk in their office. He looks up and smiles weakly as she enters, easing the door closed behind her.

'Are you okay?' Eva ventures.

'Yeah ... I mean. We should definitely savour the moment. But,' he gestures at his screen, 'I'm going through the voting records from this afternoon. We won all right but we had thirty-eight rebels from our own side.'

'Leonard said forty-nine was the problem.'

'Forty-nine would have been a disaster!' he exclaims. 'But thirty-eight isn't good, Eva. If all those people have submitted letters we're only twelve away from a proper confidence vote. To be honest, I can't see us fighting the next election.' He rubs his eyes and puffs out his cheeks.

'Well, on the plus side, at least we know who all the people are who voted against us. Right there on Hansard.' Eva points at Peter's screen, detailing the list of Conservative rebels. 'We can just lush them up a bit.'

Peter looks at her doubtfully.

'Some of these people were in my green column.' He opens his earlier spreadsheet, where he had colour-coded names of MPs. 'Which makes me think people are getting fed up. Let's just hope we get the space we need to calm things down again and get some stuff done. A fairly large wobble any time soon could cause us serious problems ...'

Across town, a fairly large wobble stalks into the Courtenays' Notting Hill living room.

'I really must thank you both for making me look such an exquisite tit today,' Daly snorts, throwing himself down in an armchair. 'Mass resignations indeed ... Charge of the Shite Brigade, more like.'

'Matey,' Courtenay moans, 'I'm so sorry. What an epic screw-up.'

Clarissa allows her husband to soothe his friend as best he can, but she is feeling quietly upbeat now that she's studied the result properly. Some of the rebels hadn't even been on Jackson's list of Courtenay supporters. It's clear the powder keg under the PM's administration could blow at any moment. This time Clarissa is ready. She explains as much to the two men.

Daly sits in silence for a moment, admitting that Clarissa has a point.

'But that may be ages away. That ministerial salary was actually quite useful, you know! That's a quarter of my income gone overnight. And how do I even know you two are going to come good on a decent Cabinet job at the end of it all?' Daly whines. 'You've mentioned Chancellor before ...'

'I swear,' Courtenay says solemnly, 'that you will have the Cabinet job of your dreams.'

Clarissa wishes all men came with a mute button.

Later, when he checks his phone in the cab back to his flat, Daly finds one interesting message from among the deluge of 'good for you's and 'you disloyal prat's (and worse) from his colleagues. It's from Jeffrey Cuthbert, of Cuthberts developers, Daly's largest donor back in Tipperton:

Looks like you could do with a job and some £££. I have something very back bench appropriate.

Thank fuck for that, Daly thinks. He stares at his response for about a minute, making sure he doesn't sound too desperate:

Sounds good. I'll call you tomorrow to discuss.

Part Two

6th April

Claybourne Terrace

Eva throws open the door. 'Welcome home, ladies!'

Bobby and Jess run up the steps and the three of them hug on the threshold. They head into the house to pick bedrooms.

Bobby's mother Elizabeth, who drove her daughter and Jess's luggage down, glances up at the imposing red-brick facades of the row of beautiful terraced houses, then busies herself pulling cases and boxes out of the car.

'Mrs Cliveden, I'm so sorry we left you out here to do all the work,' Eva cries, skipping down the steps and tugging at a suitcase. 'Let me help you ... what's *that*?'

Eva is pointing at a motorbike parked up behind the Clivedens' car.

'Oh. Jess has a motorbike.'

'Of course she does ...'

Bobby's mother follows Eva inside, taking in the beautiful wooden floors and pastel walls and elegant sash curtains. It's a funny, narrow building – listed, she supposes – that goes up three storeys and down to a basement with a small and rather wild, unkempt garden out the back. There is a threadbare look to everything, but it is clear that the furnishings are expensive, if a little dated. She can't resist wondering how much the place is worth.

'This is me, Mum,' Bobby calls, poking her head out from a door on the second floor. 'Jess and I are on this level and share that bathroom. Eva's upstairs and her dad's room is the floor below us. Don't worry,' she laughs at her mother's look of horror at the idea of Percy Cross being *in loco parentis*. 'He's away all year in America. Come and see my room.'

It is decorated in pretty yellow floral wallpaper, with matching curtains and cushions. Even the lampshades and blanket on the double bed match. The wooden floor is covered with a series of patchy rugs to cover up the holes in the carpet. Bobby points out of the window.

'Look, I can see into everybody's gardens.'

'I'm sorry it's so *Milady's Boudoir* in here,' Eva says, bringing in a box. 'Mum had a serious Laura Ashley period when they first bought it and had some cash and nothing's been touched since then as Dad's so hard up. Not that he'd change anything even if he had the money. He'd happily live in an actual pigsty. Do you know, we once got burgled – the place got completely turned over – and he didn't even notice for three days?'

'Well, I like it,' beams Bobby, pointing at the cane bedside tables. 'I think a lot of this is coming back in, anyway.'

'I hope you don't mind sharing a bathroom with Jess,' Eva continues.

'Don't be silly,' Bobby shrugs. 'Three of us share at home! And for the rent I'm paying, I should really be camped out in your shed.'

Eva notices Bobby's mother's ears have gone rather pink and

feels a stab of embarrassment. The twenty-four-year-old land-lady in her London townhouse.

'Anyway, I'll go and help Jess.'

Elizabeth ventures a glance at her daughter, who is studiously folding clothes into a chest of drawers. Bobby is thinking about her friends. They've often intimated that they're more worldly than her and now she wonders if they have a point. Physically, they've transformed. Eva has gone all yummy mummy in her expensive athleisure wear and a full face of makeup. Jess looks tougher, perhaps the stress of the Glasgow job or her decision to channel her style away from the Jack Wills of university to something closer to *The Girl with the Dragon Tattoo*. Bobby guesses they must be faking it until they make it – but as what?

Several hours later, after a whirlwind of carrying wellies and washing baskets down to the basement, or sheets and towels up to the second floor, Eva calls up the stairs from the kitchen. 'Right, who's for a drink?'

Owl-like whoops echo down to her.

'Well, you've had a busy week. You must be exhausted.' Jess saunters in carrying a cardboard box of assorted bottles, Bobby close behind. 'Here, let's open this. I've been saving it.' Jess pulls out a bottle of rosé.

'Ooh, Whispering Angel. Fancy.' Eva pulls a tray of ice out of the freezer and empties it into three glasses.

'So,' Jess begins, after the three of them have settled down in the living room and toasted their new household, 'how are you holding up?'

Eva takes a deep drink.

'Hard to say, really. The PM is essentially safe for now. But anything can happen to get these MPs whipped up,' she tips her glass back again, 'which is bad news for yours truly.'

'Unless the next person wants to keep you.' Jess plops another

111

ice cube into her glass. 'If there's a leadership contest, there's a good opportunity to jump onto somebody's bandwagon.'

'But that isn't very loyal to the PM. Just find a new host?' asks Bobby.

'Not much she can do about it. That's politics, baby.' Jess inhales from an imaginary cigarette, then flicks it away. 'Anyway, you could always join your mum on the motivational speaking circuit. Pounds for pounds.'

Eva thinks about the insane celery juice cleanse her mother is trying to convince her to do at the moment. At least she isn't doing a repeat of her TV programme about colonic irrigation. With a shudder, Eva changes the subject.

'How's your long read coming along?'

Jess updates them on the recent stories she's chronicled about women going through the justice system in Glasgow.

'Now I need to mothball it, and I was just finding my feet at the *Tribune*,' she sighs. 'This move down here is really exciting – now I've embraced it – but everyone has told me that this Ed Cooper guy is an arsehole. Apparently nobody has even managed a year with him.'

'What do your parents make of the move down?' asks Bobby.

'Well, they're not *Sentinel* readers,' Jess says wryly. 'And I'm one of seven kids, remember. Plus they have grandchildren now. And a farm to run. There's so many of us that, unless there are any real problems, we all just sort of bumble along doing our own thing. They're happy I've made the move down here, though. Progress . . .'

'Yeah, same. Mum's been harping on about me getting on with my life for ages. Although she seems to think that Parliament isn't the right kind of progress . . .' Bobby drains her glass.

'Has she met Simon Daly?' asks Eva.

'No and I'm not sure she should. She has a dim view of politicians generally and he isn't in her good books after not exactly prostrating himself before the wrecking ball over this unit closure. To say nothing of his resignation . . . '

'Oh yeah! What does that mean for you?' Jess crunches an ice cube.

'Nothing, I think. I'm dealing with him as an MP, aren't I? Not a minister.'

'Works quite well for you. He won't mind about giving the government a headache, now he isn't part of it,' Eva says, partly to herself.

'Troublemaker, eh?' Jess mutters knowingly.

'Among other things,' Eva says. Bobby frowns. 'I mean, he has a reputation.' Bobby still looks nonplussed. 'As a shagger.'

'Is he dodgy?' Jess asks, casually taking another sip of wine.

'Nah, I don't think so.' Eva yawns and turns to Bobby, who's looking stumped. 'I think the guys who screw around a lot in Westminster fall into roughly two camps: predators and opportunists. Your predators are real creeps, the ones who spot vulnerable people, like the drunkest person at a party, and zero in on them. Dodgy. Then you have your opportunists, who only push at an open door. They'll be fairly indiscriminate about who they'll jump into bed with, but they won't force their way in.' She stands to go to the kitchen and finish making dinner. 'I reckon Simon's in the latter camp.'

Bobby wrinkles her nose and follows her.

'Are you still with Jamie? How's it going?' asks Jess, serving spaghetti.

'Yep, all good. I hope you don't mind if he's around here a bit.' Eva slurps a large forkful, trying to sound casual but sensing a chance to get one up on Jess. 'I'm not sure I could manage being single. Would probably shag half of London. Jamie certainly keeps me out of trouble . . . '

When Jess doesn't bite, Eva asks if she saw anyone note-worthy in Glasgow.

'I've had a lot of fun. Most recently there was Tommy, a police officer.' Jess has another mouthful of spaghetti and wipes the back of her hand across her lips. 'You know the Thin Blue Line? Well, I can tell you that it's thick.'

Bobby tries not to sigh. The only bit she doesn't enjoy about a reunion with her friends is their vaguely competitive discussions about what they've been doing in bed. Bobby, who briefly had a boyfriend in her final year at university but was dumped after he tired of her visits home to Tipperton, is yet to have sex and so nods non-committally through these cosy chats. She can't bring herself to tell Jess and Eva that her late nights in the bedroom involve watching her ex's life with his new girlfriend unfold on Instagram.

'Sorry, I need specifics,' Eva grins.

Jess describes her first attempt at minor BDSM a few nights before with Tommy's handcuffs and speculates that perhaps her interest in being in control in the bedroom is informed by her time at university when she was, in her own words, 'Marianne Dashwooded'. Jess had been completely in love with a boy in their first year of university who led her to believe he loved her back, before unceremoniously and publicly dumping her for someone new. 'I find doing a bit of humiliation of my own very satisfying.' She takes another sip of wine, wondering aloud if this is what has drawn her to journalism, too – another way to tie people up in knots.

Eva clicks her tongue appreciatively.

Bobby, officially out of her comfort zone, gets up to pour them all glasses of water.

'All right, so you next, Bob. Are you dating?' asks Jess.

'Been quite hard with all the stuff around my dad going on,' Bobby mumbles, thinking mournfully of the Bechdel Test.

'Oh! That made me think, actually – you must meet Jake Albury.' Eva claps her hands together.

'Who's that?'

'Planning adviser. He'll know all about how these PFI contracts work. Bet he has loads of ideas to save the unit. Also,' Eva sips her wine, 'he is *hot*. Absolutely everybody fancies him. Touted as a big Conservative success story, growing up in a rough suburb of Manchester, getting into Oxford from a tough state school. And still only about 30. Very clever, very sexy . . .'

Jess wolf-whistles.

'I'm not interested in anything like that just now,' Bobby says, thinking of the dreary couple of dates she'd been on back home.

'Look,' Eva says firmly, 'you've been at a massive disadvantage. Stuck in Tipperton, not meeting anyone new. Or at least not a proper distraction. You should give Jake a ring, ask him if he'd like to join you for a drink to talk policy—'

'And screw his brains out,' cackles Jess. 'You deserve a good seeing to after your time holed up at home.' She empties the last of the bottle into their glasses.

'Hm . . .' Bobby stands and clears the plates. 'I'll give it some thought.'

'All that being said,' Eva says to Bobby's back, 'I generally advise sticking to guys outside Westminster. An ill-judged shag can damage your reputation. Plus you never know when a one night stand might pop up again in future . . .' She crouches down to select another bottle of her father's wine from a rack. 'Don't shit where you eat. It will attract flies.'

Jess and Bobby exchange shrugs.

'I suppose lots of these political relationships end in tears,' Bobby muses.

'Well, luckily tears – and indeed all fluids – just wipe straight off PVC,' Jess grins. Bobby makes a gagging sound.

8th April

Claybourne Terrace

On Monday morning, after they agree to have a housewarming party on Friday, Eva and Bobby watch Jess set off from the street on her motorbike and head to Westminster together for work.

They walk through St James's Park, taking in the spring flowers and stopping to admire a family of ducklings. Occasionally Eva points out an MP or journalist. Lots of them seem to be walking in pairs.

'I suppose they think it's all a bit *Tinker, Tailor, Soldier, Spy*,' Eva says airily. 'A totally crap version.'

'So they really just chat in the open like this?' asks Bobby.

'Yeah, well, obviously anything actually sneaky will be done in secret. And when a proper leak happens in a department, for example, there are burner phones and stuff. With MPs, I think a lot of the time these guys just want to be seen talking to a political editor. Makes them seem important.' Eva snorts. 'I suppose if you're ambitious it makes sense to have contacts everywhere. A harmless bit of gossip now and then with a junior hack about "the mood",' she makes quotation marks with her fingers, 'on the back benches and maybe you start building a relationship. One day, when you're a Secretary of State trying to squash a story and that junior hack is now an editor, that bit of gossip has really paid off. All for the price of a few cups of coffee and a bit of a dig at your colleagues. And vice versa of course. Worth lushing up lots of people if you're a journalist – you never know who might make the Cabinet!'

'Surely not everyone can progress to the Cabinet? It doesn't sound like the reward is strong enough to take the risk of getting caught.'

'Ah well, although MPs know they can't all progress, the key thing is they all think they are one of the ones that will. And you need that belief. It would be like salmon working out that statistically only some of them will make it up a river past bears and waterfalls and stuff. They'd just give up if they knew their chances. Then the whole ecosystem depending on them would die. All MPs think they can be PM – and we need them all to think that, if we're to have a chance of controlling them.'

'Still feels risky to me. Surely people gassing away at journalists get a reputation and scupper their chances of promotion?'

'Well, the gobby ones do. But journalists consider the rule of never naming their sources golden. Obviously it's ideal to get a direct quote from someone you can name. But a lot of people don't want to do that. That's why you see "a source close to the Foreign Secretary" or "a Downing Street insider" in lots of stories. It adds a layer of protection to people who want to contribute to a story but don't want to be identified.'

'I've come with low expectations but this is even worse than I thought.' Bobby kicks at a stone. 'Do these people only care about the fleeting power they hold? What about politicians getting elected to do some good?'

'Oh, there are plenty who do good. But if you don't have any power then what can you do? Becoming an MP is a start. But they soon realise you need to become a minister, then a Secretary of State – and, ideally, Prime Minister – to really get motoring. And if you aren't re-elected, you're no good to anybody.'

They stop outside the Downing Street back entrance.

'This is me,' Eva inclines her head, 'I always try to come in this way otherwise the photographers in the street take photos of you. Last year the Leader of the Lords was carrying his note-pad in without a cover on it and they managed to zoom in on his shopping list. At the top in all caps was Senokot . . .'

Bobby waves Eva off and heads past the imposing buildings of the Foreign Office and Treasury to the corner of Parliament Square. It is a beautiful day. Big Ben dominates the clear blue sky. The spectacular gothic buildings of the Houses of Parliament look delicate enough to have been spun from sugar. She checks her watch and sees she has fifteen minutes to kill until she needs to report at the Portcullis House reception. She decides to have a look at the statues – Churchill, Gandhi, Lincoln, Fawcett – on the manicured quad outside Westminster Abbey.

Bobby is about to cross the road when she hears a shout and steps back just in time to avoid being hit by a cluster of Lycra-clad cyclists. She nearly steps forward again but finds herself rooted to the spot, unable to take her eyes off another oncoming cyclist.

The figure is wearing scruffy jeans and a crumpled shirt under an inside-out-jumper; his hair, free of a helmet, is whipped back off his face by the wind. Judging by the way his lean frame is folded up like a deck chair on his tired-looking bike, he is clearly very tall. Under one arm he clutches a notepad and, sitting upright with his hands off the handlebars, he cups his hands around the cigarette he's trying to light at his lips.

Bobby can't believe how reckless and arrogant he is. Above

all, she doesn't think she's ever seen anyone so handsome before, or so cool. He stops at the traffic lights and takes a long drag, looking past her at the commuting pedestrians.

'Excuse me . . .' Bobby says quietly. The cyclist continues to survey the pavement. 'Excuse me,' she repeats, a little louder.

'Yes?' He fixes her with bloodshot green eyes.

'Um . . . your shoelaces are undone. Could be dangerous.' Bobby points at one of his scuffed trainers.

'Thanks,' he murmurs, holding the cigarette between his teeth and propping his foot against the handlebar to retie it. Bobby uses the opportunity to study his beautiful hands, his long, straight nose and his stubble jawline below slightly hollow cheeks. He's quite hard to age accurately. He just looks weatherbeaten and tired more than anything. But even with the dark, almost purple rings under his eyes there is something undeniably attractive about him. She suddenly feels a longing to reach out and touch the bare skin on the back of his neck. She shoves her hands into her pockets.

'Thought you were going to bollock me for not wearing a helmet,' the cyclist grins out of the corner of his mouth.

'Well, it probably wouldn't be a bad idea to wear one. Or to use your hands to steer. Or to wait until you get to where you're going for a cigarette?' Bobby ventures. A very light pink tinge comes to his cheeks.

'All right, well, thanks, *Mum.*' He flicks ash into the gutter, then kicks off as the lights turn green. Bobby crosses the road quickly. She'd only been trying to stop him breaking his stupid neck. But why did she say anything at all? From his plinth, Churchill's cross face surveys the House of Commons and Bobby can't help sympathising with him. She's so busy cursing politicians and cyclists under her breath that she doesn't notice the scruffy, green-eyed man craning his neck at the next set of lights to see where she's gone.

Portcullis House

Bobby's first day in the Houses of Parliament begins with a long wait in the lobby for Lucy Jeffries-Wick, a rather harried-looking woman in her mid-thirties, with frizzy hair held back by a matching yellow satin headband and scrunchie. They cross the large glass-ceilinged atrium, which reminds Bobby of the leisure centre back home where she learned to swim, Lucy all the while apologising for the wait in plummy, slightly breathless tones.

'I didn't think your first day would be quite this disorganised! Simon has decided not to come in – sulking I should think, seeing as he is now *persona non grata* around SW1 after resigning; can't stand everybody not liking him, you know – which is just as well. I don't have anything in the diary. He was due to be slipped to go to Malawi this week.'

'Slipped?'

'Oh, right. It's how MPs skip votes so they can be away from London. The Chief gives them permission to be away. Otherwise they have to hope to be paired.'

'Paired?'

Lucy then commits to a long explanation about whipping. The Chief Whip is a key figure, tasked with passing all government business in the Commons and serving as a rather Thomas Cromwell-inspired HR function for his Party's MPs. He has a team of Whips – named after a fox hunting term, whippers-in, which Bobby makes a mental note to Google later – to help him. Bobby learns that there are different levels of urgency the Chief will attach to legislation – one line up to three line Whips – and that MPs and ministers are duly punished for voting the wrong way or for bad behaviour (where the HR function kicks in) by having the Whip removed, making them Party-less independents. Pairing is when MPs hoping to miss a vote from opposite parties are paired up to essentially cancel each other out, and nodding through is when both sides agree, normally on grounds of ill health, that an MP has technically voted even if they didn't physically go through the lobby to be counted.

'Anyway, he travelled so much as a minister that it will be quite a shock to have him around again ...'

Bobby nearly asks *who* then remembers how they got started on pairing to begin with.

'But that's good, isn't it? For his constituents I mean.'

'Oh sure, although it's really Moira who takes care of things up there.' Lucy looks sideways at Bobby. 'She's quite a tartar, isn't she?'

'Um ...'

'An old tart, anyway. But you'll come to see she's a sweet one. A Bakewell. She's been such a brick to me. I've been off a few times to have my babies and she's been so encouraging about my coming back. And she's really *lived*, you know? Married three times! Knows more about men than anyone I know. Only person Simon's scared of, I should think.'

Bobby spends the morning in the Parliamentary office shared by Daly and Sackler, which is a brightly lit room stuffed with files, books and loose paper along a corridor of identical rooms shared by other MPs. Her first job is to wade through a great pile of emails from constituents about Daly's resignation, which Lucy has put in a folder on a shared email account. It's fairly straight-forward: copying and pasting a blanket response Bobby has cleared with Lucy and Moira, to the emails saying versions of 'good for you' and 'fuck off you weasly traitor'. Bobby finds she can do her work and listen to Lucy prattle on about everything from 'the cracking little Shetland' – a pony, Bobby learns – for her children to rumours of the Chancellor having hair plugs.

At lunchtime, Lucy throws down the apology note she is

writing on behalf of Daly to the Parliament cleaning staff –
'I'm afraid he can be quite imperious with those he considers
underlings. And he leaves this place a complete pigsty at night
when he has people in for drinks between votes' – and takes
Bobby down to the canteen to get something to eat. It's incredibly loud and busy and Bobby spots several people she vaguely
recognises. Luckily Lucy is on hand to point out various
big name MPs and journalists. There are also lots of people
around Bobby's age and a few who are clearly younger, particularly spotty teenage boys in dapper double-breasted suits
and loafers who bray in clipped accents about 'Mrs T' and 'the
woke brigade'.

'Don't worry,' giggles Lucy quietly, 'we have loads of those
chaps around here at the moment on work experience with
their godfathers. This is their Glastonbury.'

When they get back to the office, an extremely scruffy man
greets them, along with a beautiful, laughing woman. Next to
her shabby, greying companion she looks like a tampon advert,
Bobby thinks. They are introduced as George Sackler MP and
his wife Millie.

'You'll get to know us very well,' sparkles Millie, an expert
in making friends with other political women, 'as Simon
and George are room-mates, so we share these offices. I run
George's office. Quite common for the wives to do it,' she
replies to Bobby's raised eyebrows, 'helps us keep an eye on
their trousers. This office is a no-fly zone!' Millie and Sackler
both laugh uproariously. 'I'll let you settle in then perhaps we
can have lunch this week?'

Bobby thanks her, but before she can say anything else
Sackler interrupts.

'Is Si not coming in?'

Lucy shakes her head.

'Probably lying low,' chuckles Sackler, searching under

empty crisp packets and dirty coffee cups on his desk for some documents. His wife pouts at him and inclines her head at Bobby in a 'not in front of the new girl' attitude. 'Well, Mills, he has been made to look quite silly, hasn't he? Been left completely out to dry! Still – he'll be riding high soon enough.' Bobby notices a toe poking out of the side of Sackler's shoe. She supposes he'd be one to know what it takes to look silly around here.

'Actually, I think he's come out of it all rather well,' says Millie sweetly. 'After all, he voted for the deal. But he said there were pressures at home. It isn't an easy job to do – being abroad all the time – if you have a family. Or in his and Susie's case, *want* a family.'

Bobby turns on her computer and begins working through the rest of her to-do list: more correspondence (there is a huge backlog, so this will take most of the week) and a big job on working out exactly what the new China Trade Deal means for local businesses in Tipperton. Lucy wants to go through other bits and pieces tomorrow, like how to expense travel receipts. Bobby's plan is to race through as much grunt work as possible so she can get going on the unit closure campaign.

Sentinel Offices, Borough

Across town, Jess follows a secretary through the brightly lit, open plan *Sentinel* offices overlooking the Thames. She can see Tower Bridge out of a large window. Hopefully she won't be sent there for poor grammar.

The banks of desks fill up as they progress towards Ed Cooper's office. Cyclists untuck their trousers from socks, hangovers are nursed with coffee and aspirin. Jess's biker jacket gets some curious looks.

'Ed has an office here?' Jess raises an eyebrow. 'We're based in Parliament. Hardly seems worth it.'

'Yeah, well, he gets special treatment.' The secretary knocks gingerly on the door. 'You'll see.'

'Come in,' Ed Cooper yells. As Jess enters, Ed glances up from his phone, grunts and continues tapping. 'Give me a second.' He can't help but notice that Jess is striking. Not conventionally pretty exactly, but something going on there.

Jess takes the opportunity to gaze around the room. The walls are covered in framed front pages of iconic scoops by the man himself. There are also dozens of photographs of him interviewing politicians and celebrities: Ed Miliband, Ann Widdecombe, Gary Lineker, Donny Osmond. Jess notices there is a very small picture near the back of the desk of Ed with what must be his wife and children. Judging from his hair colour, she guesses it must have been taken about five years ago.

'Do you have Twitter and stuff?' Ed puts his phone down.

'Yeah, but I don't like it. It's like walking into a crowded room and everyone's screaming. I don't post much. Not big into the online punditry.' Jess strains a smile, thinking about Ed's Twitter profile, which is bursting with opinions on the upcoming Euros and photos of his weekend runs. Ed smarts at her words. He also knows that it's all irrelevant to his real job but he believes that if his readers feel they know him they'll be more likely to trust him as a source for news. And the more followers he gets, the more opportunities for columns and podcasts . . .

'Well, shape up. The minute you get a scoop you need to tweet about it with a link to the story. Really shoots up the traffic to the website. The high-ups like it. Speaking of which – I read some of your stuff. Not bad. But it isn't much help to you down here. Nobody gives a shit if you won a Scottish Press Award. You've got to re-prove yourself.'

'Of course.' Jess keeps her voice and gaze steady. She's decided to test out Ed's rumoured reputation. 'But I do have some ideas I'd like to discuss with you. There were a few projects I had on the backburner up in Glasgow and I wonder whether I could work on them down here. It would be a shame to waste my investigative skills from the crime beat. Don't you think—'

Ed claps his hands together and stands up. The last thing this girl needs is encouragement to become a social justice warrior.

'If your investigative skills involve going through a new MP's decades-old social media accounts, then be my guest. There's a pecking order here – I'm the political editor and then there are three of you under me: George Cusk and Mike Bain, who are in Parliament today, which is where we are usually based and where you'll head after a bit of legal and training stuff here. And now you. You'll all be told what you're covering. I advise against taking any initiative . . . That advice served your predecessors well. Now, we'd better head to your first staff meeting.'

Ed waits to see how she reacts, but Jess simply folds her arms, looking disinterested. He finds this peculiarly annoying. There have been people who have cried by now. All of them have at least looked indignant.

Jess and Ed are among the last to arrive for the meeting, which is presided over by the editor, Philip McKay. He goes round the room, quizzing different desks on their stories. Jess notices the staff cast uneasy glances in Ed's direction before revealing what they're working on to Philip and the group.

'I've got a bit more intel on these Graham Thomas expenses,' Ed says, when it's his turn. 'I think for a smaller group, though,' he says self-importantly. The assembled group exchange discreet eye rolls. The editor nods briskly. 'Oh. By the way, this is Jess Adler, my new junior.' Jess gives a little wave.

'Glad to have you, Jess,' Philip says kindly. 'I hear great things about you from Magnus. Now . . .' And he turns to the next person.

After the meeting, Jess heads to the communal kitchen to make a cup of tea when a couple of the other attendees seek her out to warn her about Ed's behaviour.

'Yes, I've heard,' she says.

'He's driven out some really good people. He's nicked stories from most of us and we're used to seeing people in your position shoved around by him. We've complained so many times but for whatever reason he's untouchable,' one of them bleats, backed up by a series of nods.

It all confirms Jess's suspicion that she shouldn't wait to see if Ed will be nice. Be professional, be tough and, if necessary, be prepared to launch a pre-emptive strike.

'Understood. Look, if you guys are doing a pool, put a bet on me for the long haul. I won't let you down.'

She hops down from her perch on the counter, picks up her mug and heads to Ed's office where he sits, thinking about Jess's leathers. She'll be an interesting nut to crack.

'Right,' Ed says. He notices she hasn't brought him a drink and briefly debates saying something. Everyone else he's worked with in the past has responded to his difficult behaviour by acting as a supplicant. This is new.

'All right, take a seat.' Ed gestures to a chair. Time to put Jess in her place. 'Let's talk about what you're up to this week. Obviously I'll be on the Thomas story. George is looking ahead at the spring statement and Mike has the immigration numbers. You'll be covering the Westminster dog show.'

Jess bites her tongue.

'Problem?'

'No, no problem. I'm on it.'

Downing Street

Eva is working her way through a sausage sandwich from the canteen when Peter marches into their shared office.

'Morning. I need you to cancel all your meetings for the next couple of hours. We're going to pay a visit to Graham Thomas with the Chief.'

Eva manages to swallow her huge mouthful. 'That sounds ominous.'

Peter merely purses his lips.

Terry Groves, the Chief Whip, is waiting for them when they reach the foyer of the Department for Transport, considerably less cheerful than he was just a couple of days before. He looks slightly deflated, like a balloon a few days after a party. All meetings the Chief has that are of a sensitive nature are uncomfortable – he's had to sit through accounts of drug use, affairs and, on one occasion, how an MP got a figurine of Nelson's Column stuck up his bottom – but he is particularly bashful about this one. Graham Thomas had been the Chief's Whip when Terry had first been elected and had needed nursing through the early stages of his Parliamentary career. Now the Chief is here to discipline his one-time mentor. The shift in relations rubs uncomfortably.

A smart young man appears and escorts them to the Secretary of State's office. Thomas looks as bloodshot and cheery as ever.

'Chief! Come in, come in.' He points to his office. 'Who'd like some coffee? Great – folks, can we get a pot of coffee in here, please?' he says to the group of private secretaries, all diligently typing away at their desks.

'Of course, Secretary of State. Do you require a PS present for this meeting, or one of your SpAds?' asks the same smart young man. Thomas looks at the Chief, who gives a tiny shake of his head and nods at Eva. She grips her notebook, feeling like some sort of political social worker.

'No, thanks. Just having a, uh, political chat.'

As Thomas closes the door, Eva sees the private secretaries exchange glances. The Chief Whip and the PM's Political Secretary coming to the department first thing on a Monday – long before the House sits down to business in the afternoon – is hardly good news.

'So, Graham, I don't want to beat about the bush. We need some straight answers out of you,' the Chief says after they all sit down. Eva has never seen Terry Groves look so serious. What on earth is going on?

'Fire away.' Thomas sits forward in his chair, his elbows on his knees.

'Well,' Peter opens his folder, 'it's like this. As you know, the PM has asked the Cabinet Office to formally investigate this Caribbean trip and the Caspar Dubois meeting. She is very grateful for your cooperation but it sounds like parts of your evidence don't match up. Or exist. For example, I think it's clear that you paid for your family's trip, the flights and so on. What isn't accounted for are the cricket tickets and hospitality, but—'

'Oh come on, is the PM going to assemble the firing squad over a couple of poxy tickets?' Thomas chuckles, pouring cups of coffee. 'Hardly the thing to question a chap's integrity over.'

'She's not questioning your integrity. She pays *us* to do that for her,' says Peter calmly. 'If Mr Dubois paid for your cricket tickets and that box, you can just declare them through the department. As soon as possible. I understand that the Cabinet Office is currently satisfied with the timeline you gave them of how you came to the decision on the East London rail link, including minutes of the official meetings you had with Mr

Dubois. They see no connection between the cricket match and the rail contract – at the moment.'

'And rightly so!' Thomas beams, clearly relieved. 'Well, I'd better get filing.'

'Good. But I said "at the moment".' Peter sips his coffee and looks at the floor. 'We understand that you and Mr Dubois might have had contact that wasn't official. That isn't necessarily anything to worry about but it is something the Chief and I need to know about, so we can protect you. Naturally it raises questions.'

Thomas looks from one to the other, nonplussed.

'The files you've sent to the Cabinet Office – which will of course be heavily redacted when they're made public – suggest there was a separate line of contact between you and Dubois. There are emails from you to officials saying things like "Dubois is on to me again, can we please hurry this up, folks?" and emails from officials to Dubois saying "as per your discussion with the Secretary of State" . . . '

'Right . . . '

'So you must have been speaking to each other. Which is fine. We're all allowed friends. But there are no accounts of these conversations. You're doing the Transport Select Committee tomorrow. You're bound by Parliamentary Privilege and they can ask you anything, including any contact you had with Mr Dubois while you were making this decision on your personal phone. We want to avoid a "gotcha" moment. It would be a shame to lie to the House, even inadvertently.' Peter looks Thomas squarely in the eye. Thomas blinks and looks away. He knows the subtext to this conversation is 'for God's sake, man, get your story straight'.

'All right, yes. We exchanged numbers at a CCHQ fundraiser a while ago. So he'd text me a bit.'

'Yes, we're aware of that. Can we see the messages?' asks Peter.

'Uh . . . afraid not. My phone has an auto-delete function. It deletes all texts ten days after I receive them.'

'Really? I've not heard of that before.' Peter frowns.

'Yup, 'fraid so.' Thomas examines his fingernails. 'So I'll just have to say to the Committee that we were in touch but the messages don't exist. And that the Cabinet Office is investigating the whole issue and we should leave it to them.'

'Well then,' the Chief slaps his hands on his thigh, 'that's that.'

'Not really,' Peter presses. 'After all, we don't know that Mr Dubois has deleted them off *his* phone. So they're still "out there", so to speak. And if he is summoned before the Select Committee or the decision to hand him the contract is judicially reviewed, he will feel under a lot of pressure to release them.'

'Yes, I see what you mean. Very difficult. Um . . .' Thomas glances at his watch. 'Look, I need to get on with my day but how about I go through my devices and see if I have anything saved?'

'Yes, good idea,' the Chief says, rising from his chair. He looks almost as relieved as Thomas that the meeting is over.

Just before they reach the door, Peter turns to Thomas once more and says quietly, 'I'm sure I don't need to tell you that the PM will take a dim view if you are lying to us about any of this, Graham. If you aren't being honest with the Chief Whip, then you aren't being honest with her either.'

Thomas does a little cringing bow.

The Chief exhales heavily as the lift doors close.

'You have no idea how awkward it is having those kinds of chats with colleagues.'

'I understand, Chief, but he was so shifty in there. Obviously something is going on. He's got to be honest with us or we can't help him.'

For her part, Eva isn't sure what to think. Thomas seemed to sweat in that meeting, but the whole system for registering gifts and so on is such a muddle that maybe it is all a misunderstanding. Something has got up Peter's nose, though. Eva can't decide if that's his old political bloodhound instincts kicking in or whether he's seeing shadows after the China Trade Deal vote.

They are about fifty feet from the building when Peter's phone rings. His face looks increasingly astonished as he listens to the person at the other end.

'You won't believe this,' he says, after hanging up. 'Graham has found the text exchange. Turns out he can retrieve stuff from his auto-delete function ... Eva, he says he's printing the exchange off for us. Will you run and get it and we'll meet you back at the office?'

When Eva gets to the department the smart private secretary is waiting for her in the lobby, holding a sealed brown envelope. He passes it to her without a word and marches back to the lifts.

Downing Street

'Well, this all seems fine to me,' the Chief says as he looks up from the sheets of the Graham Thomas/Caspar Dubois text conversation that Eva has laid out on a table. It reminds her of the dossier of her social media activity. Nothing strikes her as embarrassing exactly, but she wouldn't want the texts to be published in the newspapers if they were hers. 'Apart from "cool beans", perhaps,' the Chief chuckles, 'even I know that's cringe, as my niece would say.'

'Yeah, it does all seem to be above board,' Peter says, although he is frowning. 'You can see Dubois at various points says stuff like this, here: *Have you made a decision yet?* and

Graham is careful to respond with something like *We will signal out to all parties asap.* Even the chummy stuff is totally deniable. Graham can say he was being polite and pushing Dubois through the department. Even when Dubois directly asks, *Can you help with something?* Graham says, *Let's talk through the appropriate channels.'*

The Chief nods. 'What are these weird blocky things?'

'I think they're emojis.' Eva says. 'Thumbs-up signs and smiley faces. They just don't seem to have come through on the printout. Or maybe his auto-delete retrieval thing can't get them back.'

'It isn't ideal that Graham texted Dubois first,' muses Peter, 'although Graham said right at the beginning that he only met the guy at all because the CCHQ fundraisers seated them together at that dinner. I guess he was just being polite. And how could anyone have known Dubois would apply for the rail contract?'

'Yeah, feels like cock-up rather than conspiracy to me.' The Chief takes a gulp of tea and sighs contentedly.

'Is Dubois domiciled in the UK?' asks Eva, a thought striking her.

'Why do you ask?' Peter narrows his eyes.

'Well . . . I was wondering what was in it for Graham to get so matey with him. At the time, I mean. Okay, maybe he was being polite but it's pretty oily, isn't it?' She points to the first page of text. *'A pleasure to meet you this evening. Delighted to have your support and please know you can count on me. Do get in touch any time.* And think of the timing. It was after our first defeat on the China Trade Deal.'

'What are you getting at? That he's not playing hard-to-get?' asks the Chief.

'He thought he could tap up Dubois as a potential donor for a leadership bid,' Peter says quietly. Eva nods. 'It would explain his reluctance to give us these messages. Auto-delete indeed ... '

'Well,' yawns the Chief, 'no harm done really. I'm sure everyone was eyeing up donors back then. Different world now. PM's back on top. And that's nothing to do with government contracts.'

'Hm.' Peter continues to stare down at the texts.

'All right, well, if I'm not needed any longer, I'd better get back to my flock. See you, Pete.'

Peter waves but doesn't look up. 'See you, Chiefy.'

Peter drums his fingers on the table. 'What do you reckon, Eva?'

'I don't know ... everything seems to match up but my gut says otherwise.'

'I agree. Something fishy going on here. All right, let's chew it over for a while. We'd better crack on.'

Lower Ministerial Corridor, House of Commons

In her ministerial office in the old Parliament building, Weaver is on the phone to Ed Cooper. She isn't alone.

'This is on deep background, okay?' she says firmly.

'How many times have we done business, Nat?' Ed asks soothingly. 'Fire away ... '

There is a long pause as Weaver stifles a gasp of pleasure, holding the phone at arm's length. Her press secretary, who is pushing her against the office door, smirks and resumes his intent work between her quivering, slightly mottled thighs, using his free hand to pin Weaver's phone-less palm above her head.

Weaver covers the phone for a second. 'You can just go in the ministerial brown box if you want,' she hisses.

The press sec shakes his head and continues.

'Everything okay?' Ed asks.

'Yes ... sorry. Just sneezing. Okay, so I only know this because I know an official working on the investigation.' Weaver shuts her eyes, trying to concentrate. She wonders if her knees might give way. Being on the phone to a hack during all this really gives her an extra buzz.

'Fine, if this is enough for me to go to the Cabinet Office directly for a comment.'

'Yeah, I mean ... ahhhh.' Weaver bites her lip as her companion, moving his face next to her so he can hear what Ed is saying, sticks his tongue in her ear. 'Sorry, I ... I just stubbed my toe.'

'Right ... ' Weaver can hear Ed getting impatient. Her staffer gives a Muttley-like snigger and slips a finger inside her. She wonders if she is going to faint.

'Sorry, so I was saying ... The Cabinet Office can't find anything incriminating. I would go to Graham Thomas directly, too. He says he has something specific to tell you. The way I've heard it, he's planning to brazen it out. Feels he's having the finger pointed at him by Number Ten for no reason and he's suffering because of their botched handling.' Weaver feels herself getting close. This is dangerous. She doesn't think she can come quietly, so to speak.

'Interesting.' She can hear tapping at the other end of the line. 'Well, thanks for that.'

'No worries, Ed. Look, I've got to go.' Weaver can feel her spokesman's erection digging into her hip and she longs to get at it. He does a helicopter motion in the air with one hand, meaning 'wrap it up', while the other tackles the clasp of her bra.

'Yeah, no worries. Just one more thing—'

'No. Sorry – I've really got to run. See you!' She hangs up.

'This really needs to be the last time,' she pants after a while, pushing him into a chair and planting herself in his lap, her back to him.

'Why?'

'Well . . . it's very risky, isn't it?'

'I – don't – care,' he muffles into her shoulders, as she bounces on top of him.

Across town, Ed Cooper looks thoughtfully out of the window and shrugs. He normally can't get Weaver off the phone.

Claybourne Terrace

Bobby plonks her bag down in the hallway, her mouth watering as the smell of Jess's cooking wafts towards her. In the kitchen, Jess is laying the table while Eva paces in front of the oven, rubbing her tummy.

'Hey, how was your first day?'

'Yeah, I liked it. Although my boss didn't turn up.'

'Well, I wish mine hadn't,' Jess mutters.

'So what did you get up to?' Eva asks.

'Just finding my feet really. Most of the day was answering emails and letters about his resignation. His team is nice. And Millie Sackler too.'

'Oh yeah . . . very tight knit.' Eva raises an eyebrow.

'Meaning?' asks Bobby.

'I'm pretty sure he's sleeping with Millie Sackler at the moment.'

'*Really?*' gasps Bobby.

'Yup. And he says George is his best friend. People are weird. Honestly, some of these guys live completely different lives Monday to Thursday. They even share flats and stuff, like students.'

'Now *that* would make an interesting story. The secret life of MPs . . . ' Jess says thoughtfully.

While Jess and Eva trade theories around the intersection of sex and power – 'What's so pant-dropping about sitting on the Public Accounts Committee?' – Bobby gets a text from Simon Daly.

Hope first day went well! Apologies for being absent. S

Bobby taps out a polite reply.

Really well, thanks. Sorry you weren't in.

'Oh shit!'

'What is it?' Eva asks.

'I just . . . oh *no*. I sent Simon a text and I meant to do a smiley face but I pressed the wrong thing and . . . ' She holds up her phone.

Jess convulses with laughter. 'You sent the peach emoji?'

'Oh Bobby . . . ' Eva tries to be sympathetic. 'We've all been there.'

'What is Simon going to think?' Bobby cries, aghast. 'Oh *no*, he's replying!'

'Saying what?'

'Asking . . . ' Bobby looks confused, 'if I want to go to an event with him on Wednesday. Launch of some report in the Commons.' She pauses. 'Nice way to meet people and get going with the unit campaign, don't you think?'

Jess and Eva exchange glances, wondering the same thing. Did Daly think the peach had been more than a slip of the finger? He has a reputation after all. Bobby thinks only of what this means for the unit. Daly and his introductions are an obvious foot in the door. If that means massaging his ego a little then why not?

'Just don't go giving the whole fruit bowl away,' Eva says with a wink.

'You know, Bob,' Jess puts her hand on Bobby's shoulder

as they walk to the living room, 'if you're going to sext your boss you really should ease into it. At least get yourself on an encrypted app for this kind of thing. Eva, are you coming?'

Eva hasn't moved. Jess's words ring in her ears. An encrypted app. She texts Peter:

Can you meet me early tomorrow? I think I've worked out what Graham's up to.

9th April

Downing Street

'Okay, so the *Sentinel* piece hasn't got the real story here. Look at this.' Eva points to an exchange between Thomas and Dubois. She and Peter have holed themselves up in their office with a pot of coffee, long before the rest of the SpAds are due to arrive. 'Dubois writes, *Good evening, Graham, I wonder if you can help with something?* and then there is an emoji we can't see.' She pauses and looks sideways at Peter.

'Go on ...'

'Okay, well, imagine what that emoji could be. Or any other kind of context clue ...' Eva runs her hands through her hair and takes a deep breath. 'Look at Graham's different replies to these requests from Dubois. Each time he asks for a favour or for any news on progress. Sometimes he just says something like "Will revert back ASAP" or "Still receiving expressions of interest." But look at this.' She pulls out a pen and asterisks a few responses.

Peter reads them carefully. Eva points to a few phrases,

which Peter reads out loud. *'All indications are positive ... Red flags ... white smoke ...* These are all fine.'

'That's right.' Eva takes out a highlighter and picks out one word near the start of the conversation. *Signal.*

'Signal ... like the encrypted messaging thing?'

'Exactly. I think that they moved to Signal if there was anything sensitive to say. So sometimes Dubois messages and Graham can reply with "No news I'm afraid" or whatever. All very appropriate in case he ever has to let people know they were in touch. And then when he has something delicate to discuss he gives a sign and they switch to Signal.'

'Right. They use "red flag" or "white smoke" or whatnot to indicate to switch messaging service. Totally hidden code unless you're looking for it. Or you're a *genius.'* Peter squeezes Eva's shoulder.

'And we don't know what was discussed on Signal. For starters, you can permanently destroy messages on a timer.'

'Guess that explains his cock and bull story about his text messages auto-deleting. He obviously got himself in a muddle about what platform he'd been having these chats on so didn't want to hand anything to us until he'd checked.'

'Sneaky bastard.'

'But everyone messes up eventually. And there is no way Graham is capable of running something like this seamlessly under pressure. You're right about one thing, though: we have no idea what messages were actually sent by them on Signal. We only have his word for it and he's already shown he isn't willing to be honest with us. Or the Chief.' Peter taps his long fingers on the table.

'So what do we do?'

He refills their cups. 'We put the whole thing to a higher power.'

Sentinel Offices, Borough

Jess is chatting to the justice correspondent, hoping for some professional advice on her long read from Glasgow, but she's struggling to get the journalist off the subject of Ed.

'Honestly, Ed nicked so many of my stories when we were in the lobby together. I got so paranoid about it that at one point I thought I was being hacked! A guy who left a while ago knew Ed would steal this one thing he wrote, so he did a little code in the article, with the first letter of each new paragraph spelling out "E-D-I-S-A-C-U-N" ... you get the picture.'

Jess laughs and looks around the huge glass office. Suddenly she feels a presence behind her.

'Enjoy the Westminster dog show,' Ed says.

'Hello, boss.' Jess stands to face him. 'You should come along – I hear there are free neuterings available.'

The justice correspondent gives a surreptitious thumbs-up as Jess walks back to her desk with Ed.

Ed is unsure. This girl. He just can't seem to wrong-foot her. He tried his full set of tools yesterday: coldness, flattery, coaxing, ignoring, belittling. He feels a stab of shame at the memory of the previous night, getting into the shower at home and masturbating, frantically and hopelessly, over Jess's direct, brutish stare. The idea of her knowing about his pathetic pumping makes him feel sick to his stomach.

'I'm headed to Westminster today too,' Ed says. 'Got some further digging to do on Graham Thomas after what I think you might have noticed was a little scoop on the front page about his texts. Want to go together? Can introduce you to a few people, if you like. Your first time there, no?'

'Uh ...' Jess is a little taken aback by another of his sudden mood changes but senses an opportunity to test the strength of the small photo of Ed's family in his office. 'Yeah, that would be great. Do you want a lift?'

'Nobody drives in London, are you mad?'

'Yeah, I noticed. I've got a motorbike.' She pulls her leather jacket off the back of her chair.

'Really?' Ed takes a step back.

'Yup,' Jess says, tying her hair back in a ponytail at the nape of her neck. 'I'm going in five if you want to jump on.'

Like you wouldn't believe, Ed thinks.

Jess carries her leathers into the bathroom. Before she gets changed she stands in the cubicle for a minute or two in her gymnastics power pose. She breathes deeply, feeling strong and in control. She finds Ed to be a bit of an enigma. She's used to charming people instantly – with cheek or intelligence or toughness. His constant spins and turns are exhausting her and she's only known him for a day. She had felt Ed's eyes burning into the back of her as she walked to the bathroom. But was it with loathing or lust? She has an inkling, but having him at her mercy on the back of her bike in heavy traffic might decide it.

'Coming?' She brandishes her spare helmet.

'Uh . . . sure. It is safe, right?'

'Not really, if you believe the statistics.'

'Ha . . . right.'

As soon as the door closes behind them the remaining reporters, who have been quietly watching proceedings and instant messaging each other, burst into paroxysms of laughter and high fives. From his office, Philip McKay, the editor, makes a note to send a bottle of champagne to Magnus Campbell. He loves this new hire and she hasn't written a word yet.

'You won't like this but it's best you hold on tight around my waist,' Jess says under her helmet.

'Okay . . .' Ed feels ridiculous. Jess has made him tuck his trousers into his socks and now that he leans forward to hang onto her he notices his knees almost come past hers, like a clown on a tiny tricycle.

'This is great, I feel like I've got an exoskeleton on to protect me.' Jess points at his thigh bones. Ed feels his face get warmer under the helmet.

Jess starts the engine and pushes back a little in the saddle. As soon as they rattle off down the road Ed knows he's made a terrible mistake. His groin is pressed hard against Jess's leather-clad behind and the vibrations of the engine and the bumps in the road mean he is constantly grinding up against her. The trouble is he can't even push himself further back on the saddle or relax his grip because he is terrified of falling off as they whip through the busy morning traffic. All he can think, with his eyes shut tight in the sweaty heat of his helmet, is please don't get an erection please don't get an erection please don't get an erection.

When they finally climb off the bike he does his best to avoid making eye contact with Jess, but he can feel her looking at him intently. The sweat on his back grows cold.

Portcullis House

Bobby puts down the phone after a long and painful call with Moira Herbert about an upcoming litter pick Daly is doing in Tipperton. Once again, Bobby comes away with the impression that Moira doesn't think she should be in her new job.

'Hey, Bobby, want to take a look at the dog show? It's only round the corner,' says Lucy, the head of Daly's office, as she yawns and stretches in her seat. 'I love it. They quite often have rescue dogs from Battersea. And there's a free coffee stand . . .'

'Sounds great. I could do with a break.' Bobby tries to stifle her own yawn. She's been beavering away all morning on a new social media plan for Daly, who is due in later, and is banking on him being impressed enough with the stack of work she's done in her first couple of days that he'll be ready to sit down and talk about how to save the unit straight away. Bobby hardly thinks her idea to start a TikTok account is groundbreaking, but when she learned the only apps Lucy uses are *Horse & Hound* and Candy Crush she saw why Lucy gave her the task with a soulful 'you're young . . .'

They set off through the confusing network of corridors and staircases until they are out on a stretch of green by the House of Lords.

'Isn't it a lovely scene? The British and their animals . . .' Lucy sighs. She spreads her hands wide at the sea of dogs and smiling people. 'Ooh look, the Guide Dogs have come!' She points to a stand, where a group of photographers are snapping away at a cluster of golden retriever puppies frantically licking the face and hands of the Leader of the Opposition. Bobby finds herself momentarily starstruck by the old man, who looks surprisingly frail in real life. She realises it is the first time she's seen anybody in the flesh from TV before. She snaps a couple of photos on her phone to send to her parents.

Everywhere Bobby looks, dog owners in Hobbs blouses and LK Bennett dresses and navy suits are chatting animatedly to each other or to journalists, all the while patting and stroking and reassuring their treasured pets. Lots of them pose for cheesy photographs or sign petitions for animal charities and campaigners.

It's a wholesome scene and a good reminder that behind the *Question Time* debates and Commons heckles, MPs are civilised people with friends from lots of different political parties, and not just because they have similar policy interests. Surprising pairs are seen having drinks waiting for late votes or hobnobbing in TV studio green rooms. They have the same pressures at home and at work and on social media. More than anything, you have to be a particular kind of person to want to be an MP, let alone to become one.

'My favourite game is deciding which dog looks most like its owner,' says Lucy, bringing over two steaming cups of tea.

Bobby looks around. A tall, neat man bends to pick up his cockapoo's turd. A large woman struggles to quieten her excited springer spaniel. A skinny bald MP brushes the glorious coat of his English sheepdog.

'That one.' She points to a lean, glossy Weimaraner at the end of a lead held by a tall, handsome man. Their rangy frames and sleek grey hair, and the almost identical looks of disinterest in the goings-on around them, are remarkable. They even have the same rather blank, piercing blue stares.

'Ooh, that's Eric Courtenay. Quite a dish, isn't he? Everyone's saying he's next in line. You have great taste.' Lucy digs her elbow in Bobby's ribs. 'And that's his wife, Clarissa. Isn't she glam?' She points out the woman standing on the other side of the dog, dressed in a Burberry trench coat and a cream beret. Bobby thinks she looks like Sophia Loren.

'They're a wonderful-looking couple. I should think we'll start seeing a fair bit of them now.'

'Why's that?' Bobby doesn't take her eyes off them. Clarissa smiles serenely but seems perturbed by a nearby car, where a large group of photographers swarm like bees.

'Oh, didn't you know? Simon and Eric are best friends. Went to prep school together. Eric has promised Simon something really meaty if he wins the leadership. He owes him, seeing as Simon resigned to try and get the ball rolling!'

'I thought Simon had . . . uh, family reasons?'

'Oh Lord,' Lucy looks at her with part pity, part delight, 'you mustn't listen to everything Millie says – although she is right about the baby bit. It's not so much family reasons as

144

Simon taking a step back in order to take about three leaps forward. He is fully behind Eric and therefore so are we.' She folds her arms.

'Well . . . I'm really just here to secure the unit, so—'

'Oh, there'll be plenty of time to get into that. You just need to enjoy yourself for a bit. We'll have so much fun this year if the leadership stuff comes off. Simon thinks they'll use our office for HQ, so we'll be *right* at the centre of it all!'

Bobby looks around the crowd again and Lucy points out various MPs. Bobby is only half-listening, though. Lucy's words have woken up the ambitious little voice that has been dormant. *Right at the centre.*

The tannoy announces that the winner of Westminster Dog of the Year will be unveiled shortly, and pandemonium ensues as, along with every yapping dog on the premises, the spectators throng around the central space in the middle of the Green. A few MPs desperately try to stop their dogs humping each other, the excitement clearly getting to the contestants – or perhaps the behaviour of their owners rubbing off on them.

Bobby sees a familiar figure shaking hands with an MP and putting a notebook away before crouching down and accepting the proffered paw of her interviewee's dog. Jess straightens up and returns Bobby's wave, shrugging her shoulders as though to say 'if you can't beat 'em . . .'

The tannoy pipes up again. 'My Lords, ladies and gentlemen, thank you all for coming along and supporting this year's show. The public have cast their votes in the only election Members and Honourable Members here really mind about,' there is an appreciative titter, 'and I am sure that everyone is delighted to have our winner here today and wish him well with his recovery. The title holder of Westminster Dog of the Year is: Dennis!'

The crowd claps uproariously. The photographers finally

stand back from the car to reveal a large, chocolate Labrador lying in the boot in a nest of blankets and cushions. His thick tail beats cheerfully. His grinning, bear-like head, ruined by thick, ugly stitches and missing chunks of fur, is cradled in the lap of the PM, who rubs the heavy, loose skin around his neck. The PM's husband, holding the vet's cone of shame, kneels at his wife's feet, speaking in low, calming tones to the dog. Bobby makes out his lips saying 'good boy, you're a good boy, good boy, Dennis' again and again.

As Bobby watches assorted MPs reassure their own pets that they aren't disappointed, and listens to Lucy blow her nose between sobs, she overhears Clarissa Courtenay say in a stage whisper to her husband, 'Christ, that poor dog. Some people will do anything for a PR opportunity.'

Downing Street

'So what did she say?' Eva asks, her head snapping up from her desk, where she's been distractedly doodling. Peter has been in with the PM, the Chief Whip and Leonard Smith for over forty minutes.

'She's decided to support Graham. Tim is putting out a statement shortly and she's going to do a clip for the evening broadcast when she visits that hospital this afternoon. The Chief's convinced her that you and I have our tinfoil hats on.' He slams his notebook onto the desk.

'She doesn't believe us?'

'I think she just wants to believe this is all a comedy of errors rather than anything deliberate. You can see why – everything's finally back on an even keel. And we can't prove anything. The Cabinet Office themselves have said they haven't received any correspondence that contradicts the information he's given, now that he's handed his texts over. We haven't had to lose a member of the Cabinet over something scandalous. This is good news, Eva.' He gazes moodily out of the window.

Eva knows it isn't good news, though. The PM is staking her own reputation on Thomas, a noted idiot. Publicly. Maybe he hasn't done anything seriously wrong. Maybe he has, but nobody will ever know. But maybe this will be lighting the fuse to a huge, premiership-ending bomb.

She rubs her temples. 'Okay, what do you need me to do?'

'We need to get the message out to MPs to defend Graham in the media. One of the reasons the Chief has been so twitchy about this whole thing is that he hasn't been able to advise colleagues on what to say, so they've all had to fudge it. Meanwhile, the Labour MPs have been calling for his resignation for days now. Go round to the press team and get the lines they've prepared to brief the lobby with. We need to get it to the Whips and CCHQ so we can send it to MPs and they can flood the airwaves.'

'Gotcha,' Eva rises, 'so we're really diving in head first. God Save Graham.'

'All in. As always, MPs will go crackers if we u-turn. Defending sleaze is top of the cup of cold sick menu. We just need to hope the PM has made the right call . . . '

Covent Garden

Clarissa Courtenay gives a final brief wave then steps elegantly into the waiting taxi, being careful not to crease her vintage velvet Christian Dior evening dress as she settles herself into the seat. Her husband folds himself down beside her and pulls the door closed. Clarissa looks at his profile, picked out perfectly by the theatre lights. His high cheekbones, long nose and strong chin make him look so confident and strong. He turns towards her, his unblinking eyes beaming at her like full head-lights. As she's so often observed, they are like bright, beautiful windows to his empty head.

'Well, that was a lovely evening,' Courtenay says, taking her gloved hand. 'I like Lord and Lady Finlayson a lot.'

'Yes, and they like you,' Clarissa replies. She can't help but wonder what the younger her would have made of this evening. Lord Finlayson hadn't had a clue who she was for the first two years that she worked at StoryCorps. But he'd noticed her eventually, snared in by her curated Marilyn Monroe-esque overt sexual allure, almost girlish innocence and need for strong male protection. A relatively short amount of time – and a considerable amount of sucking that old, wrinkled todger – later and here they were, still the best of friends.

Of course, reflects Clarissa, Finlayson himself might not see it that way. It had been nearly fifteen years since Clarissa and Ed Cooper, both at the bottom of the StoryCorps totem pole, had discovered that Lord Finlayson had at one time made some ill-advised investments with the StoryCorps employees' pension pot. They'd presented him with their evidence, plus a couple of toe-curling recordings of his trysts with Clarissa, promising to keep it locked in a vault. It is a strange position for the old gentleman, who is widely regarded as one of the most powerful men in the country, with the ability to triumph or trash anyone, to be in. Clarissa, who had surprised Finlayson by switching from subservient junior to ball-squeezer in chief, had not been beneath reminding her boss of what she knew. Both Clarissa and Ed had duly received promotion after promotion – legends in StoryCorps lore – and Finlayson continues to pander to them both, pre-sumably biding his time.

Clarissa marvels at how Finlayson can compartmentalise

things so beautifully. The whole evening with his wife and ex-mistress seamlessly handled.

'I was very impressed you didn't fall asleep. Didn't think ballet is your thing.'

'Well, this shirt collar digs in so much that I couldn't really get comfortable ...' Courtenay undoes the top button and sighs contentedly. 'Especially after that big feed. I haven't had beef Wellington in ages.'

Clarissa is about to say something cutting then decides against it. She'd only picked at her Dover sole. Just like when she was a journalist hunting down a story, she finds politics has periods of feast and famine and her appetite reflects that. She'd eaten voraciously in the run-up to the China Trade Deal vote when she could almost touch the PM's demise, but now things have simmered down she's lost all interest in eating and drinking. In everything, really. She misses the adrenaline coursing through her veins.

She switches her phone back on. As usual, dozens of messages from friends and frenemies bounce up. She notices four missed calls from Jackson, Courtenay's cunning lieutenant, and immediately rings back. He picks up straight away.

'There you are. Have you got Eric with you?'

Clarissa puts the phone on loudspeaker. 'Fire away, Nige.'

Courtenay stifles a yawn.

'Where on earth have you two been?'

'Out with the Finlaysons all evening. Each one of his outlets is going to back Eric's bid to the hilt, so not exactly a waste of time. What's going on?'

'Ooh, brilliant. I'm so happy to be the one to tell you,' Jackson chuckles. 'Cast your minds back to this afternoon. The Prime Minister puts out a strong statement supporting Graham Thomas, saying she has full confidence in his honesty and abilities as a Secretary of State. She reaffirms this in a clip a little later, going even further and hinting that the Cabinet Office inquiry will exonerate him.'

'Go on ...' They can hear Jackson struggle to contain his glee.

'Well, dear old Graham went for dinner tonight at some restaurant with a bunch of his mates. A fancy place in Soho. Lots of trendy celebs and such. And he of course completely pickles himself. Starts blabbing away to his pals about this Dubois business.' Clarissa feels her heartbeat increase. 'What he doesn't realise, of course, is that one of the group of young ladies at the table next to them is some influencer type. You know, the ones with the big rubber arses? She's doing a live video for all her millions of fans. Would you care to take a guess at who is doing a lovely loud voiceover about how he sneakily bought shares in Caspar Dubois's company before the rail link decision was announced?'

'You're joking!' Clarissa gasps.

'Not joking. It's clipped everywhere now. This woman can't understand why she's trending alongside #gravytrain. Everyone's going crackers,' Jackson cackles, 'as he's both stitched up the contract and financially profited off it!'

'And the best thing is—' begins Clarissa, reading a lengthy Robert Peston Twitter thread on the subject.

'—the PM already came out to back him!' Courtenay says loudly. Clarissa could kiss him there and then. 'And it's PMQs tomorrow. She'll be crucified!'

'Exactly,' whoops Jackson. 'She can't immediately u-turn. She said the results of the inquiry were imminent and she didn't want to prejudice them but she basically said he would be exonerated. She's come out in support of him before the Cabinet Office has even reported. MPs are already going ape shit. They've been parroting the Number Ten lines all evening. A bunch of them have done supportive op-eds for their weekly papers that can't be withdrawn!'

'It's all about her judgement,' Clarissa says and places a hand firmly on her husband's knee and begins to rub his thigh. She loves winning more than anything, but the anticipation of winning is like overtaking a car into oncoming traffic. The sensation of knowing she is going to experience a moment of pure elation, tinged with just a touch of doubt about whether things will work out exactly as she hopes, makes her feel physically hungry. And horny. She runs her hand further up Courtenay's thigh and feels the outline of his hardening cock. Then she thinks of the leftover chocolate mousse in the fridge. Courtenay's eyes glow at her as she raises his hand to her mouth and sucks on one of his fingers. Her appetite is back.

10th April

Portcullis House

Sackler, loitering in the corridor outside the office he shares with Daly, is on the phone to a journalist while he struggles to safety pin the broken fly on his trousers.

'Well, I know I sound cross! The PM has made me look a complete fool ... Did you see my clip last night for Channel 4? Spouted all the Number Ten lines about what a stand-up guy Graham is ... within hours my inbox filled up with constituents asking for an explanation for how I've backed up an obvious crook ... I was wobbling on the cocking China deal and they talked me round ... Yeah, okay, gotta dash off and hand in this letter. Probably got to fight through a crowd outside Singham's office ...'

Sackler finishes his call and his DIY tailoring and steps back out into the office.

Daly has found a packet of custard creams and is offering them round the cluster of MPs who have gathered in the office.

One of them reads aloud lines from the *Sentinel*. The front page features Thomas's face superimposed onto a train with the headline *Thomas the choo-choo-chump*

'I can't believe he's managed to blow himself and the PM up so spectacularly. I mean … getting pissed and talking loudly enough to get picked up?'

Bobby keeps her eyes fixed on her computer screen, listening intently to the conversation.

'And the shame of the whole thing going online. Even my kids were talking about it this morning. We're fighting to engage with the nation's youth and this is their introduction to the Tory Party,' another MP groans into his cup of tea.

'Being clumsy enough to buy the shares in the first place is mind-bogglingly thick, though. Surely that was going to get spotted?'

'Yeah, well, not necessarily. Guess how he did it.' Daly, courtesy of his breakfast meeting with Ed Cooper, loves having the best information.

'How?'

He points to the photo of the bored-looking boy at the cricket match. 'His son. All done in his son's name.' Gasps and groans all round.

'That's crazy.'

'You'd be surprised who's capable of what, when money's concerned,' Sackler says, dabbing at a huge stain on his tie.

'Urgh, I hope this doesn't become a new expenses scandal thing. I've received three FOIs this morning already,' somebody replies. There is a general nodding of heads and exchange of nervous looks. This is exactly the kind of story that prompts a Parliamentary race to the bottom.

'Anyone catch PMQs today? Disastrous.'

Everyone agrees that the only light relief had come when one of their colleagues, a farmer from Herefordshire, hadn't realised his phone wasn't switched to silent. The notoriously poor signal in the Chamber lifted momentarily, prompting a deluge of texts to arrive, all to his loud alert – a piercing series of blasts on a hunting horn. The benches opposite had burst into torrents of laughter, mainly in anticipation of the fantastic clips they can post on social media later showing how out of touch the Tories are.

'I was on the front bench,' Hendrick says as he staggers in. 'Our side was almost silent. Just a sea of jubilant faces in front of me from the benches opposite. I just went into classic "nodding dog" mode.' He fixes a perturbed frown on his face and wobbles his head slowly up and down.

'The price for refusing to give up your Cabinet post, you coward,' teases Daly, who had dodged PMQs to harass the man from IT, who struggled to get Daly's personal laptop to connect to the wifi.

'Well, I can't resign now, can I? Would look terribly opportunistic . . .'

'Yes, very out of character.' Daly raises an eyebrow.

Everyone laughs. Hendrick shifts in his seat.

'Oh, here we go,' Sackler cuts in. 'Can someone turn the TV up? I want to watch his statement to the House . . . Shhhh.'

Via Lucy, Bobby knows a personal statement to the House is a speech an MP makes in the Chamber, generally for apologies. The key thing is nobody is allowed to interrupt or ask questions afterwards.

Sackler is shushing Daly and another MP, who are squirming with delight like a pair of schoolboys at something on Daly's phone, when there is a shout from the group of MPs clustered around the TV. Thomas has resigned.

The room erupts with ringing phones and frantic babbling. 'What do you reckon? . . . I'd better go and send in my letter . . . Aargh, it's my anniversary this weekend, my wife will go nuts! . . . My Whip's calling. What should I say? . . . Does anyone want to go to the pub?' A sense of panic and excitement hits every one of them, each thinking the same thing: what does this mean for me?

'Lord, I must just ... ah ... dash!' Hendrick beetles out of the room at top speed, clamping his phone to his ear.

'Hi, Nige.' Daly shushes his colleagues as he answers the phone. 'Yeah, no problem. I'll get down to Central Lobby now. Yeah, I'll see who's up for it. See ya.' Daly puts down his phone and pulls on a tie hanging off the back of his chair. 'The camera calls, folks.'

'What are you going to say?' asks a dazed Sackler.

'Sorry to see Graham go but it was the right thing to do. But frankly, he shouldn't have had the chance to resign. I don't know why the PM didn't sack him first thing this morning – or thoroughly investigate to begin with. Serious questions about her judgement ... and leadership. Regardless of what Graham has done, Ford has made the wrong calls over this, and even the right ones she's made too slowly. She's set the Party back ten points.' Daly brushes his hair in the mirror. 'In summary: the Bat Signal has gone up.'

'Shit. Shit, this is really happening, isn't it?' someone cries excitedly.

'Yup. The custard cream coup is in action.' Daly opens the office door. 'Catch me on the wires, fellow conspirers.'

Claybourne Terrace

Eva huddles under a blanket on the sofa. What a day. She spent most of it on the phone to MPs and Peers, feeling like she was standing on the deck of the *Titanic* at the exact moment it split in half and sank to the icy depths of the Atlantic. One after the next, it was a version of the same conversation:

'Yes . . . yes, I understand that. But do you remember the last time we spoke you raised concerns that the PM wasn't showing sufficient support to Graham? . . . Yes, circumstances do change, but . . . okay, well, thank you for your time.'

Finally, at about 4 p.m. Sir Godfrey Singham had called Peter and said he wanted to meet with the Prime Minister. It could only mean one thing: the letter threshold had been reached. Eva had valiantly tried to persuade the pompous busybody to come in discreetly through the Cabinet Office, but he was determined to have his moment in front of the cameras.

Now, Eva sits with Jess, passing a tub of ice cream back and forth as they stare at a twenty-four-hour news channel on the TV, armed with nothing but spoons.

The sound is turned down low, so they watch near silent footage of politicians going about their business in Westminster: Sir Godfrey Singham striding seriously up Downing Street, the PM at PMQs, and Thomas and Courtenay battling through huddles of journalists outside their homes – one sweaty and stressed, the other with a tight-lipped smile.

'It's so . . . *fast*!' Jess exclaims finally.

'Yeah. Peter says you never know what the issue will be but once these things go it's like a spark on a puddle of petrol.'

'It's a puddle of something, all right,' Jess mutters. 'What was it like when it happened? In the room?'

'Oh, I wasn't in there. Not inner circle enough. I probably never will be now. But as Peter has said to me lots of times, you rarely register those moments as historical. Says it's much later on that you actually absorb their significance. It's straight onto a series of other conversations and tweets and source quotes, and time flies without being able to pause for breath and soak it all in.'

'Speaking of which, I'm going to run you a bath. There's still a way to go here, and seeing as there's nothing else you can do tonight you may as well get some sleep.'

Twenty minutes later Eva lies down in the steaming water and sighs deeply. Jess has lit candles and balanced them on the sides of the bath, on the sink and the loo seat. Enya plays quietly and Eva can smell bath oils and salts. She thinks about how the Prime Minister must feel. There's going to be a confidence vote on Monday. Eva has a few days of frantic calling but, as she feels the warm water relax her aching muscles, it's hard to resist the inevitability of what is coming. When she finally slips into her sheets, Eva discovers that Jess has prepared her a hot water bottle. She pulls it into her tummy, curls into the foetal position and drops into a deep sleep.

House of Commons

Bobby follows Daly towards the sounds of indistinct chatter down the corridor in the Cholmondeley Room, where the reception is taking place. Lucy explained to her earlier that this is one of a number of rooms that Parliamentarians can book for events, generally on behalf of a charity or organisation. Daly told her on their walk over that this evening's host is Richard Hendrick, the Secretary of State for Education, and the event's to mark the publishing of some work by a think tank into mental health.

Brilliant, Bobby thinks, we're getting down to business.

Daly leads her into the room, which is packed with people. Everyone is making animated, friendly chit-chat while simultaneously glancing over their companions' shoulders, wondering if there is someone more important they should be speaking to.

As she trails Daly towards a table laid out with glasses of wine, Bobby catches snippets of conversation:

'I'll just hang out here. We have that vote at 10 p.m. Can't remember the last time we were held so late on a Wednesday. May as well stay with the free drinks until then ... I still don't understand why the Education Secretary is hosting. Oh, don't you know? He hopes it gets him in with the Royals ... He should set up his own mental health foundation, for anyone who's had to spend more than two minutes with him ... I bet Daly's feeling pleased with himself now. If Courtenay keeps his word ... I'm telling you, you can see she bought the domain name weaver4pm.com seven months ago! ... Honestly, mate, pure filth. So the next thing I know, it's absolute agony when I pee ... '

Bobby can't help but notice that Daly seems to be very popular. It takes them forever to get to the drinks table because people keep shaking his hand. After the first person, an MP from Daly's intake, turns to Bobby, saying 'Ah! You must be Annie', Daly is careful to introduce Bobby to whoever he's speaking to before they can address her.

'Sorry,' Daly says quietly. 'That chap didn't realise you were the new girl.'

Daly nearly shits himself. He really should have been more discreet about Annie.

They continue to circulate, Bobby picking up card after card from MPs who have an interest in mental health or who have similar units to the one in Tipperton. She's amazed that absolutely nobody has a good answer to what solution there might be. 'It's the free market, isn't it,' says one very red-faced man, 'if the NHS can sell it for a great pile of cash then happy days!' Daly quickly moves Bobby on.

Privately, Daly is keen to seem supportive but wants to keep Bobby off the subject of the mental health unit for now. Hopefully stuff like this reception will do the trick. He went to see Jeffrey Cuthbert at the weekend to talk about this job.

It turns out that a number of his most influential Tipperton residents form a large part of the consortium behind the PFI contract that built and maintains the unit. Now some members of the consortium, led by Jeffrey, are putting a bid together to buy the property once the PFI contract ends and turn it into a golf club and spa. The role is clear: make this closure happen. Daly had said he had to go away and think about it, hoping against hope that he can think of something to please everybody.

A large part of Bobby's evening is spent talking to Mary Jones, an MP who blasts through her assumptions about most politicians and asks whether Bobby would like to be an MP – nodding sagely at Bobby's reply, 'Possibly, but for which Party?' She explains to Bobby how she was initially selected as a Conservative candidate after running a campaign in her constituency, where she was head teacher of a school that was due to close. Entering her twelfth year in Parliament in a seat the Conservatives had never won before, Jones was handpicked by Percy Cross's predecessor as a star and was popped into a Cabinet job far sooner than expected – 'I know it was too soon, but who can say no to that?' Jones was used as a human shield by the government in its war with teaching unions over pay, her credibility chipped away by one disastrous media appearance after another. She was brutally reshuffled down to the back benches and cheerfully tells Bobby that she couldn't be happier.

'I ran that initial campaign and then realised as an MP you can get so much more done. Then I bought into that stuff about only really being able to make a difference if you have power. But now I think being an independently minded MP is the way to go. You're incorruptible! It's so freeing. I genuinely vote the way I think is right and I can communicate in my own way, not with prepared lines that clunk out of my mouth. As for campaigns – you're actually lucky that Simon is out of government to help with yours. He can reach across to the Opposition and write op-eds and all sorts. The rat race into the Cabinet is such a waste of time and energy. Not to mention a muzzle.'

Bobby repeats all this to Daly, who snorts.

'Of course Mary would say that – she's out in the wilderness.'

Bobby sulks and quietly listens as Daly continues his intent conversation with a columnist from *The Times* about the confidence vote on Monday.

A little bell goes off and the rhythm of the room changes.

'Oh Lord, is that the time? I've got to go and vote. Why don't you come and watch?' Daly drains his glass, practically throws it at a nearby waiter and joins the throng of MPs heading to the voting lobby, some considerably less steady on their feet than others.

As they walk, Daly laments to a fellow MP about his wife.

'Yes, I try to get her to come down more but she just doesn't want to ... I wonder if she's just tired of being Mrs MP and playing second fiddle ... I do wish she was a bit more supportive. It's hard to be here, there and everywhere – and it won't get easier!'

Bobby's surprised to find that she empathises a little with Daly. She takes a dim view of bed-hopping, but she certainly knows how it feels to be tied to Tipperton and the responsibilities waiting there. Watching the vote take place, she can't help wondering whether there might be a future for her in politics once the unit is saved.

12th April

Claybourne Terrace

On Friday evening, the house party is firmly under way. There had been a slight hiccup when, on entering the living room just before their guests arrived, Eva had retched loudly. Some sort of mouse or rat had died under the floorboards and the smell was terrible. A scramble for Febreze and every scented candle they owned ensued.

There had been a few wrinkled noses on arrival, but most of the guests – mainly university friends and a couple of politicos ('we must invite them, they'll just sit on Twitter otherwise') – are used to eccentric domestic arrangements at the Cross household. Percy, Eva's father, has given many of them lifts home before, which involves sitting in the back of a Range Rover chauffeured by his protection team and listening to Percy's stories with a bottle of Laphroaig. Inspired by her father, Eva has made what she calls 'rocket fuel', Cava with a shot of sloe gin, to help get everyone nicely lubricated. About twenty young people are spread between the kitchen and the living room, where they're bunched up on sofas and whispering intently in corners.

Jess is out in the garden, where fairy lights frame a group of smoking guests.

'You know,' one young think tank wonk says, studying his glowing cigarette, 'it would be quite an idea for the government to revisit its policy on smoking. I reckon post-war Britain's success was all down to the lowly fag. Think about it. With roughly half the population smoking, the Treasury raked in a fantastic amount of money in taxes. Life expectancy was sixty-five or something, so the NHS wasn't spending a load of dosh on geriatric social care and everyone was thinner. Hang on!' he shouts, raising his hand to stop the indignant interruptions and to calm the roar of approval from his supporters. 'Additionally, with everyone dying so early, middle-class people were getting their inheritance in decent time so home ownership at the age of thirty was actually possible—'

'Just one problem. You'd kill off all our voters, who are largely in the over-fifty category. Nice one, genius.'

'And you wonder why people call you lot the nasty party,' Jess teases.

The young wonk chuckles and blows a smoke ring. 'Maybe it needs a bit of workshopping.'

Upstairs in the kitchen, Jamie, Eva's boyfriend, helps Bobby shove a load of bottles into the fridge.

'Why is this place all lit up like a massage parlour?' Jamie asks, setting off in search of Eva. 'It smells like duty free at Heathrow . . .'

Eva is holding court, pleased Jess is entertaining the cluster of political people this evening. Like many of her fellow SpAds, she often feels obliged to act as an official government spokesperson at social occasions and defends all sorts of things she completely disagrees with. It takes the fun out of a lot of parties. Once people find out what she does for a living, Eva finds she can generally get through parties with non-politicos by answering a few questions along the lines of 'but what's it *like* in there?' (smaller than you think) and 'so what's the PM like?' (taller than you think). This evening she is struck by how the events of the last couple of days have registered with her friends from fashion and finance.

'It's just so trashy, isn't it?' sniffs an aspiring actress. 'It feels like we're back to the nineties. You know, with that guy who shagged the egg woman?'

'Do you mean John Major?'

The girl shrugs and knocks back the remains of her glass, wondering whether it may be time to head to the next party. She'd hoped there might be a fit *West Wing* type here but it's slim pickings. She can see why Eva has looked elsewhere.

As if on cue, Jamie joins them. The actress takes the opportunity to signal to a couple of her friends, who stroll casually to the front door and slip away.

'I hear there's at least one rat that's done the honourable thing and simply died to avoid going down with the sinking ship.'

'Oh ha ha.' Eva kisses him. 'You're late.'

'Yes, I was doing your last-minute shopping,' Jamie draws her in closer, 'and I've got you a little present.'

He holds up a plain black shopping bag, sealed with a black satin ribbon.

'What for?'

'Oh, just a new way to try and tie you down. I've not seen you for ages.'

'I know, I'm sorry. I've just been flat out with the girls moving in and everything falling apart at work. I've missed you, though.' Eva glances over his shoulder. Everyone seems to be happily occupied in conversation or self-conscious dancing.

'Want to go and open it upstairs and I can give you something in return?'

Jamie grins and allows himself to be led by Eva up to the top of the house. When they reach the bedroom, Jamie sits on the windowsill and lights a cigarette, watching his girlfriend carefully untie the ribbon and pull out the contents of the bag.

'Is it . . . underwear?' she asks.

'No,' he says quietly. 'It's a special rope. You keep saying you want to kick it up a notch after hearing Jess's story about the handcuffs . . . '

Eva runs it through her fingers, smiling faintly at his lit cigarette. 'Well, you'd better put that out, then, if I'm binding your hands up.'

'Me?'

'I'm hosting a party. I need to alert people to the fire exits in an emergency.' Eva knows she doesn't want to feel vulnerable. She's not entirely sure she'd like to do the binding either, but her strange competitive edge has kicked in and she wants to out-do Jess.

'Okay.' Jamie jumps up and grinds out his cigarette on the windowsill, then holds up his free hands. 'I surrender.'

Eva walks to him and slips her arms up around his neck, kissing him deeply. He responds immediately, running his fingers down her back, feeling around the opening of her halterneck at her shoulders and softly grazing her breast with his thumb.

Eva, still kissing, starts to unbutton Jamie's shirt. She feels the familiar nudge of his hardening cock against her. It always feels amazing to be able to arouse him so easily.

When Jamie's shirt is off, Eva pushes him back on the bed and begins kissing his chest, working her way down to his navel, where she undoes his jeans. Jamie has to lift his hips to help her pull the last of his clothes off, then he lies back with his hands behind his head and tries to relax. He's a bit taken aback by the sensation he feels next. Not the smooth, wet sucking that he'd hoped for, but a dry, tickling, slightly stinging sensation. He pushes himself up on his elbows and realises Eva is flicking playfully at him with the rope end.

'I want you to kneel, please,' Eva says quietly, 'with your hands behind your back.'

Jamie dutifully turns, stifling a nervous laugh, and allows Eva to tie his hands together. Then he waits for a long time, his enthusiasm diminishing.

'What are you doing?' he asks eventually.

'Trying to read an online guide,' Eva murmurs, her tongue sticking out. 'This may not be my strong suit, you know. I couldn't tie my shoelaces properly until I was nine.'

'How difficult can it be to tie a knot?'

'I'm more concerned about being able to untie you later . . . '

'Ah. Good point.'

Playing for time, Eva kisses the back of Jamie's neck and snakes her fingers around his waist. He immediately jumps back to attention. While Jamie's distracted with one of her hands, Eva glances at her phone screen in her other hand for the next step. She had hoped she would discover a hidden passion for bondage, but she finds the instructions confusing and her fumbling fingers unsexy. Eventually, though, Jamie is bound by the feet, hands and neck in a kneeling position.

Eva walks slowly around the bed until she's facing Jamie, who has a strange look on his face.

'Please don't put anything up my bum,' he jokes. It's then that Eva realises he's scared and so is she.

As Eva contemplates what to do next, hurried footsteps approach and there's a knock on the door.

'Eva, babe . . . are you in there?' It's Jess.

'What is it?'

'Can you come downstairs?'

Jamie looks at Eva, then they both start giggling.

'Thank Christ for that!' Jamie breathes.

'Eva . . . ?' Jess hesitates. 'Your dad's here.'

'What?' Eva jumps up and starts running to the door.

'Wait!' cries Jamie desperately, losing his balance and falling onto his face, trussed up in a stress position, completely naked.

Eva looks wildly around and spots a pair of scissors.

'Careful with those,' Jamie winces, as Eva snips carelessly at the cords. When he turns to speak to her, she's already run from the room.

As she nears the ground floor, Eva hears the slow clapping of hands and the stamping of feet and the occasional blast of laughter shoot up the stairs to greet her. Why on earth is her father back from America? She wasn't expecting him for months. Why didn't he let her know? It isn't exactly a convenient journey. A text wouldn't have killed him.

When she reaches the kitchen, Eva finds a raucous chess game in progress, a Downing Street press SpAd on one side and her father on the other. The party guests have crammed themselves in to listen to Percy's jokes and take selfies with him. Each time one of the players goes to make a move, the on-lookers drumroll with their hands and feet and then cheer when the move is made. Lots of them seem to have devised a game that involves doing a tequila shot when a piece is taken off the board. It takes a while for Eva to register the extremely pretty young blonde woman perched on Percy's knee, her arms around his neck.

'Hello, pork chop!' Percy shouts to her.

'Dad . . . why didn't you say you were coming home?' Eva says as nonchalantly as possible.

'Well, we had to head off in quite a hurry . . . '

'Yes, but it's quite a long flight. You . . . hang on. We?'

'Ah yes. I've brought Holly with me.'

'Well, I have heard so much about you!' Holly says in a sing-song Southern drawl.

The woman on Percy's lap stands and hugs Eva tightly. Holly is tall in her high-heeled sandals – perhaps a head taller than Percy – with a mass of blonde hair, a deep tan and bright, perfectly straight teeth. She is wearing so much makeup it is hard to be sure of her exact age but she is clearly a good deal younger than Percy.

'Oh Jesus.'

Eva hears the familiar voice of Jamie, who is standing in the doorway. Thank God. Jamie will know what to do.

'Dad,' Eva says, 'can I speak to you for a sec? Next door?'

'But I'm halfway through a match!'

'Jamie can take over.'

'Oh hello, young man! I didn't even see you there.' The two shake hands, Percy craning his neck up at the far taller Jamie. 'Yes, hold the fort for a minute, will you?'

As Jamie sits down, Eva notices he has rope marks on his neck and prays that nobody else sees them. What an evening this is turning into.

When they reach the now empty living room, Eva turns to her father, who is grinning bashfully. She is immediately struck by how different his smile is.

'Dad, what the hell is going on? And what happened to your *teeth*? You look like Rudy Giuliani.'

'Well, one of my fillings fell out so I went to see a dentist in LA and they weren't very happy with my gnashers. I didn't think they were too bad, but they made me feel like my mouth was Shelob's lair. Anyway, I got these lovely dentures and—'

'Okay, wait. Let's go from the top, shall we: what is going on? Is everything okay?'

'Everything's splendid, darling! I have a girlfriend.'

'Oh, you always have a girlfriend.'

'This is different. I'm in love,' Percy says simply.

'That's all very well, but what are you doing here?'

'Well . . .' Percy shuffles his feet. 'Once the college administrators found out about Holly and I—'

'Hang on, she's a *student*?'

'A Master's student, Eva,' Percy whispers reproachfully.

'Dad. How old is she?'

'Well, she's . . . she's twenty-four.' Percy bites his lip.

Same age as his own daughter, Eva thinks. She is fed up with being embarrassed by her father, who never seems to think how his actions hurt her. Percy is always pitching up with completely inappropriate Svetlanas and Conchitas, but he's always been frank about their relationships: 'stepping out', he calls it. Nothing long term. Same old stories in the gossip columns. Holly, an obvious-looking gold digger, will make a snappy exit the moment she realises the Crosses don't sit on a great pile of gold. Still, she's got skills, Eva has to admit. Her father banging on about love? He's never done that before.

'So does this mean you've lost your job?'

'Well, the Dean made it clear we couldn't be together. And I just can't be without her. So we have come home,' Percy replies, trying to look as dignified as possible, taking a deep breath and puffing out his cheeks.

Eva puts her hands on her hips and thinks hard. Holly will be on her way, soon enough. She hasn't fought with her father about his girlfriends for ages, and with Jess and Bobby in the house – plus about twenty other people at the present time – she doesn't want to break the habit.

'Where are the cops?' The thought suddenly strikes Eva. Since the day her father left Downing Street he has had police protection and will continue to do so until the day he dies.

'Ah,' Percy grins at her. 'I gave them the slip.'

'Da-ad. It's for your own safety.'

'Oh darling, I was PM for barely two minutes. Besides, it's good for them to be kept on their toes.' Percy looks at himself in the hall mirror and pats under his chin. 'Frankly, good luck kidnapping me. You'd need a whole rugby team. Do you know, I put on a stone in the US in just six weeks? Holly says it's this stuff gluten . . . '

Eva isn't listening. She calls a number on her phone.

'Hey, I just wanted to check where you think my dad is?'

'He's in the house.'

'So you knew he's here?'

'Course. It just makes him so happy to think he's giving us the runaround. I'm so relieved not to be trailing him around casinos and bars that I don't really mind . . . '

'Fair enough. See you later.'

'Are they going crackers?' Percy squirms with childish glee.

'Oh yeah . . . fuming, Dad. Crikey, you have to stop grinning. Your teeth look insane. It's hurting my eyes.'

'Anyway,' Percy changes the subject, keen to keep his daughter away from rowing with him, 'Maddie's buggered, isn't she.'

'Thanks!' Eva says.

'Well, she is. Confidence vote. I mean . . . I know how this goes.' Eva can't argue with that, so shrugs.

Before they can continue, Jamie appears.

'Hello . . . I thought I'd take everyone out to a bar. We've run out of booze.'

'In my house? What standards are you keeping here, young lady?' Percy booms, hugging Eva tight and heading back to the kitchen.

Eva cups Jamie's face in her hands and kisses him gratefully.

'You still owe me a present, you know,' he murmurs.

Once everyone has left, Jess walks to her room, checks her phone and is surprised to find that she has a text from Ed:

Strongly advise against taking bike into Parliament. Too aggressive and showy.

She thinks hard while she changes into her pyjamas. The minute he got off the back of her motorbike Jess knew exactly what was what. She has a sixth sense for when someone is into her. And, as she'd hoped, Ed Cooper is into her. But he's married and comparatively powerful. She needs to be very careful about getting this right. She has less than nine months to make her mark at the *Sentinel* and to consolidate her position in the lobby. She needs her boss behind her, so to speak. She types a reply and takes a deep breath before hitting send:

I'm surprised. You seemed to like it.

Jess heads to Eva's bedroom, where Eva and Bobby are waiting for her with hot chocolate.

'Well, I really was not expecting the evening to take this turn,' Eva groans. 'I'm sorry it's going to be a bit more crowded around here for a while.'

'I think it's fun.' Jess feels her phone buzz in her hand and feels a squirm of excitement. 'I like a full house.'

'Still . . . Holly being the same age as us. That's quite the gap,' Bobby says.

'The press will have a field day when they find out,' Jess chuckles. Then she sees Eva's face. 'Don't worry. My lips are sealed. Anyway, Jamie's a diamond. The way he got rid of everyone . . . It was great.' She looks at her screen:

What's that supposed to mean?

Jess's heart beats a little faster as she replies, thinking of Ed's hands around her waist on the bike:

I think we both know.

'I know,' Eva sighs. 'I'm sorry we disappeared for a bit, but he's had a lonely few days.'

'Good for you. God knows I could do with some fun. When was the last time you had a good old bang, Bob?'

'Mm . . .' Bobby twists a bit of old cord in her fingers. Eva recognises it instantly as a snippet of the rope she'd tied Jamie up with. She thought she'd scooped it all into a drawer before they came into her room and she's hardly in the mood to crow about the ridiculous horlicks she'd made in here earlier with it.

'Well . . .' Bobby contemplates the contents of her mug. Sod it. 'I haven't actually . . . *banged* anyone.'

Jess immediately puts down her phone and snaps to attention. 'Still? Sorry, I just . . . assumed.'

'I know. I haven't really had the opportunity.'

Bobby wishes Jess wouldn't look so surprised. Sex isn't everything.

'Does it bother you?' Jess asks, feeling her phone buzz again.

'Occasionally,' Bobby says, choosing not to say those occasions are when Jess and Eva won't shut up about their own sex lives. 'The longer I leave it, the bigger a deal it seems. I keep wishing I'd just got it out of the way in my teens or something. When it does happen I won't have a clue what I'm doing . . .'

There is a long pause while Jess reads a fresh text:

All right. I'll admit your arse looks pretty good in leather.

Jess feels a small but unmistakable pulsation in her tracksuit bottoms. Ed's walking right into this. Time to test the parameters. Her fingers fly back:

You disgust me.

Jess tucks the phone back underneath her thigh. 'It's definitely not worth stressing over.' Eva nods in agreement. 'You've got a lot on just now, so I wouldn't fixate on it.'

'Totally,' Eva nods again. 'And as for what you're doing, the right instincts just sort of kick in. Besides, most guys are just thrilled that a naked lady has agreed to go to bed with them.'

'It's true. I totally over-thought it when I lost my virginity. I acted all . . . porny, I guess. Loads of moaning and "oh baby"ing. The poor guy stopped to ask if I was okay.' Jess winces.

'Can't be as bad as my first time. We spent ages trying to tuck his balls into the condom,' Eva giggles.

Jess slides her phone out to check it. Why hasn't he replied yet? Has she scared him off?

'You must have found us wittering on about sex the whole time so annoying . . .' Eva and Bobby pick the conversation back up, Bobby feeling a weight lift off her chest and Eva carefully watching the cord in her hands.

Jess feels her phone buzz again:

I don't care what you think.

She zaps back:

We know that's not true. It can be our dirty little secret.

Jess tries not to squirm too much as her mind races. She considers telling Eva and Bobby about her plans for Ed Cooper, to have him under her thumb. After all, nothing's actually going to happen. She's totally in control. But for them, her boss might be a bridge too far. Jess is shaken from her reverie by her phone buzzing again:

What do you know about dirty secrets?

This is going perfectly. She wants to get back to her room and her rampant rabbit.

'Right, angels,' Jess says, 'time for bed.'

As soon as she closes the door to her bedroom, Jess sends her final text:

You'll see.

Several miles away in his bathroom in Blackheath, surrounded by his wife's moisturisers and shampoos, Ed Cooper bites down on a flannel as he gasps his way through another world-beating wank.

15th April

Burma Road, Houses of Parliament

Jess feels like a rat trapped in a lab experiment. She simply can't find the office that Ed told her about and is now out of breath and slightly sweaty, running up tiny staircases and along deserted corridors. It doesn't help that her chest feels tight just at the thought of seeing Ed again after their text exchange on Friday night. Finally she stumbles into a hairdressing salon.

'Oh love, you're far away from home! Let me take you in the right direction. I was nipping out for a coffee anyway,' says the cheerful stylist.

'So why is there a hairdresser in Parliament?' asks Jess, trying to steady her breathing as they march along.

'Well, everybody needs their hair cut, don't they?' comes back the reply.

'Yeah, I s'pose so.'

'You won't believe the gossip I pick up.' She lowers her voice. 'I could write quite the book! David Jenkins and David

173

Davidson in together the other day. You know they're now married to each other's ex-wives? Very awkward . . . ' She points up a staircase. 'Here we are – you'll be in one of the rooms up there. They call it Burma Road, but I've no idea why. Come in for a trim sometime!'

The stylist eyes Jess's stark fringe and black ponytail as she thanks her and sprints up the stairs.

After asking several paunchy men in slightly sagging cycling gear for directions, she finally finds the right room.

'You're late,' Ed says, studiously avoiding Jess's eye.

'Yes, I'm so sorry. It's a bit of a maze, isn't it?' She wills her normally pale face to look less flushed. Before Ed can reply, she addresses the two other men sitting with them. 'You must be George and Mike. Nice to meet you – really looking forward to working together.'

The men shake her hand and return the niceties.

'All right, all right. Can we get on, please? Bit of a big day if you hadn't noticed.' Ed clears his throat. 'So the list today . . . '

After a call with Philip McKay, the editor, Ed takes charge, dishing out orders and fielding his team's questions. Jess can't help but feel impressed and intrigued by his confidence and competence. George groans when he is tasked with speaking to the 1922 Committee executive members about how the secret ballot for the confidence vote will work, pointing to a joke Valentine's Day card, featuring a printed picture of Sir Godfrey Singham, complete with pink felt tip love hearts drawn around his puce face. 'I've wined and dined the old badger for weeks, now,' he complains. Mike is told to keep tabs on the likely challengers to the throne – Natasha Weaver, Richard Hendrick, Dev Singh – and estimated numbers for the confidence vote.

'I hardly think the vote will register. We should move straight on to leadership. Seems pretty obvious she's toast . . . '

Mike says, his tongue sticking out while he jots down notes.

'We cover all bases,' Ed says simply. 'Right – I'll cover Number Ten briefings and the Courtenay lot. Any questions?' George and Mike shake their heads.

'Yeah,' says Jess. 'What do you want me to do?'

Ed finally glances at her. She knows right away he has been trying to avoid this moment. Lust pulsates from him.

'Uh . . . the Welsh Conservatives have their Party Conference in Carmarthen this weekend. You focus on that.' Jess glances at George and Mike, who both stare intently at their boss, smirks playing around their lips. Good luck getting a story there, they think.

'Sure. No problem.'

Ed thinks about her text on Friday night. *You'll see*. Christ, he wants to.

'Good. So, uh . . . did you bike in?' Ed says casually.

'No, I took advice and walked from home.'

'Cyclist too, are you?' chips in George.

'No, although I see there are plenty of Lycra lads around here. I have a motorbike.'

'Cool!' Mike swivels round in his chair. 'What's it like?'

'Ask Ed. I gave him a lift last week.' Jess inclines her head.

George and Mike look at him, mildly confounded.

Ed shrugs. 'Yeah, it was fine. I barely remember it, to be honest. Now, can we get on? There's some news to break here, if you hadn't forgotten.'

They all turn to their computers. Ed's phone buzzes with a text:

Liar.

It's like a button has been pressed to send every drop of energy he has into his crotch. When he looks up, Jess is gazing at her computer screen like he doesn't even exist.

Before Ed can think what to do next the door swings open.

Jess turns to see a grizzled, portly man in the doorway leaning on a walking stick. With his incredible size and presence – right down to the cloud of vapour around his head – she almost mistakes him for Magnus.

'Hello, Teddy,' Ed says, 'how are you?'

'Fine, fine,' says Teddy. 'Who's this?' He points his stick at Jess.

'This is Jess Adler, our new junior. Jess, this is Teddy Hammer.'

'I know who he is!' squeaks Jess. 'It's a pleasure to meet you.'

'Charmed, charmed.' Teddy bows his head. Jess can't help but be starstruck. *The* Teddy Hammer. A veteran journalist, with stints covering war, famine, political scandal and financial collapse. He's broken some of the biggest stories of the last forty years and here he is, talking to Jess. 'Working on the leadership stuff too, are you?' He addresses the room at large.

'Yup,' Ed says firmly. He is annoyed at Jess's obvious delight at meeting Teddy, the opposite to her indifference at her first meeting with Ed. 'You?'

'Nope.' Teddy puffs on his vape. 'Not so much fun when it's about your twentieth. A young man's game.' He taps George then Mike on the tops of their heads with his stick. 'Now, miss,' he addresses Jess again, 'do you smoke?'

'I'm afraid not.'

'You drink coffee, though?'

'Oh, certainly.'

'Come on, then. Keep me company while I have some proper nicotine and tell me all about yourself. As the oldest member of the lobby I deserve to have a proper interview with the youngest ...'

Ed watches them leave, wishing he found Jess so pliable. Teddy leads Jess to his 'spot', a hidden archway on the ground floor of Parliament. She loves walking beside him on the five-minute journey. Everyone they pass greets him – all warmly and with at least a hint of fear. He introduces Jess to other journalists, MPs from every party, even Cabinet and Shadow Cabinet ministers. She feels giddy at the attention and comforted by the old-fashioned kindness. Still, enjoyment aside, Jess would be in trouble if Ed was straightforwardly professional and impervious to her unorthodox strategy to bring him round.

Once Teddy has lit his cigarette he falls into silence, moving effortlessly from vape to tobacco.

'Mr Hammer . . . ?' ventures Jess.

'Please, Teddy.'

'Sorry, Teddy. Can I ask you something?'

'Fire away.'

'Don't take this the wrong way, but . . . why is everyone around here frightened of you?'

Teddy gives a shout of laughter. Smoke billows out of his mouth and Jess sees he has a gold tooth.

'Well, reputation and mystique have a lot to do with it.' Jess nods. 'But the big thing I have in my favour compared to a little squirt starting out for the first time is really not giving a shit.' He taps his stick on the floor between each word.

Jess raises her eyebrows.

'Look at me: I'm older than Father Time. I've made myself a little pile of gold to live off. I write what I'm interested in and what I think is important. I'm not trying to build a career, so I can pretty much just go for whatever I think is in the public interest. And being independent means I don't have to give a toss about editorial direction. Someone will always buy what I'm selling.'

Jess sips her coffee thoughtfully. 'That does sound very freeing. But surely it hasn't always been like this. Didn't you have to . . . pay your dues?'

Teddy gazes at her. 'Obviously we all have to do that. But

there are ways to make a name for yourself that fall within what's fair.'

'Like what?'

'You have to work that out for yourself, kid.' He stubs out his cigarette and picks up his walking stick. 'Coming?'

'Uh . . . ' Jess keeps her eyes fixed on the last glowing embers of the butt. 'You go on ahead. I'll finish my coffee first.'

Teddy grunts and hobbles off.

As soon as he's gone, Jess bends down to pick up the cigarette butt. She's just turning to put it in a nearby bin when she hears a cough. Poking her head around the archway, she finds a hidden alcove and a woman dressed in a tabard.

'New here, are you?' the woman asks, taking a long drag on her cigarette.

'Yeah. Just joined the hacks upstairs. I'm Jess.'

'Hiya. I'm Jean. Cleaning staff.'

'Well,' Jess brandishes the cigarette butt, 'any trouble around here, it isn't me!'

'It's actually fine in this bit. It's the secret area lots of ministers who've officially quit come to, so they always clear up after themselves. You'd think we were doing DNA swabs,' Jean says.

'Well, you have a great hidey hole here.'

'Oh yeah, we pick up all sorts.' Jean takes another drag. 'To be honest, you can pick stuff up everywhere. Incredible how brazen people are about leaving things lying around in public places or saying things in front of "staff". But some of them seem to think we don't have eyes and ears, so I suppose it makes sense.'

Jess wonders exactly what Jean has seen in her time and whether she'd ever talk about it.

'You'd better get a move on,' Jean breaks into her thoughts, 'Mr Hammer will be well ahead of you now . . . '

'Oh yes! Thanks for the reminder. Well, nice to meet you.'

As she dashes down the corridor Jess checks her watch – 11.10 – and wonders whether Jean has her break at the same time every day.

Committee Room 9, House of Commons

Natasha Weaver is entering her ninety-second minute in front of the Transport Committee, a group of MPs who are in charge of holding the government to account over their running of the transport network. The room is sweltering – the ancient heating system in the Commons is on the blink yet again – and many of the Committee members are looking like they could do with a good snooze. Weaver knows that to everyone following proceedings on BBC Parliament, this looks like any other dry, procedural grilling. For her, though, nothing could be further from the truth.

'So, Secretary of State, can we move on to your involvement in the Dubois rail link contract?' the Chairman says, shuffling his papers.

Weaver crosses her legs under the desk, struggling to find a comfortable position, and thinks back to the conversation she had earlier with the Permanent Secretary – the most senior official – of her department:

'Look what I've got . . .'

'What on earth is that?'

'A special vibrating egg. It goes,' she had pointed suggestively up her pencil skirt, 'there. It's remote controlled, so you can keep me focused.'

'Hm . . .' He'd licked his lips. 'This'll be fun later.'

'Later? Let's do it now!'

'Are you mad? We're both in front of this Committee.'

'I think it will be sexy . . . and nobody will know! Come on, imagine the thrill . . .'

What a stupid fucking idea, she thinks. Sexy, indeed. She's practically foaming at the mouth with discomfort and can't seem to signal to her fellow attendee that he needs to stop. Weaver wonders whether it's possible to suffer dehydration this way.

'Of course, although as you know transport is not part of my brief,' she shifts again in her seat, 'and though I've been happy to come before you today in these special circumstances while a new Transport Secretary is appointed, I really must leave soon.'

'Indeed, but with such an important piece of the economy under your purview, you must have a view on how these kinds of contracts are being run . . . '

The Committee Chairman looks at her intently. Weaver wonders how he does it. He's chaired this Committee for years, never failing to tug at a thread until he gets the full story. Well into his seventies and fully alert in the afternoon heat.

It helps, she supposes, that he doesn't have a gentle electric shock to his balls every few minutes.

As Weaver turns the page to the right section in her folder the egg buzzes again. She crosses her legs back the other way, sweat trickling down her chest into her bra. Vibrating eggs aside, she really wants to be on her phone, getting updates on the PM's confidence vote. The whole thing is torturous.

'Well, fire away.' She tries to look relaxed and focused, aware that she could wring her knickers out into a bucket. What a day to wear a pale grey skirt.

Across Westminster, journalists can't help but remark on what a lightweight Weaver seems to be, reading most of her answers verbatim from a prepared document by her team and struggling to think on her feet for the few follow-up questions she's asked. Thankfully her Permanent Secretary is appearing alongside her, deftly answering questions she botches, building on points she makes poorly. He is rather enjoying himself, entirely aware of how uncomfortable his Secretary of State is and ruminating the hypocrisy of gleefully telling journalists about the public earful she gives civil servants about how lazy and group-think their work is, while happily accepting a private mouthful from her most senior official.

'Okay, any final questions for the minister?' asks the Chairman eventually.

The vibrating in her seat echoes each 'no, thank you for your time' as the Chairman goes around each Committee member in turn. Weaver tries valiantly to smile at each one in silence, but thinks she probably looks like she's having a series of mini strokes.

As she rises gingerly from her seat she prays she doesn't leave a stain and, as she makes her way back to her office, she hopes the gusset of her tights will prevent her from laying a literal egg in the middle of the Committee Room Corridor.

Portcullis House

'All right, chaps,' intones Jackson, his rat-like eyes glistening. The packed room of excited MPs quietens down. 'Remember we can't botch this. We need over fifty per cent of the vote or she can hang on for another year. The ballot closes at 3 p.m. so we have,' he glances at the clock on the wall, 'just under two hours for a final push.'

'Let's 'ave it!' someone bellows from the crammed sofa. There is an appreciative roar. These MPs have been waiting months for a breakthrough moment like this, languishing on the back benches feeling bored and plotting fruitlessly. Finally they can act.

'Don't you bloody *dare*,' Jackson snaps. 'Be calm. Be reasonable. It is reluctant head over heart stuff, to the media and

181

to colleagues. We'll unleash you on them, my rabid, filthy dogs, in the leadership contest!' The room explodes with howls and barks.

Once they've left, Daly lingers behind. 'Any, uh, updates on what Eric might give me?'

Jackson sighs. 'No, Simon. And you've got to stop asking. It's a nuisance for me and it just stresses him out.'

'Okay, okay,' Daly sulks. 'But I don't know why I can't just have a chat with him about it directly. I was his best man, you know!'

Jackson shrugs. 'I really don't care how far back you posh boys go. Just give him a bit of space, okay?'

Daly saunters out of the room, nearly knocking over a cleaner while he looks at his phone, wondering how he can get past this new gatekeeper to Courtenay. Perhaps he can have a drink with Clarissa.

Downing Street

Eva sits down heavily and puts her head between her knees, the blood pulsing in her ears.

The door bursts open.

'Right. It's happening in fifteen minutes. Eva, can you help me?' Tim rushes in, followed by Peter.

'What's happening?' she stammers.

'She's going to resign. Statement in the street. Peter – dash out some words. My team is sorting media. Events and Visits are getting the lectern ready.'

'What? Why? I thought we were fighting it,' Eva asks, feeling like she's been punched in the stomach.

Peter grips her shoulders, looking shattered. 'Look – we've been strategising all weekend. But what else is there for her to do? She placed her Whip behind a rotter. We've been with the Chief just now after the ring-round. There's no way she wins this vote. Why not jump before you're pushed?'

Tim beckons Eva into the corridor.

'Eva, my dear, I have a special job for you ...'

Eva follows him, as though in a daze. Months of speculation, then clutching victory from the jaws of defeat in the China vote, and now the wobble has arrived.

'The PM has asked for you to go up to the flat,' he murmurs.

'Me? Why?'

'I dunno. Maybe help pick out an outfit? Look, I just don't have time for this,' Tim says before she can protest. 'She's asked for you specifically. Just do it, okay?'

'Okay.'

'Everyone,' shouts Tim, 'we regroup in ten minutes. Peter – Leonard wants to go over the words before then. I don't want a syllable of this leaking out. For the next half hour Downing Street is officially sponsored by TENA Lady.'

Eva climbs the stairs of Number Eleven, above the Chancellor's study, and cautiously rings the doorbell, her heart hammering. She hasn't been in the Prime Minister's flat since the day she'd moved out with her mother, a few days before her father.

'Yes?' a tinny voice says through the speaker.

'Um, it's Eva Cross. I was sent by Tim ...?' The door buzzes and she pushes it open.

Eva walks into the familiar light-filled hallway, decorated with a large rug, a mahogany sideboard and an enormous bunch of lilies. She can hear voices upstairs so stands awkwardly next to the lilies, trying not to look at the personal cards and photographs dotted around.

'Hello, Eva,' the PM's husband says as he trots down the stairs.

'Hi. I'm so sorry to interrupt. Tim asked me to come up.'

'Ah yes, thanks.' He smiles kindly at her. God, he looks tired, Eva thinks. What do you say at a time like this? Eva decides to just stay quiet.

Presently there's a sound on the stairs and the Prime Minister appears in a powder-blue trouser suit. She is wearing bright red, almost orange, lipstick and has slicked her hair back off her face. Compared to her usual volumised, hair-sprayed bob – the epitome of competence and modesty – she looks sleek and defiant.

Eva gapes, open-mouthed.

'What do you think?' the Prime Minister asks her.

'You look ... I can't really describe it. It's amazing! Kind of ... punk.'

The PM laughs. 'Well, I wasn't expecting that.'

'No – it's a good thing! They'll be expecting you to ...'

'Crawl out with my head bowed?' offers the PM. 'I just wish I could get away with wearing sunglasses. What a day.'

They stand in silence, the PM digging her fingernails into her palms. Her departure had to come eventually but why like this? For a couple of precious days she had thought she was safe. Before she can dwell further, she hears panting from the next-door room.

'Ah, yes. You must wonder why we've asked you up. There is something we hoped you'd do for us.' They walk into the kitchen where Dennis stands in the middle of the room, sniffing the air.

The PM squats down beside him and lets him smell her hand.

'Do you mind sitting with Dennis while we're downstairs? I'm so sorry to ask you but we worry about him being alone.'

'Of course!' Eva copies her boss and lets Dennis work out who she is. He licks her hand.

'Thank you so much. We'll put the TV on so you can watch, if you like.' The PM rubs her dog's ears between her fingers, like she's feeling a fine velvet.

'Right, are you ready, love?' her husband asks.

'Let's go.' The PM straightens up and heads downstairs, ready to read her resignation statement one last time – she'd jotted it down early that morning, sensing the game was up – before delivering it to the nation.

Eva and Dennis settle down on the floor together. Bright red ticker tape runs along the bottom of the TV screen, under a live feed of an empty lectern in the middle of the street: *Prime Minister Madeleine Ford expected to resign. Downing Street statement shortly.* Eva can't believe it's really happening. The Prime Minister is resigning. And here Eva is – in the inner sanctum at last – watching history unfold with a blind dog and the television's burbling punditry for company.

She looks around the room wonderingly. Against a sophisticated, muted palette of pale greys and silvers pop the bright colours of cookery books and jewel-coloured kitchen appliances. Everything is homely and ordered. On the mantelpiece are a mixture of colour and sepia photographs: Michael watching on proudly as the PM makes a speech in the street on her first day in office; Dennis playing with the Queen's corgis at Balmoral; the Fords on their wedding day, standing in the archway of the church door.

Dappled light from the spring day outside gives the whole scene a strange, dream-like quality. Eva feels surrounded by memories that she has tried to force down. After all, this was her home at one time. Although it could hardly have been described as homely and ordered back then – and not just because of her mother's interior design choices, where absolutely everything was white. All that time spent thinking about her parents' arguing and how fat her thighs were. It had never occurred to her that she slept beneath her One Direction posters in the seat of power. Maybe that was a good thing. A normal teenage life. Eva thinks of the time the plain clothes detectives hustled her father out of her school play after some misunderstanding over a fake gun. Maybe not so normal.

The TV interrupts her thoughts: 'And here comes the Prime Minister.' Eva wraps her arms around Dennis, who nuzzles reassuringly into her cheek.

The Fords step out of the front door. The PM's husband stands respectfully to one side as the Prime Minister walks to the lectern, rolls her shoulders back and stares down the camera lens. Eva thinks of her father doing the exact same thing when he resigned. Bizarre that it feels so very surreal, yet also very familiar.

Portcullis House

Clarissa Courtenay arches her back against the leather sofa in her husband's Parliamentary office but doesn't take her eyes off the TV screen. She hasn't felt this satisfied in ages. She grudgingly has to admit that the PM looks good – all traces of the awkward Hillary Clinton head girl have disappeared. Clarissa had expected to see a resigned, frigid victim mope out of the front door. She clearly underestimated this woman. *I'm more humble in victory than I thought*, she smiles to herself.

Clarissa watches the PM's neon lips mouth *my resignation*. Maybe I should look at a colour like that for when I stand outside on Eric's first day, Clarissa thinks. It really pops against the black bricks of Downing Street. A shiver of delight runs through her as she casts her eye at the emerald green Catherine Walker coat hanging on the back of the door. Clarissa needs to change into it soon to stand dutifully beside Courtenay as he announces his intention to run in the leadership contest. She gasps at the thought.

'You like that, baby?' asks Courtenay, raising his head from between her thighs.

Frowning, Clarissa wordlessly pushes him back down. He needs to wear a little less product in his hair, she thinks, rubbing her fingers together. In fact, maybe he should have a fresh cut this evening. A new look altogether for the contest.

As the familiar door closes behind the Fords the BBC news presenter announces, 'So there we have it: Prime Minister Madeleine Ford has resigned. As one senior Tory said to me just moments ago – the race is on.'

Clarissa finally closes her eyes. 'I'm so close,' she murmurs.

Courtenay speeds up in response, moaning. Clarissa opens one eye in annoyance. As usual her husband can only see what is immediately in front of his nose. She glances again at the green coat, leans back and orgasms.

16th April

Burma Road, Houses of Parliament

Jess is the first to arrive at the cramped room she shares with Ed, George and Mike. After glancing at the morning bulletins she strolls around the lobby area to get her bearings. Lots of little rooms and, from the men's shower room at least (where she dubiously eyes a single very sad-looking grey towel), a rather damp, teenage boy smell.

Eventually Jess reaches the women's bathroom – it's so far away from the action she can't help but think what an afterthought it clearly is – and sits down in a stall.

'Um, excuse me?' a small voice says.

'Hello?'

'Oh, thank God,' the voice says. 'Do you have a spare tampon on you?'

'Sure.' Jess slides it under the partition.

She's washing her hands when a young woman comes out of her cubicle, dressed in a hot pink blazer dress.

'Thank you so much – you're my saviour,' she says, puffing out her cheeks. 'I wasn't sure there were any other women around here.'

'So you're new too?'

'Just temporary. I'm Camilla Baxter. From *Blush* magazine. I'm not really allowed up here. Can't get lobby accreditation. But I met a nice guy in the coffee queue downstairs who said I should just come up here and introduce myself. See how it all works. I'm doing a few pieces on the leadership contest, as we're keen to get more politics into our features. I tell you what, though, I'm going to bid for a style section. Did you see Madeleine Ford's speech?' Jess nods. 'Never been that fussed about her to be honest, but if she'd been looking like she did yesterday for the last few years I'd have paid a bit more attention. Speaking of which, you don't think this is a bit much, do you? My boyfriend called me "Legislatively Blonde" this morning.'

'No, I like it. There are some stylish women around. Have you seen Eric Courtenay's wife?'

'Yeah, good skin. I wonder how she gets that glow ... And she'll be in full Jackie O campaign mode as well. Still, plenty of fashion victims around too. Not keen on Natasha Weaver's body con efforts. Well, this is turning out to be quite the meet cute, isn't it?'

'I suppose it is.'

'So what do you do?'

'I'm the new junior lobby hack for the *Sentinel*.'

Camilla whistles. 'So I could be meeting a young Rebekah Brooks? Perhaps I should write something about the other women in Westminster too. Could do a fun profile on people like you ...' She thoughtfully dabs gloss onto her lips.

They walk back along the corridor, Camilla regaling Jess with stories about which stars are having affairs or have undergone plastic surgery. When they reach Jess's room, she reluctantly waves Camilla off and wonders how vain it is to be secretly delighted at the idea of a profile piece on her in *Blush*.

'Made it in before lunchtime today, then?' Ed mutters. She ignores him. Ed feels a stab of annoyance at her refusal to bite. She seems to have perfected the art of sending him suggestive messages out of office hours and then maintaining a blank professionalism in person. He can't resist fishing, though. 'So ... really no more motorbike?'

Jess remains fixed on her computer screen. 'It isn't really worth the trouble of parking it round here. I'm only a fifteen-minute walk away.'

'Pity.'

'Why's that?'

'I liked the leathers.' Ed bites his lip.

'Well, it was your suggestion to leave it at home ... ' Jess says disinterestedly.

Ed is saved by George and Mike charging in, dropping their bags and spilling coffee.

'Ooh, have you seen the new girl?' pants George.

'In the pink dress?' Mike gushes.

'Camilla? Yeah, she's nice,' Jess says.

'She may be nice, but I'd like her to be very nasty to me indeed. Woof!' crows George.

'Come on, get a grip of yourself. She's only here for a few weeks to write features for *Blush*.'

Mike shouts 'I'll make her *blush*!' He and George snigger.

Jess turns to Ed imploringly.

'Cha-aps. You're just over-stimulated by everything going on. Settle down,' Ed says lazily, then his eye catches a flash of bright pink as Camilla walks past. 'Jesus. What's she writing about?'

Jess can't dismiss the little pinch of jealousy. So much for liking leathers.

'She's doing some stuff about the leadership contest. Has quite a cool idea to do a style section. You know, what the candidates and spouses wear ... She got the idea from Madeleine Ford yesterday. All it had taken was one haircut – and a complete change of attitude, I guess – to make a voter take notice of the person who has been her Prime Minister for the last few years.'

'So?' Ed is quickly losing interest. Jess can see George and Mike winking at each other.

'So, putting aside the fact that women in the public eye come under an insane amount of scrutiny based on their image alone,' Jess tries to stop her voice from rising, 'there will be a lot of political reinvention over the next few weeks. People make snap decisions about whether they like a person based on a couple of seconds of footage. Their hair, their clothes, their voice. They'll all be hoping to roll out the JFK effect in the TV debates.'

'Jess, we aren't going to do a cosy sit-down with Madeleine Ford about her hair,' Ed sighs.

'I'm not saying we should. I'm not saying we need to write anything off the back of this at all. I'm just saying it'll be interesting to see what they do, with image consultants and stuff.'

'Jess,' George teases, 'you should get the inside track on all the candidates' diets.'

'Yeah, I hear Nat Weaver is on an all-sausage regime!' Mike laughs.

Jess instinctively balls her hands into fists. Stay calm, she says to herself. Pretend you think it's funny. She forces a smile.

'Now now, boys,' drawls Ed, 'no locker room talk in the office.'

Thank God, Jess thinks. She'd much rather the boss tell

them off for being misogynistic than her. I don't want them to think I'm a kill-joy, she reluctantly admits to herself. So much for changing the culture from the inside. But these guys aren't going to change tack because a junior hack is nipping at them.

'Ah, I see,' George says seriously, jerking his thumb at Jess. 'That time of the month?'

Jess sees red. She picks up the nearest thing to her – a mug – and prepares to hurl it at George's head. But before the three men notice what she's doing, the door opens and Teddy Hammer saunters in.

Jess slides the mug back onto her desk.

'Very loud in here. What kind of zoo do you run, Ed?'

'Sorry to disturb you, Teddy.'

'Well, keep it down, you little turds,' Teddy points his stick from George to Mike, 'or I'll see to it that you're banned from the press gallery.'

Jess, her face still flushed, smiles at Teddy and tries to slow her breathing down.

'Now, my dear, have you got plans for tomorrow evening?' Teddy says kindly.

'No, I don't.'

'Well, you do now. You're going to join me for dinner with the Defence Secretary. It's about time someone took you under their wing,' he mutters at the back of Ed's head.

Bellamy's, Mayfair

Eva takes a sip of mineral water and glances around the restaurant, thinking that she's probably brought the average age of the patrons down by thirty years. It feels naughty to be out for a proper lunch on a Tuesday, but now that the PM has resigned the SpAds are on a pretty long leash. Normally she'd be irritated by her father's lateness – she's worked her way through plenty of bread baskets in her time, waiting for him – but she's glad to have the time to think about what's next. Finally, Percy's plain clothes officers enter and give her a little wave.

'He's just popped to the loo. Sorry we're late, but … well, you'll see.' They grin then take up their positions at a nearby table.

Eva wonders what is going on. Then the diners around her go quiet, many with laden forks hanging midway on the journey to their mouths. She turns to see what they're staring at.

Percy shuffles towards her with his usual clumsy gait. He is wearing a floral patterned shirt – with at least two more buttons undone than is strictly necessary, showing great tufts of grey chest hair – a trilby hat, and … Eva gasps.

'Hello, pork chop.' Percy kisses her on the cheek.

'Dad … are those skinny jeans?' They are of the palest bleached denim and cling painfully to his legs, outlining his slightly cow-hocked posture.

'Yes.' Percy winces when the waistband digs into him as he sits down. 'What do you think?'

'Well, they're very … distressed, aren't they.'

'Holly says they're my dream jeans. When I'm down to my dream weight they'll fit me.'

'Well, they'll never fit at Bellamy's, Dad.'

Percy chuckles and has a long drink of water. With his head tipped back, his face catches the sunlight coming in through the window. Then she recognises the dog-biscuity smell.

'Bloody hell, Dad, have you had a spray tan?' Eva gasps again.

Eva is aware of the two officers struggling to hold a silent, straightfaced posture. She looks back at her father, who smiles awkwardly and nods.

'My God … with the teeth, too. Did you swim in a pool of the stuff? Are you … Dad, are you having a breakdown?' Eva asks, hoping she sounds gentle. As ever, she is fighting her concern and love for him with a deep rage that countless therapy sessions have failed to resolve. She'd come here for his help, not to offer hers.

Percy laughs again.

'Look, obviously I'm with a younger woman. I don't want her to think she's with some dreadful old fart. I've just . . . given the old chassis a new paint job.'

'Several coats, by the look of it.'

A waiter arrives to take their order. Eva is flabbergasted when her father orders a salad, followed by fish and steamed vegetables. He even declines potatoes. Eva raises her eyebrows at him.

'Oh, well . . . Holly is helping me with a bit of a diet—'

'Da-ad, why are you trying to change so much for this woman? It isn't healthy.'

'Oh no, you don't understand. I mean,' he points at his face, 'this was all my idea. But everything else, well . . . my ticker isn't what it used to be. Nor my cholesterol. I wasn't looking after myself before. But Holly . . . Holly really takes care of me.'

Eva thinks again about Percy's previous girlfriends. As with love, there has never been any talk of health before.

'But you can go on a diet any time you like, Dad.'

'Yes, I'm sure I can. But I've never wanted to before. Think how many times your mother tried. If anything, it made me swing the other way.'

Percy grimaces, pumpkin-like with his bright white teeth in his orange head.

'Eating and drinking is what we've always done together. What are we going to do now?'

'Well . . . Holly doesn't need to know if I cheat a little. Perhaps we could share pudding . . . ?'

The starters arrive.

'So you see,' continues Percy, forking up salad and looking doubtfully at it, 'Holly is a very good influence.'

Eva shrugs and offers him a chip. Percy pretends to hide behind his napkin in fright.

'Apart from the jeans.'

'Yes, the jeans are not ideal. So anyway, you've dragged me away from research on poor Wellie. What did you want to talk about?'

Eva stops herself just in time from rolling her eyes. Her father has been working on a biography of Wellington for as long as she can remember, the thing he returns to when he wants some peace. It was due with his publisher years ago but a great distraction always comes along and he gets sidetracked. What with all his beauty appointments, Eva suspects 'poor Wellie', as they've come to call the work, is about to be neglected again.

'Well, I want to chew over what I do next. I have a bit of time as the PM remains PM until a new leader is elected—'

'Not for me, of course,' cuts in Percy, waving his fork at her. 'Your poor old man was in too much hot water so the Deputy PM had to hold down the fort for that period.'

'Yes, I remember.'

'Still models himself as an ex-PM, you know. On the speaking circuit. As if being a caretaker for a few weeks counts. Sounds like he wipes old people's arses.' He stabs decisively at his plate. 'Still – being PM was all he wanted. So I guess he technically got there ...'

'Anyway,' Eva tries to get things back on track, 'assuming the leadership contest takes the standard amount of time, I have until the summer to find something else to do. But I want to stay in government.'

'Why do you want to work in politics at all? You certainly didn't enjoy *my* career. Crikey, don't you remember when you joined the Lib Dems on the day of my last Party Conference speech?'

'Well, that was just to annoy you. And maybe get you to pay

attention to me for once. But politics . . . ' Eva struggles for an answer. She's never really thought about it. She's just done it. 'I think it's interesting. And kind of . . . fun?'

Percy looks at her intently. He knows this world so much better than her. 'Fun' is what silly novices, intrigued by feeling like an insider and going to the right parties and having the right gossip, describe politics as.

'You know, I was once a power vampire, playing the game and constantly on the hunt. But it's fruitless. And damaging. The system corrupts, pork chop.'

Eva reflects. It was certainly true that, after all the drama had died down, her father's contentment and happiness crept up after leaving Number Ten. It was like a decades-long spell he'd been under had broken. Of course, it had also signalled the breakup of his marriage. What has never been revealed to Eva is that Percy's relationship with Jenny had pretty well hung off his ambition to be Prime Minister. Right from the moment they'd met at a literary festival, where she had interviewed him, they had formed a partnership. Jenny had been what Percy called an 'ice-breaker' – skilled at both making an instant connection with people at parties but also at forging unexpected new friendships and contacts (notably rock stars and artists once in Downing Street), like an Arctic exploration ship. Jenny's ability to create exclusive salons of politicos and creatives, coupled with Percy's natural charisma and stewardship of debates about ideas, made them popular, cool and unstoppable. But power, coupled with the nagging realisation that everything he'd scrapped to achieve, to make his family proud and enemies jealous, resulted in hard, boring, stressful work that he wasn't very good at, made Percy's ingrained need for affection get the better of him. One night in Washington – Jenny couldn't accompany him on every trip – the dam burst.

Percy has often wondered if his deluge of affairs was

deliberate self-sabotage. Backlash in the media about bad decisions (quite aside from his general gaffes) on education, health and foreign affairs coupled with in-depth polling on the specifics about why vast swathes of the public hated him eroded Percy's confidence and sent him searching for comfort in the wrong places – again and again. When it all came to light, Jenny had limited sympathy. She had committed time and energy and her own career into Percy's achievements, and public humiliation was not part of the deal. The rest, as they say, is history.

'I see what you're saying, Dad. But I just want to keep going, just a little longer. There's an itch I need to scratch.'

'Well, be careful – you can scratch down to the bone before you know it.' Percy takes a sip of water. 'So, it sounds like you need to find a way to stick around. How about joining one of the campaigns?'

'But you wrote an op-ed this morning saying that all the prospective contenders are "clots and bores"!'

'And I stand by that; they generally always are. But I'll give you exclusive advice that the readers of the *Telegraph* aren't party to: grab onto one of the candidates' coat tails and see where it takes you.'

'Dad, I'd like to work for someone I believe in. And who values what I do and who, well . . . I respect.'

'Oh Eva, this isn't the bloody *West Wing*. Real life isn't scripted. Can you imagine if my team had thought "Let Percy be Percy"? It would have been a nightmare of random decisions and u-turns – well, even more of a nightmare. None of these guys believe in anything and none of them will think they owe you anything. You'll be chewed up and spat out either way, so it's actually better to not really care about your principal. Take it from me: you can't have scruples in this world. Pick a horse and back it. Even if you lose, it will be a lot of fun.'

'But I don't want to lose!' Eva snaps. Her father looks at her carefully, recognising the familiar desire to win.

'Well,' Percy sighs, 'it's pretty obvious that Eric Courtenay will get it, despite being someone without ideas or management skills. He's got a very clever wife, who knows all the media proprietors and editors. And that psycho Nigel Jackson is running the whipping operation. He's the obvious one to help.'

Eva frowns. She's been in a desperate fight against that team for months, as they've lobbed countless grenades over the Downing Street gates to dislodge the PM. She thinks of Bobby's words from a few days ago: *You just find a new host?* Perhaps she really is little more than a parasite, moving onto the next viable life source, shedding her principles in the process.

Portcullis House

'Oh, I can't stomach any more of this waiting around. It's five o'clock so nothing's going to happen now. We'll find out our marching orders from Simon and George tomorrow. Bobby, will you come for a drink?' Millie pokes her head round the door.

Bobby shrugs. She emptied her inbox half an hour ago and is waiting for Daly to appear so she can sit him down and talk about the unit closure. He lets Bobby tag along to coffee with journalists and lunchtime receptions in Parliament, but every time she brings up the ideas she has for the unit, Daly disappears like a submarine. He and Sackler have been holed up with the rest of the Courtenay team at a hotel suite in Victoria, laying the foundations for their campaign.

'Sure. The Red Lion? Two Chairmen?'

'Oh Lord, no. I need a proper drink. Let's go to the Corinthia for a cocktail.'

Bobby bites her lip. She can barely afford a glass of orange juice.

Millie brandishes Sackler's wallet. 'My treat.'

Fifteen minutes later, two elegant martini glasses and a bowl of smoked almonds in front of them, they settle into easy conversation. Millie isn't quite as buoyant as usual, but still manages to have the barman gawping at her when she orders.

'So are you enjoying your new life down here so far?' Millie takes a long sip of her new drink and stifles a little burp.

'I am,' Bobby nods. 'Simon is being really generous about taking me to stuff with him. It saves a lot of time on meeting people and understanding how things work. I've not made much progress on the unit, though ...'

'Well, Simon owes you – not least for the wonders you must be doing for his rep. He probably even feels better about the thinning patch on top of his head. Anyway, he's promised you help and this contest is ideal to activate that.' Millie indicates to the barman that they'll take two more drinks. Bobby, still halfway through her first, wonders at Millie's directness about her lover.

'Still, I wish I had some more policy ideas for the campaign.'

'You know who you need to meet?' Millie plonks her empty glass down. 'Jake Albury.'

'I keep hearing about him,' Bobby says, wondering what this mysterious guy looks like. She has secretly Googled him but there are no social media accounts, no photos. Just a load of policy papers he has written over the years. Bobby is getting increasingly curious about him.

'Oh, he's got a lot of buzz around him. He was the planning guy at Number Ten, but he's just agreed to run policy for Eric's leadership bid. Super smart.'

'Why is he so important to me?'

'You silly doughnut. He's going to be in charge of laying out what Eric would do in government and then put it into practice when he wins, if all goes well. If you get Jake on side with protecting mental health units then it's job done.'

Bobby frowns.

'Here, I'm going to text George now to set up a coffee for you.' Millie taps away on her phone, always confident that fixing the right people up is what gets things done. She should charge commission.

'Thanks!' Bobby gets a little rush. It's only a meeting, but she can't help but feel her hopes rise. She's itching for some progress. Plus Eva's description of Jake has intrigued her. 'How can I repay you?'

'Drink with me,' Millie sighs. She slumps down in her chair.

'Are you ... okay?' asks Bobby gently.

'Not really,' Millie slurs slightly as she drains her glass. Bobby takes a great gulp of her own drink. It hits the back of her throat like a punch and makes her eyes water.

'So what's wrong?'

'Oh, man troubles.'

'Oh ...' Bobby isn't sure what to say so just takes Millie's hand in her own.

Millie gives her a doleful look.

'So ... well, I'd heard that perhaps you and Simon were ...'

'Alas, not any more. As of today,' Millie says, her voice wobbling.

'I'm so sorry, Millie. I think. I mean ... What happened?'

Millie steals a sip from Bobby's untouched second glass.

'It all started after George and I decided to have a third child. We aren't blessed with cash, but we thought we could manage a third. We had always wanted lots of children. Anyway, it turned out to be twins! We decided we didn't need any more accidents – though a wonderful accident, of course – so George said he'd get a vasectomy. They're reversible, you see, and perhaps one day we'd win the lottery and ... *anyway*, there's an absolutely tiny, tiny,' Millie squints her eyes down to minute pinpricks, 'chance that something can go wrong. And it did. Poor George is impotent now.'

Bobby gapes.

'Yup,' Millie says, surveying Bobby's glass and finally just sliding it over in front of herself.

'But where does Simon come into all this?'

'Ah, right. So, George – sweet man that he is – was very concerned about my ... womanly needs. He suggested I have what he calls "boyfriends".'

Bobby pauses the conversation to order a third round, feeling it's necessary.

'Where was I ... yes. Boyfriends. We have ground rules, though. He can veto anybody. And we have such a giggle talking about things on the long car journeys to and from the constituency. In a way it has brought us closer together. George is ...' Millie searches for the words and finally shrugs, 'kind.'

'I'm still at a bit of a loss about Simon. Aren't they best friends?'

'Oh, right. Yes. They are. So we approached Simon about it and he agreed.'

'But what about his wife?'

'How would I know? Good luck to them. George and I made a decision early on that it was for other people to be honest with their wives about their arrangement with us. In fact, married men with something to lose were the people we really felt we could count on for discretion. So I don't think Susie has any idea at all. At least, she's certainly never said anything to me about it. As I said when we first met, she has her own problems ...' Millie gratefully takes a slug of her fresh glass.

'Well, it all sounds ... like it was going fine. What happened today?' asks Bobby, taking a sip of her drink too. She is starting to feel light-headed and is amazed that Millie is still upright.

'Simon gave me the bullet. After being talked into resigning for no reason, he thinks he's owed a big job if Eric wins and he's worried about media scrutiny. Maybe he thinks Susie is getting a whiff of what's going on . . . whatever the reason, it's finito.'

Bobby reflects that everybody seems to owe someone something in SW1.

'Millie, I'm sorry you're upset about it. Think about it this way, though: this isn't really about you. He's obviously got his own reasons for wanting to end things. You're lovely and beautiful and funny. And he's ambitious. And, you know . . . your husband is his best friend. Maybe it all got a bit weird for him?'

'Yes,' Millie hiccups. 'That's true. Maybe he needs to conserve his juices for his baby-making.'

Bobby is grateful her mouth is full of almonds.

'You've made me feel so much better,' Millie beams at Bobby, her eyes unfocused. The thought enters her head that the Courtenay stuff is rubbish and Daly has in fact decided to upgrade to a younger model, like the one sitting in front of her now. She feels like the Marquise de Merteuil from *Les Liaisons Dangereuses*, still beautiful but no match for sodding Michelle Pfeiffer. 'I'm going to go home and give George a big sloppy kiss.' She picks up her handbag.

'Well . . . he sounds like he deserves it.'

'Oh, he does. You,' Millie suddenly looks at Bobby with perfect focus and lucidity, 'you won't say anything to anybody, will you?'

'I promise I won't,' Bobby replies, looking earnestly at her. Then she grins. 'I can't imagine anyone would believe me, even if I did tell.'

'It's quite extraordinary, isn't it?' Millie falls against the bar, trying to get her arm inside her coat.

'Truly.' Bobby, not very steady herself, takes Millie's arm and guides her to the door.

As they wait for the doorman to hail Millie a cab, Bobby turns to her.

'You know, I think it's pretty cool, what you and George are doing. I don't know much about this sort of thing. But you've been presented with a problem and you've found a solution. You're . . . you're getting yours, uh, girl.' She opens the cab door.

Millie falls inside onto her hands and knees, her skirt hitched up and a shoe falling into the gutter. Through shouts of laughter, she manages to crawl into the seat and pull the door closed.

'Oh yes,' she hoots through the open window as the cab pulls away, 'I am the very picture of a modern major feminist!'

17th April

Portcullis House

The following morning, Bobby, Millie and Lucy squeeze themselves onto a windowsill to listen to the first meeting of the Courtenay leadership campaign. As predicted by Lucy, Daly and Sackler's shared office is being used as HQ for the Parliamentary whipping part of the campaign, while policy and media work will take place in the Courtenays' Notting Hill home. This arrangement will last as long as it takes to whittle down the dozen or so contenders to two, which could take days or weeks. There will be a ballot of the Parliamentary Party every Tuesday and Thursday and candidates who don't get enough support from their colleagues will have to drop out. Once the final two are chosen, the campaign moves to the 100,000 or so Conservative Party members across the country for several weeks. The public will be heading into September with a new Prime Minister.

Last night, Courtenay confirmed his decision to stand in

the race with a beautifully made video on Twitter, packed full of black and white photos from when he was in the Army. The camera loves him. It also seems the microphone loves him too, as his voice sounds deep and honeyed as he reads the carefully prepared script about leadership, vision and passion. The whole thing, including his strong message about his personal values of integrity and honour and his focus on standards in public life – 'I'm not going to do things like they've been done before. It's time to sterilise with sunlight' – has gone down very well online and with MPs, who have gratefully jumped on the message to push at their constituents as proof that the Conservative Party still has some good chaps in their ranks.

The office is so full of jostling MPs, their eyes alert and their grins maniacal, that the room resembles a clown car.

'Okay, so we have our runners and riders,' Jackson, who is leading what he calls the 'MP love-bombing campaign', announces. The room quietens down. 'Richard Hendrick.' The room erupts into boos.

'Natasha Weaver.' More boos, plus a few cat calls.

'Dev Singh.' Muted chatter.

'Gosh, he's very young to be standing,' Lucy whispers. 'He's jolly good, though. He was the guy on *Question Time* last week. You must have seen the clips – the audience loved him.'

'Mark Norman.' Exaggerated yawns.

'He's the Defence Secretary. He's all right but a bit of a bore. Sits well with the right wing of the Party, though,' Millie mutters on Bobby's other side.

Jackson reads out another half a dozen names. Most trigger the same boos from the group. A couple elicit shouts of laughter.

' . . . and the future Prime Minister of the United Kingdom of Great Britain and Northern Ireland: Eric Courtenay!' The MPs stamp their feet and hammer their fists on the desks.

Bobby glances across at Courtenay. He looks as handsome

as ever, but she notices a muscle tick in his cheek. His wife stands next to him, the picture of serenity. Their eyes meet for a moment and Bobby gives her a small smile. Clarissa looks through Bobby like she doesn't exist.

'What are you doing tonight?' Millie asks Bobby.

'She has a date!' hisses Lucy.

Bobby nods. 'I decided to join one of those apps. You know, to get out there a bit. So I'm going for a drink with someone.'

'Oh to be young again,' sighs Lucy. 'Just the one man for us forever now, Mills ... I never got to try the apps.'

'Yeah ... me neither. We'll have to live vicariously through this one.' Millie gives Bobby a meaningful look.

'I'll tell you everything. It can be our secret.'

Millie smiles.

Once the meeting is over, Courtenay is whisked off by Jackson and Daly to the Members' Tea Room (a sort of common room for MPs) to kick off their charm offensive.

' ... a-and the thing is, I really believe that passion is more important than experience. Leadership is ...' Courtenay is struggling with an ex-Cabinet minister, who was a couple of years above him at Eton and looks as though he still considers Courtenay to be the same old squirt.

Jackson artfully slides over and takes Courtenay's elbow.

'Eric, can I borrow you a second? Good to see you, David ...' He presents Courtenay to a new group of younger MPs.

' ... vision is so important, don't you think? And passion ... leadership ...'

Wherever Jackson takes Courtenay, the man panics and trots out random snippets of his launch video. When MPs ask him questions on policy positions or problems in their patches, Courtenay has to be rescued by Jackson or Daly, fobbing the person off with 'Oh, we'll be announcing all that in due course' or 'Will you come and see me after this? Sounds like this needs a proper conversation and we're running late for something.'

It doesn't help that Mark Norman, the Defence Secretary, is working the room like a pro. He might be dull, but he has clearly done his homework and is experienced. Whatever each MP needs to personally get re-elected, Norman knows about it: junctions, station platforms, A-roads, hospital expansions. Even his launch video, which has been ridiculed by young media types on Twitter, has struck a chord with his colleagues. Clearly taken on an iPhone, Norman does a simple piece to camera, reeling off his experience as a businessman before Parliament and his delivery record as a minister. He comes off as a very safe pair of hands.

Jackson, aware that presenting the contrast of his man with Norman for all to see is a mistake, quickly hustles Courtenay away from another valiant effort at conversation:

'Well, I'm the anti-sleaze candidate . . . play with a straight bat . . . sterilise with sunlight . . .'

It doesn't occur to him that the MP he's speaking to is currently being investigated by HMRC for fraud.

As they head down the corridor, Jackson puts an arm around Courtenay's shoulders. 'Well done, mate, but when you talk about being passionate, maybe don't sound like you've just been neutered . . .'

Claybourne Terrace

'I can't believe both of you are out tonight.' Eva is lying on her stomach on Jess's bed, her chin propped on her fists. 'Holly is making dinner for me and Dad. She called it a "family night in".'

'Cute. Bit of a muddle if you both call him "Daddy",

207

though.' Jess, dressed in black silk trousers, a black polo neck and towering suede heels, kneels on the floor and begins applying eyeliner in front of the mirror. She is having dinner tonight with Teddy Hammer and Mark Norman, the Defence Secretary.

Eva screams into the duvet.

'I think she's pretty nice, you know. I mean in the vast universe of women your dad has dated . . . ' Jess raises an eyebrow.

'I won't be out for long. It's only a drink,' Bobby breathes, zipping up her jeans over an orange silk halterneck. 'Can I borrow those gold earrings?'

'Sure,' Eva stretches out, 'they're by my sink.'

Once she hears Bobby on the stairs, Eva whispers, 'I hope this date goes well.'

'Yup,' murmurs Jess, dabbing on concealer. She suddenly swivels around. 'Hey, are you going to this Welsh Conference thing at the end of the week?'

'Yeah. Are you going?'

'Yup. My first assignment. Is it interesting?'

'Uh . . . regional conferences of the Conservative Party are definitely an experience, babe.'

'Oh, I see.'

'Yup. Although I guess this is a pretty well-timed one. You can speak to quite a few members and get a sense of which candidate they're moving behind. They'll be the ones deciding, in the end. Sounds like the smart money is on Eric Courtenay but strange stuff happens. Mark Norman is polling well on Conservative Home.' Eva rolls onto her back. 'I'm quite looking forward to it, actually. Peter and I are going to stay in this lush hotel the night before. A sort of final hurrah.'

Bobby saunters back in and flops down on the bed next to Eva.

'What's wrong?' Jess stands to examine herself.

'Oh, it's just this Tinder guy. I have a feeling this is going to be a waste of time.'

'How so?' Eva asks.

'He keeps messaging stupid stuff like "hope you've made an effort haha".'

'You may as well just go anyway, right? No other irons in the fire.'

Bobby decides not to tell them about Jake. After all, it's only a meeting.

'Exactly,' nods Jess.

Eva grins. 'It's only for one drink, like you said. Then you can run back to me and—'

'Hugh Hefner and his Playboy Bunny?' offers Jess.

Bobby rolls over. 'Yeah, maybe I will go. Just for one drink.'

'Atta girl.'

18th April

St James's Park

'So all in all,' wheezes Jess, springing out of her final burpee, 'really quite boring.'

The girls are doing an early morning circuit session.

'How can it possibly have been boring? You were having dinner with a member of the Cabinet and a lobby legend,' Eva pants, picking up some pads. 'Besides, I quite like Mark ever since he sent me flowers on my fifteenth birthday – although he was probably sucking up to Dad to get a job.'

'Being a member of the Cabinet doesn't mean you're interesting. In fact,' Jess pulls on some boxing gloves, 'if this guy becomes Prime Minister the whole country will go into a *Sleeping Beauty*-style coma.'

Jess thinks about the conversation she had with Teddy Hammer after dinner, where she had laid hard into Norman's chances of winning the leadership on the grounds that Eric Courtenay is young, photogenic and popular – characterised by his slick launch video. Teddy had slapped her down by reminding her that Jess isn't the target audience. Right now the people to win over are MPs, and he pointed out how much detail Norman knew at dinner about each MP's banal wants and needs. Assuming Courtenay does reach the final two, the audience changes again to a largely old, white and male electorate – an army of Mark Norman gammons, who hardly want slick and stylish.

'Well,' puffs Bobby, changing her rhythm with the skipping rope, 'I'll take a boring evening over a disastrous one.'

She proceeds to tell them, through furious bouts of skipping, about her evening. It started with a civil drink at a pub, but ended with Bobby making a run for it after the guy sent her a picture of his penis from the loos.

'No!' Jess breaks from raining punches down on Eva. 'There in the bar?'

'Yes,' says Bobby firmly, starting a set of lunges and speaking over her shoulder. 'It wasn't a total waste, though. I ended up going to meet Simon at a book launch. It was pretty good fun. He was really amusing about Brian and introduced me to lots of interesting people. I met Andrew Marr,' she pauses for a rest, 'and Emily Maitlis.'

Eva looks meaningfully at her.

'Oh come on, I'm not an idiot! He's just being nice.'

'I didn't say anything,' Eva tuts.

'Look, I need Simon to help me with Dad's unit and so it's in my interest to be on good terms with him,' Bobby scowls, stretching her calf muscles before they start walking back to the house. 'No different to Jess going out with Teddy Hammer . . . '

'Hey, leave me out of this! We're lunch buddies.' Jess raises her hands.

'A lot of dinners for lunch buddies. Aren't you going out with him again tomorrow evening?'

'Yeah. Richard Hendrick this time. Then loads of the lobby are meeting for drinks later, so I'll go on to that afterwards. Try and get Mike and George to warm to me.'

'I think you're taking the right approach.' Eva unlocks the front door. They had discussed in depth the night before whether Jess should have called out her colleagues' sexism. 'Why be the unpopular one? You can't have too many friends in this world.'

'I wish you saw it that way with me and Simon,' Bobby flushes.

'She wants to be in the lobby more than anything else, right? So that requires a certain amount of rough with the smooth. It's a careful line to tread.'

'And what do you think I'm doing?' Bobby is getting sick of the implication that she can't manage her relationship with Daly. She knows what she's doing.

Eva pauses for a moment then shrugs. 'Sorry, you're right. I just don't trust Daly.'

'You're both right,' cuts in Jess, putting on the kettle. 'These guys are powerful, okay? But beauty and youth and peachy asses have their own kind of power. So long as we're all in control then why not go to dinners with Teddy and parties with Daly to help our careers?'

Besides, Teddy's the last thing on Jess's mind. She wonders how sustainable the current situation with Ed is. The sexting keeps him on a tight leash but that can't go on forever. Is it time to up the ante?

Part Three

19th April

Paddington Station

The train inches out of the station on its way to Swansea. Eva and Peter have a table to themselves and have spread out a Pret picnic and several sheets of heavily annotated documents.

'So, how's the housemating with your dad and his missus?' Peter asks, watching the scenery change from urban tower blocks to lush English countryside.

Eva blows a raspberry. 'Well, the media have clocked that he's back in the UK. The *Mail* has these pictures of him and Holly out shopping together. He actually looks in physical pain, waddling around in his stupid jeans.' She squashes a biscuit crumb angrily under her finger.

'How was dinner with them the other day?'

'Fine. But I just don't see the point in making an effort. All Dad's relationships crash and burn eventually – as soon as they find out he doesn't have a bean . . . '

'But Eva, you must know that Holly's got plenty of her own money?'

'What?'

'A cursory Google. She's the heiress to some Texan farm machinery dynasty. She's basically Jane Deere. Her family are absolutely rolling in the stuff!'

'Jesus. I had no idea.'

'Well then,' Peter says a little haughtily, 'perhaps you should be less judgemental. Now,' he says, before she can reply, 'we'd better carry on with this speech for tomorrow.'

'Oh, we must get a joke in about Richard Hendrick and the letter "y" . . . '

Eventually the train pulls into Carmarthen station. Peter and Eva find a taxi and fifteen minutes later they drive through the gates of a spectacular country house.

Peter stretches. 'This is just what I need. Look, I think there's a terrace bar.'

But when they get to reception they discover there is no booking under either of their names. And the hotel is full up for the night.

'I . . . I can't think what must have happened,' stammers Peter.

'May I see your confirmation email, sir?' asks the receptionist. Peter hands over his phone. 'Ah, I see the problem. This is Myrddin House. You're booked into Myrddin Farm. It's about three miles away.'

'Oh no . . . ' groans Peter, thinking of the drinks terrace.

'We can ask our driver to take you. He is picking up some guests from that direction shortly.'

Eva and Peter stand outside, listening to the fountain splashing.

'Arse,' Peter hisses.

*

Ten minutes later they step out of the Mercedes into a farmyard caked in cowpat. Peter stands with his head bowed as the car drives away.

'Bore da! Careful of your shoes, there. The buggers squirt it out faster than I can clean it up,' shouts a cheerful voice. 'Here from London, are you?' The farmer eyes Peter's flawless black leather shoes as he jumps down from his tractor.

'Hello. I'm Eva, this is Peter.' Eva offers her hand.

'Oh, I wouldn't, love. Just had it up one, I have. Checking a calf.' Eva tries not to laugh at Peter's look of complete horror. 'I'll take you to my wife.'

The farmer leads them out of the yard and onto the lane. They follow him through a bright blue gate and into a gorgeous kitchen garden, alive with flowers, herbs and the lazy hum of bees. A kind, pink face pokes out of a front upstairs window.

'Welcome! I'm Morag. Wait there, I'll be down now, in a minute.'

Moments later she zips out of the front door, so bright and fast and little that Eva can't help but find her an instantly reassuring figure. The sort of attitude you want from a beautician at a well-overdue bikini wax appointment.

'Come on, mun,' Morag says casually to a sheepdog, who is sunning himself on the warm flagstones, as she leads Peter and Eva back out into the lane.

'Guess we're in a cottage,' mutters Peter under his breath, struggling with his small wheelie suitcase on the pot-holed road.

Morag continues walking, finally pushing open a gate. She lets the sheepdog run ahead down a little path, arched by ivy. They enter a clearing, where two large yurts nestle together, surrounded by apple trees and long, wildflower-filled grass.

Peter spins around. 'I'm terribly sorry, but I think there's been some kind of mistake. We thought we had rooms booked for us.'

'Oh yes, you did. But you booked luxury.'

'This is *luxury*?' he stammers.

Pulling back the canvas flaps of the yurts, it is like stepping into Narnia. Both have enormous wrought iron double beds with thick feather duvets and linen sheets. There are Persian rugs, bookshelves of classic novels and comfortable armchairs. Best of all, each yurt has a large copper bathtub and log burner. Morag shows Eva and Peter how they can pull a cord to separate the tent tops to reveal the night sky while they lie back in their beds. The only drawback is the compostable loos, which use sawdust instead of flushing water. Peter and Eva exchange looks at the thought of the inevitable rustic thud.

They head back outside, Morag explaining that she'll serve a full breakfast in the morning made of produce from the farm.

'We only do bed and breakfast, but I booked you a table at the pub. It's under a mile, if you walk across the fields. There are wellies in the cupboard, there.' She eyes Eva's suede ballet pumps.

'So, anything you're hoping to do while you're here?' asks Morag, as they pull on their borrowed boots.

'Well, we're here for work . . . '

'Work?'

'Yes. We're here for a political conference. We work for the Prime Minister.' Peter hopes these words will re-establish his position with his host.

'Oh . . . righto.' Morag crouches down to investigate a hole by a tree stump. Rabbits, she suspects. 'Never seen much point in politicians, myself. My husband's been waiting for his knee op for nearly two years now, but every time I turn on the telly there's a load of nonsense about some bugger getting his knob out. Whoever can sort out the NHS and bring down the cost of tractor diesel would be fine by me.'

Peter, debating whether to launch into the government's policy on fuel duty, is rescued by his phone ringing.

'Ah, it's the PM. Do excuse me . . . ' He dashes off. Eva can hear him disappear down the path. 'Hi, PM. Yes, we've just arrived. Sort of. We seem to be ... uh, glamping. Glamping, it's – never mind ... has he? Right ... yes, no problem. Do give him my number ... okay, understood ... '

Morag, looking nonplussed, checks her watch. 'Now, I need to get back to the house. I'll pop down while you're at the pub and get your stoves going, so you'll have lots of hot water for baths before bed. You've got plenty of blankets but just give me a shout if you need anything else.'

Eva longs to lie down on the bed and breathe in the fresh grass and manure. She can hear the tinkling of running water somewhere. And birdsong. She pulls on her coat and heads out after Peter, following the path back onto the lane. Peter is standing at a stile, reading emails on his phone. He points at a signpost above his head: *Pub/Tafarn*.

'Tafarn. The only Welsh word I need to know,' he chirps, considerably more cheerful now that a local ale and a pie are less than a mile away.

They start walking.

'Everything okay with the boss?' asks Eva.

'Oh yeah. She's got all sorts of people trying to speak to her just now. Just palming someone on to me.'

'Gotcha. Resignation honours, eh?'

'Bingo.'

The Prime Minister is able to nominate the great and the good for honours twice a year: New Year and the Queen's birthday. She also has the chance to make a list for her resignation. It is the perfect opportunity for people who feel she owes them to come out of the woodwork in a last ditch attempt to get a knighthood or peerage. On the train, Eva and Peter had discussed the letters from so-called supporters that have been pouring in for the last couple of days, reminding the PM of all their good works.

They trudge on. Eva is glad to have the wellies on. The grass is drenched in spring rainwater and the number of cowpats makes avoiding stepping in one impossible.

Peter's phone rings again.

'Ah, good evening. Great to speak . . .'

Eva tunes out. Instead, she listens carefully to the birdsong, distant livestock and insects. Rabbits dart across the field ahead of them. She feels sure the familiar vine in the hedgerow is wild asparagus and tries to identify as many plants from the banks as possible. She spent some of her summer holidays at her grandparents' house in Essex and she is pleased she remembers fritillaries, bluebells, cow parsley and wild garlic. It seems that absolutely every plant has woken up from a winter sleep to greet them. The smell is incredible.

She hears a gentle plodding sound behind her and turns to see a young bullock following them cautiously. He is a beautiful mushroom colour, with large dark eyes and long eyelashes. Eva stops to admire him. He stops too. She pulls out her phone and takes a photograph, the evening light glancing off his haunches. The meadow behind him is a mass of green and gold. Just in shot is her long shadow cast by the evening sun.

Eva puts her phone back in her pocket and jogs to catch up with Peter. The wellies and thick grass make her feel like she's running through treacle.

'Yes, well, I quite take your point and I will discuss it with the Prime Minister. Obviously there is a very rigorous process and these things take some time . . .' Peter is saying into his phone. When Eva catches up with him he rolls his eyes. She knows the look well. Someone's getting testy.

Eva hears the gentle thudding behind her again and turns, walking backwards, to see the cow has caught them up, maintaining a distance of twenty feet or so. A dozen friends have joined him, all adopting the same careful pace and lowered, curious heads. One of them emits a gentle, mournful moo.

Peter looks round at the noise. 'Aren't they beautiful?' he mouths ecstatically.

Eva mimes taking a bite from a burger. Peter aims a kick at her.

'Yes, I quite agree. There is precedent ... Well, I hope you can understand that patience is extremely important here ... Quite, some things never change, do they ... a moo? No, it must have been a car horn ...'

There is another, longer lowing.

Eva looks over her shoulder again and sees that perhaps thirty young cows are now following them. They all move with uncertainty, egging each other on like a gang of teenagers doing a dare. They push and shove to have a closer look. Occasionally one trips and canters forward to regain its footing, sending a ripple of excitement through the herd. Eva cranes her neck and sees that dozens more are coming down from the top of the field to join the fun.

One of them snorts and Eva grasps Peter's arm.

' ... yes, everything needs to go through the correct committees, of course ... just for propriety, you see ... of course not, I'd never imply they would have reasons to reject you, I – sorry, do excuse me just a moment.' Peter presses the phone to his chest. 'Eva, what is it?'

Eva points up the hill.

'Jesus! Where did they come from?' he squeaks, taking in the advancing herd. They seem to be gaining the confidence of numbers. The sound of hundreds of tons of bovine muscle and bone compacted into tight hooves rumbling over the hillside sounds like thunder.

'I don't know, but they're only babies. They, uh, won't do us harm, will they?' Eva glances ahead at the gate, about thirty yards ahead of them. 'We can't outrun them from here, not in these clodhoppers. Let's just ... keep walking slowly. Keep your voice calm. I'll try and ... shoo them.'

'Shoo them?' Peter hisses.

'Just get that person off the line, will you?'

'Look, I'm terribly sorry but now isn't a great time,' Peter stutters, turning and stumbling backwards with her as the cows steadily gain on them. 'No, please! This isn't a fob off at all. It's just ... ah ... well, of course ...'

Finally, they are ten yards from the gate, and the cattle, sensing their fun may be over, suddenly plunge forward.

'Run!' yells Eva, whipping round and sprinting as fast as she can towards the gate. Her boots clump heavily against the ground. She can hear the thunder of hooves and the angry snorts of the herd.

'I'm terribly sorry, but – I'll have to call you back – I think I'm about to be crushed by a herd of cows. Cheerio!' Peter yells into his phone as he charges along beside her.

A couple of hours later, full of sausages and mash and several pints of local beer, Peter and Eva accept a quad bike ride back to the farm from some friendly locals, who have several tips on future cow wranglings. They stumble up the path to their yurts, guided by a delicious, appley smell from their log burners. Morag has left them large, steaming pots of hot chocolate.

Eva runs the bath, experimenting with the different salts and oils on a tray. Her yurt seems to swell with the scent of lavender and rosemary. She strips off and steps into the water, easing herself in up to her neck, and takes a sip of hot chocolate. It is thick and creamy and rich. She can't remember the last time she felt this peaceful. Through several layers of canvas she can hear that Peter is playing Chopin piano concertos on his phone. Eva lies back and closes her eyes.

When she has towelled herself down and brushed her teeth, she wraps up warmly and pulls back the canvas roof to reveal the stunning night sky. She switches off the bedside lamp and climbs in under the duvets and quilts, lying on her back. It hadn't even occurred to her that there are places in the UK where the stars are this clear. It makes her feel small and insignificant but in a strangely comforting way. Politics suddenly seems very fleeting and unimportant.

Gradually, her body snug and her face feeling the cool air, Eva's eyes droop. As she rolls over and falls into the deepest, most refreshing sleep of her life, she vaguely wonders who Peter had been speaking to when they'd made their escape from the cows.

20th April

Paddington Station

The following morning, Jess arrives at Paddington with plenty of time to spare before her train departs. It isn't a very bright day but she still needs her sunglasses on. She can't remember the last time she has felt this hungover. After dinner with Teddy Hammer and Richard Hendrick, she'd joined the rest of the lobby for drinks in Soho and didn't get to bed until 3 a.m.

'It's astonishing,' she'd shouted over the tequila-fuelled chatter to George and Mike, after arriving at the bar, 'Hendrick genuinely thinks he's going to be PM. Cold hard polling numbers mean nothing, he says he just *knows* people love him. He kept talking about how he was "the one to bring the country back together".'

'He's evangelical about himself, all right,' George had nodded.

'Yeah,' slurred Mike, 'he has this disgraced-junior-Congressman-from-Missouri energy. "I've hurt myself, I've hurt my family – but most of all I have hurt God."'

It was a terrific atmosphere. A leadership contest is exactly

224

what all the hacks have been waiting for. Months of speculation about the PM's position and a fall in circulation as readers have got tired of the stagnation in Parliament got them tetchy. Now there will be reams of copy coming at them every day as each candidate's team pours out their vision and feeds the mountains of dirt they have on their opponents.

Jess met the broadcast reporters, the women beautifully made up for the studio lights wearing jewel colours, the men laughing about their new knowledge of foundation and powder. The man who seems to be perpetually asleep at his desk in the next room on Burma Road turned out to be a cheerful regional journalist, with lots of horse racing tips to plump up Jess's meagre salary. There were several reporters from magazines looking to make friends and break into a national paper (Jess is reminded how lucky she is to have landed her gig). Without exception, everyone asked in a furtive way how she is getting along with Ed.

'Oh, he's perfectly easy to keep under control. He just needs his balls squeezed from time to time,' she had said to the gang from the *Mail on Sunday*.

'Good luck breaking this one,' chortles one of them, speaking above Jess's head.

She knew he'd come eventually.

'Can I get you a drink?' Ed had asked, his voice casual.

Jess had taken the large, colourful cocktail glass from Ed's hand and carefully rotated the rim around so that her lips touched the exact spot where he had been drinking from. Ed was momentarily lost for words.

'Delicious,' Jess had whispered.

The evening had continued, the group splitting off and rejoining in twos and threes, trading gossip and spreading fun. With the flashing disco lights, it was like a human kaleidoscope. Jess realised how, once they had a few drinks in them, everyone let their guard slip. Grumbling about bosses. Stories about MPs and other journalists. Crushes. Through the fog of Ed's stream of colourful cocktails, she noticed a few hands lingering on waists.

Things had come to a head when George and Mike, learning Jess had a gymnastics blue, dared her to do the splits. After ample encouragement from the assembled group, Jess had climbed onto the bar, kicked off her shoes and executed five perfect backflips along the top of it. As she took a bow, the place went wild. Even by lobby standards, this was high jinks.

'That's my girl!' Teddy had cried, whacking people out of the way with his stick. 'This calls for one thing – karaoke!'

As the group swarmed out into the street, following in Teddy's wake, Ed fell into step with Jess, who pointed out a thick leather collar worn by a mannequin in the window of a sex shop. Ed had very carefully brushed his finger against her hand, feeling a nudge of lust.

Crazy to think all that was just a few hours ago. Jess's throat hurts from belting out Tina Turner and Cher along with everybody else. She still isn't certain she didn't dream that Teddy Hammer had sung Sir Mix-a-Lot's 'Baby Got Back' without needing to consult the lyrics on the karaoke bar screen. She doesn't want to touch tequila again. She could have broken her neck.

Still, there is a four-hour train journey to settle her stomach and to think about what she wants to write. Jess walks slowly to M&S for water, crisps, chocolate biscuits and cocktail sausages before picking up an enormous coffee. Her phone buzzes. George on their *Sentinel* WhatsApp group, sending a photo of Jess mid-backflip and several hearts. She can't help grinning, even though it hurts her head. Jess wanted to be accepted and had been willing to bend over backwards to get there – she just didn't realise she'd have to do it literally.

When the platform is announced, she settles down in her seat and listens to David Bowie as the train eases out of the station. She doesn't know if it's the increasingly green landscape opening up in front of her, or the coffee and chocolate biscuits, but she finds her throbbing head is easing. She manages to read the news on her phone and, around Cardiff, writes a few notes about the questions she wants to ask conference attendees, but becomes absorbed by the view once the train hits the coast. There is a strange, eerie beauty to Port Talbot, where the rugged coastline meets the smoke and lights of the steelworks. The stretch from Llanelli to Carmarthen, where at certain points she thinks the train might tip into the sea, is wondrous. She doesn't even mind when the train is delayed because sheep are on the tracks.

Jess's phone buzzes. It's Ed:

I've bought you a present. Would you wear this for me?

He is holding the collar from the window display the night before.

Jess grins, the remnants of her hangover evaporating.

Twenty minutes later Jess is walking into the conference venue when she bumps into Eva.

'Christ, you look dreadful,' Eva says, hugging her tight.

'Thanks.' Jess takes off her sunglasses. 'A long night.'

Eva's phone rings. 'It's Dad. Just a sec, okay?'

Jess shrugs and reaches in her bag for her notebook.

'Hi, Dad, is everything okay?' Eva steps into the sunshine.

She returns moments later, microwaving rage from every pore, doing her best to speak as calmly as possible to Peter, who she has gripped by the elbow. It turns out it had been her father on the phone to Peter the night before, fishing for a peerage. The idea of her father asking for an honour feels somehow worse to her than any of his past scandals. Percy himself has always referred to those who had asked him for a gong during his time as PM as 'hopeless grubbers'. Peter does his best to soothe Eva, insisting that the PM has no intention of putting Percy in the House of Lords, but she fumes.

'It's *her*.' Eva stamps her foot. 'You've said it yourself – Holly's already got money. A title is something else altogether. Look, Dad can be a complete nightmare but he has never cared about this sort of thing. In the same way he's never cared about his clothes or his teeth. Now he's going to be ... Lord Oompa-Loompa.'

'Well, not on my watch. I've already told you the PM has said no.'

'Darling, your watch isn't much longer. You wait,' Eva rages, 'he's really got the bit between his teeth with this woman. No matter how stupid it makes him look.'

Portcullis House

Bobby sits at the café table, skimming her notes on NHS costs and planning laws and wondering if she looks okay. She's finally meeting Jake Albury and is nervous that she'll say something stupid. Worried she's made a bit too much effort, she pulls out a tissue and quickly wipes off her lipstick. A bag slams down on the floor next to her.

'Sorry I'm late,' says a half-familiar voice. 'Got caught up with Eric.'

Bobby looks up vaguely. It's the cyclist from her first day, as scruffy and sexy as ever.

'H-hi,' she stammers. His eyes have widened in recognition. 'Nice to meet you ... properly.'

They shake hands. Bobby feels very aware of his skin touching hers.

'So, uh, George Sackler said you had a planning question,' Jake says as he pulls out a notepad.

'Right, so . . .' Bobby pushes her well-thumbed collection of documents towards him, detailing the full sorry story of the Tipperton Mental Health Unit. 'Perhaps you don't mind giving these a read, while I get some coffee?'

'Sounds good. I'll have a flat white.'

'Great. I'd start with that.' She points to her letter to the Prime Minister she drafted for Daly two weeks ago. It occurs to her only now that he never signed it.

Bobby heads off, grateful to have a couple of minutes to pull herself together, then brings back their coffees and some KitKats.

'Thanks,' Jake murmurs, continuing to read and take notes.

Bobby is struck by how tired Jake looks. He carries it off, though. The lilac shades beneath his green eyes set off his olive skin. His shaggy dark hair, peppered with silver, hangs over his forehead as he works. From time to time he runs a hand absentmindedly through it. From across the table, Bobby tries to concentrate.

Occasionally Jake asks Bobby a question and she feels her face burn as their eyes meet. The most pertinent enquiry is of course why the unit can't just be moved to another building in Tipperton. The answer is easy: the NHS simply can't afford to do that without a massive injection of cash.

'So look,' Jake says eventually, reaching for a KitKat. 'These PFI contracts are tricky and funding is . . . funding. But I think this comes down to how ambitious you want to be. Christ knows how many other PFI contracts like this will collapse soon . . . If you want to save this particular unit then you're really best to focus your efforts on the local authorities—'

'But I've already done that!' Bobby interjects. 'Besides, this shouldn't happen anywhere. Why not make a blanket law?'

Jake leans in towards her. For a confused, hopeful moment she thinks he might be about to kiss her.

'Look – I'm writing the bulk of Eric's policy plans for the leadership—'

'So you can sort this out?'

'Not exactly. Rolling this out nationally to save all of them is a serious amount of money. That being said, we'll be pushing for proper funding for public services and opening up planning laws—'

'But public services ... planning – this *is* about planning, right?'

'Partly, yes. Look,' Jake pauses for a beat. 'I won't be able to persuade him to include something like this without—'

'Without what?' Bobby nearly shouts, desperate to grip the situation. 'How do I make this happen?'

Jake is wondering how sensible it is to be as honest as he is preparing to be with this very new acquaintance. Bobby has a touching naivety to her that he finds endearing – 'this shouldn't happen anywhere' rings in his ears – and he wants to help. Truthfully, Jake's finding it almost impossible to talk properly about policy or strategy with the Courtenay team. They seem completely agnostic on specific ideas, with Courtenay hardly engaging and Clarissa and Jackson just wanting to announce anything popular with members that will help them to win. The campaign isn't going as well as anticipated, Courtenay still struggling to connect with his colleagues, so they're jumping on anything they consider 'red meat'. Bobby is so refreshing by comparison, laser-focused on doing some good.

'Please,' Bobby says softly. 'I'm running out of time.'

Jake looks at Bobby properly for the first time since his arrival, something he'd been desperately trying not to do. He'd regretted not turning back to speak to the girl who told him off at the traffic lights and now here they are. He can't remember the last time he had a proper conversation with someone who was on a mission to get something done, impervious to the game-playing of politics. He wants to see more of her. Helping her could lead to anything.

'Without MPs asking for this to happen. A proper campaign that captures the public, so that the candidates feel they 'must' support it. It's happening already.' Jake runs his pen down the margin of a page in his notepad. 'MPs are organising themselves and preparing to push the candidates for guarantees on their pet policies. Flexible working, drugs, parental leave ... services for the homeless, green taxes, fox hunting. The point is, you need to get MPs talking about your campaign. The more candidates they push on this the better. Then it just becomes accepted that this legislation is a no-brainer for any new PM.'

'But how?'

'You've got this far already, haven't you? You're clearly a very good campaigner. Just expand it out. You need to persuade a core group of MPs – I'd start with Simon Daly and the other MPs with these units in their patches – to take this issue forward. It doesn't require heavy legislation. We can probably fold it into the Planning Bill or even something within health or social services – and it's extremely emotive. But the money is a clincher so you need a strong sense of momentum to get it over the line. MPs first – then use them as vehicles to take it to the public.'

There is a pause while Bobby scribbles down a few things, thinking about what Mary Jones said about being an MP – 'You can get so much more done'. She feels Jake's eyes on her and wills her face to stop flushing.

'Simon said he'd work with you on this. What has he done so far?' asks Jake. Bobby looks up and notices that his eyes have narrowed.

'Well ... obviously he resigned just before I started, so his attention was on that. Then everything blew up for the PM and so . . . well, he just hasn't had the time to really talk about it yet.' As she speaks, Bobby realises Daly has done very little. Why didn't he tell her about getting the MPs on board? He must know it's important. 'He's been great at taking me along to parties and things to meet people, though.'

Jake's face darkens.

'Is something wrong?' asks Bobby.

'No, no. It's just . . . it sounds textbook Simon to go big on parties and not much else.' Jake coughs.

Bobby feels a sting of humiliation. She'd wanted Jake to come away from this meeting impressed, not pinning her as a Parliamentary party girl. The annoying thing is that Jake is right – Daly hasn't actually done anything to help her yet and she's been here nearly a month.

'Well,' Bobby, embarrassed, stands up and gathers her papers, 'thanks very much for your help. I'll let you get on.'

She leaves as quickly as possible, unaware that Jake sits perfectly still at the table, gazing at the seat she'd been in moments before and wondering what he said wrong.

Swansea

Jess is feeling down in the dumps. Her hangover has returned, leaving her with a cracking headache and mild nausea. The Prime Minister delivered a solid farewell speech to the Welsh Conservatives, who only had pleasant things to say about her. The membership seems pretty squarely to support Courtenay. The only real sniff of a story she has is Percy Cross begging for a peerage, but she knows she can't possibly do anything with it. When they got on the London-bound train together, Eva had specifically made Jess promise not to whisper a word to anyone about it.

Jess looks moodily out of the train window, wondering what spectacular gymnastic feat she'll have to do when she tells the boys that she doesn't have any copy beyond a boring, factual account of the day.

Eva suddenly appears at her seat, grinning.

'Do you fancy a drink?'

'No way. I don't think I want a drink ever again ...'

'What if it was with the Prime Minister?'

'What?'

'Peter and I told her you've just started with Ed Cooper and that you're on the train. I don't know whether it's because she's not a big fan of his or that you're a new girl starting out, or maybe she's just demob-happy ... Anyway, she's asked if you'd like to join us.'

'Shit! Really? Uh ... sure.' Jess quickly gathers her things together. As she picks up her phone her eye catches a text from Ed:

Just heard Graham Thomas will endorse Natasha Weaver for Leader in exchange for a big job.

'Um ... I'm just going to duck into the loo.'

Once inside, Jess calls Ed. He explains that, via a source he won't reveal on pain of death, Weaver and Thomas brokered a deal late the night before. For a suitably senior role, Thomas has agreed to be Weaver's campaign manager, unleashing his old Whips Office skills and his transport-related wish list of what MPs want – everything from where they stand on a Heathrow expansion to disabled access platforms in their local train stations. It could be the perfect formula to bring a chunky list of MPs on board Weaver's campaign. In a surprising extra, Thomas has insisted that he consults on all other ministerial appointments. Westminster is bursting with MPs anxiously wondering whether they can buy the man a drink to make up for their lack of support over the Dubois contract mess.

They stagger up the jolting train, Jess's headache banished. When they reach the right carriage, a couple of police officers nod at Eva, who leads Jess to where the PM, her face animated as she tells a story to her team, sits at a table.

'Prime Minister, this is Jess Adler from the *Sentinel*.'

The PM and Jess shake hands and trade pleasantries.

Eva's phone rings and she excuses herself. Jess is left awkwardly swaying.

'Please, join us.' The PM indicates a seat across the aisle from her. 'So you're working with Ed Cooper now. How are you finding him so far?'

'Fine, really. I was covering the crime beat in Glasgow before this, so Ed is an angel compared to some of the characters I've come across.'

They chat earnestly about policing, the PM reminiscing about her time as Home Secretary. Peter brings a large tray of drinks and crisps.

'Prime Minister, can I ask you something?' ventures Jess.

'Hang on, we aren't doing any official interviews,' snaps her press secretary.

'Of course. This is all off the record,' says Jess hurriedly.

Madeleine sips her gin and tonic. 'Shoot.'

'I've just heard that Graham Thomas has endorsed Natasha Weaver for the leadership.'

'Has he indeed. Well, Natasha has been very supportive of him these past couple of weeks.' The PM takes another sip. 'So what's your question?'

'Well ... he's the reason that your own premiership has come to an end. He's the first big beast to endorse somebody. I suppose I just wonder ... what do you think about it?'

The PM looks at Jess carefully. Then she fixes her eyes on the little bubbles of her drink.

'I think ... If Graham brings Natasha half the luck and

loyalty he brought me then I wish her well. I'd advise her against making him Chancellor, though, or the nation's finances will likely be entrusted to his eleven-year-old son. Now that,' she turns to Jess, 'can be a direct quote.'

Jess can't believe it. After thanking the PM she is subjected to an extremely firm word with the Downing Street press secretary about exactly how she will be using the quote. As she wobbles back to her seat, she texts Ed to let him know she has some great words coming – he replies to tell her Philip McKay is holding the front page.

Jess sinks heavily into her seat, switches on her noise cancelling headphones and pulls her laptop out of her bag. She doesn't notice that Eva is looking out of the window, biting absentmindedly at a hangnail.

Eva has a decision to make, her mind moving as fast as her eyes, which dart back and forth following individual trees and houses as they race past her.

The phone call had come from Jackson. He has offered her a job on the Courtenay leadership campaign, overseeing the spreadsheet of supporters, planning the summer tour (if he gets down to the final two), coordinating the policy and media teams so they're making sense. Money. People. Plans. It all needs managing.

It is definitely tempting. Courtenay is the frontrunner and Jackson had hinted heavily that she would remain a SpAd if he wins – perhaps get promoted, depending on her performance on the campaign. Eva has never worked on a leadership campaign before and would have a seat at the table for every strategic decision.

However, it hardly means job security. Within the rules of Conservative leadership campaigns, Eva would have to work for free – and forgo the three months of severance she would get at the end of the current PM's administration (in that instance she loses her job, but to work on the Courtenay campaign she'd

have to resign). It also leaves her with an unpleasant acknowledgement of how disloyal she would feel, telling the PM that
she was officially jumping ship to help someone instrumental
in her own demise to win.

After a long time, Eva thinks about her father's advice. She
wants to take her life into her own hands. Pausing to smooth
her skirt, she heads down the train to speak to Peter – then the
Prime Minister.

22nd April

Burma Road, Houses of Parliament

'I still can't believe she gave you that quote. It was in every Sunday paper too, did you see? Amazing.' George stands in the middle of Burma Road, sweating after his cycle ride in.

'Thanks.' Jess swings her bag off her chair. 'Are you going to Natasha Weaver's campaign launch later? Don't really understand why she's having one. Everyone knows she's running.'

'Not sure I can stomach it. Judging by her team's briefings so far it's going to be a wailing of rhetoric and policies targeted at the nutters among the MPs and membership. Revisit capital punishment, sterilise the uneducated . . . anyway, they all have them. Blows a decent chunk out of their campaign budgets, but it's their chance to explain their vision and get on TV.'

'Bit of an SW1 circle jerk in my view.'

'Yeah . . . hey, shall we go to the Burger Awards tonight? I feel like getting wrecked.'

'The Burger Awards?'

'It's really fun. Food. Beer. Loads of MPs and journos. Oh, and maybe see if Camilla wants to join us? Nice to include her.' George tries to sound casual.

'Sure, I'll ask if she's free. Did you see her piece on Saturday – Downing Street Style? They even made a video of ministers walking up to the front door, set to catwalk music. Brilliant. Apparently all the leadership contenders are hiring stylists and stuff off the back of it.'

'I could do with a stylist.' George examines the various creased shirts he has hanging in the office storage cupboard.

'Where's Ed? I haven't seen him since before I went to Wales,' Jess asks, hoping she sounds disinterested.

She keeps thinking about the photo he had sent her of himself over the weekend, wet from the shower with just a towel slung around his hips. He certainly isn't in his twenties – or even his thirties – but he looks in surprisingly good shape. Jess told him to send it and he had done as she asked. She wonders what else she'll be able to get him to do before long.

'Oh, he's been tied up with legal at HQ for the past few days. He's got some stuff that's proving quite hard to get over the line.'

'What stuff?'

'I dunno exactly. I reckon he's got hold of something dynamite, though. He's got himself all quivery and excited' – I'll say, thinks Jess – 'but old Finlayson is very jumpy about being sued. Ed will need to be on pretty firm ground.'

'Fair enough. Did you see the *Crash* website this morning? My friend Eva Cross is starting on the Courtenay campaign today.'

'Percy Cross's daughter?'

'Yeah. I actually live with her.'

'No way! And her old man? And the fembot?' Mike tries not

to spill a tray of coffee as he kicks open the door. 'Morning, by the way.'

'She's not a fembot. She's all right.' Jess takes the tray from him.

'What's it like living with them?' Mike has a gleam in his eye.

'Don't even think about it,' Jess says flatly. 'The Crosses are off the table.'

Before George or Mike can protest, Ed sails into the room.

'Right – gather round, children,' he looks dizzy with elation, 'I have something to show you. Shut the door . . .'

Notting Hill

Across town, Eva glances once again around the attendees of her first meeting on the Courtenay campaign. She is astounded at how quickly she has found herself here: she left Downing Street on Saturday, swinging by the office after the train back from Wales to grab her belongings, and here she is on Monday, in the Courtenay's OKA living room in Notting Hill.

The exclusive group of Eva, Clarissa, Courtenay, Jackson, Jake Albury, who is running policy, and Nick O'Hara, Courtenay's bullish press man, are discussing their launch event. They are desperate for it to go well, as, despite being the frontrunners with the membership, the Defence Secretary, Mark Norman, is well ahead of them with his number of MP backers. They must get into the final two. Eva has already been shocked by the silly mistakes the campaign is making: not registering with the Information Commissioner or writing a GDPR policy or carefully listing donations for registration. She sees now why they were so keen to hire her. Nobody else was paying attention to the painful practicalities. The atmosphere is chaotic and scrappy and everyone is primed to blame each other for failure, should it occur.

'We can't do it at the Carlton Club. I want the backdrop to be fresh and new, not Phileas Fogg's drawing room,' says Clarissa from the sofa.

'I was wondering about outside,' suggests Nick, thinking about how the broadcast pictures might stand out compared to everyone else's boring backdrops.

'I want to launch at the Army and Navy Club,' Courtenay says, the first time Eva has heard him speak all morning.

'Eric, please—'

'Clarissa, I don't care what else you want but I am launching there.'

His wife surveys him carefully. 'Okay – Eva, please call them.'

Eva, who is reading a text from Jess, looks up from her phone. 'Yes, will do. I just— '

'What is it?' snaps Clarissa. Eva wonders yet again why Clarissa seems to dislike her so much. Could she be threatened by a younger woman? Maybe she should talk more about how much she loves her boyfriend.

'It's just ... Nick, have you heard anything about Natasha Weaver?'

'Her launch is in about an hour,' Nick mutters, scribbling something down. 'Why?'

'I've just had a text from someone at the *Sentinel*. It's going to break at any moment.'

'What is?' Clarissa demands.

'Well, she ... I don't want to sound judgemental – this is said with reverence if anything – but ... it looks like she's been having an affair. Or – affairs.'

'What?'

'There are photos.'

'*What?*'

They all jump to their feet and pull out their phones.

'Oh my God, she's right,' shouts Nick, who has flipped open his laptop and is looking at the *Sentinel* website.

'Just let me savour this moment.' Jackson closes his eyes, his face saint-like.

'I ... I can't believe it,' stammers Courtenay.

'Oh, I believe it all right. I just can't believe it's all caught on camera,' Clarissa smirks.

They all gather around Nick's laptop. He scrolls from photo to photo of Weaver, each one different. Different men, different positions, different times of day. The one thing they have in common is the setting: her Parliamentary office.

'This has been going around for ages, but there's never been anything concrete. Plus she has a good lawyer. Photos? Wow. Someone must have made a fortune,' Nick muses.

'Unlikely,' Clarissa snaps. 'Must have been a jilted lover or something.'

'Let me make some calls.' Nick disappears into the garden.

'Jesus,' Eva mutters, without thinking. 'I mean, on a basic human level can you imagine what it would be like to see pictures like this of yourself everywhere?'

'No, I can't,' Clarissa replies coldly.

'Woah,' Nick says, stepping back through the door. 'Sounds like she's pushing ahead with the launch. Brazen it out.'

'Brazen it out?' laughs Clarissa.

'Yup. Apparently she has an open marriage with her husband. He's fine with the whole thing. She's going ahead. Maybe even make a virtue of it. Time for a modern woman and so on.'

'Modern woman? She's trying to become Prime Minister! You think we can have a PM heading off to the United Nations Security Council when everyone's seen her naked?'

'Well, she's not technically naked in these,' remarks Jackson.

'One thing's for sure,' Eva says quietly, 'she can push

whatever message she likes in the media. But the Party members will absolutely hate this.'

'Particularly the women,' nods Clarissa. She looks off into the middle distance, thinking of the bristly-bottomed old prudes in Courtenay's Association.

'You want to say anything about it?' Nick asks. Eva is surprised to see he directs the question at Clarissa and not Courtenay. 'I reckon we no-comment it.'

'No,' Clarissa says slowly. 'Let's say something. Nothing disparaging. We want to recognise her right to a private life and condemn the distribution of the images. Women's bodies, blah blah. But reiterate our stuff on sleaze and traditional values, too.'

'That seems to cover all the bases.' Nick taps on his phone. 'How's this?'

Clarissa reads his screen and nods.

'I still can't believe she's going ahead with it,' breathes Courtenay, still looking at the pictures.

'Well, in a way, why not? Rumours have been swirling about plenty of the other candidates for ages. Did I tell you about that SpAd walking in on David Bathurst hanging out the back of one of his researchers in the Slug and Lettuce bathroom in Victoria?' laughs Nick. 'Must be the only reason he hasn't thrown his hat into the ring.'

Clarissa makes a note. 'It seems that every contest is dubbed the "sleaziest ever". This could really raise the bar. Hats off to Nat.'

'Well, that's that,' says Nick.

'Tell me about it,' Clarissa replies.

'No, seriously – that's that. She's just withdrawn.' Nick holds up his phone, showing a brief statement on Weaver's Twitter profile.

'Well, then – that's one down. Only ten to go.' Jackson rubs his hands together.

'You don't seem at all surprised by this, Nige,' Courtenay says, biting his lip.

'My job, Erico. I know everyone's dirty little secrets. You wait until the contest really heats up – people will do anything under duress—'

'Eric – you need to send Natasha a text,' Clarissa cuts in. 'Get Eva to help you write some guff about her feelings and the invasion of her privacy.' She stretches on the sofa like a cat. 'Endorsing you will make her and her supporters feel so much better.'

Eva, shell-shocked at such a rapid series of developments in just a couple of minutes, sits down next to Courtenay, who looks equally stunned. The GDPR policy will have to wait.

Jackson slaps his thighs and rises from his seat, wiggling his eyebrows at Clarissa. 'Well, I'd better be going.'

'I'll show you out,' she smiles and takes his arm.

When they reach the privacy of the front hallway they grin and give each other the thumbs-up. The campaign has begun in earnest. From now on each candidate will be ducking to avoid media Molotov cocktails thrown by the guerilla-like rival camps. For weeks, their days will be plagued by the constant need for a strategic grip on their campaigns and a hungry search for MPs they can pick off like gazelles. Their sleepless nights will be characterised by late drinks with donors and long, anxious calls with their teams about a throwaway comment. Then, at the end of it all, they'll lick each other's wounds and pretend that serving in the government of the enemy they've been attacking for the last eight weeks is their dearest wish come true.

23rd April

Westminster Bridge

'Hey, what are you doing here?' Jess nearly bumps her coffee over Eva, who is absorbed in her phone in the street.

'Sorry, mind elsewhere,' Eva sighs, slipping on her sunglasses. 'Just been at CCHQ. They gathered all the different campaigns together to explain how the national part of the contest will work. You know, when it's down to the final two. Lots of travelling around the country for stump speeches and debates. I hope Eric's voice doesn't give out.'

'He looks pretty healthy to me.'

'Yeah, he's holding up well, even if the campaign itself is a bit of a disaster. We're practising for the first TV debate later. Lucky he's handsome, as he doesn't have a huge amount to say,' Eva laughs.

'Is it going well then?'

'It's not really been the start we wanted. I think that the Weaver stuff has actually made the MPs miss Madeleine Ford.

She was just so clean, you know? The last person you can imagine getting caught up in a scandal. And then there's the relentlessness of the whole campaign. I've divided up Eric's diary into fifteen-minute pow-wows with different MPs and it's killing him, having to be "on" like that all the time. But this is nothing compared to how it will get on the road in the final two. Luckily he's a pro at power-napping. Throwback to grabbing a bit of rest when he was in the Army, I suppose . . . Anyway, have I told you that Jamie has invited you, me and Bobby to this crazy-sounding party in a couple of weeks? Very exclusive guest list. His boss, Jeremy Spears, has one of those vanity foundations in his own name and this is their summer bash. I went to their Christmas one and it was completely wild. The exact kind of City squillionaire party that you'd expect: girls in silver bikinis handing out drinks; vodka luges on every table; Shirley Bassey performed!'

'Sounds amazing. I wonder if I can get Camilla to open up the *Blush* fashion cupboard for us . . .'

'You really think so?'

'Sure.' Jess's phone rings. It's Ed. 'I'd better take this. Good luck with the debate prep.'

'I'm starting to think that you don't need luck when you have Nigel and Clarissa . . .'

Portcullis House

In the Daly/Sackler Parliamentary office, Bobby clears her throat. After a month on the job she finally has her first meeting with Daly to talk about the Tipperton Mental Health Unit and by the end of their thirty-minute slot she wants him to agree to launch the campaign.

Daly, of course, has been trying to dodge this conversation

since the beginning. Now he finds the whole issue heating up. When he was in Tipperton at the weekend he'd had lunch with a couple of donors, hoping they might contribute to Courtenay's campaign. Jeffrey Cuthbert is still piling on the pressure for him to join the consortium, promising fabulous dividends. As tempting as this is, a Chancellorship in the offing promises deep media scrutiny – of his finances, of his personal life, of his personality. With Courtenay's promise to weed out sleaze and corruption, Daly needs to stay cleaner than a vicar when the bishop is visiting without putting Jeffrey Cuthbert's nose out of joint. Relying on his dexterous stakeholder management skills, born out of juggling several girlfriends at any one time in his twenties, he's trying to carry the confidence of both Cuthbert's consortium and Bobby and her campaign without actually having to commit to one at the expense of the other. So he's just done nothing.

'How are you finding everything so far?' Daly finally puts down his phone. The incoming on the Legislative Lads WhatsApp group will have to wait.

'Really interesting,' Bobby smiles. 'And I like everyone a lot.'

'Even Moira?' Daly asks, looking at her knowingly. He has a habit of conspiratorially asking different team members what they think of each other, seeking confidences.

'I'm just trying to focus. It's been so easy to get swept along by the parties and gossip and everything else going on. I started almost a month ago and you've been so generous with taking me to things and introducing me to people, but this is the first conversation we've had about protecting the unit, and the PFI contract ends soon. You know,' Bobby thinks of Jake, 'I'm here for a reason.'

'Of course,' Daly replies, 'but the parties and gossip have their place, you know. Information ... anecdotes ... booze. All currency in Westminster. It's what brings people together.'

'Sure, but isn't it time to take that on a step? I reckon it's time we launched this campaign. I've spoken to a few people,' Bobby decides not to mention Jake, 'who think we should organise a group of MPs behind us and campaign to protect every unit nationally with the right legislation and funding. It's a big ask, but with a disciplined group of voices we can get the leadership contenders to commit to it. I've made a list of MPs who have a similar unit to the Tipperton one in their constituencies.' Bobby slides a piece of paper across the table.

'Well, that's wonderful,' Daly says. 'Did I tell you I'm doing *Newsnight* tonight? Spinning for Eric post-debate.'

'Yeah, very cool. Are you nervous?'

'Nah, I'm in mid-season form.' Daly chews over how to distract Bobby for a while longer. 'Want to come with me to the studio?'

'Oh . . . well, I was planning to watch it on catch up.' It's very tempting. Bobby's never been to a TV studio before.

'Ah, another hot date?' Daly smirks.

There is no way that she is going to tell Daly that her plans after the TV debate are to sit down with Jess, Eva and Holly to listen to Percy talk loudly over *Air Force One*, his favourite film. He had told them that morning that he used to fantasise about the headlines he would have got if he had fought terrorists off the UK Voyager plane while he was PM.

'No! Nothing like that. I, uh . . . are you sure?'

'Of course!'

'Great. In the meantime, are you happy for me to put together a launch plan and approach these people?'

Daly picks up the list of MPs and sighs. 'Sure.'

'I've also taken advice on the legislation itself. I wonder if we can look at whether there's a mechanism to get some of the money back from the consortiums behind these different PFI contracts. That's what got our unit into a financial scrape to begin with. And then I was thinking about the land and building. What if it was bought and then leased back to the NHS on a manageable, reduced rent?'

'Which new owner is going to want to do that?'

Bobby explains that landlords might be willing to, in exchange for a new tax break. They continue back and forth, with Daly venturing one of Jeffrey Cuthbert's ideas: selling the current site for such a hefty amount that the NHS can take the money to buy a new unit in Tipperton. Bobby dismisses it. Aside from the legal nightmare they would be bogged down within no time, it would require a sale far over the odds to pay off the PFI debt and have enough to buy, build and maintain somewhere new – plus it would be a one-off for Tipperton. Daly latches firmly onto this idea, desperate to make legislation that is national, not specific to his constituency. Bobby supposes it is for him to have safety in numbers with other MPs. Whatever his reason, he suggests that Bobby prepares messages for him to send to her list of MPs and that they invite in some experts – lawyers, developers, councillors – to test the plans. He'll even chat the idea over with Courtenay at their next squash game.

Finally, he agrees to a soft launch of the campaign, while the details are being worked out.

Bobby is just thanking him, thinking this is much easier than she was expecting, when Daly jumps up from his seat.

'Oh, Susie!'

Bobby turns and recognises the rather dishevelled-looking woman standing in the doorway as Daly's wife. She is carrying an overnight bag and an umbrella. In her hurry, she has worked up dark rings under her arms and has sweated off her makeup, leaving her face pink and shiny.

'Hello, Mrs Daly.' Bobby stands up. 'I'm Bobby, Simon's new researcher. Can I take that for you?'

Susie clutches her bag rather stiffly. 'No, thank you.'

'A cup of tea?'

'Uh ... yes, thank you. That sounds lovely. I walked from the station, so I'm a bit tired.'

Daly kisses his wife on the cheek. Bobby is glad to busy herself with the tea things. After everything she knows about Daly and Millie, she hardly knows where to look.

Over the boiling of the kettle, Susie says that she's heard about Daly spinning for Courtenay on *Newsnight* after the TV debate and has come down to offer moral support.

'Oh, really? I wish you'd warned me, Suse. I've just offered my space in the car to Bobby ... '

'Oh, please,' Bobby says quickly, 'Mrs Daly should take my space after coming all this way. I'll catch it on TV.'

'Lovely. Thanks, Bobby.' Susie straightens herself up. Daly clenches his jaw. 'Oh Si, I've brought down some documents from Jeffrey Cuthbert. He dropped them over this morning and was keen for you to take a look.' Daly takes them from her and stuffs them into a drawer, spilling tea and knocking over a bin in the process.

Susie stoops to clear it up but Daly stops her.

'We have cleaners to do that, for God's sake.'

'You can't leave that mess!'

'It's their job, isn't it?' Daly snaps. Lucy wordlessly prepares a fresh apology note to the cleaning staff.

Susie looks awkwardly around the room.

'So, uh, Mrs Daly – I hear you have a psychiatry doctorate? I'm doing a campaign to save mental health units ...'

'Ah, never completed it, I'm afraid ...'

Bobby and Susie are soon talking earnestly about the Tipperton Mental Health Unit and the new campaign.

Daly, sensing trouble ahead, gazes moodily out of the window, his arms folded. He needs a way to make good on all of his many promises.

Claybourne Terrace

Eva, Bobby and Jess gather around the large TV in the living room to watch the first televised leadership debate. While the bulk of the Courtenay team are at the studio with their candidate, Eva will be the digital nerve centre for the campaign. She checks her laptop is fully set up one last time, with tabs open on Twitter, where she'll be live-tweeting from Courtenay's personal account, a Google doc that Jake and Nick will be filling with soundbites and suggested tweets for her to post, and WhatsApp, so Eva can post suggested tweets for Courtenay's supporting MPs on a group she has made with them all.

'Want to play debate bingo?' Percy asks, strolling in with a bottle of red wine. 'You know, every time one of them says "let me be absolutely clear" or "magic money tree" you take a drink.'

'I thought Holly wants you off the booze, Dad,' Eva says tersely, not looking up from her computer screen.

'She's upstairs doing an at-home spa session and is not to be disturbed.' Percy plonks himself down in an armchair.

Bobby glances over Eva's shoulder and sees that Jake is writing in the live Google doc. 'Oh, I forgot you work with Jake,' she says casually. She has not forgotten. 'Is he doing okay?'

'Yeah, good . . .' Eva keeps her eyes on her computer screen, her fingers flying across the keyboard.

'Great. You know, I—'

'I'm so sorry, babe, but now really isn't the time,' Eva says apologetically, her focus fixed on the TV screen as the moderator appears on a bright blue studio stage.

'Good evening and welcome to the first debate of the Conservative Party leadership hopefuls. Previously, we have waited until the final five candidates before we host a debate, but tonight we're bringing you the opportunity to see all eleven candidates (previously twelve, of course, before Natasha Weaver withdrew) in action before they formally launch . . . '

Eva quickly types out a message to the MP group:

OK, folks, here we go . . .

At the fifteen-minute ad break, Eva sits in shocked silence. The majority of the first section saw each candidate give a one-minute pitch, then they faced questions on the issue of sleaze. After a perfect, well-practised introduction, where he billed himself as the standards in public life champion, Courtenay didn't open his mouth once while the other candidates got stuck in debating Weaver's indiscretions, Parliamentary expenses and disciplining MPs. There are already jokes online about his team sending a cardboard cut-out of their candidate while locking the real thing in a cupboard, and someone has posted a clip of twenty whole seconds where he doesn't move at all.

On the Courtenay team WhatsApp, Nick has messaged:

Tell everyone not to worry. I'm going to go and wake him up.

Eva hopes Nick has a car battery to attach to Courtenay's balls.

Jess says nothing. Her WhatsApp group with Ed, Mike and George is fizzing with forwarded messages from horror-stricken MPs.

Before anyone can dwell any longer, the ad break is over and the debate is back on.

Nick certainly wasn't joking about giving Courtenay a wake-up call. The moderator has guided the debate to defence spending and he's arguably getting rather too passionate, interrupting his fellow panellists and getting increasingly flustered. He and Mark Norman, the Defence Secretary, are at each other's throats, both determined to be the foreign affairs candidate. Norman keeps suggesting that Courtenay's military career is nothing compared to his own experience in the Cabinet. At one point he even makes a comment that suggests Courtenay's service record might be blemished in some way.

Courtenay pushes back hard, each statement he makes beginning with 'As an ex-serviceman ...' Unbeknown to him the Twittersphere immediately responds, Percy helpfully piling in with, *Finally get why people used to go and watch public executions for entertainment.*

'Well, Eric,' David Jacobson, a rank outsider, says, 'you keep talking about being in the Army. Of course I want to thank you for your service, but I don't think it necessarily means you deserve to be Prime Minister. Have you ever run your own business? Were your family on benefits? While you were sitting at Eton with a silver spoon in your mouth, I was fighting my way into grammar school ...'

Courtenay, apoplectic with rage, struggles to respond. Every one of the other candidates piles in on him and the poor moderator struggles to bring the group back under control.

Percy slaps his thighs. 'Ooh, I've not had this much fun in ages ...'

'Oh piss off, Dad,' Eva says. What a shit show.

A couple of miles away, Daly's debate wrap-up appearance on *Newsnight* doesn't boost his profile in the way he'd hoped. He is repeatedly asked if he agrees with an anonymous Conservative MP that 'Eric Courtenay revealed himself to be a useless flesh puppet this evening', finally attempting to argue that 'flesh puppet' is a term of endearment and respect in Conservative circles. Yet again, Daly smarts at having his own credibility on the line in public because his old friend hasn't got his act together. In a sure sign of an unmitigated disaster, the Labour MP who is on to give balance to the programme doesn't even bother scoring points, instead simply giving Daly a sympathetic pat on the back. So much for mid-season form.

26th April

Portcullis House

Bobby is by herself in the Parliamentary office, deleting nasty comments under the video of Daly's disastrous *Newsnight* appearance on his Facebook page. It's a Friday, so the Dalys and Sacklers are back in their constituency homes and Lucy is working from home. As no MPs are in town, everyone from the Courtenay campaign has decided to work in the Notting Hill house. Bobby is happy to be alone for a while. In the last twenty-four hours Daly has launched the 'Save the Units' campaign online and she's managed to make contact with all the MPs on her list. She's thrilled by the amount of interest but she needs to think of next steps in peace.

There is a knock on the door.

'Come in,' Bobby says, deleting a comment that reads *u smarmy fuck*

'Hey.' She looks up and sees Jake Albury. She hurriedly runs a hand through her unbrushed hair.

'Sorry to interrupt,' Jake twists his watch strap around his wrist, 'I can come back another time . . . '

'No!' Bobby jumps up. 'Please . . . ' She gestures around the office then stops. 'Uh. Nobody's here.'

'Well, that's easy. I've come to see you.'

'Me?'

'Yeah,' Jake coughs and rubs his chin, 'I wondered if you fancied a cup of coffee?'

'Now . . . ?'

'No worries if you can't. I just thought I'd see if you were free—'

'I'm free!' Bobby nearly shouts. 'I'm free. You just caught me by surprise.'

'Great,' Jake smiles.

Bobby picks up her bag, cursing herself for not bothering with any makeup today. Despite the warm day, she pulls on a jumper. She's forgotten to wear a bra.

'So how is the campaign going?' Jake asks, trying to pick up the conversation again once they've bought their coffees and headed back to the office.

'Good,' Bobby replies. 'Thanks for all your advice. We've launched now. And the MPs I've approached are all interested. Simon is putting in some additional calls this weekend.' She shrugs. 'I guess this is all actually much easier than I thought. I know you think the drinks and receptions and tea room chatter was a silly talking shop. But at some level it really is all about relationships and just getting the ball rolling. People will do the right thing once you point it out to them. It didn't even occur to these MPs – even the ones who are big on mental health stuff – that these units needed protecting. The worry has been the national number of beds, not the geographical spread. It's only because ours is at risk that they can see this gaping hole.'

'I know what you mean. It's fashionable to bash all MPs for

being intrinsically self-interested or lazy or rotten. But that isn't true. There are so many talented people around, trying to do the right thing. At the very least, everyone must agree that nobody is solely bad or good. There's a lot of grey in the middle.'

Bobby nods vigorously. 'Like Simon.'

'So Simon's being helpful, is he?'

'He's being fantastic.' Bobby unlocks the office door and turns to face him. 'The minute I asked him to launch and contact these MPs, he did it. What is your issue with him?'

Jake sits down heavily on the sofa. 'He once dated a friend of mine and really hurt her.'

'Well, he's my boss. Not my boyfriend.'

'Speaking of which . . . ' Jake decides to cut to the chase. He has work to do, after all. 'Have you heard about this Spears Foundation party next week? Sounds kind of stupid, but I'm being roped in and I get to bring a date. It's black tie . . . could be fun. Want to go with me?'

'I'm actually going to that.'

Jake drains his cup and stands up. 'Oh. No worries . . . '

'But I'd like to go with you!' Bobby's brain catches up with what Jake has said.

'Great.' Jake leans against the door frame. 'See you there.'

He puts her number into his phone and leaves.

After a couple of hours of online dress shopping, Bobby reluctantly returns to her to-do list. She and Daly are meeting their planning experts on Monday and she needs to prepare. Just as she's settling down, her phone pings:

Really looking forward to the party next weekend. And Eric's launch. Maybe we should just go in black tie to both . . . Jake x

29th April

Burma Road, Houses of Parliament

Monday morning in the *Sentinel* Parliamentary office, and while George and Mike talk about football Ed keeps glancing at Jess, wondering why she's ignoring him. Jess's mind is out of the room. She found a note under her keyboard this morning:

I have something for you. Come to you know where at 11.

When Big Ben bongs eleven times, Jess wordlessly gets up from her desk and walks to the stone alcove. After a minute or two, Jean appears and signals to follow her into a hidden archway.

Before Jess can say anything, Jean hands her a plain envelope. Jess begins to unfold it but Jean stops her.

'Not here.' She glances around furtively. 'Look, I've not done this before. Given anything to a journalist, I mean. And trust me,' she pauses to light her cigarette, 'there's been plenty of stuff.'

'So why now?' Jess's mind is racing about what – and who – this could possibly be about.

'Look, we put up with our fair share of bad behaviour as "staff", but this chap takes the biscuit. He's . . . ' Jean stares into the middle distance, frowning.

'Who is it?' Jess asks.

Jean clamps her cigarette between her teeth and types a name into her phone.

Simon Daly.

Jess chews the name over.

'So what's this?' She brandishes the document.

'You'll see.' Jean flicks her ash.

'Jean, why are you doing this? You know we can't pay you, right?'

'It isn't for money!' Jean hisses. She shakes her head and takes another puff. 'My understanding is he's in line to become a pretty powerful man, if Eric Courtenay gets in. You can see where the man's headed. He's got the haircut and the suits and the smile. He's going to fall upwards the same way so many around here have.'

Jean drops her cigarette butt and stamps on it and continues.

'I'm retiring this week. It makes no odds to me what you do with that,' she inclines her head at the document in Jess's hand. 'I found it plain as day in a waste paper basket. It struck me that you could have too. This isn't revenge for the usual rudeness, you know. I call it a public duty.'

Jess walks quickly to the nearest bathroom, closes the door on a stall and opens the envelope. The headed paper reads *The Pearl Clinic, Harley Street*. It's a letter to Daly, confirming the date of an appointment several weeks ago for an abortion. Jess frowns. There's no way a newspaper can publish something like this. Aside from the strict rules on medical confidentiality, an appointment for an abortion (which could well be for Daly's wife, anyway) surely doesn't meet the requirement to be in the public interest. Jess turns to the other piece of paper, which is crumpled and grubby.

'Shit,' she whispers under her breath.

It's a handwritten note:

As discussed, here is the appointment for next week. I strongly advise you to take it. I will pay. If you don't you can expect a world of legal pane.

It's unsigned and unaddressed but the misspelling of 'pain' lets Jess safely assume that this was a first run at a note to somebody. If the author is Daly (and she assumes it is), famed for his large brain and turn of phrase, it would be pretty in character for him to scrap a ransom note on the grounds of a spelling mistake.

Jess sits in the cubicle for a long time, looking from one page to the other, before finally admitting to herself she's out of her depth. She tucks the papers back into the envelope and carries it carefully back to the office, feeling like she might be stopped at any moment and forced to hand it over.

Ed is alone when she arrives.

'Ed ... I've got hold of something I need to show you.' Jess closes the door behind her and lays the two documents out on her desk.

'Look at the date. Early March.'

'Where did you get this?'

'I can't tell you. Is that Daly's handwriting?'

'Haven't a clue.' Ed taps his fingers on the desk, wondering the same things as Jess. Can they publish this without being sued? 'We're going to have a lengthy chat with our lawyers, that's for sure.' He keeps looking at the pages.

'Surely this doesn't meet the threshold for being in the public interest to publish?'

'I dunno about that,' Ed says, leaning in closer to the pages, as if hoping to see a hidden code. 'Daly's big on women's rights. Abortion access, support for single mothers. The DWP child support stuff ... this jars pretty badly with "a woman's right to choose" – given the threatening nature of the hand-written note.'

'Kind of exciting, right?' whispers Jess, her warm breath tickling the back of Ed's neck.

His mouth twitches.

'Very.'

Portcullis House

Bobby uses her bum to push open the door of the Parliamentary office, her hands full of milk, biscuits and Diet Coke. The first of the meetings she is having with Daly and a series of planning specialists, lawyers and policy advisers to talk about Bobby's proposed unit legislation is about to begin. It's a 'stress test' according to Daly, to reveal any flaws in what Bobby's come up with. He wants Bobby to lead off on present-ing the plans, on answering the bulk of the questions and on asking a few questions of her own. He's even asked Lucy to arrange a large meeting room for the day. Bobby checks her phone and sees a good luck message from Jake. Since their coffee on Friday, they've been messaging all weekend, getting increasingly flirty.

What Bobby doesn't know is that over the weekend Daly had another meeting with Jeffrey Cuthbert, who is coming down for one of the meetings today and wasn't pleased about Daly's soft launch of the 'Save the Units' campaign. Daly had assured Jeffrey that the campaign would get very little momen-tum – which is true so far, the online interest is tiny outside Tipperton – and finally came clean about his deepest concern: the money would be very welcome, but with the chances of

Daly becoming Chancellor getting increasingly likely, the scrutiny isn't worth it.

Jeffrey Cuthbert had looked at him carefully, and said, 'Hm ... do you trust your wife?'

'She's a lead-lined box.'

'Leave it with me ...'

So for now Daly is still trying to reconcile Bobby's campaign to save the unit with Cuthbert's interest in tearing it down. He's hoping today's meetings leave everyone thinking he's on their side.

'Now, Roberta,' Daly says, 'are you all set for our day of brainstorming?'

'Ready,' replies Bobby brightly.

'I'm here to support you, remember? We're starting with Cuthberts, who are the biggest developers in our region,' Daly says, as they walk together down the corridor, Bobby carrying the tray of drinks, her papers tucked under her arm. 'I'll make the introductions and stuff – butter them up – but then I really want you to go for it.'

'Okay, I will.'

By lunchtime Bobby is on cloud nine. She dominated the discussions with professionals who have challenged her and – she feels sure – been impressed by her. Daly has even taken to introducing her as a 'whizz kid'. She hasn't felt this intellectually stretched and satisfied in ages.

'Shall we get some lunch?' Daly checks his watch. 'We've got time before the next meeting.'

They make their way to the Adjournment restaurant. As Bobby consults the menu she notices they are getting a few curious looks from other diners. On a high after her morning of winning minds, she is getting tired of the significant glances she and Daly generate whenever they're seen together. She glances at Daly's wedding ring. As if.

'So what do you think?' Daly pours them both a glass of wine.

Bobby takes a sip. She doesn't really want any – not least because it must look extra cosy to gossipers – but she also doesn't want to seem unfriendly. She needs to focus on the rest of the meetings coming up this afternoon.

'It's pretty encouraging how little resistance there seems to be,' she says. 'At least, I think I managed to see off the different challenges they raised.'

'Oh, absolutely. I've known all these guys for a really long time – when election time rolls round I need to get some cash out of them! So I know when they're impressed.'

'I can't believe they came all this way.'

'I said it was important,' Daly says earnestly. 'Plus I promised I wouldn't bring Moira with me. She's managed to completely blow some of these relationships. And they're important people in Tipperton.'

'So word is you're likely to get a big job if Eric Courtenay wins,' says Bobby, keen to keep Daly cheerful ahead of the afternoon's discussions. She really needs him to push the campaign a bit more publicly. It's getting very little traction so far. Perhaps she should try and get him to host an event like Hendrick did in the Cholmondeley Room a few weeks ago.

'That's what I'm told,' Daly frowns.

'What's wrong?'

'Well . . .' he sighs, 'it's a big opportunity, obviously. All I've ever really wanted, in fact. Finally down in the history books. But I'm worried about it. Mainly home stuff. It is so difficult . . .'

'I'm so sorry to hear that, Simon. You know, you don't have to take the job.'

'What would be the point of the last few years? I know I want to do it. More than I want kids, truthfully. It's Susie who is the keen one on that front . . .'

Bobby, wary of the personal direction the conversation has gone in, quickly fills her mouth with a large forkful of curry.

'Sorry, I shouldn't have off-loaded to you about what's going on at home. I just feel like I can trust you. And I don't have many people I can talk to about it. I'm sorry.'

Pull the other one, Bobby thinks. You hardly know me, let alone trust me.

'Don't worry about it. I'm no expert, but for what it's worth I think you'd make a great minister. But you do have a choice, remember?'

'You don't understand what it's like, do you?' Daly suddenly flares up. 'This has been it, for as long as I can remember. The great race. All the way through boarding school and Oxbridge and the back benches ... I've been with the same guys since I was thirteen. Some of them since before that. Whether it's exams or sports or girls, we're conditioned to win, okay? You opt out, you're a loser.'

'Simon ... ' Bobby says, wide-eyed.

He takes a deep breath and battles to get a grip of himself. His usual manner returns.

'It's a very strange pressure we put ourselves under. To make our fathers proud. To be a perfect man ... ' He smiles earnestly at her. 'I'm sorry, I'm being so dreadfully self-indulgent. You're far too good a listener, Bobby.'

Bobby continues to look at him, wondering whether a session at the Tipperton Mental Health Unit wouldn't go amiss.

'Come on, the next meeting is at two.'

As they head back to the meeting room, Daly rattles off anecdotes and shouts cheery greetings to MPs walking the opposite way. On the inside, his mind is racing. No more drinking at lunchtime. He'd nearly veered completely off his carefully laid rails.

Claybourne Terrace

Heading home after a long day, Eva checks her to-do list once again. Tomorrow is Courtenay's launch event and she can't recall having ever felt this stressed before. Clarissa has Eva's phone number now and is incessantly peppering her with messages about where she wants to sit, what the lighting is like and how she will be escorted through the building. On no account is she making her own way to the venue, so Eva has had to hire a car to drive her. After the disastrous first TV debate all eyes are on the Courtenay team. With Nick handling media and Jake on policy (plus Lucy, Bobby, Millie and a couple of Courtenay's researchers for operational support) the event itself seems in hand. But Clarissa has been clear that anything going wrong will, in her view, be Eva's fault. Her phone pings again.

Is your father coming? I'd like him to be there. Under no circumstances is he to bring his child bride.

Eva rubs her eyes.

She wonders why Clarissa would want Percy there at all. He's hardly been helpful to any of the candidates so far and his analysis of the first TV debate had been withering – 'great dynamism and bravery from all the candidates in scrapping tediously over the centre ground'. He's so active on Twitter, basking in all his adoring followers and cheerfully rowing with the less adoring ones, that as predicted the Wellington book has been neglected again. It seems that every time Percy settles down for some well-paid work that promises to pull him out of his financial woes he manages to veer off in a way that gets him plenty of attention but which scares corporate sponsors. The leadership contest is simply proving irresistible.

Eva pushes the front door open and heads to the kitchen for a glass of water. Percy is sitting at the kitchen table, looking slightly glazed.

'Everything okay, Dad?'

'Oh hi, pork chop. Just thinking ... ' Percy's eyes focus on his daughter. 'Holly has gone back to the States to see her family. Turns out old Pa Mayhew isn't entirely keen on his little girl shacking up with yours truly.'

'Hm, sensible man.' Eva puts her glass in the dishwasher. 'By the way, Clarissa Courtenay wants to know if you're coming to Eric's launch tomorrow.'

'Yes,' Percy perks up, 'yes, I'll be there.'

Keen to vent on someone, Eva considers having a crack at her father on the peerage. But he doesn't know that she knows about it – and for her to say so would break the confidential conversation he'd had with Peter. What Eva doesn't know, however, is the reason for Percy's sudden interest in joining the House of Lords. Holly has nothing to do with it.

Percy has worked hard to bury his ambition and competitiveness since being booted out of office, going out of his way to joke about how hopeless he had been as PM. But with the recent political earthquake in SW1, his dormant instincts are waking back up and he can see a route back to power, or some power at least. Eric Courtenay will likely be Prime Minister but he is weak and dependent on the skills and ideas of others. Percy, always with an eye to posterity, spots the opportunity to reinvent himself as the statesmanlike kingmaker.

It is technically possible for a member of the House of Lords to serve in the Cabinet – with the added benefit of not going through the bother of getting elected to the Commons – and if he positions himself well then Percy, when Courtenay faces the inevitable 'reset' moment in his premiership, can swoop into the political annals and public consciousness once again.

'Cool. Okay, I'm going to have a bath before supper.' Eva trudges up the stairs to her bedroom.

As the door closes behind her she feels her phone buzz. Clarissa again:

What the hell is your mother doing interviewing Natasha Weaver during Eric's launch tomorrow?

Eva frowns.

I don't know what you're talking about.

Ping. *I've just been told that Jenny Cross is doing a sit down with Natasha Weaver for a special Morning Show segment on open marriages, cheating, taboos, etc. Do you think this is helpful???*

Eva has had enough.

Obviously not. I don't know why you think my parents' schedules have anything to do with me.

Ping. *You've only got this job because of your parents.*

Eva is really getting sick of this woman pushing her around.

What are you talking about?

Ping. *You have this job because your father called me to beg. We've taken you in exchange for his support.*

Eva sits down on her bed. Before she can stop them, fat tears spill from her eyes. All her anxiety about nepotism, her rage at her parents, her exhaustion and frustration at the last few days seems to burst out in thick, ugly sobs.

After a few minutes she manages to calm down. She digs around in her knicker drawer, finds a packet of Jamie's cigarettes and settles down on her windowsill with her phone.

She calls Peter Foulkes.

'Well, duckie,' Peter says, after Eva's explained why she's sniffing so much, 'there's a reason your father always referred to her as *kalon kakon* when she was at StoryCorps.'

'What does that mean?'

'A beautiful evil.' Eva chews the words over. Her father is right – Clarissa is somehow both dangerous and fascinating. Like a poisonous flower. Eva knows deep down a large part of what bothers her is that she doesn't have Clarissa's favour.

'Look,' Peter continues, 'there is every reason to be worried about her, but my experience of Clarissa is she's only aggressive

265

towards people she's threatened by. She wouldn't give you the time of day if she genuinely thought you were a tiny pawn on the board.'

'But why am I even bothering with this job if I've only got it because of my dad? As soon as Eric wins they'll just bullet me.'

'Then make yourself indispensable. You've got a real opportunity here, Eva. You are exceptionally good at what you do. Show them.' Eva stares moodily at a pigeon on a nearby rooftop. 'And it could be worse.'

'How?'

'You could be married to her.'

Claybourne Terrace

Later that evening, Jess prepares dinner, thinking deeply about her day of discussion with the *Sentinel* legal team about the contents of Simon Daly's bin. Bobby lays the table, thinking about Jake, who she has been texting all day.

'You know, I really feel like me and Simon are getting to understand each other,' Bobby says. 'The meetings today were just ... fantastic. And after work he took me to the Red Lion for a drink and introduced me to a load of journalists. Obviously Simon's doing a lot of spinning on behalf of Eric Courtenay just now. It was really cool to watch him work. The whole day has helped me understand why people want to be MPs. It must be so satisfying.' She decides to leave out the part about the campaign making very little impact so far.

'Mm, yeah.' Jess is typing on her phone, the corners of her mouth twitching at the conversation she's having with Ed.

'How about you?' Bobby balances the bowl on her hip while she gets some salad servers out of a drawer. 'You look like you've had a good day.'

Jess looks up guiltily. 'Yeah, good. I mean, I haven't had any big breakthroughs,' she blushes slightly at her lie, 'but I really feel like Ed and I are getting the hang of each other. We spent a lot of today at HQ speaking to executive folk. We're working on a project together and he really let me take the lead. Super empowering. He was so impressive, just with everything he knew. I learned a lot.'

Jess decides she won't add that when she gave Ed a lift back to Westminster on her motorbike they had nearly hit a lorry after she started to grind her leather-clad back against him. He's been texting her incessantly since, now firmly under her spell.

'Such a great feeling, right?' Bobby gushes.

'Hm-mm,' Jess says, glad that Bobby isn't a mind reader.

They eat in silence. After a while Eva glances up and notices Bobby looking at her strangely.

'Are you okay, Eva?'

'Yeah. I am. Just a bit frazzled. Hasn't been the best day, to be honest. And I'm really nervous about tomorrow.'

'It's going to be great, okay? Besides, I'll be there to help you.'

'And look at it this way,' Jess looks at the time on her phone, 'in about fourteen hours it's all done anyway.'

'Good point. Are you coming?'

'I'm probably going to be stuck at HQ again, but Ed will be there.'

'It's a bit weird to have you doing something else when there's a leadership contest, no?'

'Yeah ... but,' Jess thinks hard; she doesn't want to lie exactly but she can't tell the truth, 'I'm new, so they insist on a load of rubbish training.'

'Oh, cool,' Eva shrugs and goes back to her phone.

Bobby looks at Jess, sure that she's hiding something. It's an altogether strange evening but, Bobby reasons, maybe this is just the reality of the three of them hitting their professional stride.

30th April

TIME TO CRACK DOWN ON SCHOOL BULLYING/
WORLD WHEAT SHORTAGE

Army and Navy Club, St James's

Eva is out early at the beautiful wood-panelled room where
Courtenay's launch is about to take place. It would be perfect
for a club dinner, or perhaps a wake for a decorated general,
but the oil paintings, rich carpets and marble fittings clash
horribly with the zesty pop-up banners screaming *Eric! Time
for Change!*

There are several TV screens dotted around the room, tuned
to different channels. Millie, Bobby and Lucy are glued to one
in particular.

'Welcome back to the *Morning Show*. Now, some of you may
have seen that last week Industrial Economy Secretary Natasha
Weaver, a frontrunner in the contest to become the next
Conservative Party Leader and our Prime Minister, withdrew
from the race after photographs of her,' the host stiffens, 'were
published in the *Sentinel* newspaper. It has started a fiery conversation online about open marriage and cheating, as well as

the treatment of women in the public eye. Jenny Cross, a great friend of the show and herself no stranger to the perils of political marriages, sat down with Ms Weaver earlier this morning.'

Eva's mother appears in what looks like a fancy hotel room, wearing a turquoise skirt suit and a fixed smile. Her gaunt face is heavily made up and her helmet of blonde hair glitters in the studio lights. Jenny Cross is on a mission. After years as Percy's number 2 – dexterously hosting MPs' wives for wine in the Number Ten flat and charity coffee mornings in the State Rooms, as well as being the heart and soul of the G7 and G20 spouse programmes – she wants to forge her own career as a writer and broadcaster. Her diaries are due to be published soon and she hopes that a few TV gigs and podcast appearances will lead to her own show, a turn on *Strictly* and who knows what else? She lies awake at night chewing over the words 'national treasure'.

Eva turns away from the screen but can't resist keeping an ear out for the dialogue. She's terrified her mother is about to sabotage Courtenay's launch.

'So, Natasha, there are those who say an open marriage is just cheating. What do you say to those people?' And they're off.

Eva busies herself with straightening chairs and checking glasses and cups for cleanliness. The different TVs blast her with sound bites: 'Well, Jenny, in my experience of serving the British people, the value of fairness is perhaps what we all have in common. We don't like cheats . . . What's crucial is that this part of the campaign is exclusively about appealing to MPs. Courtenay is popular with the membership, but can he get through this stage? . . . What my husband and I have is very special. It's an agreement we've made as a couple, based on love and trust . . . Yes, so we're hearing that the Permanent Secretary in question has handed in his resignation and is expected to become the Ambassador to the Philippines . . . Ex-PM Percy

Cross has taken to Twitter this morning to clarify what he meant by previously referring to Eric Courtenay as "a massive weapon", saying "I meant he's a force to be reckoned with" ... What about emotional cheating? Texts. Letters. Online messages. An open marriage might seem taboo or peculiar to people, but surely it is more honest than sneaking about on a dating app or something?'

'I think that's fair enough,' interjects Lucy. Millie nods, not taking her eyes off the screen.

'Yes, Courtenay is the acknowledged frontrunner but there is a lot hanging on his launch. The big criticism of him is lack of experience and, I hate to say it, any real substance ... The Leader of the Opposition is in Grimsby today, launching ... A series of really quite damning nude photos ... I think it is extremely difficult to be a woman in politics. You have to be perfect. And with regards to sex, you're held to a completely different standard to men. JFK, Clinton ... But these photos. Why hasn't Weaver resigned? ... Why should she? She's not done anything illegal ... So why did she quit the race? ... I felt it would become a distraction from my record of delivery. In truth, I think this was deliberately done by someone to discredit me. One hour before my launch event? Please! ... Speaking of which, it's Eric Courtenay's leadership launch event this morning. Will you be going along?'

Eva stops and listens.

Weaver looks at Jenny roguishly. 'Oh, I wouldn't want to be a distraction ...'

'Well, will you be supporting him?' presses Jenny.

Eva wheels around and stares at the screen helplessly.

'I think it's only fair for everyone to launch their campaigns first. I want to hear what they all have to say so I can make an informed decision.'

'Blah blah blah,' yawns Millie.

Eva exhales as she hears her mother plug her upcoming book to finish the segment.

'All right, guys – show's over. Guests arrive any minute.'

Lucy and Bobby jump up and take their positions at the door, guest lists at the ready. Millie nips to the loo to brush her hair and rearrange her bra to put her V-neck dress to best effect. She's still down about Daly and hopes that picking out a new 'boyfriend' will improve her mood.

Nick O'Hara appears, accompanied by a camera crew. He directs them on where to set up, so that Courtenay's speech can go out live to all the different broadcasters. He explains to Eva where he wants volunteers with microphones for the Q&A bit.

Eva walks round the back of the stage to a private room and knocks.

'Come in.'

Courtenay and Jake Albury look up as she enters. They're both standing over a table, making minor edits to the speech. Courtenay is drinking Red Bull and looking ashen. Eva's mouth twitches as she catches a faint strain of 'Lose Yourself' by Eminem coming from his headphones.

'Can I get you anything? We've got water and cough sweets on the lectern. You know . . . just in case.'

'Thanks, Eva. I'm fine with this. Clarissa said I should drink it to give me a kick. Making me feel even more nervous, to be honest.'

Eva checks her phone. The WhatsApp group she has made for the event is coming alive. 'So just to let you know, guests have started arriving so we're still on track to begin at 10.30, so in about fifteen minutes' time.'

'Okay, great.' Courtenay goes slightly green.

Eva raises her eyebrows at Jake, who gives her an imperceptible wink, before heading back to the main area. Nick high fives her on his way to pump up the quivering Courtenay.

'Looking great out there. Nice one.'

The room is now full and buzzing with conversation. Some MPs and Peers are weaving their way through the rows of seats, guided by Lucy and Millie to reserved places. Eva picks up strands of conversations through the hubbub:

'It really was the most wonderful constituency surgery I've had to date. Honestly, a neckline down to her navel ... yeah, I did her Association dinner a few weeks ago. The raffle included a signed Percy Cross book. You know, *Boadicea: Barbarian Babe*. Good luck getting an unsigned one ... Nah, I think Eric's an idiot, but he's the only candidate we have who stands a chance of keeping my seat at the next election ... Of course I'm not going to drop the cottage hospital campaign, David. That's why I got elected in the first place ... Apparently Ford is trying to cement her legacy, go down in the history books. Labour are doing a great job of painting it as killing off public services ... She said she's leaving me, mate. Tired of me pinging around between London, home and the constituency. She calls it the Bermuda Triangle as I keep disappearing ... I feel like I'm running out of time. We'll have an election soon and I haven't done half the stuff I said I'd do – to say nothing of getting even an inch up the greasy pole. The minute I was elected, all my energies should have gone into getting re-elected ... '

Bobby chats with the earnest Mary Jones about the 'Save the Units' campaign.

'Well, of course it could all be a bit louder – but Simon has a different style to me. He knows what he's doing. I'm sure he'll know when the time's right to draw more attention to it,' Mary says kindly, when Bobby reveals her worry that the campaign isn't getting much pick-up. 'He has the ear of this guy, after all.' She jabs her thumb at the large poster of Courtenay's name.

Clarissa arrives with Jackson, wearing a magnificent

navy-blue military-style cloak over a silk burgundy wrap dress and neon orange stilettos. Her hair and makeup have been professionally styled to look natural in photographs, so she looks a little overdone to the naked eye. The snappers go wild.

Eva texts the group:

Princess Margaret is in the building.

Burma Road, Houses of Parliament

Ed flops down in his chair and yawns.

'How was it?' Jess asks him.

'Heavy going,' he replies. 'Courtenay's an all right guy but he didn't exactly capture the imagination.'

'It was like watching an aged orca at SeaWorld,' Mike says. 'Going through the motions but you could kind of tell he wasn't in his natural environment. Just going round and round his tank with his dorsal fin all floppy.'

'Oh dear . . .'

'Yeah. Just not really a public speaker. He did a bit better in the Q&A, but all in all not impressive.'

'It was the Gettysburg Address compared to Dick-Dick's launch,' laughs George, holding up his phone, and shows Jess a picture of Richard Hendrick standing in front of his campaign slogan, *Richard Hendrick > Taking Britain Forward*. He has managed to get his head positioned so that the photographer has got a perfect photo of the arrow pointed at Hendrick's face, which covers the 'r' in 'drick'.

'Did you see Natasha Weaver's interview with Jenny Cross?' Jess asks.

'Yeah. She's done quite well to get it onto the violation of the photos being published and away from the actual misbehaviour. Our lawyers aren't concerned, though. Anyway, feels like old news now ... can you believe the Graham Thomas stuff was only a couple of weeks ago?' George yawns.

'On which note, we'd better get going if we're going to make Mark Norman's launch. Apparently he's pissed off that Courtenay got the Army and Navy Club. Obviously thinks defence is his thing.' Mike stands and stretches.

'Why isn't he doing it there too?'

'They won't have him,' George grins, 'he's only a reservist. Still, I'm told he'll have substantial snacks. We'd better hurry or they'll all be eaten.'

Mike beckons George, who picks up his jacket, clicks his heels and gives a little salute before they head out together.

Ed closes the door behind them.

'So, how did you get on with the legal eagles this morning?' he asks.

'Not well,' Jess says sullenly. 'They think Daly has strong grounds to sue the paper if we print the story without more to go on. We could probably prove the handwritten note is from him, but who is it to?'

'You know what? I think we should just have a punt.'

'How?' Jess asks.

'Just go fishing. Call the Daly office and see if anyone bites ...'

Jess runs through the possible scenarios. The worst that can happen is the Daly team tell her to piss off and threaten legal action. On the other hand, she might get a bit more out of them. She wonders whether to ask Bobby but reasons it's unlikely she'll know anything, seeing as she's only just arrived. Plus she'd like to keep home and work separated as much as possible.

Jess nods.

'Christ,' Ed exhales, 'this gets me so pumped.'

'Me too,' Jess moves slightly closer to him and holds out her arm, 'look, I've got goosebumps.'

The room seems to have suddenly emptied of air.

Ed runs his fingertips softly down Jess's wrist. She looks unblinkingly into his eyes. Ed can smell her hair from here. He desperately fights the urge to kiss her.

'Jess, do you want to . . .'

She smiles up at him. 'Look, Ed, I'm enjoying this cat and mouse. But we can't sleep together.'

'Sure . . . of course.' He gives his head a little shake, like a dog trying to get water out of its ears.

'But that doesn't mean we can't have a little fun . . .' Jess steps ever so slightly closer to him. Ed feels his heart rate jump up.

'Meaning?' He tries to keep his voice steady.

'Well . . . obviously you can't touch me and I won't touch you . . . but I don't see why you can't touch yourself.'

'Uh . . . it sounds a bit weird.'

'Oh, no doubt it's unusual,' Jess smirks, 'but I thought you'd quite like that.'

For a long moment their eyes are locked together. They stand close enough that Jess feels Ed getting hard against her hip, the bustle of Burma Road rumbling away just the other side of the door. Eventually Jess walks slowly to her desk and sits down.

Ed remains fixed to the spot, his eyes not leaving her. For a moment, Jess has a flutter of panic. Has she finally overplayed her hand? He could fire her on the spot.

'So . . . what do you have in mind?' Ed says finally.

Jess swivels her chair round to face him, flooded with relief.

'Depends.' Very slowly, she slides her legs apart, revealing bare thighs beneath her skirt. 'Want to try something different?'

Ed's mouth feels unbelievably dry. 'I think I already am,' he manages to grin.

'Sit down.' He does as he's told.

Jess feels a delicious thrill of excitement. She rises from her seat and strolls over to him. Without thinking Ed reaches for her.

'No touching, remember?' she says, stepping out of range. 'Do whatever you like to yourself, but I'm off-limits.'

'Sorry. Yes. Okay,' Ed mutters.

He senses Jess sit down behind him.

'I've thought about doing this since my first day, you know,' she whispers, anticipating what will excite him.

'Really?'

'Yes. And that first bike ride ... Bet you weren't expecting that, were you?'

'It's definitely refreshing ... So when do you think about it?'

'Oh, everywhere. But it depends on where I am for whether I do anything about it. If I'm in public, or buying lunch or in a meeting ... I put it to one side. But if I'm alone. In bed ... or the shower, then ... '

'Then what?' Ed can feel his chest tighten. His fingers, gripping the armrests of his chair, are dying to move to his trouser zip. The idea of this young woman thinking about him like that is intoxicating.

Jess's breath tickles his ear. 'I do whatever I want with my fingers ... or the shower head ... or a toy ... until ... '

Ed lets out a tiny whimper. His hands dart to his crotch, where he fumbles with his trouser button and zip.

'Sometimes, halfway through, I text you.' Jess grins.

Her words send Ed into overdrive. He begins rhythmically stroking himself.

'And I know that gets you off, too.'

'It does ... it does,' he manages.

'I bet you feel filthy, wanking to your junior's text messages,' Jess whispers, trying something out. She can't quite believe the effect these words have on him.

He emits an involuntary, hopeless wail. 'Jesus ... ' he says through clenched teeth.

'How does it feel to know that I could end your career?'

'Oh God . . . you couldn't . . . ' he hisses.

'Really?' Jess steps back around so she faces him. 'You don't think it would mean something if I told our editor, maybe Lord Finlayson himself, that you'd exposed yourself to me,' his hand moves even faster, 'wanked yourself off like a disgusting little pervert . . . in our office?'

Ed's face is a mosaic of fear, rage and pleasure.

'You'd be a social pariah. Your marriage would end. You'd presumably be fired . . . '

Ed doesn't know what to do with himself. He's desperate to stop but he just can't. He's never experienced anything like this before. He must get to the finish line and back to his senses.

Jess sits down in front of him and slides to the edge of her seat, pulling her skirt up to reveal that she isn't wearing underwear.

'You disgusting,' Ed bites his bottom lip, his face purpling in effort, 'shameful,' he closes his eyes in a painful wince, 'filthy man.' He springs forward and in a series of juddering, helpless spasms he orgasms on Jess's legs.

Ed falls forward onto his knees on the floor, panting.

When he finally composes himself, he looks up at Jess, who's been waiting for his attention to return. Without saying a word she pulls her skirt back down and turns back to her computer, as though nothing has happened.

Claybourne Terrace

'Thank you so much.' Clarissa accepts the large glass of wine from Percy and settles back in an armchair in the shabby living room.

'My pleasure,' cries Percy. 'You must be exhausted.'

'Well, we've hardly got going really. But cranking darling

Eric along is really very tiring. He doesn't have your talent for oration.' Clarissa smiles graciously.

'You're very kind. I think he did well, though. After all, nobody really cares about the launches outside Westminster. I'll of course be penning a glowing write-up about him in the *Telegraph* tomorrow.'

What a shambles, Percy thinks. The guy would have been less wooden in a coffin.

What do you want, you brown-nosing old has-been? thinks Clarissa.

'Thank you so much.' Clarissa takes a thoughtful sip of wine. 'Tell me – is there something you want from me?'

'Well, it's more that I think there may be something that you want from me. You just don't know it yet.'

'Go on.' Clarissa raises an eyebrow. 'Another daughter to employ, perhaps?'

'Not quite. I see that Mark Norman is picking up rather a lot more MPs than your dear husband, and catching him up in the members' poll.'

'Correct.'

'What if I told you I possess a certain picture of our respected Defence Secretary enjoying some lines of . . . Daz at university?'

Clarissa smiles wickedly. 'Well, that depends on the picture. We'd have to be sure it was him. And that the Daz is in fact . . . detergent. We used to practise with sherbet when I was at school . . . '

Percy saunters over to his desk and unlocks a drawer. He slides out a photograph and hands it to Clarissa.

Although the photograph is in black and white there is no question the man sitting at a table holding a rolled-up bank note is Mark Norman. There is also no question of who his companion is.

'But Percy, that's you with him.'

Percy nods.

'What do you want us to do ... crop you out?'

'Oh, I don't think so,' Percy says casually. 'I'm pretty resilient. I see dear old Mark's launch kicks off shortly. It might be worth planting a question with a friendly journalist about whether he's ever taken drugs before. I bet you a case of champagne Mark says no. It would then be most unfortunate for this photo to appear in the public domain ...'

'With you in it?'

'Of course,' Percy shrugs. 'How else can the story be verified?'

There is a long silence while Clarissa looks at Percy carefully.

'This is showing great generosity of spirit, Perce,' she says eventually. 'But I hate to be in debt to anybody. Surely there's something we can do for you.'

'Oh, well,' Percy keeps his voice light, 'I suppose if the next Prime Minister were to see fit to squeeze me into the Upper House I'd be honoured to serve him in any way I can ...'

Clarissa smiles. She hadn't taken Percy Cross to be such a vain old fool. Selling what is left of his reputation for a peerage. There was talk of him making a comeback a while ago but it fizzled out the moment he got used to kicking back in first class on the way to Davos. 'I'm sure he'd be delighted to.'

'Well, that's terrific.'

Percy heaves himself up and refills their glasses.

Clarissa toasts him. 'Lord Cross.'

2nd May

Burma Road, Houses of Parliament

By Thursday morning, after going round in circles speaking to the *Sentinel* lawyers, Jess is finally ready to call Daly's office. A real problem has been trying to catch Ed for advice. He was so busy darting around after the Mark Norman cocaine story that Jess struggled to get his attention. Eventually she'd suggested meeting in the lobby briefing room, up some rickety stairs above the House of Commons Chamber, for a repeat of their private meeting in the office. She knew he wouldn't be able to resist coming, so to speak, somewhere so risky. Hot on the trail of big scoops and constantly fearful and thrilled by this strange new arrangement, they both seem to have come alive.

Jess closes the office door and stands in her customary power pose, enjoying the peace. After a few deep breaths she sits down at her desk and dials the number for Daly's Parliamentary office, praying that Bobby doesn't answer. Jess has privately decided that if Bobby does answer she'll just play it straight and ask to speak to Daly. For the hundredth time, she wonders what possessed Daly to just put the letter and his note in the communal bin rather than shredding or burning it.

The line rings for about fifteen seconds, then a woman answers. It isn't Bobby.

'Hello, this is Jess Adler from the *Sentinel*.' Jess's nerves seep away as she gets down to business. 'Please can I speak to a media representative for Mr Daly?'

'Oh, I'm afraid everybody's out and about just now.' The woman pauses. 'Could I take a message, Miss Adler? Then someone can call you back.'

'Yes, great. So we have a few questions about a couple of documents that have recently come into our possession. It's an appointment letter for the Pearl Clinic on Harley Street addressed to Mr Daly for an abortion. There's also a handwritten note, which we believe is from him, suggesting that he is threatening someone with legal action if they don't take the appointment.'

The woman on the phone doesn't say anything, presumably scribbling it all down, so Jess reads out her name and number and promises to send an email too. Before she can finish, though, she's interrupted.

'These seem to me to be highly spurious, entirely unsubstantiated claims. I hope you have some very good lawyers, Ms Adler. I recommend that any further correspondence comes through them.'

Susie Daly slams the phone down and stands motionless in the middle of the room, still wearing her coat. She feels like she has been looking at one of those optical illusions and seeing a lamp. Just one phone call has switched everything in her brain. Now she sees faces. Women's faces. A hot coil of anguish and rage seems to wrap suffocatingly around her.

As Susie stands frozen, wondering how she will ever move

again, the door rattles open and her husband strolls in, texting the Legislative Lads WhatsApp group, followed by Bobby, Millie and Lucy.

'Oh, hello, darling,' Daly smiles. 'Down early for the fundraiser tonight, are you?'

He stops when he sees her face, sensing trouble.

'Simon,' Susie says, her voice eerily calm, 'I've just had a journalist on the phone, wondering whether you have an explanation for why you recently booked an appointment at a Harley Street clinic for an abortion.'

'Suse, I—'

'Don't interrupt me!' Susie hisses. 'You may be familiar with the name of the place. The Pearl Clinic. If you'll recall, it's the place I've been begging for us to go for IVF for the last year. The place you think is too expensive and ostentatious. Apparently it is perfectly adequate for one of your WHORES!' She screams the last word.

Millie, Bobby and Lucy look desperately at each other. Lucy inclines her head towards the door. She inches out and the other two begin to follow her.

'No, please don't leave on my account!' says Susie loudly. 'I think you all ought to hear this, seeing as one of you is going to have to call the paper back.'

'Susie, darling,' Daly is finally able to speak, 'I think there's been a mistake here. What on earth is going on?'

'Simon, stop *lying*.' Susie starts to cry. 'I know this is true. It's the first thing I know about you that is. I've always shrugged off your flirting with other women as innocent, a bit of risky fun . . .'

Bobby sees that Millie has started to shake. It suddenly occurs to her what has happened. Millie must have become pregnant during their affair. Daly can't tell his wife the truth without going into Millie and her husband's arrangement. And how would Sackler feel about his wife having a termination?

Daly has done the halfway decent thing to protect his best friend and his wife by picking up that bill. The Sacklers are hardly blessed with money.

Susie sits heavily down on the sofa, her face in her hands. 'I've pushed off your reluctance to get proper help to conceive a baby for ages. An abortion? You know I would do anything to have a child. Even raise one that isn't mine.' She begins sobbing in earnest.

'Darling,' Daly croons softly, 'I promise, this isn't what you think . . . '

It's like watching an accident happen in extreme slow motion. Bobby glances at Millie, who seems to be paralysed.

'Simon, what the bloody hell else could it be?' Susie groans. 'This Jess Adler woman has the whole thing laid out . . . '

There is a long silence, broken only by Susie's sniffles.

'Mrs Daly . . . ' Bobby says in a small voice, her mind racing. 'It's me. That clinic appointment. It's for me.'

Everyone in the room looks at her open-mouthed.

'It isn't what you think, though. What I mean is, it isn't anything to do with Simon at all.' She looks at the floor, trying to get her thoughts together. 'He very kindly sorted it out for me. And I'll repay him through my wages. I . . . got myself in trouble. He helped me. I'm so sorry you're upset. I didn't mean to hurt anybody.'

Susie looks at her suspiciously.

'I know Jess Adler. Let me call her and explain. They can't write about this.'

'Well then,' Daly takes Susie's hand, fighting a whoop of relief, 'I think I should take you out for a lovely lunch, my dearest. Bobby – I'm sorry this has all come out, but remember that you're among friends here.'

Daly wipes his wife's face with his handkerchief and guides her out of the room by the elbow.

As Bobby steps into the cupboard next door to call Jess she notices Millie looking at her strangely.

Claybourne Terrace

'I still don't understand why you're protecting him.' Jess hands Bobby a huge gin and tonic. 'You don't owe him anything. You sounded so odd on the phone, you know. I knew you weren't telling the truth. Aside from knowing your stats on the action front, the dates don't even match up! What's going on?'

Jess and Bobby are sitting in the scruffy garden of Claybourne Terrace, enjoying the warm stones in the evening sun. Eva is out at a fundraising dinner for women candidates, and Percy, pining for Holly, has gone for a solitary research session at the British Library.

Bobby is getting tired of Jess's constant needling and is dying to ask her how much she enjoys going through people's bins, but suspects that could lead to an argument and all kinds of stuff tumbling out. She guesses this is why Jess was acting so strangely the night before Courtenay's campaign launch.

'I can't tell you,' says Bobby. 'You know I would if I could. But it isn't just to protect him. There's a bunch of people who would have very painful, private parts of their lives exposed if this were printed. I know this is frustrating, but you've made the right call.' Bobby hopes this draws a line under the discussion. Privately, she's hoping her quick thinking might get Daly to put a bit more energy behind the unit campaign. The other MPs involved seem very nervous about stepping on his toes. If Daly is a bit more strident then perhaps more of them will speak out. Little does she know that the more ambitious ones are waiting for a clear signal that Courtenay will back the campaign – something he's unlikely to do until the final two.

Aside from disappointment at losing the story, Jess wonders whether Bobby is out of her depth. She knows her friend is a kind, loyal person but she also thinks Bobby's naive. There's no way she can manoeuvre her way through this unscathed. That handwritten note was no joke.

Once Jess had got off the phone with Bobby she'd sat down to talk it over with Ed immediately. There's no way the story can be printed on public interest grounds as it currently stands.

'Look, I'm telling you it has nothing to do with this girl Bobby, okay?' she'd said, repeatedly.

'How do you know?'

'I just do. She's one of my best friends … I know she's protecting someone. The dates don't even work – she hadn't even met Daly when that letter was sent! What I don't understand is why she is saying otherwise.'

'Well, one thing's for sure, this whole story is scuppered. If what she says is true, we can't use it. And if she won't tell us more, it's dead in the water. I can't believe you never said you knew someone who worked in that office.'

'She's only just started and hardly knows the guy. There's no way she would be answering press enquiries. I'll work on her but I don't feel comfortable pursuing my friends for stories.'

'You'll feel differently in a day or two, when the high has worn off and you're back to trying to pick up any titbit about the new Highway Code. Simon Daly is going to be the next Chancellor. Everyone knows the deal is done. You could blow this whole thing wide open.'

'Do you think all I care about is getting stories? I happen to think proper journalism is about genuinely informing the public. Holding on to a moral compass that our readers agree with. Doing the right thing. Reporting real news.'

'Oh come off it – where's your killer instinct? I saw how

buzzed you got this week, although maybe that was down to a couple of particular highlights . . . ' Ed had smirked.

'If you think my highlights were watching a middle-aged, married man wank himself silly, you need your head looked at.'

She'd picked up her bag and marched out leaving a red-faced Ed to fume.

Dorchester Hotel

Eva, having a quick scroll through Twitter in a loo cubicle, decides she ought to get back to her table, where an increasingly drunk Susie Daly is waiting for her. She is about to flush when she hears two women enter the ladies and can't resist listening to their conversation.

'Well, Diana tells me they were in the Parliamentary office where, after a generous amount of Famous Grouse, they were having a very nice time indeed.'

'Who?'

'You know Diana Packer. And her husband – dear old Bertie? Anyway, the bell goes for a vote and the sweet old chap toddles off, zipping up his large trousers and completely forgetting about the cock ring he's wearing that Diana so kindly gifted him to, in her words, "improve his attention span".'

Both women giggle.

'Such is the size of these large trousers, or the comparative size of his honourable member, that none of his colleagues notice his carefully maintained erection as he waits to vote, swaying ever so slightly.'

More laughter.

'He's at a tricky age – very tricky when whisky comes into it – and with the struggle to make it down in time and vote the correct way, he's horrified to register a considerable relaxation below the belt buckle as he potters into the Chamber to hear the result. Cursing his commitment to boxer shorts rather than secure briefs, he tries to make it to a bench to sit down before disaster strikes. Diana says she watched on TV as he ... ' the woman stifles another laugh, 'John Waynes his way to a seat, feeling the ring slipping, slipping ... slipping ... then the cock ring plops down right in the middle of the Commons! Not missing a beat, an energetic young Whip tosses the loose change from his pocket onto the floor to disguise the ring and spare the old chap his blushes. Diana says she's sent the Whip in question a case of champagne to thank him for his discretion!'

The women laugh for a good deal longer, finish touching up their makeup and leave.

Eva leaves shortly after and dashes back to her table, delighted to have a fun story to relay to Susie Daly. But when she gets there, Susie isn't in the mood for gossip.

'Fill her up,' Susie burps loudly, holding out her empty wine glass. Eva calculates this to be the seventh time that evening that she's done a refill. Susie, no longer the kind, gentle woman from Chequers of a few weeks ago, is getting curious looks from the pearl-wearing donors at nearby tables. Fuck you, Susie thinks, as she sloshes a great quantity of her fresh glass down her front, where are *your* husbands right now?

Eva's had enough.

'Susie, is there something the matter?' she asks.

'Oh,' Susie hiccups, 'I had a terrible run in with some-one today.'

'What happened?'

'I toddled down to London early for this,' she gestures round the room, 'wretched affair. Nobody was in the office when I arrived – busy bees indeed – and the phone was ringing so I answered it. Some ghastly journalist from the *Sentinel*.

Claimed to have some correspondence about an appointment for an abortion at a Harley Street clinic addressed to . . . ' Susie pauses for a moment, apparently unable to remember Daly's name, 'my husband.' She misses her mouth and tips wine down her chin.

'Susie, I'm so sorry,' Eva says. At least the poor woman isn't being strung along any longer.

'It's fine! It's fine . . . turns out it's nothing to do with him . . . all a misunderstanding. He was just doing someone a favour . . . poor little tart from the Parli office.' Susie seems to lose her train of thought. 'I'm so sorry, what were you saying?'

'Nothing. Just that I'm sorry. How very stressful for you.'

'Yes, and it's so sad, you see, because Simon is so dreadfully worried someone will try and make mischief with it and cause him problems. He's been promised high office by Eric Courtenay, you know.' Susie grins a wide red-wine smile.

As she guides a glazed Susie to a cab, Eva turns over in her mind what she's just learned. No doubt Clarissa will be well abreast of all Daly's affairs, but will she know this interesting development? Eva's been around uneasy power dynamics long enough to see that Clarissa is weary of Daly's purchase on her husband. This bit of intel might be just what Eva needs to get Clarissa on side – and kick Daly out of the picture.

3rd May

Notting Hill

The Courtenay campaign are having their usual morning meeting in the Notting Hill house. It's safe to say that energy is low. Courtenay himself, tired of being the stalking horse for the other campaigns, is struggling with the pressure of constant anonymous jabs at him in the media. Yesterday he had a hustings event for the 1922 Committee – a private Q&A in front of every Conservative MP where all the hopeful candidates make their pitch – and got in a muddle, repeatedly referring to the Queen as 'Her Highness' and not 'Her Majesty'. His colleagues had been ruthless in their assessment of his sophistication. Mark Norman, the now ex-Defence Secretary (he felt he'd had to resign as well as drop out of the race after the cocaine photo surfaced), responded by tweeting a photo of himself and the Queen, inspecting a tank.

'This is outrageous!' Courtenay slams a copy of *The Times* onto the table. Mugs of coffee tremble. 'I didn't serve in the Armed Forces for fifteen years to get shat on by this ... this TA twat!'

Eva has read the story already but can't help glancing at the front page, featuring an old photo of Courtenay on deployment somewhere hot and sandy, brandishing a large gun. Norman has done an interview about his failed candidacy, where he has gone one step further with what he said in the first TV debate about Courtenay's service record and made a vague but concerning allusion to a mysterious incident in Somalia. The blogosphere is churning with the words 'possible human rights violations' and Jacobson, the surprising outside prospect, has been quick to call for transparency from Courtenay about the rumours.

'Don't worry, boss,' Nick says soothingly, piling spoonfuls of sugar into his tea, 'we'll fix this. He's just having a punt because he thinks the coke story came from us.' Nick is always chipper in these meetings, but privately he is worried. He'd come over in person late the previous night with Jackson to ask Courtenay what had really happened in Somalia. Courtenay won't divulge a single detail, even to Clarissa. He'd just kept repeating, 'Classified means something, okay?' That won't work if Norman stays on the rampage.

'Well, it wasn't us. Besides, he shouldn't have snorted it in the first place.' Courtenay rubs his eyes. Clarissa had made becoming PM sound pretty easy. Three days since his launch and he feels like he's been repeatedly rear-ended by a monster truck.

'Pity he stopped taking it. The TV debates would be a bit more lively.'

'Speaking of which,' Clarissa says, 'that's what you need to focus on now. The next debate is on Monday. Only you, Singh, Hendrick and Jacobson next. Singh is faltering. We've prepped for Hendrick. You guys need to focus on Jacobson. We didn't count on him getting this far and he seems to be carrying a lot of the do-gooders with him.'

Eva casts her mind back to her long and painful chat with David Jacobson at Chequers. She'd written him off as a bed-wetting, Lib Demmy mouth-breather. Clearly he has something to him that she missed.

'No problem. I'm spending Monday morning with the spinners too. Graham Thomas is willing to say anything we want if it means he stays in the Cabinet. Literally anything. Bring back the death penalty ... dump his wife ... get a microphone in front of that man and we're good to go.' Nick laughs and shakes his head at the ex-Transport Secretary's willingness to go from one campaign to the next like a (spud) gun for hire.

'Thank God for cannon fodder,' Clarissa grins, joining Nick in trying to lift the mood. 'Nige, how is the whipping going?'

'Well, it helps to have the lovely Eva,' Jackson beams. Clarissa doesn't react. 'She's a good cop and I'm the baddie. We're feeling very confident, but I'm holding back a few plum job offers and a couple of Ks in case Jacobson plays a blinder next week. The troops are jittery about this Somalia stuff in *The Times*. Norman is kicking it at anyone who'll listen. We don't want it running into the weekend. And the Nat Weaver stuff is still sticking in their inboxes. Worries it'll become a new Pestminster thing. Lucky you were strong on it with your launch video ... '

Eva is careful not to make eye contact with anyone. She knows that Jackson is being airy but he's lying through his teeth about being confident about MP numbers. They're nowhere near where they needed to be after the launch and the first TV debate. The performance of their candidate is one thing, the cloud over Courtenay's military career another. However, the Weaver story, the scrutiny of every remaining candidate's sex life and tolerance for misbehaviour is front and centre in everyone's mind. Eva knows from her conversations with influential grey beards that Courtenay must double down on his 'zero tolerance for sleaze' message. It's the only thing that is working for him at the moment.

'Leave *The Times* to me,' Clarissa sighs. 'It's a disgrace that the ex-Defence Secretary is allowed to make these kinds of accusations – not to mention a National Security threat. Desperate measures . . .'

Clarissa has given the Weaver stuff some thought. She needs something more on it to feed the media beast over the weekend while she gets to the bottom of exactly what the hell her husband was doing in his tin hat in a sandpit . . . But she can't quite find the missing piece.

'Exactly!' Courtenay stands up again. 'It is total bollocks, but because he doesn't have to prove anything, everyone thinks there must be something to it!'

'Calm down, my love,' Clarissa says gently, stroking his hand. 'You've got work to do. Leave this with me.'

She heads to the kitchen. Jackson joins her, indicating to Eva to follow. She ducks in behind him.

'Excuse me, Clarissa,' Eva says quietly.

'Yes?' Clarissa raises her eyebrows.

'We need a word, Clazz.' Jackson sits down heavily. 'It's much worse than we thought on the MP front. Eric needs to show up. He sat there like a lemon at the last TV debate.'

Clarissa seems to deflate before them. 'I know.'

'Well, young Eva has something to cheer you up.'

'An idea?' Clarissa doesn't look hopeful.

'Gossip,' Eva says, leaning against the counter conspiratorially, 'but it's sensitive.'

'Gossip? I'm not Martha Mitchell—'

'You need to listen to this,' Jackson cuts her off, jabbing his thumb in Eva's direction.

Clarissa says nothing but her eyes narrow a little. Eva is

taken aback by the transformation from tired and vulnerable to hungry and alert in seconds.

'So last night I sat next to Susie Daly – Simon's wife – at dinner. She had a lot to drink. I'm not even sure she'll remember what she said . . . but anyway, she told me that the *Sentinel* has been sniffing around some story about Simon. Apparently they found a letter from a Harley Street clinic, confirming an appointment for an abortion a few weeks ago.'

'Really . . . ' Clarissa's lip curls.

'Susie said the story has been squashed and that it was all a misunderstanding. Something to do with a researcher.'

'Ah yes, I hear Simon has some pretty young innocent following him around,' Jackson chuckles.

'It's not her,' Eva says quickly. 'The new girl. It definitely isn't her. I know her. She didn't even know Daly until a couple of weeks ago.'

'Okay, but unlikely to be his wife . . . '

Clarissa's eyes find Jackson's. There's no need for telepathy. If this story comes out somehow and Courtenay is ruthless about following through on his anti-sleaze promise – going as far as disowning his best man, no less – then everyone will agree that he is made of proper leadership material. The other candidates will only have platitudes. He will have action. And a story. For Clarissa, there is the added benefit of cutting Daly down to size. She doesn't like his influence on her husband, and to have the control of the Treasury is, in her view, to have too much control. There are only enough strings for one puppet master.

'Well, this is very interesting,' Clarissa keeps her voice steady, 'although I don't see what can come of it if the *Sentinel* won't publish. I know from experience they have very jumpy lawyers.'

'That's true, but we don't need a big paper like them to publish,' Jackson says eagerly. 'After all, we only really need to speak to MPs, seeing as it's them doing the voting at this stage. We need to distract them for a few days while we get to the bottom of this military stuff. Can't you think of a creative solution? Just for the bubble . . . Aside from the fact it's unlikely that it was for the woman he's married to, Simon has been pretty vocal about women's issues. Don't forget the DWP fiasco last year. Someone with a higher appetite for risk might enjoy this.'

There is a long pause while Clarissa works out how she can resuscitate the story.

'Of course,' she looks innocently through her lashes, 'Simon is a dear friend of Eric's. And hopefully our next Chancellor. This will need to be handled with complete care and discretion.'

'Absolutely,' Eva replies. Jackson merely nods.

'Well then, I'd better get Nick to fix up an interview slot on the radio tomorrow morning for Eric.'

'That's right,' Jackson grimaces. 'Gotta punch the sleaze bruise.' He's thrilled to nobble Daly. Membership of every conceivable London club hardly means you're entitled to a key Cabinet role.

As Eva is leaving the room, Clarissa pats her on the arm.

'Very good, Eva. Very good . . .'

4th May

Claybourne Terrace

Jess, Eva and Bobby wait in their dressing gowns for Camilla to come from the *Blush* offices, where she has chosen dresses for the three of them to borrow for tonight's party. Jess, as anxious as the other two about Camilla's cryptic message – *I've gone full fashun* – tops up their Prosecco glasses. She and Eva idly discuss the response to Eric Courtenay's renewed hard line on sleaze on LBC that morning – 'politicians are always promising to be tough on slipping standards but the moment it's time to act – particularly with someone you know – the easy road is taken. Not with me . . . ' MPs, Party members, the media and the public at large couldn't have received Clarissa's world class, zero tolerance wordsmithing better.

Bobby is excited to see Jake but otherwise calm after a normal day in the office yesterday, following the drama from Jess's phone call the day before. Daly has headed into the weekend promising earnestly to work away on a stack of reading material for the mental health unit campaign. Lucy made a few jokes about Bobby being a dark horse, but mainly focused on how much bigger their office will be once Daly becomes Chancellor. She's already started to pack cardboard boxes in preparation.

The doorbell goes.

'Ladies!' Camilla trills, stepping over the threshold, her arms stuffed full of suit bags, a wheelie suitcase behind her.

As she accepts a fizzing glass from Jess, Camilla mystically describes the *Blush* fashion cupboard: shelves of shoes, hats and bags alongside rack after rack of dresses; feathers and sequins, chiffon and silk in every imaginable colour; furniture draped with scarves and belts.

'That doesn't even include the beauty cupboard. And you should see the jewellery. There's this amazing diamante wig I tried on yesterday, but unless I go as Cher for Halloween I don't know when I'd ever get to wear it,' Camilla says, starting to unzip the different bags. 'Now . . . who's first?'

A couple of minutes later Eva cocks her head to one side and surveys Jess, who is wearing a floor-length sleeveless black leather dress in front of Eva's bedroom mirror. The bateau neckline, modest on the chest, shows off her toned arms. She takes a step forward to reveal a long slit up one side then turns, revealing a deep V down the back.

'Oh fuck me,' gasps Camilla. 'You look stunning. And I got these to go with.' She holds up a pair of large green drop earrings.

'Those aren't real emeralds, are they?'

'Sweetie, this isn't De Beers,' Camilla laughs. 'Eva . . . '

Eva pulls on a dove grey Grecian dress, made of the most delicate hammered silk. She turns to reveal a floor-length cape at the back. Camilla pulls out a handful of what looks like cobwebs and explains that they are tiny chains, which can be threaded through Eva's hair by the stylist coming later.

'Do you think this is too much?' Camilla has put on an enormous hot pink mesh dress. It is a perfect fifties silhouette: a hidden corset in a sweetheart neckline straps her waist firmly in and a full skirt, cut to mid-shin at the front and dropping into a slight train at the back, accentuates her waist even further. The neon colour and layers of mesh give it a modern twist.

'No way. I love it,' Jess says, still admiring herself in the mirror. She shouts through to the bathroom. 'Bob, how are you getting on in there?'

Bobby shyly steps out and stands in front of the mirror. The dress, as red and shiny as a fresh cherry, hangs perfectly on her frame and brings out the colour in her pale cheeks. She turns to admire the back, the bow at her neck ending at the top of her bum. She has never felt so beautiful.

'Christ, that looks good. Why did I opt for Journalist Barbie?' Camilla gasps. She checks her watch. 'Right – we have a glam squad coming in thirty minutes. I'm off to roll around in a paddling pool of instant tanner.'

Notting Hill

'Ed, darling, can you hear me?' Clarissa lies back in a steaming bath. She reaches up a finger to delicately scratch the tip of her nose without disturbing her face mask.

'Yes, hello, my dear, all well?' Ed Cooper's voice rings out tinnily from the speaker phone.

'Just having a nice soak before this party later. Are you going?'

'You wicked girl, putting a picture in my head. Yes, I'll be there.'

'Wonderful. But I have a little something to discuss before that. We don't need to set tongues wagging with too much chit-chat in person.'

'Go on . . .'

'A little birdie tells me you have a cracking story on ice about a certain MP . . . and a certain clinic?'

There is a pause on the other end of the line.

'So you've seen the letters?'

'Letters plural?'

'There's the clinic letter with the appointment and then there's a handwritten note. It isn't signed but it's pretty clearly a threat of legal action if whoever it is doesn't . . . acquiesce.'

'Are you going to publish?' Clarissa splashes water as she soaps herself. This is getting very interesting.

'Nothing doing, I'm afraid. Our lawyers won't touch it on public interest grounds. You know the StoryCorps lot. We don't even know who the girl is, though I'm assured it isn't the current pup running round with him. All we can do is join the dots right now and they want more.'

'Well . . . there are places where dot-joining is just fine. Finlayson still owns the *Crash* website, doesn't he?'

'That's a gossipy rag, Clarissa . . .'

'Read by every single Conservative MP. Obviously you don't need to write anything in your unimpeachable name. Just get this out there, okay?' Clarissa sits up, water sloshing around her.

'I see,' Ed smirks, pausing to let her dangle for a moment. 'Well, I'm sure you have your reasons. Leave it with me.'

He hangs up and, inspecting the ironed shirt his wife has hung out for him, texts Iain Atkins at *Crash* to make sure he'll be at the party.

Clarissa lies back and allows the warm water to wash over her. It had taken some effort to get her husband in the right place to go hard on the radio this morning with what is now being referred to as 'a plea for abstinence'. Courtenay simply hadn't thought it was necessary. Too used to chaps being issued slaps on the wrist at every institution he's been part of since birth. But polling numbers convinced him in the end, they generally always do, and he'd agreed that Party members didn't rate him on 'good leader' and 'shares my values' – and that MPs just didn't rate him. Now, unbeknown to him, there will soon be a chance to put his money where his mouth is.

Clarissa is impressed by the rejuvenating powers of good press on her husband, who had been as down in the mouth as a cone-shamed dog all week. At lunchtime, he'd screwed her so hard against their fridge that Clarissa wouldn't be surprised if she has a little 'SMEG' bruise imprinted on her lower back. How she loves to make her husband happy.

Just thinking about it makes Clarissa reach for the shower head.

Claybourne Terrace

'Oh pork chop, don't you look wonderful,' beams Percy. He is sitting on the floor of the living room with his legs straight out in front of him, Winnie-the-Pooh-style, spooning Nutella from a jar.

'Dad, why don't you come with us?' Eva struts around, admiring herself in the mirror. Her hair has been plaited into a wreath around her head, the tiny silver chains criss-crossing it like a net.

'Oh, that's very sweet but I don't want to drag you girls down ... plus, with Holly away I am making very good progress on poor Wellie.'

Before Eva can respond, the others file in one by one. Percy clangs his spoon against the Nutella jar in riotous appreciation for each outfit. Jess's hair is styled in loose waves, her fair skin glowing against the green earrings, black leather and crisp red lipstick she's chosen. She's also wearing an interesting belt, covered with chains and studs, that the others haven't seen before. Bobby's hair is drawn into a neat chignon at the back of her head. She catches sight of herself in the mirror and is taken aback by how different she looks with heavy, smoky eye makeup. For the dozenth time she rubs the rich, scarlet fabric of the dress between a finger and thumb to calm her nerves. Camilla, her straight blonde hair drawn back in a flawless ponytail, her makeup dewy and bright, inches carefully round the room, trying to avoid knocking over little tables and vases with her enormous layers of pink mesh.

'This reminds me of when I met the Spice Girls,' Percy beams. 'All so different. Gosh, I wish Holly were here. She'd love all this. Anyway – pictures!'

The girls pose in front of the fireplace, Percy struggling with their different camera phones.

'You don't realise how much you have your photo taken as Prime Minister,' he confides. 'So many shots of you walking and things. I always knew when a newspaper editor was cross with me because they'd choose an absolutely appalling snap of me gurning . . . '

'Girls, our taxi's here,' Eva consults her phone. 'Dad . . . can you help us into the car? Camilla's dress is massive.'

When they are all packed inside, Percy waves and walks back up the steps to the front door, his shoulders slumped. Eva lowers the window.

'Are you sure you'll be okay?' she calls.

'Yes,' he smiles. 'I've got a lovely curry coming. And I think I'll watch *Where Eagles Dare*.'

'Again? You've been watching it all week.'

He spreads his hands. '"Broadsword calling Danny Boy". Have fun!'

Eva cranes her neck as the taxi speeds away, watching Percy

go back inside the house. She has a nagging worry at the back of her mind about him. He's miserable without Holly around.

'Funny position your dad finds himself in,' muses Camilla, muffled by the layers of fabric around her. 'I mean, he's still quite young, relatively speaking. What does he do now?'

'Bits and bobs. Writes books and articles. Gives speeches. I know what you mean, though. All he ever wanted was to be PM. Then he did it. Not very well, but he's in the history books with the rest of them. Now he's sort of rattling aimlessly around,' Eva says ruefully.

She spends the rest of the journey watching the city pass by, dipping in and out of Camilla's long explanation about why she has dumped her boyfriend.

'He basically admitted I'm just a trophy girlfriend,' she rants. 'He was totally fine with all the fashion stuff, but now I'm writing more about things like politics, he's got the hump. Sorry it makes you feel insecure that I have a brain!'

'Oh God,' squeaks Bobby. 'We're here!'

The cab sweeps through the gates and joins a queue of vehicles up the drive of Jeremy Spears's huge Hampstead mansion.

Hampstead

They manoeuvre their way out of the cab as elegantly as possible (Camilla's voluminous pink skirts make everything quite hard to do inconspicuously) and climb the steps to the open front door, which is decorated with a beautiful flower arch. A waiter offers them champagne and directs them to the garden. As they walk, Eva explains a little about Jeremy Spears: made all his money through property; an incredibly wealthy donor to the Conservative Party and to several galleries, museums and creative institutions; a long-standing member of what Jeremy himself calls 'the City's gay mafia'. Incredibly vain, he's constantly throwing parties in his own honour – 'Tonight's for his foundation, which currently has something to do with getting kids off video games and into chess.'

They follow the noise of the party and enter a stunning long gallery, made of glass panes and filled with what they take to be priceless ancient Greek statues and sculptures.

Jess gasps and points at one of them. It is of a young, muscled man aiming a bow and arrow into the middle distance. It's surely the Greek god Apollo, but the face is strangely modern. Jess is pointing out how massive and erect the penis is when Eva clutches her arm and whispers, 'It's Jeremy Spears! That's his face!'

They wheel around and see that every statue is of someone current. The men, for the most part, fantastically well endowed. They cluster round each one, stifling laughter. Bobby points at an Athena in full armour wearing a set of pearls: Margaret Thatcher. Fiona Bruce, examining a golden apple like she is on the *Antiques Roadshow*, as a demure Aphrodite. Robert Peston in winged sandals as Hermes. Gordon Brown, hammer aloft, as Hephaestus. Eric Courtenay as a sleek Ares, kitted out for all-out war. There are also a decent number of giant-cocked rock stars and actors that Jeremy seems to have thrown in for good measure.

'I've found the winner!' cries Jess. She has found a small, fat Dionysus. Pot-bellied, with a large cup of wine in his hand, sitting in the same unmistakable Winnie-the-Pooh pose and gazing down at a tiny, mushroom-like penis is Percy Cross.

'There you are!'

The girls all turn to see Jamie marching towards them, looking like a harried Ralph Lauren model in his dinner jacket. When he gets closer he stops. 'Ah, so you've found Jeremy's little collection.'

302

'Has he really had all these made of marble?' asks Bobby.

'Oh Christ, no. Plaster. He gets them done all the time. Always with the great big doodahs. Except your pa, of course – the price for holding back on a knighthood. My word, you all look sensational. You, my love,' he kisses Eva, 'look like a real-life Greek goddess. Come and say hi to Jeremy.'

He leads them away from the sculptures towards the chatter of the crowd out in the garden. They pause for a moment, taking in the scene. It is a wall of sound, colour and smell. There are easily eight hundred people before them on the lawns, dressed in every colour and texture imaginable. The scent of the riotous flower beds battles over several different perfumes and the sizzling pan-Asian canapes. A pianist at an enormous white grand plays Chopin beneath the hubbub of animated conversation and laughter. While the girls stand, framed by the doorway, several people look up and admire them. Eva nods and smiles in recognition at many of the faces. She sees Jackson circling like a shark around a small cluster of MPs. He'll get those votes for Eric if it kills him. Bobby's eyes frantically search for Jake, but she can't see him. Jess glares out, doing her best to look uninterested. There are ex-Prime Ministers, minor Royals, captains of industry, Rod Stewart and Mick Jagger, artists, journalists and authors. All three of the women realise that if it weren't for Jamie, they would never have been invited.

A tanned, silver-haired man standing at the bottom of the steps looks over his shoulder at where his companions are staring. He turns to face the girls and forces his heavy Botox into a smile.

'Jamie, dear,' Jeremy Spears drawls, 'you really have outdone yourself. What an exquisite bunch. Welcome to my humble abode, ladies. Now, do tell me which is your mare?'

Eva, well used to this kind of thing, steps forward. Jamie introduces each of the others in turn. Jeremy makes a great show of kissing their hands and discussing their outfits. He recognises each designer by sight.

'I'm just so pleased you've made the effort. I said black tie, but some people look,' he inclines his head at Susie Daly's maroon Monsoon cocktail dress a few feet away, 'cheap.'

'Well, we can't all fall back on the *Blush* fashion cupboard,' smiles Eva.

While the group chats, Bobby feels a gentle touch on her shoulder.

Jake is standing behind her, holding two glasses of champagne. He couldn't look more handsome. He is wearing a faintly worn-out double-breasted dinner jacket that hangs perfectly off his tall, lean frame. He's shaved and had his hair cut.

'You look ... amazing,' he grins.

She beams back at him and kisses him on the cheek, taking one of the glasses.

'Ah, you know this young lady, do you, Jake?' blurts out Jeremy, keen to remain the centre of attention. He starts singing a loud and tuneless rendition of Chris de Burgh's 'Lady in Red'. Groups of people nearby turn to see what is going on.

Bobby, wishing the ground would swallow her up, thanks Jeremy for the invitation to the party, knocks back the contents of her glass in one gulp, and leads Jake away by the hand. She feels Jake's thumb give her palm a reassuring squeeze.

'Crikey, who's that?' Camilla whispers to Jess, pointing at a woman stalking towards them.

The woman is incredibly thin, every sinew of her bare arms and neck strained, like a whippet. Her shiny bob and heavy makeup are dramatic and unmistakable, her heels sky-high.

Before Jess can answer, Eva sighs. 'Hi, Mum.'

'Eva, darling,' Jenny Cross offers a bony cheek to be kissed. 'You look ... smart.' Eva immediately feels relieved to have most of her body covered with draping material. She had forgotten that her mother, a serial mingler, would be invited.

'Thanks. These are my friends. You've met Jess before at graduation. This is Camilla. She writes features at *Blush*.'

Jenny smiles vaguely at Jess and immediately turns her attention to Camilla, sensing a commission.

'How fun. You know I'm writing a piece for you just now on the star sign diet. It's fascinating. Now Eva here, as a Leo, should really avoid dairy. But it's pretty clear *that* isn't happening!' Jenny gives a little laugh, then sighs. 'God, I looked good before I had a child . . . '

'Well, I think you look wonderful, Jen.' Jamie puts a protective hand on Eva's shoulder. 'Now remind me of your star sign. *Saggy*-tarius, isn't it?' Before Jenny can answer he turns to Eva. 'Will you introduce me to your new boss?'

Eva gratefully takes his arm and they head off into the crowd in search of Courtenay.

Jess listens politely to Jenny and Camilla's earnest conversation about diamond dust facials but can't help glancing around at the other guests. She spots Nigel Jackson clenching an MP's hand, the knuckles white. After a couple of seconds of the MP speaking she sees Jackson grin, release the MP and pat him on the back, moving on to new prey. Next she spies the horn-rimmed glasses of Philip McKay, the *Sentinel* editor, who beckons her over.

As Jess walks through the throng she feels very aware of being in floor-length backless leather. At least she has a sensible neckline. As she gets closer she recognises the person standing with Philip. The *boss*.

'Hello, Jess,' Philip smiles. 'There's someone I'd like to introduce you to. This,' he indicates the upright older gentleman next to him, 'is Lord Finlayson.'

'My Lord,' Jess shakes his hand. 'Or, should I say, my Overlord.'

Lord Finlayson roars with laughter. 'Well, it is a pleasure to meet you, Miss Adler. Although I'm sad to say it looks difficult for you to perform any Cirque du Soleil acrobatics this evening in that dress.'

'I'm afraid so,' she says. 'This is a special occasion and that was just a normal Friday.'

Finlayson laughs again. Philip spots the Home Secretary in the crowd and excuses himself.

'So, how are you finding things so far?' Finlayson asks genially.

'I'm enjoying it,' Jess replies. 'And I'm so grateful to you for the opportunity.'

'My pleasure. I'm very pleased with what you've produced so far. And I've never heard Ed Cooper speak so generously about one of his colleagues before. You seem to have tamed him. I'm sure the HR team thanks you.' He beams at her.

'Well, there's always a danger he'll maul me at some point.'

Finlayson sips his champagne, well aware that Ed, along with Clarissa, could go for his jugular at any time. He wishes he was the type to set some ex-Mossad goons on them.

'So, are you enjoying the leadership race so far?' he says, changing tack.

'It's definitely eye-opening. But I hope to move around a little in the medium to long term.' She wonders how hard to push and then shrugs, unsure of when she'll next get to make her case. Years, probably. 'I really want to expand my repertoire. Write some longer pieces. Investigative journalism. Perhaps a book one day . . . I have a warm project—'

'About your working girls in Glasgow? Magnus told me all about that.'

Of course the two men know each other. This old chap's tentacles spread far and wide.

Finlayson fixes her with a gimlet eye. 'It's possible, what

you're talking about. But it takes time and requires some investment from us, which you need to earn.'

He takes another sip of champagne and waves at someone behind Jess. She feels a stab of disappointment. She's overplayed her hand and is being dismissed.

'Lord Finlayson.' It's Ed.

'Hello, Ed. Have you seen Clarissa yet? I'm keen to say hello.'

'She's just over there,' Ed points. 'Can I guide you over?'

'No, no. I must take Margaret. She needs rescuing from Richard Hendrick. Now, young lady,' Finlayson takes Jess's hand. She feels a little card transfer to her palm. 'I'll think about what you've said. Time is one thing, but impressing me? That's quite another.'

As Ed follows Lord Finlayson's retreating figure, Jess glimpses at the card – Finlayson's personal mobile and email, AKA the golden ticket. She slips it into her clutch bag, buzzing with a new sense of purpose. Lord Finlayson wants to be impressed. She'll knock his cashmere socks off.

'Great dress,' Ed says, finally tearing his eyes away from the old proprietor and Clarissa Courtenay. He recognises the belt around her waist as the collar he bought in Soho. He longs to reach out and grab it. 'I suppose you recall that I'm a fan of you in leather.'

'Yeah . . .' All Jess can think about is what she should do next. Now she's met the big man, Ed seems irrelevant. She spots Teddy Hammer in the crowd. She is just about to step away when Ed forces his way into her thoughts.

'So the clinic story's back on.'

Jess's head snaps around, immediately focused on him. 'In the *Sentinel*? In my name?'

Ed puts his finger to his lips. 'Are you mad? No – *Crash*. It's the sort of thing they can get away with. We're nowhere near it.'

Jess looks intently at Ed. He has shielded her. But not everyone is protected.

'How is it being reported? Is Bobby named?' She allows her finger and thumb to gently jingle one of the little chains on the belt.

Ed tears his eyes away from her waist and surveys the crowd. He gives an imperceptible shake of the head.

Jess breathes a sigh of relief. She knew the very idea of Bobby being involved was rubbish. And with the story no longer even appearing in the *Sentinel* she is nowhere near it. Jess wonders whether Ed is right about her lacking a killer instinct.

Eva rushes into the loos, where Jess and Bobby are reapplying makeup.

'Bob, I have someone I want you to meet,' she cries and taps Jess on the shoulder. 'You come too.'

Jess is happy for the interruption. She's been making chit-chat with Bobby but feels like a cork trying to keep in a shaken bottle of champagne. It isn't fair to tell Bobby what's coming, as it puts her in a dilemma on whether to warn Daly about it. Besides, Jess doesn't actually know how it'll be written up by *Crash*. It probably won't even name the guy.

Bobby and Jess exchange glances and follow Eva back to the room with the statues in it.

'Prime Minister,' Eva's voice reverberates off the tiled floor and glass ceiling, 'this is Bobby Cliveden.'

The PM and her husband turn away from Peter Mandelson as Hades. 'Bobby, how nice to meet you.' The PM smiles and offers her hand.

Bobby shakes it wordlessly. She feels winded.

'And Jess, great to see you again. Glad you put that quote to good work.' The PM winks.

'Prime Minister. You look . . . *awesome*.' Jess struggles for any other word.

The PM is wearing a cream silk blouse tucked into

high-waisted black satin cigarette trousers, high heels and the sleek hairstyle she'd chosen for her resignation statement. Most strikingly of all, she wears a heavily embellished cropped matador jacket and matching cummerbund.

'Thanks. What do you think of this?' She points to the statue her husband has moved to, a copy of the Boudicca statue by Westminster Bridge, except with the PM's face. There is even a little figurine of Dennis in the chariot beside her, his tongue lolling as though his head is sticking out the window of a moving car.

'Can you keep it?' asks Eva. 'You should keep it.'

'I don't know . . . will your father keep his?' the PM asks dryly.

'He claims he's lost weight, so I should think he'll only want it if he can persuade the artist to shave some material off the pot belly and use it to give him a . . . poll lead.' Eva grimaces.

'So,' the PM turns to Bobby, who is staring at her, 'Eva tells me you have a campaign running. Tell me about it.'

'Well, Prime Minister . . . '

Eva and Jess drift away to give Bobby some space, having fun looking at the other statues with the PM's husband. Jess is pointing out how the figurine of Ian Hislop as Prometheus is bearing a rolled-up *Private Eye* rather than a flaming torch, when she looks up and digs her elbow into Eva's ribs. It is Clarissa Courtenay, wrapped in an exquisite dark green Vivienne Westwood ball gown. The corseted waist and off-the-shoulder neckline expose her gorgeous creamy skin. Her dark hair has been sleekly blow-dried. Rubies glitter at her throat and ears. She looks like a soprano on opening night at the Royal Opera House.

Clarissa walks straight ahead, not acknowledging anyone, but when the PM's husband calls out to her she swivels round, acting as though she hadn't seen him.

'Michael, how lovely to run into you.' She kisses him on

the cheek, ignoring Eva. 'Tell me, how is your poor mangled doggo?'

For a split second, the PM's husband looks taken aback, his mouth hanging open slightly. 'Fine ... fine. I just wanted to say hello and, if everything goes to plan for Eric, I'd be pleased to take you out for lunch and chat about what life's like in the madhouse. I had a ... fascinating discussion with Jenny Cross when I was going in. I'd be delighted to pass the spouse baton on.'

'That is so incredibly kind, but one doesn't wish to count one's chickens. Anything can happen. How about I get in touch through Evie, here,' Clarissa inclines her head, 'nearer the time?'

'Of course. Have a good evening.' The PM's husband watches her leave, frowning slightly.

' ... I am fully supportive,' the PM says, as she strolls back over with a starry-eyed Bobby. 'I suppose it will be introduced with my successor, but I'm remaining as an MP so I'll certainly back it. Perhaps we can speak once the dust settles to see how I can help?'

'Oh, I can't thank you enough.'

'Well, I'm just sorry this wasn't addressed during my own premiership.'

'I suppose Simon reasoned it was a bit trivial to raise just one unit with you. And it wasn't until I dug a bit deeper that we realised it had the potential to be a national problem. Luckily no harm has been done. Yet.'

'Yes, that's true. Still, it's refreshing to fix something because it needs fixing and not because the damage is already done,' the PM sighs, taking her husband's arm. 'Well, enjoy your evening.'

Bobby watches the Fords leave, her back to the other two. She feels overwhelmed, picturing herself a month ago learning she'd soon be pitching her campaign to a sitting Prime Minister.

'Sorry,' Bobby blinks several times, pulling herself back together, 'think I've had too much champagne.'

'Or not enough! Come on – let's re-enter the fray.' Eva leads them back outside, where the sun has gone down. The garden is now glowing with tea lights and tiki torches.

Jamie is loitering at the bottom of the steps. 'There you are! Come and dance, girls.'

They follow him through a long, candlelit archway of trellised roses, towards a huge marquee. Jamie suddenly stops in his tracks. 'Shh! Sounds like somebody's having some fun!'

There are two figures tussling in the bushes. For a moment, Eva thinks Jamie is right and that this is a romantic embrace. Then she recognises one of the whispering voices. She waves her friends on into the marquee and presses herself against the roses, straining her ears.

'... make your mind up, mate. I'd hate to have to push out that unfortunate rent boy stuff. Not sure your wife would be too pleased ...'

As her eyes become accustomed to the dark, Eva sees that Jackson has a man pinned against the other side of the rose arch.

'Are you so desperate for votes that you're resorting to blackmail?' Eva thinks hard but can't place the person with him.

'You get special treatment, David ...'

Eva keeps walking, shivering a little. No wonder they had so much trouble keeping rebel MPs under control in Downing Street. Jackson is so ruthless that the government whipping operation had no teeth at all by comparison. Who wouldn't rather be disciplined by the Chief over seeing their darkest secrets made public?

She follows the music into the marquee. 'Crocodile Rock' mixed with a familiar hip hop track blares from the speakers.

'The DJ has been shipped in from Miami, apparently,' yells

311

Jamie, 'does mash-ups. We've had Jay-Z, Rick Astley, Rolling Stones . . .'

'Bobby!' Jake tears himself away from the dancefloor. He's taken off his bow tie. His hair is scruffy again. He has colour in his cheeks. Without thinking, Bobby slips her arms round his neck and kisses him. Jake is surprised for a second, then he is kissing her too, his arms wrapped around the small of her back.

Jess and Eva exchange gleeful looks, before Jamie drags Eva off to the dancefloor.

Jess enjoys being alone for a moment, turning the evening's events over in her mind, but it is only for a moment.

'I saw you having a nice cosy chat with Finlayson,' says a now familiar voice. It is Teddy Hammer, fixing her with a beady eye. 'Everything okay?'

'Yeah. It is.'

Teddy doesn't say anything but continues to look at her.

'Finlayson likes what I do and when I pressed him on diversifying my projects and stuff he gave me his card . . .' She holds it up.

'Personal number. Very good,' Teddy murmurs. 'Nothing else?'

Jess sighs. 'I dunno. I just wonder if I'm cut out for this. I like hunting down stories and stuff but . . . I'm not sure I have the killer instinct to be a journalist.'

'Hm. Ed's muddied the waters, has he?'

'How did you know?'

'Young Edward has his own way of doing things. He likes to have someone egging him on. Let me guess, he's called you a chicken?'

Jess stares at the lights pinging off the spinning disco ball and nods, avoiding Teddy's kind but meaningful look.

'Pure brinkmanship. He'll do for himself eventually . . . Right, my dear. Home time for me. Hold on to that card – I know Presidents and Prime Ministers who would kill to have it.' Teddy hobbles off.

Jess watches Teddy's retreating back, wondering exactly what he means by 'he'll do for himself eventually'. Would he say anything if he knew about Ed's strange power dynamic with Jess? She shrugs the thought off, reasoning that it's much worse for Ed – who is married and is technically gratifying himself in front of a subordinate – and, grabbing a glass of champagne off a passing tray, heads onto the dancefloor to join Eva.

At a nearby table, Bobby and Susie Daly sit, talking earnestly. Jake hovers awkwardly to the side.

'Bobby, I just wanted to say one more time … I'm sorry for jumping to such a silly conclusion. I've had some fertility issues, you see, and … well, I'm just a bit all over the place,' Susie says, her eyes full of tears.

'Please don't apologise,' Bobby babbles. 'I'm just so sorry to have upset you. I'm really glad we've been able to clear the air.'

'So, all going well with the unit campaign?'

'Yes, thanks to Simon. You know, the PM – the current one – is going to support it!' The thought briefly crosses Bobby's mind that this was not through Daly's efforts.

'Oh, how wonderful. Yes, Simon is working his socks off. He's always on the phone to lawyers and developers and councillors about it. A real passion project.'

'Well, I'm extremely grateful. I was at the end of my tether a month ago.'

Susie nods at Jake. 'I think this young man would like you back, now. Thanks for talking with me.' With as much dignity as she can, Susie rather unsteadily gets to her feet and sets off in search of her husband.

'Want to go home?' Bobby murmurs in Jake's ear.

'My home or …'

'I'm not taking you back to Percy Cross working his way through a chorizo ring and *Top Gun*.'

At the bar, speaking quietly over the thumping music, Ed is having an intent conversation with Iain Atkins, the editor of *Crash* and the wiles behind the daily gossip email. So fat that he's almost spherical, Iain is a strange Westminster creature who seemed to simply materialise one day with a Substack and Twitter feed. He's willing to write the tantalising stories that others won't, avoiding key legal scrapes by relying on innuendo rather than names and facts. His blog, *Crash*, remains the same one-man gossip machine, though bolstered now with advertising revenue after he sold forty-nine per cent of it to StoryCorps.

'So tell it to me one more time,' Iain says, blinking his piggy eyes through his beer goggles.

Ed grits his teeth. 'A letter from a clinic confirming an appointment for an abortion is sent to Daly. A second letter, which is likely Daly writing to a woman who is not his wife, suggests he is going to take legal action against this woman if she refuses the abortion and comes to him later claiming paternity and asking for money.' His eyes follow the bondage collar sashay across the dancefloor on Jess's waist.

'Gotcha.' Iain examines the gold signet ring jammed on his chubby finger. 'And the view is it's his researcher? The cute one he's had around him lately?'

'No. She's only just started working for him. Timing doesn't match up. Although,' a thought hits Ed and he decides to plant a seed in the little toad's mind, 'she is from his patch, so maybe they knew each other before . . .'

'Iiiiiiinteresting,' Iain smiles. 'Well, looks like we can have a bit of fun here, mate. Mr Values might be heading for a bit of depreciation . . .'

'Remember – this didn't come from me, okay?'

As Ed watches Iain's enormous retreating back, his jacket straining over his shoulders, he texts Clarissa:

Mission accomplished.

Brixton

As the taxi fare ticks steadily up, Jake takes Bobby's hand. 'Are you okay? You've gone very quiet.'

'Just tired,' Bobby smiles in the darkness. The warmth from his fingers trickles through her and her nerves relax.

When they arrive, Jake dashes ahead of her, kicking at shoes in the hallway and chucking used pans into the kitchen sink.

'Sorry, I wasn't expecting company so it's a bit of a mess . . . My flatmate's away for the weekend, so I can't even blame it on him.'

Bobby clutches her bare arms, hugging herself. She feels self-conscious in the bright kitchen lights and worries that her heavy makeup looks clownish after all the dancing.

'You look cold. How about some tea? I've got some herbal stuff somewhere . . . ' Jake digs around in the back of a cupboard.

He brandishes a box of chamomile teabags and flicks on the kettle.

They stand in bashful silence, just the water boiling and Jake's nervous fingers drumming on the countertop for company.

After what feels like an age, Jake fills two mugs and leads Bobby through to the living room. They sit on the sofa, Bobby holding her mug between her hands. Jake can't help gazing at her, but she carefully studies everything else in the room – books, lamps, rugs, pictures.

'This is nice,' she says and takes a sip of tea. 'I was an idiot not to bring a coat or something.'

Jake quickly puts down his mug and pulls off his dinner jacket. Bobby leans forward so he can drape it round her shoulders.

'Thanks.'

They look at each other. Bobby feels her chest tighten. Very slowly, Jake leans in and kisses her, his hand slipping down beneath the jacket to her waist.

'Stop!' Bobby jumps like she's been electrocuted.

'I'm sorry.' Jake pushes himself away against the sofa arm. Has he misread something?

'Sorry? Don't be sorry. It's just,' Bobby puts her mug down, 'I want to tell you something. Look,' she turns to face him, 'I haven't had sex before. So I have no idea what I'm doing.'

'Bobby . . . ' Jake tries not to laugh with relief. He takes her hand in both of his. 'We don't have to do anything if you don't want to, okay?'

Bobby nods.

'I've got an idea,' Jake smiles gently. 'How about a nice bath?'

'Men are all the same . . . anything to see a girl naked,' Bobby laughs.

'You've got me.' He holds up his hands. 'Wait here, I'll be back in a minute. Got to find some clean towels . . . '

Once he's gone, Bobby kicks off her shoes and, snuggling into the warmth of the jacket, finishes her tea. She's glad to have got that off her chest.

'Okay! Ready . . . '

Bobby gets up and follows the sound of Jake's voice down the hallway. She hesitates on the threshold to the bathroom. The bath is full of steaming water and bubbles. A couple of candles sit on the shelf next to the bath, flickering against a bottle of whisky and a pair of tumblers. A bath caddy straddles the inviting water. Nico plays quietly from a speaker by the sink.

'And you . . . have a bath caddy?'

'I do all my best thinking and reading in the bath. You can't beat a caddy for balancing a book. And a drink.'

They stand there awkwardly for a moment, both wondering what to do next.

'Anyway, do you drink whisky?' Jake moves towards the bath.

'Yes, please.'

When he turns to hand her a glass, Bobby has her back to him, her chin over her shoulder.

'Will you untie me?'

Bobby feels Jake's fingers fumble nervously as he gently unties the bow at her neck. She lets the fabric fall to her waist, wiggling slightly to help the dress slip down over her hips. Jake's breathing, slightly ragged now, plays on the back of her neck. Bobby, feeling like she can see and hear and smell everything more clearly than normal, steps carefully into the water. As she slides down into the bubbles she turns to look at Jake, who is staring at her, his hands still raised from where he undid her dress.

'Are you joining me?'

Bobby makes a big show of putting her hands over her eyes, her ears keenly listening to the rustle of clothes coming off, then one foot after the other stepping into the water. She feels the water rise around her as he sits down.

They sit together, clutching their knees.

'You're right. The bath is a great place to think,' Bobby says, lying back and sipping her whisky.

*

An hour later, the water now tepid, Jake passes Bobby a towel.

'Can I borrow some clothes? A T-shirt or something?' she asks, pointing to her red dress. 'I didn't bring anything . . .'

'Go for it – take whatever you need from this drawer.' He leads her to his bedroom and points, before disappearing back into the bathroom to blow out the candles.

Bobby chooses some boxer shorts and a cricket jumper, which comes to the middle of her thighs.

'Bit small for you, eh?' Jake leans against the door and grins at her knees.

Bobby walks to the bed and sits down. 'Your bed smells nice.'

'You're in luck – I change my sheets on Saturdays.'

'Luxury ...' Bobby gets in under the covers, pulling the duvet up to her chin. Jake continues to stand awkwardly in the doorway. 'Jake, you're making me nervous. Can you just get in?' She pulls back the blanket.

As they lie facing each other Bobby can hear his heart hammering as hard as hers.

'This is nice,' she whispers.

Then, with just a lamp offering a dim, golden light, they begin to kiss.

5th May

UK CHILD LITERACY RATES DROP/
RARE SNOW LEOPARD SPOTTED

Brixton

'Are you hungry?' Jake asks, his thumb stroking Bobby's side as they lie facing each other.

'Starving,' she laughs, realising she is able to centre on a familiar sensation in her body for the first time in hours.

Jake leans in and kisses her on the ear, mumbling, 'Wait here.'

He disappears from the room, pulling on his boxers as he goes. Presently Bobby hears the industrious sounds of pans clanging and water running.

She rolls onto her back and smiles. Her body is tired – very tired; they haven't even dozed – yet satisfied, like a spring that can finally relax after being tightly coiled for some time. Her heart rate and breathing have steadied; she has been a deep sea diver, holding her breath, and now oxygen is coursing cleanly through her once again. Every normal sensation in her body feels somehow purer and more defined than usual and as she stretches – a delicious, tingling sensation – she feels a small echo of the orgasm she had minutes before.

After gazing at the ceiling for a while, reliving the long night, she starts to tune in properly to what is going on around her. Jake is still moving around in the kitchen and, as Bobby sits up, she gets a waft of bacon. Footsteps come down the passage so she pats under her eyes, pulls on Jake's cricket jumper from the floor and looks expectantly at the tray he carries in.

Claybourne Terrace

Bobby has her key in the lock when she hears a shout behind her. It's Jess, dressed in gym kit and dripping with sweat.

'You've been out for a run?' Bobby asks incredulously, pushing the front door open.

'Only way I can deal with a serious hangover. You have to squeeze it out of every pore.'

'How?' groans Eva from the kitchen. 'I can barely see ...' She is wrapped in her dressing gown, her feet tucked beneath her on the counter, leaning with her back against the window.

'So how was it?' asks Jess, pouring boiling water into the teapot.

Eva's head snaps up. 'Yes! I completely forgot,' she says, gratefully taking a steaming mug from Jess.

'Blissful,' Bobby grins, folding her arms. She'd rather not get into post-match analysis with them.

'Excellent ...' Eva glances out the window. 'I've got an idea. How about we lie in the garden and sunbathe today? The weather's gorgeous. I'll pop to the newsagent and get some magazines and stuff.'

'I'm in. I could do with a decent nap ...' Bobby says dreamily.

'Young love ...' Eva yawns, shuffling upstairs to get changed.

*

They have a lazy Sunday in the garden, taking it in turns to get iced lollies and drinks from the kitchen. Bobby talks non-stop about the party for about twenty minutes and then conks out. Jess can't nap. She tries to distract herself with books and magazines and horoscopes, but, now she's sober, she feels far less flippant about her conversation with Teddy. Plus, as the day drags on, she becomes increasingly anxious about exactly what *Crash* will write about the Daly story.

'Are you sure you don't want me to order you some pizza?' Eva asks. 'You've not eaten anything today.'

'I know, I just can't,' Jess says. 'I feel really sick.'

'I've gone the other way,' groans Eva, watching the pizza's progress on an app. 'Still in the kitchen. Are they grinding the flour themselves? Oh!'

'What is it?' yawns Bobby, roused from her snooze.

Eva holds up her phone to show a story on *Crash*: *Which MP, a vocal ally of the sisterhood, has recently booked an abortion for an unwanted lovechild? Crash is reliably informed that the young lady in question is a pretty Parliamentary aide . . .*

There is a moment of horror-struck silence as they read.

Jess feels a coward, so relieved at being nowhere near the story that she didn't insist Ed tell her exactly how it would be written up. She could have warned Bobby – or pushed her harder for the truth. She kicked off the whole saga with the documents from Jean and that phone call with Susie Daly. Teddy's words haunt her – she's allowed herself to be egged on.

Eva wishes she'd thought more carefully about how Clarissa might use her gossip from Susie. Eva had been clear it wasn't to do with Bobby but that didn't mean the piece couldn't heavily imply otherwise. Her real worry is that Bobby finds out that, inadvertently of course, Eva has poured petrol on the situation.

Bobby feels horribly trapped. She's certain the story is about Daly – surely no other MP could have got in the same mess – and herself. She's made it believable, swanning around with Daly at parties and cosy lunches. In protecting Millie and ignoring the advice of Eva she's torpedoed her own reputation. After all, she said so herself to Daly's wife and team. And a journalist . . .

Bobby gives Jess a hard look.

'Jess, you didn't have anything to do with this, did you?' she whispers.

'N-no. I promised you I wouldn't touch it after we spoke.'

'It's going to be okay, sweetheart.' Eva puts her arms around Bobby, praying she doesn't start asking her questions too. 'It's just a shock. We all know it's bollocks. Anyway, nobody will be reading *Crash* on a Sunday. We just need to get the truth out there.'

'But I don't know what the truth is,' sniffs Bobby, 'I just wanted to protect my friends.'

Bobby explains the whole story, Jess chipping in at different points, shocking Bobby with the detail of the threatening note, though keeping her prior knowledge about the *Crash* piece under wraps.

Eva sees how the situation has spiralled out of control. There's no question that Daly is in fact firmly in the 'dodgy' camp, and he may have got away with it if he'd been less careless in disposing of those documents. Character is destiny, and he may still have scraped through if he wasn't always so rude to the cleaning staff. Jean, on the eve of retirement, had clearly had enough. Jess did her job and poor, misguided Bobby had thrown herself into the mix to shield Millie and to keep the show on the road for her campaign. Without Eva's attempt to ingratiate herself with Clarissa the story would likely have fizzled out.

'Who is this really about?' Jess wonders aloud. 'It could still be Millie . . .' Bobby's refusal to reveal the truth now makes some sense.

Bobby, the initial shock over, is still puzzling over how this story has come back at all.

'I don't care who it's about. As far as I know it *is* Millie. What I want to know is why this story is out there at all.' She points at Jess. 'We're all ambitious but I thought even you wouldn't put your career before your friends.'

'I promise you I didn't publish this, Bobby,' Jess says, ashen-faced.

Bobby, exhausted and angry, runs inside. Jess chases after her.

Eva sits on the blanket, glassy-eyed. In her lap is her phone, open on a text from Clarissa, who has been having a joyous twenty minutes, pointing everyone she can to the *Crash* website:

Nice tip. Perhaps you'll go far after all.

She's done nothing to dispel the belief that the story is indeed about Daly and his pretty aide.

Eva feels overwhelmed with shame and horror. She can hear Bobby sobbing upstairs. She makes a decision, deleting the message from Clarissa. She'll bury this deep down and never tell a soul.

When the pizza arrives she carries it out into the garden and wolfs it down as quickly as she can, tearing off handfuls at a time. The hot tomato sauce scorches her tongue, making her eyes water.

Notting Hill

'Well, that was the worst phone call I've ever had.' Courtenay slumps in his chair. He's just been on the phone to his oldest friend, Daly, to tell him he is going to publicly condemn the actions of the unnamed MP in the *Crash* story. Daly has not taken it well.

Clarissa places a gin and tonic in her husband's hand and rubs his shoulders like a sensual boxing coach. 'I know, baby, but you had no choice. Everyone's been clear that the next administration must be sleaze-free. If Simon were squeaky clean then this *Crash* stuff probably wouldn't stick, but absolutely everybody knows he's a wrong'un. Being top dog is tough.'

'Si says it isn't even true. Nothing to do with this girl at all!'

Courtenay thinks back to Daly's acidic response to the Legislative Lads WhatsApp group earlier:

Si, you dirty dog! Bringing your home squeeze to work is a new one.

SD: *This is bollocks and I will personally sue if you suggest otherwise to anyone.*

LL: *Chill out, mate . . .*

'Which girl is it then? Not his wife. Trust me, darling,' Clarissa moves her hands down inside her husband's shirt and starts massaging his chest, 'this is going nowhere good. You're absolutely right to cut him loose now.'

Courtenay, despite his grinding guilt, can't help but respond to his wife's supple hands. He feels blood start to leave his aching, worried brain and migrate down to his trousers.

'You'll make sure we are very nice about him if it comes out, won't you? Talk to Nick for me?' Courtenay bleats.

'Oh yes,' soothes Clarissa, stepping round and kneeling before him. As she unzips she considers exactly how aggressive her husband's statement should be in reiterating his zero tolerance sleaze pledge. It would be fabulous, she thinks as her jaw starts to ache, if Daly's name could be firmly out there. Still, she can at least make clear that this unnamed MP has no future senior Cabinet career. As Jackson had texted her earlier: *The MPs will come a-flocking.*

6th May

Portcullis House

Bobby makes her way through the large atrium as she has dozens of times before. Usually she goes unnoticed, but it seems clear that every single person queuing for coffee has read *Crash*, identified Simon Daly as the unnamed MP in question and Bobby as the mysterious aide. She may as well be wearing a red A badge.

She makes it to the lift and is exhaling when someone sticks their foot in the doors just before they close. Jake.

'How are you?' Bobby asks, venturing a weak smile. She hasn't heard from him since the previous morning and holds on to a tiny hope that he hasn't seen the article.

'Fine.' Jake stares ahead.

'Jake . . . I—'

'Bobby,' he swings round, 'is it true?'

'Well . . . ' Bobby hesitates for a moment. Does he mean the whole story? Or just the rumour about her? She really doesn't want to tell him the whole thing. After all, she thought she could trust Jess but perhaps she was wrong.

'It's a pretty clear yes or no answer, Bobby.' Jake had been expecting an outright denial. It simply hadn't occurred to him that Bobby would prevaricate in any way.

'Yes, but you see it takes a bit of explaining—'

Jake hits the open button and steps smartly out of the lift at the next floor. 'See you around,' he mutters over his shoulder.

Bobby stands in appalled horror, considering whether to call in sick and go home. Just in time, Millie appears.

'Here, sweetheart, I got you a strong one.' Millie hands her a cup of coffee.

'Thank you,' Bobby croaks gratefully. She follows Millie, who seems to be handling the situation very well, down the corridor. 'I hope you don't feel too upset.'

Millie sits on the office sofa. 'What on earth do you mean?'

'It isn't you?' Bobby asks.

'It isn't *you*?' Millie stammers.

Bobby starts to see everything clearly. She'd had her suspicions. After all, why would Daly send Millie a threatening note? Her marriage is on the line.

Millie cups her chin in her hands. 'So, who is it?'

'And what should we do now?' Bobby asks.

'Well, Simon is, understandably, staying away from London. Eric's campaign has completely crushed his career.' Millie can't help smiling regretfully. 'Still, it's great for George, who's going to have a crack at spinning for Eric at the final debate later. You know, this story blows the potential Cabinet wide open . . .'

'I meant what should we do about this story. It isn't true!'

'Well, are you prepared to go out and say something?' Millie asks.

Bobby considers. For starters, she now definitely has no idea what the truth is. And does she want to risk pushing Daly, her most important advocate for saving the unit, even further down into the sewer along with his reputation? Seeing as she's not actually been named, saying something might make a mountain out of a molehill. Perhaps the best thing is to just sit tight and try and squeeze the last bit of Daly's credibility into the campaign.

Bobby feels like she had forgotten why she's really here. She's been swept along by the current of political promise, obsessing over Jake and going to parties with Daly and falling into the *Crash* gutter. She just needs to swallow her pride, stick this out for one final push and then she can go home. It was her plan all along.

Notting Hill

Eva stands at a makeshift lectern, pretending to be Laura Kuenssberg. The final TV debate of the MPs stage is this evening, a crucial performance before tomorrow's vote, when MPs will choose the two candidates that will take their campaigns to the Conservative membership. The team is preparing in the Courtenays' living room but it isn't going well. Courtenay himself is making silly mistakes about NHS bed capacity numbers and the national debt. The spiniest issue has been questions about sleaze, which Courtenay had initially point blank refused to answer any questions about – 'I'll just stonewall' – until Nick finally lost his temper.

'This is the issue we've built your bloody campaign on! Look, nobody has been named in the *Crash* piece so you can't be asked a direct question about Simon, even though everyone knows it's him. But you will get questions on conduct nonetheless. Okay,' Nick had snapped, when Courtenay pugnaciously folded his arms, 'let's just do a practice run then. Mr

Courtenay, you have committed to zero tolerance on sleaze. If you become Prime Minister, will you remove the Whip from the unnamed MP in the *Crash* article, if their identity comes to light? Yes or no question.'

'No.'

'Really? So you agree with coercing someone into an abortion?'

'No ... yes. Ah, I don't know!'

'See? This is why we practise ...'

Eva is struggling to focus, having hardly slept. All she can think about is Bobby's reaction if she finds out Eva is in any way involved in the *Crash* story.

'Hello, Earth to Eva?' Nick barks. He, like everyone else, is feeling tetchy. Courtenay still hasn't revealed what happened on deployment to Somalia all those years ago and it makes Nick feel nervous. Thank God Daly dropped such a colossal bollock at the opportune moment to keep interest elsewhere.

Eva pulls herself back into the room. Nick, Jake and a handful of other staffers sit on the sofas and armchairs, pretending to be audience members with questions to fire at Courtenay. He stands at a makeshift lectern alongside Jackson, Sackler and Graham Thomas, who are reading scripts in the roles of Dev Singh, Richard Hendrick and David Jacobson. Clarissa, who is finally civil – warm, even – towards Eva, loiters at the back. Eva would gladly take her usual spitefulness to reverse those few fleeting moments of conversation about Daly.

'Okay, we've been at this for ages,' says Nick after another hour or so, 'let's take a break for lunch. Meet back at 1 p.m.?'

Eva scoops up her bag and heads out before anyone speaks to her. She walks quickly to the nearest newsagent, buys a packet of biscuits and heads to a bench underneath a tree. She crams biscuit after biscuit into her mouth, scrolling Twitter for any developments – the crunching drowning out every thought in her head – until the packet is empty. She sits on the bench for a few more minutes, full of regret.

Her phone buzzes in her pocket. Nick on the Courtenay WhatsApp group:

Everyone – come back ASAP.

When Eva gets back to the Courtenays' house, Jake is at the door. He stands aside to let her in ahead of him. He looks dreadful and had been over an hour late to the debate prep. She thinks of Bobby's inconsolable sadness from the past couple of days.

She pauses. 'Jake, I—'

'Nope. Please, no. We have work to do.' He looks straight past her to the sitting room.

'Come on, arseholes, we have a development!' yells Nick, beckoning them with a phone in each hand.

'What is it?' asks Clarissa, spooning taramasalata onto a piece of buttered toast.

'Has the debate been cancelled?' Courtenay asks hopefully.

'We've got the full report into your deployment in Somalia,' Nick addresses Courtenay. 'Full exoneration. Boss, why didn't you tell us you saved a load of kidnapped schoolgirls?'

The group emits a series of gasps and admiring glances.

'Well, it was classified. It wouldn't have been appropriate—'

'Eric!' snaps Clarissa. 'What—'

'That's not all,' Nick cuts across her. 'Some absolute legends from your old regiment have written a letter, with everyone from ex-chiefs of the defence staff to squaddies who served under you condemning the Mark Norman attacks and backing you to the hilt as a national hero.'

Clarissa is shocked into silence.

Courtenay stands up. 'I want to address it in my opening statement.'

'It's not a bad idea,' Nick says, looking to Clarissa for

confirmation. 'Quite a good foil for the Daly stuff too. Prepared to take the tough decisions even if you don't get credit ... loyalty ... willing to be unpopular if it means doing the right thing.' He debates with himself about whether he should brief Courtenay's modest reluctance to recount what had happened to his team, then decides against it. It wouldn't do for journalists to think that Nick doesn't have his boss's complete confidence.

'I wonder if we can get all the other candidates to sign up to your Veterans Pledge,' Jake says thoughtfully. 'You should ask them live on air why they haven't already. Particularly Jacobson.'

Broadcasting House

'Listen to this,' Clarissa shouts, breaking from browsing Twitter on her phone. '*Turns out Eric Courtenay has serious depth. Decisive win for him this evening.* Andrew Neil. Well done, darling!' She wraps her arms around her husband, who looks exhausted but happy.

The Courtenay team are in their green room, chattering raucously and drinking wine. The debate couldn't have gone better, from the moment when Courtenay walked into the studio building past a group of protesting Labour activists. One threw an egg and, his expert cricketing instincts kicking in, he caught it and lobbed it back. The Courtenay digital team immediately blasted out the footage, captioned 'a safe pair of hands'.

A TV screen shows the spin room a few doors down, where the loyal lieutenants of the different candidates are parroting the line that their guy won fair and square.

'You smashed it, mate,' Jackson says, patting Courtenay on

the back. 'If there's one thing Conservative MPs care about as much as the Queen and the Union it's the Armed Forces. We just need to keep punching this bruise ahead of tomorrow. Who won't vote for a national hero?'

'Sounds like Dev's going, Nigel,' Eva says, feverishly tapping on her phone. 'His team has been in touch about an endorsement. Will you ring them? And Hendrick – wow . . . Do you think he's on meds or something? Weird how he kept making that whistling noise with his teeth.'

'What a tit,' Nick sniggers. 'Check this out – someone's already parodied him.'

Nick holds up his phone, which plays a series of clips of Hendrick, eyes bulging with effort, clicking and fidgeting over Snoop Dogg's 'Drop It Like It's Hot'.

'I tell you what,' Jackson points to the TV, 'George is doing a superb job next door. I didn't realise he was such a performer.'

' . . . of course, Eric Courtenay has already served his country once before. He therefore really knows what duty and sacrifice mean. If you've seen action in a real conflict zone I hardly think being supposedly "untested" within political ranks matters at all. People like to think they play with live ammo around here but I think the public recognises real-world experience as far more desirable than how many jobs you've clocked up sitting around a green baize table . . . '

'Bloody good,' agrees Nick, 'let's get him on the morning round tomorrow. And yes – we double down on military service. If we're left with Jacobson, he's wet on security, defence, law and order, etc.'

'Where's that file on him?' Clarissa asks, replying to countless congratulatory texts.

'We've got it,' Nick hands it to her, 'but let's take a moment to enjoy this, right? Jacobson's exactly who we want to be up against. He's made of jelly!'

'Nick, we're potentially at our most dangerous point. Jacobson has nothing to lose and he's been incredibly vicious about Eric so far. And he's come from nowhere ...'

Clarissa sits down with the file and begins reading about the former charity worker, Cambridge graduate and unexpected Tory sensation. In normal times she feels certain she could crush him but at this stage she's leaving nothing to chance.

7th May

Portcullis House

'How're you doing, mate?' Courtenay opens his Parliamentary office door and shakes Daly's hand, then pulls him in for a hug. He still feels desperately guilty – not least because he hasn't told his wife that he's meeting with Daly – and is just happy that his old friend doesn't greet him with a punch.

Daly is cleverer than that, though, and thinks of the long game. 'Congratulations, matey,' Daly grins. 'Final two, eh? Home straight now.'

'Jacobson's a funny one, though. Really wasn't expecting him to get this far. And all those Lib Demmy areas like him a lot. And he got Hendrick to endorse him.'

It's true. Although Dev Singh has backed Courtenay, Hendrick has rowed in behind Jacobson – it will either pay off with a big job or quite possibly finish him.

'He's a pushover. Now all everyone's talking about is your sparkling military record, he hasn't got a chance. Big mistake for him to have weighed in so hard behind Mark Norman's stuff. Completely the wrong side of public opinion.'

'Hm . . .' Courtenay points to an armchair. 'Have a seat. Do you want a drink?'

'What are you having?'

'I've got this green juice. Clarissa is keeping me pumped up with vitamins and stuff so I don't catch a cold. I'm struggling with the pace, to be honest. These regional hustings are going to absolutely kill me.' He thinks of the exhausting series of stump speeches he has done so far. Soon, it will be the same again but followed by coffee mornings with moustachioed old ladies and donor dinners with that particular county's biggest bores. When he should be napping, Courtenay can't resist checking on Twitter to see how everything is landing, which generally swirls him into a whirlpool of panic and self-loathing. Nick and Jake in particular are getting tired of his late-night calls after the next day's newspaper front pages drop. By contrast, when he has a snatched conversation with Jacobson behind the scenes, he just seems to be thoroughly enjoying himself.

Daly hands him a glass of green juice. 'Best to hold your nose. The smell – and taste – is terrible.'

'Chin chin.'

They both drink. Daly gags.

While he wretches, Courtenay drains his glass and takes the opportunity to say his piece. 'I'm still so sorry about that call on Sunday night, pal. It all seemed to happen so fast.'

'I know this game. All is forgiven.' Daly wipes his streaming eyes. 'God, that's grim.'

'So ... what do you want to talk about?' Courtenay scratches his chin. He had assumed Daly had come to demand an apology.

Daly, who's been trying to get a bit of the smoothie out of his back teeth, suddenly gives his friend his full attention.

After a bruising couple of days, he has finally given in to Jeffrey Cuthbert's charm offensive and agreed to join the group to buy the unit and build the golf club. Cuthbert has introduced Daly to a lawyer, who has found a way around declaring anything to anyone: a blind trust. The lawyer has also suggested the blind trust should be to the benefit of Susie, rather than Daly, so he really can plead ignorance to any of its workings or profits. After all, everyone knows Susie's family are the ones with money and trustees and so on. Too distracted to read the papers, Susie had quietly signed everything like a lamb this morning.

Now Daly needs to make sure the sale of the unit building and grounds goes through – and at the lowest possible price. Otherwise it will all be for nothing.

'It's like this,' Daly says, still able to feel a bit of fibrous matter tickling his throat. 'Do you remember that mental health unit in my patch I told you about?'

'That bill you want me to support? It's all sorted – Jake said it's one of my policy announcements in the next couple of weeks.'

'Well, I've been given some polling of our members on it. Long story short: they hate it. You know their views on planning and value for money on public services. It's crazy to pledge to cut red tape on land use on the one hand and then effectively hold taxpayers and landlords hostage with the other. It'll go down like a shit sandwich.'

'Hm. That does make sense,' Courtenay says with uncertainty. 'Even with these units disappearing? Doesn't everyone want more NHS beds?'

'You can see it all here.' Daly pulls a sheet of paper out of his breast pocket and hands it over. 'I guess there have never been any issues before, so people are reasonably not seeing it as a priority. Plus, when it really comes down to it, who really wants a load of nut jobs loose in their community anyway?'

Courtenay glances at the paper. 'Shit. Well ... We'd better bin it then. I'm sorry you've done all that work for nothing.'

'It happens.' Daly shrugs and sits back in his chair, waiting while Courtenay tucks the polling sheet into his pocket. He has to fight to hide a smirk – it's remarkable what a bit of 'polling' can achieve with politicians.

At just that moment Courtenay glances up and feels a jolt of pity, misreading his friend's twitching mouth for a wobbling attempt at a stiff upper lip.

'Oh matey ... I just feel awful about all this. First the sleaze stuff, now this mental health unit bill being kicked into touch. Listen,' Courtenay clasps his friend's hands, 'is there anything I can do to cheer you up?'

Daly pauses. He wasn't expecting this turn of events. Still, he knows Courtenay's weakness to emotional manipulation. He feels suddenly greedy.

'Well, it's like this,' Daly manages. 'You're my oldest friend. And obviously I want what's best for you, you know. And I know we discussed the Chancellor job ... '

Courtenay grimaces. 'Matey, you know that can't happen. I mean ... of course I knew all about Annie, but I really thought you'd have the brains to take care of that properly. You know, give her a decent amount of cash and send her on her way. Generosity always pays. And on top of that, dumping those letters in the open bin? Epic fuck-up!' He slaps his thigh.

'Thanks for the advice,' Daly snaps.

'Well, there's no way this Chancellor job can happen now ... ' Courtenay examines the dregs of his glass.

'What I want to know is – is this it? Should I just shove off, stand down from my seat and leave you to it? Is there any future hope for me?'

Normally Courtenay would discuss this sort of thing with Clarissa and Jackson, but they aren't here and he really doesn't fancy them finding out about this secret meeting. The significance of the words 'stand down' ring in his head. What this means is a by-election right at the beginning of his premiership – triggered by a key ally. Surely Clarissa would agree that it must be avoided at all costs. So what can he do? Obviously a Great Office of State is out of the question. But does it really matter if Daly's in at a lower level? Courtenay had said zero tolerance on sleaze, but really – if he truly takes that approach, who *will* be able to serve in his government?

'Of course there is, chap. I still want you. For a big agenda. Industrial Economy?'

Daly wrinkles his nose. Not long ago he would have taken any job he was offered. But the back benches with his nice new pay packet would be far preferable to slogging along to factories every Friday. Daly runs his hands through his hair. Perhaps he can manoeuvre Courtenay. He gets up and begins pacing.

'Aren't you pleased?'

'Um ... not really, matey. Until recently I was preparing to meet with the heads of the IMF and the World Bank ... the G7 and G20 finance ministers. I didn't bin off my career – for you, I might add – to get back to square one clearing up the mess made by Nat Weaver.' Daly kicks at a chair leg.

'Yes, I see your point ... ' Courtenay nods solemnly, thinking of his meeting with Weaver the day before when she came in to pitch for Health, taking care to wear a low-cut top that showed off her crêpey cleavage. 'Well then, what do you want?'

'I suppose I'd consider Secretary of State for Housing and Communities,' Daly says casually. The idea just dropped into his head. He may as well go in for a penny with this blind trust business and pull whatever levers he can. Who knows what other opportunities may crop up for the minister overseeing every major planning decision in the country? Even if he gets caught out, what else has he to lose? He'd be back as a lowly MP – exactly where he is now.

'A key job,' Courtenay says, immediately warming to the idea. 'It's very important to me, you know. I want to cut red tape. I want people to own their own homes. Big legacy stuff ... Do you really want it?'

Daly pretends to be thinking it over. Aside from the job itself, Courtenay is mad to budge even slightly on his sleaze pledge. Still, why does Daly care? He owes Courtenay nothing now.

They shake solemnly, Courtenay giddy with relief at so artfully dealing with this potential wrinkle. Clarissa and Jackson don't know everything, he thinks.

'I really am sorry, you know,' Courtenay says one more time. 'Public opinion's a fickle thing.'

'It is. So let's stay on the right side of it, matey.' Daly winks and bounds down the corridor to his office.

Both men pat themselves on the back for services to diplomacy.

Within minutes, Daly is back in his office. Immediately, he summons Bobby imperiously into the little side room. Everyone stares as she follows him in, her head bowed. They haven't managed to speak since the *Crash* piece appeared.

'How're you doing?' asks Daly, leaning against the printer.

'I've been better.' Bobby manages a smile. 'How about you? Must have been a difficult few days.'

'Oh, you know ... you develop a thick skin,' he says airily. Bobby frowns. 'I've just had some pretty bad news, though.'

Bobby sits down.

'So I may as well just spit it out. I've just been with Eric and I'm afraid that he's dropping support for the mental health unit bill.'

'What?' Bobby cries. 'Why?'

'It's not a vote winner. Our members hate it.' Good old members, Daly thinks, these nameless hordes taking the blame for so much.

'What about all those MPs who support it? They've all done op-eds and letters and—'

'They're here to represent their constituents and associations—'

'What you mean is you're going to call every one of the MPs we got signed up and change their minds!'

Daly smiles. His face looks like a cold, glazed mask to Bobby. Inside he is churning with shame and guilt but this has to be done. 'If Eric isn't backing it then they're just wasting their breath.'

'What about all those developers and lawyers?' Bobby asks. 'Cuthberts?'

'They certainly enjoyed meeting you and couldn't be more grateful for your time. But I'm afraid they're going a different way – to the soon-to-be-announced Tipperton Golf Club and Spa.'

'You bastard!' Bobby screams, before she can stop herself. 'You never intended to help me, or . . . or to save the unit – or anything!'

She is on her feet, her fists clenched.

'Oh, I did, Bobby,' Daly protests, 'but reality bites some-times and this is what Eric wants.'

'I can't believe you would do this – after all I've done for you!'

'Such as?' Daly feels suddenly impatient. He wishes Bobby would stop screaming like a banshee.

'Such as? Oh, I don't know . . . covering for you with your wife to the media about this clinic? And your affair with Millie?' Daly doesn't even flinch.

'Well, I'm very grateful,' he says tonelessly. 'Now, we've got some work to do.' He claps his hands together.

'You can't honestly think I'm staying here now?'

'What are your other options? Back to Tipperton to do nothing in particular? This is the game, Bobby. You can't win every time. We'll think of a cunning wheeze to move your father to another unit somewhere perfectly nice.'

'You think this is only about my father, you fucking sociopath?' Bobby howls.

She marches to the door, then turns round to speak to him one last time.

'I hereby hand in my resignation. Thank you *so much* for everything. I truly look forward to watching you come to a suitable end. I don't mean up in flames. I don't mean flying too close to the sun and crash-landing in a blaze of glory. I mean a *suitable* end: a slow, steady decline into obscurity. Cold and alone. No books about you. Nobody to spend Christmas with. Nobody to change your adult nappy in your old age. A sad, soulless obituary to no one. From the bottom of my heart: go fuck yourself.'

Bobby strides out into the office, picks up her bag and leaves, wishing she had never arrived in the first place. She heads straight for King's Cross station. It is time to go home.

8th May

Burma Road, Houses of Parliament

Jess groans and sits back in her chair, wondering whether a
Twix will cheer her up. She feels out of control and irritable.
Bobby's gone and unlikely to return – or fully trust Jess – any
time soon. She has no big stories in the pipeline, and is tired
of researching David Jacobson's boring business interests for a
hint of scandal. Ed is so distracted, running around after the
leadership contest, that he didn't even notice that Jess is wearing the collar as a belt again. She needs a way to get herself back
on an even keel but can't help eyeing her phone, wondering
whether to send Ed a message to see if he'll bite. Playing it cool
makes her feel crabby and desperate.

As if by magic, a text pops up on her phone. Tommy:

Hello, Jess. How's it going down there?

Twenty-something male in uniform. She couldn't have
picked a more perfect distraction from the classifieds.

She closes the door and calls Tommy.

'999, which service do you require?' Tommy's deep Scottish voice slides from the phone.

Jess bites her lip. 'Police. I need you to get me off.'

She hears Tommy's exhalation. He's sitting at his desk in the open plan office, eyeing a large pile of paperwork. He gets up and saunters outside to his car.

'Sounds like you need Fire instead . . .'

When he's outside he starts asking Jess questions but she cuts him off.

'I'd prefer to do the talking, if that's okay.'

'Okay . . .' Tommy grins, happy to be taken on a trip down memory lane by Jess. She always likes revisiting past hits.

'Do you remember that time we went for a picnic in the woods?' Jess slides a chair beneath the door handle. 'It was an insanely hot day. We drove out into the countryside and went for a walk. I went ahead of you.'

Tommy, now in his driving seat, closes his eyes and takes himself back to the smell of mud and Scotch pine and the vision of Jess's short skirt.

'So as you walked up the trail, you found my knickers . . .' Jess listens carefully to how Tommy responds. 'And there I was, sitting on a gate, my knees apart . . .'

'But you hopped over and stayed ahead of me,' Tommy whispers, glancing round the car park and unzipping his trousers.

'We kept going, deep into the forest . . .'

'It started raining.' Tommy's voice sounds more urgent.

'We got soaked and ran for cover into the trees . . .'

Tommy, the memory of Jess's outlined bare tits through her soaking silk camisole, moans softly.

'And I finally let you touch me . . .'

'Jess,' Tommy groans, 'I'm so hard.'

'Good,' Jess whispers, grinning at his grunt of pleasure. 'Finally, you pushed me against a tree . . .'

'Jesus . . . oh . . . ' Jess's ears strain, listening to Tommy release as quietly as he can.

After she's said goodbye to Tommy, Jess has some fun of her own. She's so worked up that it takes no time at all. Afterwards, she sees a text from Ed:

Free now? I want to see you wearing that collar. And nothing else . . .

Jess taps out a reply as she removes the chair from the door, realising how much more clearly she thinks once the fog has lifted:

Busy, I'm afraid. Maybe some other time.

Tipperton

Bobby sits at the kitchen table with a mug of tea, talking to her mother about the last few weeks. The more she talks the more removed she feels from London and its pointless, fast pace. Her mother interjects with things like 'What's *Crash*? We didn't hear about that up here' or 'What do you mean "everyone" says? I don't!'

Bobby feels disappointed with herself that she's failed to save the unit. She's humiliated at the realisation that the bulk of her time has been spent monitoring Daly's media accounts, writing him fob-off letters to constituents and booking him restaurant reservations and massages – and in return for what? Bobby also hasn't heard a peep from Jake. She was so used to her phone pinging and it be him that she hears phantom pings and buzzes now, feels a fleeting wisp of hope and then a miserable sink when it isn't Jake.

The only person she's heard from in SW1, apart from Eva and Jess, is Mary Jones:

Hear rumour campaign being wound down. Anything I can do?

Nothing springs to mind, Bobby had replied. She wonders if any of the other MPs received the same news with anything more than a shrug.

Bobby dunks a digestive biscuit into her tea and bites off the soaked bit. 'What's Dad going to do now? And everyone else who needs the unit?'

'Well, let's not think about that today. Or this horrible man Simon Daly. I knew I didn't like the sound of him.'

'You were right as always, Mum. I should never have left.' Bobby mournfully pops the rest of the biscuit into her mouth.

'What rubbish. I hope I haven't raised my daughter to just give up!' Elizabeth scowls out of the window. The doorbell rings. 'Ah, that must be the postman.'

She returns to the kitchen, followed by Susie Daly and Moira Herbert.

Bobby stands awkwardly. 'Susie. Moira. What a . . . surprise.'

Moira nods briskly.

'Hi, Bobby.' Susie clasps her hands awkwardly. 'Look, we're sorry to barge in on you like this but we really need to talk to you.'

Bobby leads them into the living room. They sit down.

'I suppose I should start by saying that I'm sorry you quit, but I completely understand why. A lot has happened in the last couple of days and Moira suggested we come and see you.'

'We'd like to ask you some questions,' interjects Moira. Bobby is tempted to say, 'Of course, officer', but decides against it.

'Fire away. I'll answer anything you ask. Can't do me any more harm.'

'Okay. So,' Susie gets up and begins pacing, 'I suppose I'd like to start with . . . There's no easy way to say this . . . were you, are you, have you ever had sex with my husband?'

'No. Never have, never will and have never wanted to. Someone once even warned me about him but I was too stupid

344

to listen . . . I can say with all sincerity that I hate your husband with the fire of a thousand suns.'

'Join the club, love,' mutters Moira.

'I'm sorry, but I felt I had to ask. Then the story in *Crash*. About the clinic. You said it was for you but I know that isn't true. Why did you cover for Simon?'

'I wasn't covering for him. Not really. I was trying to protect someone else I thought was involved. Turns out I was wrong and it was for nothing.'

Susie nods.

'So we also found out why you resigned, Bobby,' Moira says, keen to get down to business. 'Lucy heard the whole, er, conversation through the walls. Sounds like you really socked it to him.'

'He went back on his promise.'

'Well, this is really the crux of what we wanted to talk to you about,' Moira says. 'It wasn't until now that I really started paying attention to this whole business about the mental health unit. I fix Simon's meetings up here. Donations are handled in Parliament. I spent the morning going through his Parliamentary register of interests and the constituency diary. Guess who happens to be his biggest donor and most regular contact? Jeffrey Cuthbert.'

'The developer?' Bobby frowns.

'Yup. Turns out Simon has been meeting with Cuthbert a lot. Fancy lunches and dinners. Wimbledon. Lord's . . . they've put in a huge bid to buy the unit's building and lands from the NHS and have planning permission, courtesy of dear old Simon's council contacts, to make this enormous—'

'Golf club and spa,' Bobby says, her final chat with Daly springing back to her. 'But what's in it for Simon? It isn't like he can take commission!'

'Well, not exactly . . . ' Moira looks at Susie.

Susie runs her hands through her hair. 'It turns out he stands to make quite a lot of money . . . through me.'

Bobby looks from Susie to Moira.

'You see,' Susie gets up to pace again, 'over the past couple of weeks he's been having me sign various bits and bobs, for the house or insurance or "work" things . . . I realise he's been picking his moments beautifully. You know, just as he's dashing out the door back to London or when we're in a hurry to leave home for something . . . Since the *Crash* stuff I've done a bit of reading. Turns out I've got all sorts of things in my name that I didn't even know about, which now include shares in this bloody golf club.'

'Knowing your fucking husband – no offence –' says Moira, 'you're probably exposed to all kinds of risky things. A blind trust? God knows what else he's up to.'

'Well, we have time. We need to learn everything we can about this planning deal. Maybe we can zap it . . . ' Bobby says thoughtfully.

'Okay,' Moira says, standing. 'I'm going back to the office to see if there's anything I can get hold of.'

'Good idea – I'm going to call a solicitor,' Susie says. 'Regroup in a couple of days? In the meantime, I'd better get back to playing the dutiful little wife.'

Pimlico

'Well, it's nice to have you to myself for a change.' Jamie unzips his bag and hands Eva a bottle of water. Eva has managed to get away from the Courtenay campaign for a couple of hours and she and Jamie are playing tennis on the courts of the Claybourne residential square. 'You've become much fitter . . . anything I should know about?' He picks at the strings on his racket.

Eva laughs and takes a long drink. 'Jess makes us do circuits with her in the park a couple of mornings a week. You build up pretty strong lungs if you're prattling through a conversation while you're doing burpees.' She sits down on the bench next to him and wipes her face with a towel.

Jamie takes her hand. 'I mean it, though. When do we normally spend this much time together?'

'I'm sorry, J. You know it's been a crazy couple of months for me.'

'Yes, but would it kill you to—'

'Please don't get at me about this. I know I should see you more. But,' Eva leans in and softly kisses his cheek, whispering in his ear, 'I make up for it when I see you, don't I?'

Jamie gives a sulky smile.

Before he can reply, Eva's phone buzzes. Jamie groans.

'It's Holly. That's weird, she never calls.' Eva puts the lid back on the bottle, stands up and gives her racket a swing.

'She's in America, isn't she? Aren't you going to answer it?'

Eva scoffs. 'Why? She probably just wants to witter on about skincare or something. She's just . . . ugh. Awful.' Eva gives her racket another swipe at nothing. 'Come on, then—'

Eva's phone rings again.

'Eva—'

'Just ignore her.'

'No . . . it's the protection team.'

Eva feels her mouth go dry. They never call her. She snatches the phone from Jamie and answers.

'What is it?'

'It's your dad. He's . . . we think he's had a heart attack. We're just following the ambulance now.'

'Oh my . . . to . . . ' The phone drops out of her hand.

Jamie picks it up. His voice sounds far away from Eva. 'Shit . . . Which hospital? . . . Okay, we'll be right behind you.'

Eva seems to walk into fog. Someone could blow a horn in her face and she wouldn't react. Her next stream of consciousness comes in front of St Thomas' Hospital, where she momentarily comes to her senses and realises she's still clutching her tennis racket. There is another great chunk of time missing until she finds herself standing outside a private waiting room. She has been in such a heavy fugue that she doesn't know the point at which Jamie left her side. Or the tennis racket. All she can think is that her father is going to die and there is nothing beyond that one, clear thought.

When Eva enters, Holly is standing at the window, her arms wrapped around herself. Her shoulders are heaving.

'Hi,' Holly whispers through sniffs.

'Hi,' Eva replies and sits down on a lumpy sofa. 'What happened? Is he alive?'

Holly joins her. 'He's alive ... at the moment. I don't know what happened exactly. I came back early to surprise him. We were making lunch in the kitchen and he was totally fine. Then he just ... kinda grabbed at his chest and collapsed.' Holly gives a heart-wrenching sob. 'I screamed my head off and the cops came runnin' ...'

Eva sees it all in her mind's eye. Percy could have just died in that house alone, not yet sixty. Thank God Holly had been there. Eva has been so determined to hate this woman and yet she had been the one at his side when it counted most.

They sit in silence for a long time, Eva's hand gradually creeping out to hold Holly's.

'You know,' Eva whispers, 'he really missed you while you were away. I've never known anything like it. He was like one of those dogs that sleeps on their owner's grave after they've died, pining away.'

'I was really nervous about meeting you. You should hear the way he talks about you. On paper he's achieved a lot ... but

348

you're all he really lights up about. He's so proud of you . . . and so full of regret. It's real sad.'

'As a child he could have told me he'd been the first man on the Moon and I would have believed him. But I was angry with him as a teenager,' Eva concedes. 'He was such a public figure of fun . . . I didn't get him at all. It's funny how you understand your parents better as you get older. They're fallible, imperfect people. But that's okay. He's sacrificed a lot, not least his happiness.'

'There's a lot of trauma being carried around in the Cross family for sure . . . ' Holly sighs.

'Yes. I want him to be happy, you know.' She turns to Holly. 'And you make him happy. So now you've got your own Cross to bear.'

There is a knock on the door and a consultant enters and introduces herself.

'Hello. Ms Cross, Ms Mayhew?' She shakes hands with both women. 'I'd like to update you on Percy's condition.'

'How sick is he, doc?' Holly sniffles. 'That was one heck of a heart attack.'

'No, it wasn't.'

'Excuse me!' Holly flares up. 'I think I know a big one when I see it. My pa's had three! And quadruple bypass surgery.'

'Sorry, you misunderstand me,' the doctor says calmly. 'I mean he hasn't had a heart attack at all. He's had gallstones and kidney stones, in tandem. Likely caused by some rather unhealthy lifestyle habits . . . '

'But his chest?' Holly says, confused.

'Not taking his inhaler.'

Eva looks down and realises she is still clutching Holly's hand. All this fuss because her father's been eating like an asthmatic pig.

'Doctor, are we allowed to see him?' she asks.

'You may, but he's asked that, uh, you're both easy on him.

He's being rather silly about his daughter or his girlfriend seeing him in a backless gown. Says he feels exposed, poor dear.'

The two women are led down the corridor to a private room.

Percy is in bed, drinking from a glass of water and watching *Cash in the Attic*. His skin looks grey and sallow and bloated, like he's recently been pickled in a jar. He has clearly been in a lot of pain and had a serious asthma attack, but he is otherwise fine.

Eva stays an hour or so – long enough to join Holly in a bollocking about his late-night feasts – before heading back to Claybourne Terrace.

Despite the lack of danger, the hospital is keeping Percy in overnight to run some tests on his heart (the perks of being an ex-PM with serious health insurance, Eva reasons) and Holly has decided to stay with him. Eva has promised to return the next morning with a bag of 'essentials': clothes, vegan snacks, organic beauty products and a selection of self-help books that Holly intends to read aloud to Percy. Percy has asked for earplugs.

When she gets home, Eva walks into the kitchen and sees the lunch preparations are lying untouched on the work surface: a half-chopped cucumber, a lettuce sitting in a colander in the sink, the fridge door ajar. It's like walking onto the deck of the *Mary Celeste*.

Despite her father's temporary stay by the executioner, Eva can't help but feel emotional about the afternoon's events. What would she do if she lost him? Percy needs to take care of himself better and Eva is starting to see that Holly is the one he will listen to. Eva and Holly had got to know each other in the hospital and it turns out they have a lot in common. Difficult fathers. Vain mothers. Challenging teenage years. Holly is considering transferring her college credit to the UK, and Eva found herself encouraging her warmly to do it. She's all right.

Eva trudges up the stairs, then finds herself pausing outside her father's door. She hasn't been into his room for years. It's hardly trespassing, as she needs to go in to get the things Holly wants tomorrow, but she hesitates. She really wants to just touch something of his.

Eva goes in. There are definite signs of Holly, but it is still unmistakably Percy's room. His threadbare childhood teddy sits on an old leather armchair, a twenty-first birthday present from his parents. Stacks of notebooks he wrote in over the years, charting everything from unemployment benefit meetings he'd chaired as Prime Minister to Eva's birth, are piled in a corner, ready for his memoirs. A number of photographs – Percy's parents, Percy with the Queen at a State visit, an old school photo, a stunning black and white shot of Holly – are propped up in frames around the room. On Percy's bedside table is a pretty silver frame, home to a pencil sketch he did himself of Eva as a little girl. She picks it up and sits down on the bed.

It seems to fall away beneath her, throwing her backwards and churning around, making it impossible for her to sit back up. There is a strange sloshing sound as she manages to regain her balance and stand.

She bursts into great, uncontrollable heaves of laughter, and wonders how the White Company would feel about their sheets being used on a water bed.

Covent Garden

Clarissa steps gingerly into Mountain Warehouse on the Strand and heads to a rack of anoraks, where Jackson is loitering. She feels nervous because when she'd suggested they meet for a drink at the Savoy, he had insisted they come here, somewhere they definitely won't be spotted by a Westminster insider.

Clarissa is laden down with Jermyn Street shopping bags, full of new clothes for her husband. Ties, shirts, boxer shorts. Now he is down to the final two candidates she wants to give him every possible edge.

'Well, my dear,' Clarissa says, dropping her bags on the floor and giving Jackson a peck on the cheek, 'this is all rather mysterious. I thought your work was done, now that we're finished with the MPs.'

'Clazz, I don't consider my work done until our boy is waving outside that famous black door.' Jackson pretends to be checking the size of a jacket.

'Oh come on. Even Mark Norman has withdrawn his remarks on Eric's service record.' Clarissa examines the sleeve of a bright pink cagoule.

'Yes, well, it's Mark Norman I wanted to talk to you about. He, ah,' Jackson speaks from the corner of his mouth, 'he knows the cocaine story came from our camp.'

'Ah. I see.'

'And he's rather cross with us just now. So he's going to say it was us. As in you and me.'

'Oh dear. Does he have proof?'

'Does he need it? He can say what the hell he wants.' Jackson holds a lime-green poncho against himself, as though to ask Clarissa's opinion.

Clarissa tries to look calm but she feels a flutter of panic in her chest. Norman could cause serious problems. She doesn't want the rest of the campaign to be dominated by questions about her and her influence. One thing's for sure, should the floodgates open on everything in her past, she'll be hounded out of London.

'This is a problem, isn't it,' she whispers, running her fingers through a rack of children's waterproofs. 'I wonder ... what if we tell the truth?'

'Have you gone mad?' Jackson hisses.

'Listen,' she leans in, 'we can concede that it was someone in our camp. And then we *make* it someone in our camp. Plenty of outrage – this isn't how we like to play, totally unbeknown to us, etc. And we move on. A half-truth is better than a full lie sometimes.'

'But who?'

'Eva Cross.'

Jackson starts to object but Clarissa cuts across him, pulling a large woollen balaclava onto his head.

'Who else could have got that photograph? Percy probably has all sorts lying around … and she did give us that gear on Simon Daly and the abortion stuff. Then I'll chuck in everything else. Brief it all. That way the stuff she can't deny gets mixed in with the cocaine story and a bunch of your other tricks. She's too young and dumb to spin her way through such a muddle.'

'But Clazz … she's all right, you know?'

'Nigel. Dear Nigel.' Clarissa presses her fingers against the steel tips of a pair of cleated mountaineering boots. 'Has it occurred to you that it's us or her? She'll bounce back. She's very well connected. And fairly bright. Lord,' she scoffs, 'we can give her a SpAd job anyway once Eric wins. But we need to do this now.'

Jackson, the corners of his mouth creased down, gives a small nod.

9th May

St Thomas' Hospital

Eva steps out of the hospital for a bit of fresh air and checks her phone. She has dozens of missed calls and text messages from journalists. Word of Percy's stint in hospital had to get out eventually.

The phone rings in her hand.

'Hello? Eva, this is Bruce Shillington at the *Mail on Sunday*. How are you doing?'

'Not too bad, considering the circumstances. I suppose you're after a statement? All Dad's PR is handled by his agent, so you'll need to call him.'

'No ... I wanted one from you.'

'Oh, well, I would really rather not speak on the record about his health.'

'Sorry, Eva ... do you know what I'm calling about?'

'My father,' Eva waits a beat for an answer, 'no?'

The journalist sighs. 'No ... look, there's a story being

pushed around that you're behind a lot of the negative brief-ing coming out of the Courtenay camp over the past couple of weeks of the leadership contest. All unauthorised. The Norman cocaine story, for starters. Obviously your dad is in the picture so it's being suggested that you got it from him ... that weird Simon Daly abortion thing. You live with his researcher and apparently you've been telling everyone it's her ... some blackmail stuff – I've heard you threatened to out an MP.'

Eva seems to have stopped breathing. Pure, undiluted panic courses through her.

'I assume you deny all of it?'

She feels like she is in a heavy, sickening dream. She tries to tear herself back to the present but her mind is slow and foggy.

She knows the cocaine stuff is nonsense. But the Daly stuff ... that's partly right. Who in their right mind issues a statement saying 'not all the allegations are true'? She feels trapped. For one second, she wonders who could have done this to her but it is only for a second: Clarissa.

Without giving Bruce an answer, she turns her phone off and stumbles through the London streets in a daze.

Claybourne Terrace

'Eva?' Jess calls from the front door. She checks the living room and kitchen, then runs up the stairs to Eva's bedroom.

The curtains are drawn and the lights are off. Eva is curled up under the duvet.

'Are you okay?'

'Please go away,' whispers Eva.

'I'm not going anywhere.' Jess sits down on the bed. 'This is all bollocks, all right? You need to issue a strong denial.

Everyone knows that coke photo came from your dad. It's nothing to do with you.'

Eva curls up even tighter. 'It's not all bollocks . . .'

'What . . . really? Which bit?'

Eva pokes her head out so she can see Jess. She can't bear admitting that she'd done nothing to persuade Bobby that Jess hadn't turned her over.

'Okay.' Eva sits up. 'So you're right: the cocaine thing has nothing to do with me at all. Or any of the blackmail stuff. It's that fucker Jackson who has been threatening MPs for their votes! But the Simon Daly story . . . I sat next to Susie Daly at dinner a couple of weeks ago. She got pissed and told me your paper called the office that day and asked them some questions. I didn't know it was you who called and I certainly didn't know Bobby would be sucked into it. I told Clarissa about it,' she grips Jess's arm, 'but if I'd known Bobby . . . I was just trying to get Clarissa to . . . that *snake*. So it *was* me, in a way. And then when the story came out and it was about Bobby I was so ashamed I didn't say anything.'

Jess watches her friend intently.

'It's not ideal, but I can see your thinking. Bobby's in this mess because, for some reason, she wanted to shield that fucker Daly.' Privately, she feels she can afford to be magnanimous. She'd rather not reveal that she knew the *Crash* story was coming nearly twenty-four hours in advance.

'Exactly! I mean, I didn't know her involvement. After all, I *knew* it couldn't be her having an abortion . . . and now everyone thinks I'm this terrible, back-stabbing gossip. I never meant to hurt anyone. Just cause a bit of mischief . . .'

The doorbell rings.

'It's probably a journalist,' groans Eva. 'Tell them to piss off, will you?'

Jess goes down the stairs to her bedroom and looks out of

the window. It's Jamie. She buzzes him in and he bounds up the stairs.

'I'm a stupid, bad friend, J,' Eva whispers. 'I've been running around Westminster like Emma Woodhouse, thinking I know what I'm doing when in reality I'm a total amateur … and I've abandoned you for months. I've made a terrible mess of everything.'

'Shh, don't be silly,' Jamie strokes her hair. 'Who cares about all this nonsense? You think I love you because you're in politics? You're heaps better than all these dreadful people. You need to just get back on an even keel.'

'It's true,' Jess agrees. 'And I know where we need to start. We need to go and see Bobby.'

'What?'

'We've hurt one of the only good people in Westminster. She came here to do something and through a combination of our idiocy and this rotten place she's failed. We need to fix what we can and that starts with an explanation to your friend – preferably before she reads Clarissa Courtenay's version of events. If you're being called by journalists then we haven't got long before it breaks. Look, I've not exactly covered myself in glory either. We all need to sit down together, away from this ridiculous petri dish, and talk. I'm tired of us all tripping up over ourselves. Time to put our heads together.'

Eva throws off the duvet. 'You're right. I'll be ready in twenty minutes.'

'You go girls,' Jamie murmurs.

10th May

UK HAD HOTTEST APRIL ON RECORD/
US CONGRESSMAN DENIES AFFAIR

Tipperton

Eva's eyes are only open a few seconds before she remembers why she's lying on a blow-up mattress in Bobby's childhood bedroom. After she and Jess arrived the previous night, they had sat down and told Bobby everything: Eva's misguided attempt to ingratiate herself with Clarissa Courtenay; her ignorance about Bobby's involvement; how wrecked her own reputation is now; how miserable Jake is (this had cheered Bobby for about three seconds, before it occurred to her that Jake could have been in touch at any time and had chosen to stay quiet). They had talked for hours, reasoning out how all three of them had been snagged in different people's webs and how to turn things around. There were no obvious ideas.

Eva unlocks her phone and checks the time: 5 a.m. It will be a long while until the house stirs and, though she is exhausted, she knows she won't sleep again. Despite Jess and Bobby's advice to the contrary, she can't resist typing her name into Google. There are dozens of bitchy news items about her. *Crash* has found anonymous ex-school friends and people she'd hardly known at university willing to tell spiteful stories about her. There are also plenty of 'Tory sources' condemning her alleged dirty tactics and even a Courtenay team spokesperson announcing that she's 'been let go as a volunteer on the campaign' – the first Eva has heard about it.

Perhaps worst of all is reading the comments underneath each piece and the various tweets about her. She lies on her side, thinking about all the hateful words, wondering if this will ever pass. Panicky heat starts to build up from her stomach to her chest. Will she ever get another job? Has she been permanently cancelled at twenty-four years old?

A few hours later, Eva, Bobby and Jess are clustered around the Cliveden kitchen table. While Bobby's mother busies herself with a frying pan, the others turn their attention to a little TV set in the corner, which is switched to a morning politics show special called 'Countdown to a New Prime Minister'.

'. . . And of course Westminster is alive with the leadership contest, which is now in its final stage of two candidates . . .' says the polished host.

'Hey, isn't that Ed Cooper?' Bobby points to the TV.

'Yup.' Jess hasn't heard from Ed outside their work-related conversations. He has been busy and, not wanting to upset the balance of power, Jess hasn't dared text him. The situation is delicate.

Bobby turns the volume up on the TV.

'. . . and of course it will be an interesting few weeks ahead. We have two very different men vying for the keys to Downing Street here in David Jacobson and Eric Courtenay—'

'But both are fairly untested, no? Neither have held Cabinet positions,' says the host.

'That's right,' Ed twinkles at her.

'We've seen a torrent of anger in the last twenty-four hours from Conservative Party MPs and members, who have disagreed with David Jacobson's criticism of Eric Courtenay's military service, including a petition of about 25,000 members to the Party Chairman, calling for Jacobson to apologise. He is of course due to make a statement responding to that petition shortly. Ed, is Jacobson on shaky ground?'

'I don't think so, Rachel.' Ed stretches his hands behind his head. 'Eric Courtenay is favoured to win but traditionally these leadership contests have a pattern of throwing up a rank outsider. David Jacobson has a good chance to push through with the Party members. If I know anything then—'

'Sorry to cut you off, Ed, but we are going to turn to David Jacobson's doorstep right now for his statement . . . '

Jacobson appears on the doorstep of his pretty redbrick house, wearing a linen shirt and reading glasses. He looks haggard.

'I wish to publicly apologise whole-heartedly to Eric Courtenay for any offence I may have caused for comments about his military service that have been taken out of context. Members of my team and members of my Party have been clear that this is unacceptable. With the number of signatories to the membership petition hitting 30,000 this morning I feel I must withdraw from the race. Eric Courtenay has my full support, congratulations and admiration and I feel proud to . . . '

In the Cliveden kitchen, there is stunned silence. Bobby mutes the TV.

'Well,' sighs Eva, 'that's it then. They've won. We're irrelevant now.'

Bobby can't help but agree. They've been timed out, along with her hopes of making up with Jake. Now that Courtenay has won, Jake will be too busy to give her a second thought.

'Rubbish. You're more relevant than ever. Sure, they're now at their strongest point but that also means they have a lot to lose. Oh come *on*,' Jess throws her hands in the air, 'winning over MPs and Party members is one thing, but they've got to win over the public now. A completely different kettle of fish.'

'And we're due a General Election soon ...' Eva tears thoughtfully at a pancake.

They spend the next hour discussing their meeting with Moira and Susie, who are dropping in shortly, while the muted TV shows a shell-shocked Courtenay give his hastily prepared acceptance speech. This is their last chance to salvage the situation.

Tipperton

Susie and Moira dive straight in when they arrive with the news that Annie, Daly's old Parliamentary researcher, has been in touch. Bobby casts her mind back to the Cholmondeley Room a few weeks before. It's all clicking together.

'She's the person connected to that bloody clinic appointment. Turns out she was ...' Susie sighs, 'involved with Simon. And ever so young. She insists it was consensual but when you're twenty-one and hoping for a career in politics and the guy's a minister ...' The others all nod, understanding the power imbalance. 'Anyway, she's gone against my charming husband's advice and is keeping the baby. She needs money and help but Simon isn't responding to her calls. She's been getting increasingly desperate.'

'Susie, I'm so sorry,' Bobby whispers.

'Oh, it gets worse!' Susie cries, pulling out a handkerchief and blowing her nose.

'Perhaps I should take over,' says Moira gently. 'Annie told us the whole story. But there's more. Letters. Texts. Emails. Denying paternity, terrorising her with legal threats and gagging injunctions. Makes that first note sound like a sonnet. Very nasty stuff and all from Simon.'

'Will she talk publicly?' Jess asks.

'I doubt it.'

'Who'd want to?' Eva adds. The group nods again. Sitting at the centre of a big debate about sex and power dynamics is the last thing any of them would want.

'Will she give us the letters?' Jess asks. 'Perhaps we could redact Annie's name and publish anyway. I have the StoryCorps lawyers on speed dial these days . . .'

Moira reaches into her handbag and pulls out a folder with the letters safely tucked inside. 'Worth a try.'

With half of their agenda complete, the group spends a couple of hours on what can be done to save the unit. They pore over the different documents Susie and Moira have brought with them. Each new bit of information makes the picture a little clearer, like a 5,000-piece puzzle. It is clear that Daly has been busy in the last couple of days. They all agree he has been foolish to accept the role of Secretary of State for Housing and Communities, which he'd gleefully told Susie about at breakfast that morning, because he opens himself up to so much scrutiny.

What is clear is that, judging by a series of emails Susie has found ('he thinks I'm such a trustworthy dope that I have access to everything!'), he had been counting on the remaining few weeks of the leadership contest to tie up the loose ends of the golf club deal, so that he wouldn't have to declare any meetings on his ministerial register of interests. They wonder aloud what he will do now that time has run out. As for the finance side of things, it's all in Susie's name and she can legally do what she likes with it. Turns out that for Daly, she's the wrong kind of lead-lined box.

Although the picture is getting clearer, a way to save the unit still eludes them.

'Look,' Eva says during a tea break, 'they've just announced that the handover from Ford to Courtenay will be midday on Tuesday. Four days away.'

'Simon has to move pretty fast then,' muses Susie.

'So he'll probably make mistakes. Although it needs to be a big one, if we're to have a chance,' Bobby says, poking sadly at the stack of documents in front of her. 'I can't find anything here that helps us.'

'At least he's going to get savaged over his treatment of Annie,' Eva mutters.

'They aren't mutually exclusive, of course,' Jess says. 'I wonder what will happen to the golf club consortium if we take him out. Cut the head off the snake, as it were. Cuthbert may well crumble on the deal if the main broker is ousted like a social leper.'

'Exactly,' Moira says. 'We can't give up. Bobby – tomorrow you and I are paying a visit to every person on this list. Councillors, developers, businesspeople … you've impressed them once before, why not again?'

11th May

Tipperton

It is remarkable how the personal stock of a politician can be followed like any other share. Just a few weeks ago, Simon Daly MP had been a PUS at the Foreign Office and worth putting a bit of long-term money on, like an ISA. Natasha Weaver, Secretary of State for the Industrial Economy and leadership hopeful, was worth shorting if you'd done a bit of insider trading and knew her sex life would likely blow up. Both Daly and Weaver investors have experienced a Black Friday level crash over the past few weeks. However, by lunchtime on 11th May, they're holding steady again: Daly has been duly confirmed as Secretary of State for Housing and Communities and Natasha Weaver, still a firm favourite with the Party faithful, is Party Chairman and Deputy Prime Minister. Hendrick, who backed Jacobson to the hilt, has seen his career consigned to the political oubliette, where he will make loud cries for attention but everyone will let him fester.

While Daly takes a lap of honour around his new department and favourite London clubs, Susie, Moira, Jess, Eva and Bobby are busy in Tipperton, working to make sure Daly's spell of pleasure is as short-lived as possible.

Bobby returns home for lunch after driving around the constituency with Moira, working their way down their list. It hasn't gone well: none of the developers will drop their plans, especially now that Daly has been formally announced to the Cabinet; the few councillors they managed to track down simply ran away and hid. Local residents are cross about the unit closure, but aren't clear what they can do about it.

Bobby dumps her bag in the hallway and heads for the kitchen, where her mother is arranging a vase of flowers.

'Jess and Eva are out with Susie Daly, visiting some Association people,' says Elizabeth, 'and we've one extra for lunch.'

'Who?' asks Bobby, after draining her glass.

Elizabeth points out of the window to the bottom of the garden.

Bobby looks and almost drops her glass. Jake Albury is sitting on a bench with a glass of rosé.

This is the sort of thing that happens in Richard Curtis films, not Tipperton housing estates, Bobby thinks, as she quickly checks her reflection in the living room mirror. She has a strange, fizzing sensation, like she might cry and skip at the same time.

'Hello,' she says, when she is a few feet away.

Jake smiles apologetically in response. Bobby sits down beside him.

'I'm sorry,' Jake says in a quiet, desolate voice next to her.

'I am too,' Bobby whispers. 'I should have explained properly. I thought someone would get in trouble . . .'

'I didn't even give you a chance to. I was proud and stub-born. I've seen how Daly operates and . . . Well, I was jealous and stupid and I've been completely miserable ever since.'

'I have too. I've missed you. And now here you are.' Bobby takes his hand. 'I hope you haven't come all this way to say "I told you so".'

'I wouldn't dare . . .' Jake grins. 'I wish I'd come to see you before now, but I just couldn't quite be brave enough.'

'So what changed your mind?'

'Well, my phone hasn't stopped ringing. I had Susie Daly and Eva on to me last night. They told me everything. Then first thing this morning my friend Annie called—'

'You know Annie?' Bobby asks in amazement.

'Yeah . . .' Jake sighs. 'She's why I'm not a big fan of Daly. I knew her when she worked in Parliament. She fell completely in love with him. I mean real, heartfelt infatuation. She got it into her head he would leave his wife for her . . . the lot. I hate Daly because of how upset she was when he dumped her. I had no idea about the baby, though.' Jake clenches his fists. 'I'd like to break his jaw . . .'

'Well, you may get the chance . . . Is she okay?'

'She'll be fine, if Daly follows through on his responsibili-ties.' Jake clears his throat. 'Anyway, that isn't all. I've had a bit of a brainwave.'

'For the unit?'

'Yup,' he smiles. 'Do you remember when we had the coffee and I wondered if other PFI contracts were coming to an end? I've looked into it and I'm afraid my suspicions were right. A bunch of them are about to end and there's simply no fall-back plan, meaning many of these units could collapse imminently. But I think we can use that to our advantage . . .'

He hands Bobby his glass, and she sips and listens intently as he outlines his idea.

When Jake finishes she looks at him doubtfully. 'Can it really be done?'

'In theory. I've never seen it in practice but I don't see why that should hold us back.'

'But where do we start?'

'We've already started.' Jake points back up to the house, where Susie, Moira, Jess and Eva are talking earnestly at the picnic table. Bobby watches as her mother proudly places her vase of flowers in the centre and feels overcome with a delicious, hopeful happiness.

'Thank you,' Bobby murmurs.

'Don't thank me yet,' he says, turning her face up to his and kissing softly at her lips and cheeks and the tip of her nose. 'We've got the busiest forty-eight hours of our lives coming up.'

Downing Street

Dennis hears a familiar voice and shuffles awkwardly across the Downing Street rose garden to Eva. He licks her hand in recognition. After a series of phone calls with Peter Foulkes and Leonard Smith, Eva has come with Jake and Bobby to pitch their idea to save the mental health units. It is strange to be in the building on a Saturday, particularly in the garden. It reminds her of the stifling weekends during Percy's tenure.

'I've told you before that you have my full support,' the PM says, relaxed in a white linen shirt tucked into jeans, her reading glasses perched at the end of her nose. 'Besides, I quite fancy going out with a bang. What do you think, everyone?'

'I've won tougher votes for you, PM,' grins the Chief Whip, Terry Groves.

'Worth a shot, isn't it?' Leo, the chief of staff, rubs his hands together.

'It can be done ... it can be done,' Peter, the Political Secretary, says thoughtfully.

'Let me at 'em,' Tim, the press man, says grimly, throwing punches at thin air and thinking of some journalistic scores he has to settle.

The three men are keen to have some fun in their final couple of days. It's all coming to an end six weeks sooner than expected and they're all nervous about the furore that will be made over the gongs they're getting in the PM's resignation honours list.

The PM's husband says nothing, but when his wife meets his eye he nods slowly, his eyes shining.

'Well then,' the PM stands and grins roguishly, 'if you'll excuse me, I have some phone calls to make – beginning with the Leader of the Opposition. Chief, shall we?'

She chirrups to Dennis, who follows her inside. The Chief Whip jumps up excitedly and joins her.

'Right,' Leo says, his veteran campaigning instincts kicking in, 'Jake and Bobby, please dig out your draft text and turn it into a bill with legislative affairs. We need it to be perfect – we can't afford to get stuck in ping pong between the two Houses, so there's no wiggle room for objections over a few silly words. Pete and Eva, you need to get onto the Commons and Lords Whips, the Leaders of both Houses, Opposition Whips, the smaller parties . . . everyone. Help them get scripts together for their people. Tim, I'm going to listen in on the PM's calls with the different party leaders and the Speaker. Get your team teed up so we have our messages ready. We need every newspaper backing this, every broadcaster primed so that (assuming we get the green light) they carry our story this evening.'

Everyone gets to work.

*

An hour later, Bobby thanks the Downing Street custodian as he opens the famous Number Ten front door so she can leave with Jake and Eva.

'It's lucky there aren't any cameras out here,' Eva whispers, 'I'm practically vibrating with excitement.'

'They'll be out soon enough,' Jake mutters. 'Leo says the other party leaders are in agreement. They're all going to see the Speaker this evening.'

They decide to head back to Claybourne Terrace, where Jess has stayed, reasoning that it would raise all sorts of questions if a junior member of the lobby was meeting with the Prime Minister on a Saturday. Hardly press impartiality. Besides, she has work to do with Susie and Moira, who have stayed in Tipperton and are calling her every thirty minutes or so with updates.

When they arrive, they are greeted with a chaotic but cheerful scene: Percy and Holly are home – Percy under strict instructions to change his ways before his insides turn to black pudding – and have been fully briefed by Jess. The three of them are in the living room, Percy wrapped in a quilted dressing gown on the sofa, ready and waiting with notebooks and phones for instructions from the Downing Street delegation.

They're all settling down when the doorbell goes.

'I'm sorry to barge in like this,' Mary Jones says breathlessly, 'but the Chief told me what's going on and I just had to come. How can I help?' Greeted as a hero, she pulls off her coat and plops into an armchair.

Eva gets Moira and Susie on speakerphone, then explains to the group that the PM has decided to support their idea. They should try to get as many of the great and good in Tipperton (Moira and Susie), political bigwigs like ex-PMs and editors (Percy) and every MP imaginable (Eva, Mary and Bobby) on board to build a sense of momentum.

'What do you mean by "support"?' Mary asks.

Eva checks her watch, walks over to the TV and turns on the twenty-four-hour news. Then she settles down next to her father to watch the PM (still in her jeans) and the other Westminster party leaders (in a selection of weekend casual clothing – the Westminster leader of the SNP still in his dress kilt after racing down from a family christening) file in to meet with the Speaker of the House of Commons.

Presently they all file back out, smiling broadly, and cluster around a microphone that has been set up. After a few minutes the Speaker appears and steps forward.

'I have just met with the Prime Minister and the leaders of the different Westminster parties and am reminded of a predecessor of mine, who I have often tried to emulate – William Lenthall, who was the first Speaker to truly defend the liberty of Parliament. I have been asked by these folks to recall Parliament first thing on Monday, to have an emergency debate on,' he pauses to read off a piece of paper in his hand, 'the Health Services Bill. I am persuaded of the emergency by the imminent collapse of many key institutions around the country and of the consequent urgent need to provide stability. After careful deliberation I can choose no better words than those of Mr Lenthall himself: "I have neither eyes to see nor tongue to speak in this place but as this House is pleased to direct me whose servant I am here." Parliament shall sit at ten o'clock on Monday morning and we shall debate this bill.'

13th May

Notting Hill

'What the *fuck* is happening?' howls Courtenay, throwing the TV remote onto a pile of newspapers, all carrying leader columns, colourful family stories and letters pages supporting the passing of the so-called Health Services Bill. Bobby's limping campaign has been given a massive adrenaline shot. #saveourunits has been shared hundreds of thousands of times, including by footballers, actors and musicians. A video by Stephen Fry has gone viral. It's about the worst thing to stand against just now, up there with climate denial. 'How can she do this?'

'It is possible . . . ' Jackson says quietly. 'If both Houses waive it through with minimal debate and no amendments, it need only take twenty-four hours.'

'But she isn't even Party Leader any more,' Clarissa spits.

'She's still Prime Minister, though. Until midday tomorrow.'

'But . . . I don't even understand why she thinks she has

371

everyone's support!' Courtenay yells. 'How can I be the only politician in Westminster whipping against this? Simon told me that our members hate it!'

'Who gives a shit what the members think now? A hundred and fifty thousand people is nothing compared to several million.' Jackson inclines his head at the stack of newspapers. 'They've bundled in every mental health unit in the country! Anyway, I don't see what made him so sure.'

'Yes, he came to see me a few days ago. Showed me some polling. They hate it.' Courtenay digs around in a bag and finds Daly's sheet of paper.

'What polling?' asks Clarissa. 'I didn't even know this was an issue until today. Frankly, I didn't know we had a stance on it.'

'Actually, Simon was all for it originally. He has one of these units in his patch and it was in danger of being sold off to developers ... Anyway, he told me we should drop it after all because Tory members don't want meddling in the natural progression of the free market ... or something.'

Jackson glances at the paper Courtenay hands him. In small text in the corner is who has paid for the poll: Cuthberts. The developers have likely chosen the questions and picked the focus group participants. The numbers couldn't be cooked more if they were fried in onions.

'That bloody fool Simon,' hisses Clarissa. 'And bloody *you*! Why didn't you tell me you'd met with him? And why didn't you say you'd pulled this policy off the table?'

'He's a pal,' Courtenay laments, 'and I was going to tell you – but everything happened so fast that I forgot.'

It is a fair point. The contest ended far sooner than any of them were expecting, so a discussion to confirm Courtenay's announcements for the membership part of the contest never happened. The unit campaign just evaporated. Even in the steadiest times of experienced government, this kind of thing happens. Someone falls off the reshuffle board or one spending decision inadvertently bashes into another. Cock-up, rather than conspiracy, generally prevails. The problem for the Courtenay camp is that this one's a doozy – and friends and foes alike will capitalise on any opportunity they can. Graham Thomas has just sent out invitations to a selection of MPs for 'Chat with Nat' drinks on behalf of Weaver, a revival of her pre-leadership contest gatherings.

'What do I do now, then?' Courtenay says petulantly, crossing his arms. 'Obviously I'm going to have to back this thing. What a bloody great way to start my premiership.'

Clarissa and Jackson look at each other grimly.

'You can't support it,' Jackson says.

'Why not?' Courtenay rubs his eyes. 'I thought we're meant to weave baskets and talk about our feelings all the time now!'

'Because you'll look unbelievably weak,' mutters Clarissa. She feels tired. What a pointless thing to be caught out on. 'U-turning before the car's even started? I don't think so.'

14th May

ONE-MONTH WAIT FOR DENTAL APPOINTMENTS/
SKIRMISH ON INDIA–PAKISTAN BORDER

House of Commons

Bobby looks at her watch. 11.20 a.m. She calculates she hasn't
snatched more than a couple of hours of sleep since Saturday
night. She sits next to Eva in the small area in the House of
Commons known as the Box, behind the Speaker's Chair on
the government side of the Chamber. Peter and Leo are there,
as are a couple of legislative aides. Up above the Opposition
benches sits Jess, between Teddy Hammer and Camilla from
Blush, in the packed press gallery. Every national newspaper has
backed the bill in the last twenty-four hours, driven by their
readers' interest, and the reporters all want to give first-hand
accounts of how the action unfolds. Bobby's eyes travel down
to the end of the room to the public gallery, where her parents
are crammed in with Percy, Holly, Susie, Moira, Lucy, Millie
and the PM's husband. She knows that Jake is watching from
his new office in Downing Street. As the new PM's Policy Unit
Director, he feels it would be best if his meddling wasn't known.

The Chamber is absolutely rammed for the outgoing PM's final appearance, her swansong. MPs who haven't been able to find seats sit on the steps in gangways or stand around the entrances. They had met at ten o'clock yesterday morning and, after heartfelt speeches from MPs across the House – some with highly personal revelations about their own mental health – they had passed the bill last night. The most optimistic, least cynical have fresh hope for issue campaigns of their own, which they thought were fizzling out and dying. The most jaded have just got swept up in feeling part of history and the emotions for their constituents. Parliamentarians have enjoyed bashing the creation and collapse of PFI contracts. All of them have now congregated to hear whether, after a full night of debate, the House of Lords will follow suit.

Unusually, the Speaker has allowed MPs to watch the progress of the bill in the Lords Chamber (which is equally packed) on the screens around the Commons that normally broadcast the subject of debates and votes. The general consensus is that it will pass without a problem, but the noble Lords are taking their time to scrutinise and the clock is ticking down to midday. With a new Prime Minister waiting a little less than a mile away to see the Queen at Buckingham Palace – he and Secretary of State Daly had notably skipped the debate yesterday in favour of a visit to a building site – and the possibility that Madeleine Ford could be timed out in her final act as Prime Minister, the mood is electric.

At 11.44, when the Lords rise from their benches to vote, MPs who have been chatting to colleagues quickly return to their seats. Conversation continues, but in hushed, excited tones. Bobby clutches Eva's hand, silently urging the Peers to hurry up as they settle back down in their seats to hear the result. The Commons Chamber falls into total silence. Nobody even dares cough. 11.56.

The next few seconds seem to slip into ultra-slow motion. A ringing, aged voice reads out the result: the Lords have passed the bill. The legislation is through. The Tipperton Mental Health Unit – and every such unit in the country – is safe. Guaranteed funding for an even spread of mental health beds up and down the land. Security at the end of PFI contracts. A number of clever funding and safety measures that Jake has cooked up, including a programme of apprenticeships for young patients and tax breaks for companies that provide utilities, maintenance and interest-free loans to NHS properties that need them.

But those thoughts come to Bobby much later. In the moment, she leaps to her feet as the result is read out and is nearly knocked backwards by the roar of approval from the benches around her. MPs are standing up, clapping, stamping their feet and cheering. Many bow or wave their hands above their heads in acknowledgement at the benches opposite them. The clerks dash around the Chamber floor, aware of the scant minutes they have to finish the job. In the Box, the press gallery and the public gallery, everyone is cheering. The PM slowly closes her red folder for the last time and walks steadily to the centre of the Chamber, where she meets the other Westminster party leaders and shakes hands with them, before bowing to the Speaker and returning to the despatch box.

When her colleagues have simmered down, she speaks – ready to mark the end of an era.

'Mr Speaker, I have been a Member of this House for nearly twenty years. We have had to make a great number of important and difficult decisions. War. Sanctions. Taxes. There has been plenty to disagree about and many opportunities to disappoint the public. What has happened today is not the passing of the most complicated or lofty piece of legislation this House or the other place have ever scrutinised.' She looks around at the smiling faces. 'What has happened is the right thing. I'm so proud that in these,' she looks at her watch, 'remaining few seconds as Prime Minister, we were able to unite and do the right thing. We should remember this moment when we are faced with those difficult, divisive questions in the future. There is more in this House that unites us than divides us. Please, to all Members here and in the other place – don't stop fighting for the causes you believe in and which need your help. Listen to your constituents who have ideas. Work together across the House to champion those that need us most – that is how we will get things done.'

17th May

RAIL AND BUS FARE RISE MOOTED/
UN ANNOUNCES CLIMATE CATASTROPHE

Tipperton

'Are you ready?' Daly says, patting Susie on the shoulder. She fights the urge to shrug him off and continues brushing her hair.

'Just another minute, if that's okay.'

Susie gazes around her living room, her home of eight years. She feels like her mind is separated from her body. She has tried so hard to make her marriage work, sacrificing the chance of a career in psychiatry and a great chunk of herself, she now realises. It makes her feel sad to think of the many nights she has sat here alone, miserably eating chocolates and watching Jane Austen adaptations, waiting for her husband. At least she'll be doing that for pleasure now.

Out in the hallway, Daly studies his face carefully in the mirror. He seems to have aged ten years in the last week. It is now Friday, three days since Courtenay officially started as Prime Minister and Daly's Cabinet career is already over. At his first oral questions in the Commons on Wednesday he simply couldn't work out why he was getting so many queries about his register of ministerial interests. Unfortunately for him, he had lied (or, as he claimed, 'inadvertently misled the House') when quizzed on whether he 'directly or indirectly' owned shares or interests in any property companies. Somehow, in a way that mystified him, the documents and legal advice about the blind trust had become public.

As a result, after a difficult phone call with the new PM that evening, who had pompously told him, 'My hands are tied, matey – I said I'd drain the swamp!', Daly had resigned from his post, making him the shortest-serving Secretary of State in history. What had stung the most was that he was replaced by George 'Sack' Sackler, who was, according to every pundit, already doing a terrific job.

But things had gone from bad to worse for Daly. On Thursday, the Commons passed a motion calling for him to be investigated by the Privileges Committee and his correspondence with Annie was released, prompting several anonymous young women to speak to *Woman's Hour*, detailing their experiences of relationships they'd had with Daly in Parliament. They all conceded that the relationships had been consensual, but all told of similar patterns of him using his ministerial status, his power as an MP or simply the promise of introductions and jobs to essentially transact a sexual relationship. Each time he had rowed back on his promises. The papers had dubbed him the 'Cabinet Minister for Casting Couches' and carried dozens of quotes from furious Tipperton constituents and Association members, who had been nicely riled up by Lucy and Moira, calling for him to stand down as their MP.

To top it all off, the golf club deal has fallen through and the consortium has dumped him, so his hopes of filling his coffers have died. Not only that, but he has agreed to take a paternity test when Annie's baby arrives so he is shortly to have a new dependent to cough up for. Still, Daly is cunning to the end. He drove down early from London this morning, having spent last night in the Prime Minister's Downing Street study, arguing with Jackson (the new Chief Whip) and Clarissa, who were urging him to stand down – 'It's just a matter of time. Go with dignity before the Privileges Committee sets you on fire and there's a recall petition!' – while the new PM sat in dumb silence.

Eventually Daly had pulled out his phone and scrolled through to the Legislative Lads WhatsApp group.

'Look,' he held it up so they could see the five names, the PM and two other new Cabinet ministers among them. 'I wonder ... Clarissa, you're a PR whizz. Would it be a good thing or a bad thing for the new and improved swamp-draining Prime Minister if screenshots of this group were released onto Twitter?'

Daly held his screen up again, showing a photo of the Shadow Education Secretary showing a small amount of cleavage on the front bench. Courtenay had replied with several laughing faces, a cow emoji and *nice udders*.

'Trust me,' Daly had said, putting his phone away, 'that's the tamest thing on there.'

Clarissa had rounded on her husband, hissing like an angry goose. 'You idiot!'

'Don't fret, dear Clarissa,' Daly had said coolly. 'This needn't go any further than this room.'

'In exchange for what?' she'd sighed, while her husband sat at his desk, goggling at the scene. Clarissa was privately kicking herself for being so fearful of a u-turn about the Health Services Bill. Perhaps they should have just backed it after all. Of course, what they really should have done was hold the line on keeping sex pests and sleaze bags out of government.

'I will stand down as an MP and delete this ... *stuff* the moment I have, in writing, the promise of a peerage.'

The others had exchanged doubtful glances.

'Come on now,' Daly had smirked. 'You help me, and I'll commit hara-kiri.'

'Done,' Clarissa had breathed.

As he was marched out of the room, Daly heard the PM, his head buried in his arms on the desk, groan, 'I don't think I can manage two whole years of this ...'

Back in the living room, Susie applies lipstick and reflects on the way her husband had relayed the Downing Street meeting to her. And the way he replayed all the events from the past couple of weeks. He was still stumped about where crucial pieces of information had come from about his business interests, or who had persuaded the young women to speak out, or planted the questions in the Commons, or had organised the local campaign against him in the constituency. Susie realises in that moment that her husband doesn't even respect her enough to think she would have had the guts or brains to take him out. Let alone underestimate her, he hasn't once apologised for anything. She's easily been able to hide what she has done over the past few days and what she is about to do next.

Susie is pulled back to the present by her husband's despondent call from the hallway. 'Come on, Suse. Let's get this over with.'

She follows him out of the front door and onto their driveway. There is a clattering of shutters as the photographers catch every step. When Daly reaches the press microphones, Susie stands a few steps behind him, the dutiful wife, and tunes out of his glass-eyed prepared speech, standing down as an MP. Her ears buzz and she feels a little light-headed. She can't believe she is about to do this. She fights the urge to smile as Daly, finished with his statement, tucks his note cards in his pocket.

'Have you got anything further to say, Mr Daly? How are you feeling about the peerage?'

'I won't be taking any questions at this time.'

'Susie, are you looking forward to becoming Lady Daly?' another calls.

Daly turns and reaches for his wife's hand, but she ignores him and takes a step forward.

'What was that?' Susie asks in a small voice. 'Could you repeat your question?'

Mike from the *Sentinel* raises his voice, fully prepped by Jess. 'Are you looking forward to becoming Lady Daly?'

'No.' The photographers begin clicking frantically as Susie smiles widely. 'But I'm very much looking forward to becoming Dr Coleman when I return to university and complete my PhD in the autumn.' She clears her throat, hitting her stride. 'While you're all here, I'd like to announce that Simon Daly and I are separating and will soon be divorced.' The photographers go bananas, capturing Daly's appalled expression. 'Like the other citizens of Tipperton, I look forward to being served by someone better.'

As she turns to go, Mike shouts, 'Will you be putting your name forward to replace him as the Member of Parliament?'

'No. I'm delighted to say that, alongside completing my studies, I'll be working part-time at the Tipperton Mental Health Unit, which, thanks to a very generous donation from Cuthberts, a highly valued local developer,' Susie's eyes twinkle, 'will be expanding to help serve patients with even better care.'

'Sounds like you'll have your hands full,' yells another journalist.

Susie nods. 'I would like to endorse the perfect candidate, though,' she says loudly, 'Moira Herbert, who has proudly served this community as de facto MP for years. I think it's time she gets a chance to do it in earnest.' She points at Moira, who is standing at the back of the group with her arms folded and ready to take questions.

'Thank you very much!' Susie turns and marches back to the house, closing the door behind her and leaving her husband on the doorstep, wondering what on earth has just happened. After an agonising couple of minutes of banging on the door – all captured by the nation's media – he climbs into his Audi and drives off, scattering gravel at the gleeful press pack.

Epilogue

Eva slips out of the Chief Whip's House of Commons office and walks to the House of Lords, smiling and nodding to MPs and Peers as she goes. She's been in the Chief's office for several weeks now and the Parliamentary Estate is feeling like a second home. Eva can't help but think that, like Downing Street, Parliament has a blueprint that guarantees certain behaviours. In Number Ten, which is made up of a series of terraced townhouses, information can flow poorly between the small rooms of advisers and officials – which is why everyone is either vying to get into or loitering outside the PM's private office – and the heavy security required to enter means it can feel like a bank safe once you're inside, encouraging a clam-like bunker mentality. Parliament, with its many dark corridors, cramped staircases and secret hidey holes, invites intrigue, plotting and, after a few drinks, bad behaviour – and Jackson wants to know it all.

Eva had considered carefully whether to take the job as the Chief's SpAd. Jackson had, after all, played a part in the unpleasantness about her in the spring. But after consulting with Peter Foulkes, the ex-Chief Whip Terry Groves and her father – Percy shrugging and saying, 'A whip? Never been one, never owned one' – Eva had agreed. She had been summoned up to the Number Ten flat on her first evening in the job to be lushed up by a very friendly Clarissa who, over a bottle of wine, clearly understood the problems Eva could cause if she revealed the truth behind the tactics of the Courtenay campaign during the contest. 'You know, it's an interesting choice, taking down Simon. The enemy of your friends. I do hope this means you aren't planning to take down the friends of your enemies ...' Clarissa had looked at her carefully.

When Eva reaches the Peers' Lobby, she spots an enormous fuchsia hat belonging to Holly, who has bought it from the Duchess of Cornwall's milliner and teamed it with a matching Valentino skirt suit. Looking like her Met Gala chaperones are Bobby, fresh off running Moira's successful campaign in the Tipperton by-election, and Jess, back from an agreeable lunch with Lord Finlayson, who has just commissioned a podcast series about her work in Glasgow to run alongside her lobby job.

The group is escorted to a special gallery up some stairs so they can watch the Right Honourable Percy Cross become Baron Cross of Molton and Georgetown. Molton for his old constituency, Georgetown for his birthplace in Washington DC.

'Did he find an okay ermine to rent in the end?' Eva asks Holly, referring to the white-fur-collared scarlet robes that Members of the House of Lords wear for ceremonial occasions. These are so expensive and rarely worn that lots of Peers choose to borrow these from the House.

'Well,' Holly looks shifty, 'I went with him to try them on but Eva, honey, it just all looked so sad. And they *smelled*. So ... I bought him brand new ones as a gift.'

'Holly!'

'Well, there's all this talk about using fake fur in the future ... I can't bear the thought of him smelling of piss or wearing *faux*.' Holly wrinkles her nose.

They are hushed as proceedings begin below them. The Chamber is stunning, with ancient intricately panelled wood, an ornate ceiling, rich red leather benches and an enormous golden throne from which the reigning monarch makes their speech detailing the government's proposed legislation for the new Parliamentary term. Judging by the packed galleries, several new Peers are being announced today. Bobby, surveying the nodding white heads below her, hopes the new recruits will bring the average age of the Lords down by at least a decade. Several sitting Peers seem to be asleep. She scans around and then clutches at Jess's arm, stifling a laugh. Directly below them one of the noble Baronesses, who Bobby estimates to be about eighty years old, appears to be engrossed in a document in her leather-bound folder. In actual fact, she has tucked her iPad inside it and is joyfully devouring a novel on the extra-large font size familiar to tech savvy grandparents the world over. It is hot stuff, if you're a dedicated Parliamentarian. The words 'dis-Honourable Member', 'Black Rod' and 'red box' scream up at them.

Luckily the whispers coming from their group are masked by the little stir created by the arrival of the ex-PM, Madeleine Ford, to watch the ceremony. Eva, who sees her frequently and still struggles not to address her as Prime Minister, guesses that she must be coming to watch Peter Foulkes and Leonard Smith be introduced – as well as several Davids, who have stood down from their seats and triggered by-elections. Ford is followed by the new PM, Eric Courtenay, who has taken a short break from another miserable, own-goal-filled news cycle (the latest is that a Downing Street insider has said the PM is looking to appoint a 'useful idiot' as his new Ethics Adviser) to watch his old friend Simon Daly be elevated. As members of the Privy Council, both famous behinds are allowed to sit on the steps of the golden throne to watch proceedings, but the eagle-eyed press are quick to observe that the PM and his new back bencher do not speak to each other.

Kettled outside the Chamber, the group waiting to be ennobled huddles together excitedly, comparing robes and titles. Daly, who struggles to make conversation with many people, thinks of the lucrative offer he's had from beleaguered companies who need a Lord on the board. This is step one in revamping his political brand. Peter and Leonard, resplendent in their robes, nod stiffly to him. Percy as an ex-PM gets plenty of attention. There are going to be late nights of voting ahead and he's going to make the place considerably more fun. He chats away about his most recent trip to America to meet Holly's family – 'the father is Jock Ewing reincarnated! Of course, he's the one who's so keen on me joining the Lords. Basically thinks I'm royalty now . . .'

Presently, they are asked to line up in order and, with great solemnity, file into the main Chamber, then the ceremony begins.

One by one the group walks forward and is introduced to the House, taking an Oath of Allegiance. Percy steps forward wearing an inscrutable, Mona Lisa-like expression, when it is his turn to speak. When he sits, now Lord Cross, between Lords Lawson and Lamont, he gives his party in the gallery a little thumbs-up.

A hundred yards away on Burma Road, Ed Cooper returns to the small *Sentinel* office after lunch with Moira Herbert, the newly elected MP for Tipperton. After an extremely rocky start to his premiership, Moira's by-election success is being touted by Number Ten as a sure sign of the new PM's election-winning magic. Ed suspects otherwise. The tough old bird wouldn't give much away but it is well known that Moira's team did their best to keep the new Prime Minister away from their voters for the majority of the campaign.

Ed stumps over to his desk and nearly cries out. There, out on display for anyone to see when they walk by the open door, is a sleek black strap-on. Jess has left a note:

Let's kick it up a notch . . .

Ed checks over his shoulder, then picks it up. The enormous rubber cock is heavier than he would have guessed. The leather belt is sturdy and, with its various buckles, vaguely menacing. He's heard there's an underground trend in SW1 for pegging just now, and he supposes that this would still fit within Jess's parameters of no touching. Just the thought makes him reflexively move his hand to cover his bottom, more terrified than aroused, officially out of his comfort zone. Ed thought he had the whip hand over Jess – but it's clear she wants to take back control.

Acknowledgements

It wouldn't have been possible to write this book without the support of Tom, who has been incredibly encouraging and patient – even if he was clear about dying of shame if this book were dedicated to him.

Thank you also to: my family, who have been so positive about my new career and who will be receiving special light-weight copies of this book with all the embarrassing stuff cut out. My friends, both from within politics and without, who, if they were hesitant about admitting to knowing me before, are going to feel actively embarrassed about it now. Caroline Michel, perhaps the most elegant woman on the planet, and her fantastic team at PFD. James Gurbutt, the most wonderful editor and friend, who had to have some appalling conversations with me (the easiest of which began, "okay, talk me through the cock ring . . . ?"). Tamsin Shelton for her amazing copywriting. The fabulous team at Corsair, who have so patiently pulled me along the journey to becoming a published author. Finally, to the many wonderful – anonymous – civil servants who were such a pleasure to work with in government and who have the hottest gossip out there.